A novel with
one girl,

??

two blokes
and
three endings

LOVE STUCK

LOVE STUCK

SUSIE GILMOUR

FLAME
Hodder & Stoughton

First published in Great Britain in 2001 by Hodder and Stoughton
First published in paperback in 2001 by Hodder and Stoughton
A division of Hodder Headline

A Flame Paperback

10 9 8 7 6 5 4 3 2 1

A CIP catalogue record is available from the British Library

ISBN 0340 79356 2

Typeset by Palimpsest Book Production Limited
Polmont, Stirlingshire
Printed and bound in Great Britain by
Clays Ltd, St Ives plc

Hodder and Stoughton
A division of Hodder Headline
338 Euston Road
London NW1 3BH

In fond memory of my dad
Robin Gilmour (1943–1999)
to whom I owe so much.

Acknowledgements

I sat down and wrote a list of all the people I wanted to thank. There were eighty-four of them. To prevent this from turning into the telephone directory, I am especially grateful to:

My agent, Simon Trewin, who rescued this book from drowning in the slush pile and who has stuck by me with patience, encouragement and humour.

My editor, Philippa Pride, and all at Hodder for their time, expertise and accomplished handling of three endings, two covers and one novice author.

All my wonderful friends for never giving up on me: Fiona – my soulmate – because I couldn't have done it without her; Garrett, for his overwhelming generosity, kindness and support; Lindsey, for her help, companionship and many fruitful discussions on 'compromise'; Lisa, for going to China and sowing the first seed of this book; Candy, for inspiring me; Libby, for feeding me; Matthew, for phoning me; and Ches, Emma, Gray, Janet, Layla, Sarah, Sonja and Whid for making the solitary hours of writing so much more enjoyable.

I owe any abatement in my overdraft to Nomura who were kind enough to employ me, and to Allison and Terrie for always asking me back.

Above all, I would like to thank my family, my brothers Jonathan and Richard and especially my sister, Lucy. She has been my trusty sounding board from word one and has tirelessly and good-naturedly read every draft, providing much invaluable advice along the way.

My greatest debt, however, both personal and financial, is to my mum whose constant belief in me gave me the confidence to write in the first place and whose continual support and encouragement meant I never gave up.

Finally, a note to all family friends and relatives who have not yet read this book but who have so kindly expressed an interest in doing so. I fear it will not be the novel you are expecting from the daughter of such a learned man as my late father, but I hope that nevertheless you might still enjoy it.

LOVE STUCK

Pretending not to be waiting for James to call
Running back and forth from the fridge still relishing
  the novelty of finding things in it
Plucking stray hairs from my left eyebrow

Dear Alex,
  Five and a half days and:

You have	**I have**
Flown to Beijing	*Walked to Superdrug*
Scaled the Great Wall	*De-scaled the kettle*
Observed the rich tapestry of Chinese street life	*Watched* EastEnders *omnibus*

And I imagine you are currently cruising down the Yangtze in a ferry with tinkly Irish Pan-pipe music and a Chinese Leonardo DiCaprio.

I, on the other hand, am alone in my bedroom plucking. I have been doing this for half an hour now, stopping intermittently to peer into my Holly Hobbie mirror and squeeze some premature spots into bulbous red lumps, then shuffling through to the bathroom once they start oozing blood. Had a particularly nasty experience on my last trip, however, when I noticed something decidedly wrong with my face – more wrong, that is, than normal. I thought perhaps it might just be the recently created mosquito-attacked effect then realised, to my utter horror, it was my eyebrow. In keeping with the general trend that nothing in my life should go even marginally right, I have just plucked away half my left eyebrow.

I am now in a quandary. Do I hazard more plucking in the vain hope of achieving some kind of symmetry or should I just wear my hair over the left eye until my mono-brow sprouts back?

Of course I would not be plucking at all if James had called when he said he would. I cannot believe that after a perfectly trusting year-long relationship I have regressed to post-first-snog stage where one phone call dominates an entire evening. The trouble is I have convinced myself he is going off me and have done such a good job that the slightest thing he does or doesn't do confirms I am right. Evidence so far:

- *Wednesday night's call when he made a joke about being bored with me. Was it a joke?*
- *Saturday afternoon's call when I asked him who was at Chris's party and he just said, 'Usual people,' and wouldn't give details even though he knew what I really meant was, did he fancy anyone?*
- *Monday night's call when he seemed distant.*
- *And now no Thursday night call at all.*

Am I being paranoid? Or just very, very perceptive? Or paranoid because I am very, very perceptive? Or is it more that – ahhh, thank goodness, the phone. He is exactly one hour and twenty-three minutes late. I am not going to pick it up and make him think I have been waiting for this call. Instead I must decide whether to be pissed off that he didn't ring when he said he would and risk sounding like a moany, naggy, no-life sort of person, or be a happy, carefree spirit who thinks relationships should not be weighed down by the likes of prearranged phone calls.

Mum has got it. I think I will be the happy person. Back in a mo . . .

It wasn't James. It is some friend of Mum's who is causing her to shrill, 'How lovely to hear from you,' in a way that suggests she will spend the next three hours doing so. I bet he tries to get through now. Oh, God, I wish I'd come to China with you. I would now be absorbed in edifying new cultural experiences and concerning myself with the plight of poor Chinese people rather than stagnating at home plucking, eating and obsessing over a phone call.

It's because I'm unemployed, that's the problem. If I had a normal job like all other normal graduates I'd be fine. Busy making a success of my life, not bored making a mess of it. I've even resorted to drawing up 'Must Do' lists to give my empty existence some focus. Here is the current one:

MUST DO
(1) *Get job.*
(2) *Buy nail-polish remover.*
(3) *Copy friends' new numbers from cheque-book cover, receipts and old chewing-gum wrappers into one address book.*
(4) *Speak to woman in post office about green money-off form.*
(5) *Wipe dust off all spider-plant leaves.*
(6) *Put photos into photo album (NB if any make me look pretty or popular or both – put up on noticeboard).*
(7) *Sort out noticeboard: messy noticeboard = messy head.*
(8) *Look into Spanish classes.*

I have singularly failed to accomplish any of the above save a feeble stab at no. 7, which I quickly abandoned when I realised the bulk of the mess constituted out-of-date party invitations from uni (put up as proof of a social life) and that chucking them away would be admitting we have all moved on.

Only I haven't. I seem to be moving backwards with frightening rapidity. For example, compare the above with how fun my life used to be when we were at uni (found this stuck to a recipe for 'Puker's Punch' where the only ingredient not measured in % vol. were the ice-cubes):

MUST DO
(1) *Write and thank lads for superb dinner party.*
(2) *Get 2 tickets for ball.*
(3) *Get 1 man for ball.*
(4) *Get 1 man!*
(5) *Take advantage of fantastic 12 Beck's for price of 8 before whole student pop. discovers it and Oddbins withdraw offer.*

3

(6) *Buy tiny V-neck tops everyone is wearing.*
(7) *Make appointment at student health centre – NB free condoms!*
(8) *Remove traffic cone from lounge.*
(9) *Take Charles out for drink – if don't manage to get entire Foucault essay out of him at least secure salient points.*
(10) *Work out what to wear to Jane's fancy-dress party (theme – sexual positions).*

I can now only remember uni as a heavenly paradise of booze, sex and twenty-four-hour parties. Three months of suffocating home-living and I have forgotten that a large proportion of time was spent sobbing over wanker-of-the-week who, after giving every indication he was keen, had just snogged 'n' scarpered. Or the six essays, deadline last term, and the discovery that some arse-licker had emptied the library of every book on the list including optional/only-if-you-want-to-shag-tutor section.

But right now any of that is preferable to being trapped in a bedroom with Jungle Book *wallpaper where, other than on Baloo's back, the only escape route is via the jobs section of Monday's* Guardian.

The routine is still the same: Mon = Go mad and cut out eight TV jobs, four PR ones and one for obscure small-animals charity. Agonise over which to take if offered all thirteen. Tues = Rank TV jobs according to salary. Send off for small-animals form. Get rid of two PR ones – hadn't read ad properly – cannot claim five years' experience unless went to uni early, in which case would be super-child and therefore already have job. Wed = Start inventing perfect CV and planning five hundred words on 'Why I want to earn nothing working as trainee tea-maker on Les Dennis's Family Fortunes'. Thur = Receive small-animals form – forget being charitable person, job is based in Hull. Fri = Send off two of original thirteen applications – what is the point? Will only get rejection letter in one month's time. Sat = Rejection letter.

4

Today's offering was evilly disguised as an acceptance, i.e. fat envelope promising juicy new job info rather than anorexic one stamped Reject. Mum presented it to me over breakfast – my breakfast, her lunch – with a look that suggested she had already added 'Jess's fantastic new job' to the other brags she'd concocted for this year's impersonal our-family-is-better-than-yours Christmas circular.

I did the usual it-probably-won't-be smirk as if it were Valentine's Day and I had just been handed a red envelope, then opened it and, in much the same way as discovering Dad's signature beneath 'I love you,' found my returned CV and letter.

Was all set to make one of my melodramatic I-am-a-failure exits when Dad came charging into the room and did not so much steal my thunder as create his own gale-force electrical storm. He just stood there glaring at me through flaring nostrils demanding to know James's phone number. For a fleeting moment I thought he had taken it upon himself to goad James into commitment and, in a very un-Woman of the New Millennium way, quite liked the idea. Then I noticed he was clenching something that looked decidedly like a bill and realised he had an altogether different agenda.

'But he's on Friends and Family,' was all I could squeak, then waited in silence for the explosion – which came: 'At two hundred and eighty bloody four pounds ninety he is no fucking friend of the family.'

As a result I spent the rest of the day in morbid contemplation of suicide, wandering the streets getting rained on trying to convince myself I was too distraught to notice. Eventually returned home doing lots of stroppy teenage door-banging to a note saying, 'Becky rang. Good news.' With restored faith in fate, and more specifically Becky, I began imagining an array of exciting scenarios eventually plumping for the she's-got-me-a-wonderful-job-at-the-BBC option. I had not for the faintest second considered the good news might refer to her life and was forced to fake pleased happy-for-you sounds when she told me she was now Becky worth-ten-grand-

5

a-year-more-with-a-snazzy-little-company-Clio-to-prove-it Bradshaw.

I am a failure who hates everyone else's success. Actually, I wouldn't want Becky's job. She has to be up at six. And be nice to wanky people.

I hope travelling in China is better than unemployment in Inverness. Fingers crossed this letter reaches you. I can't believe that in this modern world of global communication we are still having to resort to pen and paper: let me know if you find anywhere where e-mailing access actually works.

Lots of love,
Jess
xxx

PS I have just phoned James. Disaster. I am the epitome of the failed Cosmo *woman:*

Do you and your partner really understand each other?

Q1. *You are feeling insecure about the relationship.*
    Do you:
    (a) Wait for the right moment to bring
         it up.   10 points
    (b) Phone him at midnight in a
         paranoid panic.   0 points ✓

Q2. *How does he react when he knows you*
    want to talk about things?
    (a) Says, 'I've got all the time in the
         world,' in a loving way.   10 points
    (b) Says, 'Can we do this later? I've
         got too much work on.'   0 points ✓

Q3. *How do you present your insecure feelings to him?*
   (a) In a calm, balanced and rational manner.   10 points
   (b) In a high-pitched squawk and erratic tearful outbursts.   0 points ✓

Q4. *What is his reaction?*
   (a) He assures you there is nothing wrong. You are the most important thing to him.   10 points
   (b) He dismisses everything you say as irrational and assures you his work is the most important thing to him.   0 points ✓

Q5. *How do you feel at the end of the conversation?*
   (a) Happy – of course he loves you.   10 points
   (b) Miserable.   0 points ✓

PPS For crying out loud, I'm going to go mad in a minute. I've just heard Mum say she will get 'one of the kids' to go to Safeway with her tomorrow. I cannot stand the fact that I am an adult when she needs to make up numbers at a dinner party but a child when she requires a slave. I will not let her treat me in this way. I am not going to Safeway.

Jess was standing outside Safeway with a shopping trolley that seemed to want to head, along with the rest of her life, straight for the gutter. 'Come *here*, you moron,' she shrieked, as it hurtled enthusiastically towards a shiny BMW parked for no obvious reason in the disabled-only space. As usual she seemed to have selected something whose wheels took after Take That: all four of them were going off in their own separate way, some more successfully than others.

None of the other shoppers had this problem, she noted, finally manoeuvring into the shop where her mum was choosing a cucumber. They were all gliding through the aisles in a Mary Poppins-esque manner smiling fondly at gooing infants.

'These look nice melons,' her mum announced. She was someone who used 'gay' to mean merry and carefree. A male attendant looked up enthusiastically. 'Are they juicy?'

Jess always felt protective towards her parents whenever they were exposed to anything sexual. It was as if they'd spent their lives believing in Santa Claus and it was her duty to shield them from ever thinking otherwise.

'Lovely!' her mum declared, tossing two melons into the trolley with the cucumber to form an image that would send most men reeling to the floor with inadequacy. Then she marched off up the lonely-meals-for-one aisle.

Jess, meanwhile, under the pretext of needing some shampoo, scampered off out of sight only to find herself face to face with ranks of sanitary towels discreetly labelled 'Feminine Hygiene'. If sanitary towels were their idea of hygienic, she thought, it would not be a wise move to buy anything from their Fresh Produce counter.

'Can I help you?' a voice chirped from behind a pack of Bodyform Ultra with wings. She'd been trying to read the back of a Persona pack without looking as if she was – still at the stage of finding contraception-buying slightly embarrassing and certainly not ready to discuss it with a twelve-year-old Safeway attendant.

'No 'anks . . .' she murmured, into the shelf, thrusting the pack behind some vitamin tablets, which had been placed next to the condoms, she decided, so that people like her could pretend they were looking for an iron supplement rather than Durex.

'Think you'll find they're doing a special offer on the Durex. Two shags for the price of one.'

Jess turned round and went spontaneously red. It was Brad.

Brad had been the heart-throb of Swallow Street Primary School and thirteen years on still appeared to be enjoying the title. He had blond hair and blue eyes and looked a bit like Denise van Outen.

'Hi!' she said, wishing she wasn't wearing a Snoopy T-shirt.

The crowning moment of Jess's school career had been when she and Brad had been on milk duty together. He had told her he loved her and wanted to kiss her. She had told him she loved him too but would only hold hands, due to a particularly confusing episode of *The Birds, the Bees, and All That Biz* where the lady had kissed the man and pretty much immediately produced a baby. Such was the extent of his love for her that he had promptly performed the same procedure on Stephanie who, as far as Jess knew, was still with him and who evidently, from the multi-coloured, multi-flavoured, multi-textured assortment in his basket, was up for more than just hand-holding.

'Hi there, gorgeous,' he gushed. Brad thought everyone was gorgeous, most noticeably himself.

'Hi.'

There was a moment's silence during which they did the

human version of bottom sniffing and Jess tried to think of something witty and interesting to say.

'So . . . how are you?'

'Fine. How are you?'

'Yeah. Fine.'

There was every danger that the conversation was about to follow a pattern similar to that of her French oral exam and she had no desire to go down the 'What are your hobbies?' route. Besides, it was blatantly obvious from the contents of his basket where his interests lay.

'Nice Snoopy T-shirt, eh?' she said, lest he thought she always dressed in a BhS nightie. It was her custom to fill awkward silences with remarks that rendered her more embarrassed than she would have been had she said nothing.

'You look fabulous,' he said, stroking Snoopy in a manner that wasn't, Jess decided, purely nostalgic, 'but you're not going to get out of my bad books that easily.'

'Really?' she said, intrigued. She wondered whether he could be referring to the milk-duty incident. After all, it had functioned as a silence-filler before.

'Because, you little devil, you nearly split Steph and me up last time we saw you.'

A large grin spread across Jess's face as she began to see herself as the woman Brad had always loved. She cast her mind back to the last time she'd met him. It had been in a restaurant and she'd been with her parents celebrating her birthday and he'd been with fifty friends celebrating that he had fifty friends. She'd tried to hide behind a pillar all night until her mum shouted, 'Isn't that Bradley MacCormack?' at which point everyone had turned round and stared.

Right enough, though, Stephanie *had* been weird. Why hadn't Jess twigged it was jealousy? She imagined a series of images featuring herself as the evil 'other woman': Stephanie throwing a saucepan at Brad screaming, 'Why do you still love her?'; Brad on his knees wailing, 'I can't help it, I can't help it'; Stephanie in an apron cooking him steak and pleading; Brad weeping into a milk bottle.

Suddenly she realised Brad had been talking. '. . . and I don't think Steph liked it much.'

'Liked what?'

'You going on and on about Trudy.'

Jess squinted as she struggled to fit Trudy into the over-crowded love triangle. 'What's Trudy got to do with it?'

'Quite a lot. I shagged her on and off for a year,' he said, as if Trudy were a tap. 'Steph's still paranoid about it.'

Jess stared blankly, crestfallen.

'It's OK, though,' he added quickly, mistaking her disappointment for concern, 'we're getting married.'

Jess grimaced, feeling as if she'd been punched on one side, staggered up and immediately punched on the other. 'You and Trudy?' she said, when she felt able to deliver it without sounding bitter. It wasn't that *she* wanted to marry him. Obviously. Just that it would've been nice to have had the option.

'Me and Steph.' He guffawed.

'That's nice,' she replied, as if her back teeth had been irrevocably clamped together.

'So. How are you and . . . Jasper, is it?'

'James,' she said, sourly.

'Wedding bells too?'

'We've decided to pursue meaningful ambitious careers first before giving in to middle age,' she replied, in a prepro-grammed monotone.

'Right . . . well,' he said, after an uncomfortable pause, 'I'd better be off. Things to do,' he added, nodding pointedly at the basket and planting a saliva trail down her left cheek. 'Great to see you again, gorgeous. Send my love to Jasper.' And with that he flounced off down the aisle, grabbing another couple of packets of Durex for good measure.

By the time Jess found her mum she was standing at the

checkout with a trolleyload that could quite comfortably have alleviated most of Sudan's famine.

'D'you think we've got everything?' she queried, as the old man in front placed his one tin of economy baked beans on the counter and counted out 11p. Jess felt as though she'd just removed £30 from a cashpoint then told the homeless person sitting under it that, sorry, she didn't have any money.

Watched by an inactive checkout woman, they emptied most of the trolley contents on to the conveyor belt, using the Moët as a brake to prevent the Camembert being squashed by the box of luxury Belgian chocolates. Once they'd crammed on everything but the fresh strawberries, the woman reached under the desk and pressed a buzzer. This seemed to give her *carte blanche* to sit with her arms folded and stare at the exit sign.

'Is there a problem?' Jess's mum hazarded, in the way that one asks somebody with tears streaming down their face if they're OK.

'Till receipt,' she said, then hit the buzzer again as if she were a contestant in *The Price is Right*.

It seemed to be a prerequisite of supermarket shopping, Jess decided, that no matter how often you thought you'd found the quickest queue, whenever it was your turn to be served there was always something wrong with the till.

After several more buzzer rounds a large woman with a beard appeared and started helping herself to a stack of £50 notes. Jess wondered whether it was Safeway's policy to employ women with facial hair: she had spotted a checkout girl two aisles along with the kind of growth James would have been proud of.

It wasn't until they made it home, however, that she found out why they had bought up most of the shop, bar the bearded assistants. They were expecting the McAllisters for dinner which, she realised miserably, meant two things:

(1) They would get out all the posh plates and silverware from the back of the cupboard, place them in fancy arrangements around the table, pretend they were accustomed to doing this and then wait until everyone was seated for her brother to say, 'Why have we all got four forks?'

(2) The McAllisters would talk *ad nauseam* about how their multiply talented daughter, Kirsty, was being head-hunted by so many firms she was confused by the choice, while asking Jess if she was still getting nowhere with the job search. Jess would try to explain how difficult it was and they would look at her as if she had just taken the year off work with self-diagnosed ME.

On balance, Jess decided, as she made a quick bolt for her bedroom, she would rather watch her own colonic irrigation.

'. . . and then guess who I met?' she prattled into the receiver three hours later, when she'd finally escaped what had degenerated into a baby-sitting-group coffee morning, with everyone agreeing that Kirsty's salary was advanced for her age and Jess's dependency on parental handouts indicative of a late developer.

'I can't.' James hated guessing games.

'Try.' Jess loved them.

'You don't know anyone in Inverness. I don't know . . . Your hairdresser?'

'Better-looking,' she said, cleaning her toenails with a fork. The day videophones were introduced, she thought, would be the day many long-distance relationships ended.

'Um . . . that girl you go swimming with . . . Ally?'

'Abbey. No. Better-look—' She stopped. 'Why? D'you think Abbey's pretty?'

'Not really.'

'What. Not at all?' She was offended. Abbey was her friend.

'Well . . . she's quite sexy, I suppose. Anyway, I thought I was meant to be guessing. Ummm . . . drippy Moira?'

'Sexy? Abbey? But she's got a fat bum! *And* a funny chin.'

'She can still be sexy.'

Jess paused as she recast Abbey in the role of lusted-after sex-goddess. She hated it when blokes picked at random some dumpy girl wearing jeans that tapered at the ankle and a Laura Ashley cardigan and announced that she was sexy. She was much happier with the Big-Tits-Blonde-Hair formula – at least she knew what she was aiming at.

'Well, sorry to disappoint you but it wasn't *sexy* Abbey,' she said, as if by admitting to finding her attractive James had also expressed a desire to sleep with her. 'It was sexy Brad.'

'Oh, right,' he mumbled, faking a doesn't-bother-me yawn. 'And who's he?'

'Just this guy.' Jess waited excitedly for the barrage of jealous questions. She'd teach him not to fancy her friends.

After a fairly long pause, a funny rustling sound started coming from the receiver. Maybe it was a tissue. Maybe he was crying. She softened a little. 'What you doing?'

'Checking the *Radio Times*. Apparently there's supposed to be some kind of *X Files* special on but I can't seem—'

'*James!*' she exploded. 'We're having a conversation.'

'Oh,' James said, sounding slightly surprised by this.

'Yeah, anyway. Brad. Yeah, he's very good-looking and sexy in a really understated kind of way and . . .' She paused to see if this was working.

'I see,' James inserted, in a voice that sounded remarkably like it was still coming from the *Radio Times*.

'And heaps of girls seem to fancy him, and stuff, and you can see why. I mean he's a real flirt, was like practically trying to shag me in the shop but nice with it, so it isn't really offensive, more kind of sweet and he's – James, are you listening?'

14

'Ye-es. He isn't really offensive, more kind of sweet. He sounds nice.'

'Aren't you jealous?'

'No, why should I be? I trust you.' Jess wasn't sure that she wanted to be trusted. 'And besides,' he continued, 'I think it's good for you to see people your own age. You can't spend your entire life with your mother.'

Jess sighed, feeling like a balloon three days after the party: deflated, shrivelled and not even worth stamping on. James was supposed to be eaten up with envy, turn a lurid green and weep I-love-yous down the phone. Not say Brad was nice and suggest she see him.

'Anyway, listen, I've got to go. I was supposed to be at the pub half an hour ago.'

'But . . . we haven't talked.'

'Jess! We've been on the phone for forty-five minutes, what else have we been doing?' James occasionally forgot the phone *was* the pub for most women. He, along with the rest of the male population, treated it as an efficient means of communicating X via A to B, where X is a straightforward arrangement, while women saw it as a relaxing leisure pursuit where X is introduced by A, squealed about by B, squealed about by A, enquired about by B, minutely detailed by A, analysed by B, re-analysed by A, theorised by B, pondered about by A, counter-referenced by B until someone else needs to use the phone or *Friends* is about to start, where X, most frequently male, is anything but a straightforward arrangement.

'Have a nice time, then,' Jess said, in a violin voice.

'Will do,' he chirped. 'See ya.'

She then sat and listened to the dialling tone, feeling sorry for herself until a lady-cum-intelligent-parrot told her, 'Please hang up and try again. Please hang up and try again.' She wondered whether this advice related to the phone call specifically or her relationship with James generally, and went off to bed to cry.

Happiest day of my life!!!!!
Except for getting 1 per cent more than Lucy Piles
 in Standard Grade Biology
And almost snogging Kevin at the Lit. Soc. Ball
 in second year (if the lights hadn't come up
 during Whitney's 'I Will Always Love You'
 creating an atmosphere of the stopping-to-put-
 on-a-condom variety)

Dear Alex,
 I've got a job!
 A job!
 I can't imagine this simple little three-letter word pleasing me more – except, perhaps, if it was prefixed with 'blow', accompanied by a ravishing blonde, and I was male.
 I am so unused to being happy I'm going a bit mad, kangaroo-leaping off my bed and doing high-pitched yelping as if I have just won a radio phone-in quiz. I know I would be calmer if I could just tell someone, but my parents, never normally more than half a millimetre away, seem to have taken my 'leave me alone's literally, and all my friends are in a meeting. (The fact that I am told this after the secretary has taken my name and put me on hold is something I will reserve to get paranoid about at a later date.)
 It all started this morning when I woke to find this insane message from my brother: 'Alien called – Job?' I was unsure whether this meant (a) an alien came to visit during the night on the off-chance I wanted a job, (b) there is an alien called Job or (c) my brother, an oft-suspected alien himself, had finally reached communication meltdown with humans and had left us for his friends

on planet *Job*. This was far and away the most appealing explanation.

Then, just as I had cleverly executed the balancing act of a mug of tea on one arm of the chair, a glass of orange on the other and a bowl of muesli wedged somewhere in the depths of my crotch, in time to catch the opening theme tune to Neighbours, *the phone rang. It was Aileen from Green Fingers Productions. She'd called earlier but been told I was 'in my pit' and wouldn't budge till* Neighbours.

'*Do you always begin your days at lunchtime?*' she asked.

'*No,*' I lied, lunging at the telly in a frantic effort to drown out the warblings of the latest model-turned-particularly-bad-actor, and recalling my interview six weeks previously where I'd enthused about being an early-morning person, 'never.'

Aileen is that friend of James's aunt, the one who gave me a sympathy interview after *she'd given the job to her unbelievably dull niece, Cynthia. She works with her husband Brian. At least, I think he's her husband. They show all the obvious signs of being married, i.e. familiar and slightly bored, but not sexual.*

Anyway, they do weird gardening programmes: a series I've never heard of called Gardener's Grotto *of which I claimed to be a fan – which felt a bit like pretending to get a joke then being terrified you might have to explain it – and a seven-minute slot on* Richard and Judy *commemorated, Royal Wedding style, on all their mugs.*

Apparently, unbelievably dull Cynthia couldn't cope. She found the job unfulfilling and walked out yesterday afternoon taking the cappuccino-maker in protest. How can anyone be so ungrateful? Does she not realise that most people would carve out their reproductive organs for a tea-making job in telly? I actually said that to Aileen and she seemed to like it. It is remarkable how quickly two people can unite over a shared dislike of another.

And then it came. She told me they would like to make me their new office manager and did I have any questions. An obvious one sprang to mind: 'What is an office manager?' but according to my CV I had been one last summer, so instead I asked what I should wear. Now I'm paranoid she'll think I'm vain. I have to admit, though, I have thought more about outfits than the job but this is only because I have got the job but not, as yet, any outfits.

So I am planning to buy the following:

1 orangey suit (Cosmo says orange is this season's power colour)

1 black suit (in case Cosmo is wrong)

1 pair of shoes that do not make my ankles look pinny, give me blisters, cause my heels to bleed, make me walk funny or encourage revolting growths to sprout out at odd angles from my toe joints, but instead look chic, comfortable and expensive

2 for the price of 1 plunge-neckline tops, currently pinned to the pertly bosomed mannequin in Top Shop's window (dubious as to where they might plunge on a non pertly bosomed human, hence £2.99, but I can't resist the bargain)

1 briefcase

1 bumper pack of streaky black tights – which will not look streaky in the packet but will once I have put them on and walked out of the front door

I have a budget of £200 so I might have to forgo the briefcase. The thing is, I've got completely obsessed with images of myself dashing between meetings in a flowing trench coat, clutching important documents and swinging a nice, leather, professional-looking briefcase.

Oh, I am so happy. I cannot decide whether I'm happy about the job because it is a job or because it is in London and means I will no longer be a sad graduate living at home with my parents. Also, am I pleased because it fulfils me personally and intellectually or because it is an answer to the 'What do you do?' question at parties? Tricky. Either way, I cannot wait to start talking about work as if it's a normal thing. It'll be weird to say 'work'. I've been practising in front of my mirror while doing handshakes with *invisible people and have just compiled a what's-in-what's-out list of sayings in the manner of a trendy fashion magazine.*

Phrases out	**Phrases in**
'in between jobs'	*'call me at work'*
'a few things in the pipeline'	*'meeting a few friends from*
'taking time to consider	*work'*
my options fully'	*'meeting'*
'chasing up promising	*'sorry, got held up at a*
contacts'	*meeting'*
	'salary'

Mmmm . . . I particularly like the last one. I'm not sure what it'll be as I didn't want to seem vain and *greedy by asking but I don't think it can be anything less than twenty – a managerial position, after all. I can't wait to feel rich and buy Clarins rather than Superdrug, Karen Millen rather than Miss Selfridge.*

And no more sucking up to the State for money either. Or my parents, for that matter. Actually, come to think of it, I'll still have to suck up to my parents because in my excited kangarooing I ripped up my signing-on book, which was unbelievably satisfying until I remembered I hadn't collected my last wodge of benefit and had therefore just shredded up £51.35. Clarins and Karen will just have to be patient.

Shit, doorbell. That'll be Moira. Back soon . . .

Oh, God, help me. I am in a completely foul mood (a) with James and (b) because I went shopping. I don't know what it is about shopping but I will always start off feeling perfectly fine and then within about forty-five minutes become crippled with the most blindingly furious temper that makes me want to kill everyone in sight including myself.

I made the mistake of taking drippy Moira with me, which was an unimaginable pain. (I have consequently decided that shopping compatibility should be a major consideration when selecting friends – not that I would class Moira as a friend exactly,

19

more a shit-I-haven't-called-Moira person though she confessed I was her closest ex-schoolmate yesterday, which made me feel both sorry and guilty – in that order.)

The problem was that she insisted on foraging at length in every lingerie department (she has finally got a boyfriend but only recently, and is therefore still at the stage of wearing nice underwear) and refused to help me sneak eight suits into the changing room at once. So I kept having to run out in my *underwear (certainly not nice) to retrieve the next set of three. I hate this rationing business. Surely if I'm going to steal clothes when I'm in the changing room I would be more imaginative than to pilfer eight navy suits?*

We ended up combing all the shops including, in a state of desperation, Dorothy Perkins. Naturally there was nothing. Why is it that whenever you go shopping with money and the intention of spending it there is never anything you like, but the minute you have no money and no intention you like everything and want to buy up the entire shop?

I found a lovely suit in this posh designer shop, which we had only gone into because Moira was feeling drippy and they had a comfy sofa and magazines. It was a sophisticated slate-grey thing with buttons running diagonally down from the shoulder and a rather tantalising price tag poking out from its accompanying neckerchief that seemed to suggest the whole thing was only £125.

Jubilant, I was about to try it on when an immaculately dressed Sloaney sales assistant pounced on me and asked, in a very uninviting tone, if I needed any help. It was dubious from the way she was looking at me whether this offer was directed at my shopping or my life in general. So I pointed to the suit and was told immediately that they didn't have it in my size. I was going to ask if she could order one, forgetting we were not in the mass-production world of M&S, when she pointed out that they sold the jacket separately at £800. I queried the maths of the whole ensemble including the neckerchief = £125, the jacket on its own = £800, to be told that the £125 price tag belonged to the neckerchief only. Humiliated, we skulked out, Moira badly disguising the fact she'd stolen the Clinique toner sachet from their Marie-Claire.

Predictably, therefore, I ended up in a frantic rush at 5.27 buying the first suit I had tried on and discarded in the first shop we'd gone into, thus rendering the previous five hours completely futile. It is not the wacky orange number Cosmo *sent me in search of but a maroon, tweedy thing that is totally not me. In fact, it is exactly the sort of thing Moira would wear. I despair at my susceptibility to the foul taste of others, culminating, in this instance, in the purchase of said gross suit. I look on this buy as Moira's revenge for my phoning her only when I have no one else to go out with.*

When I made it home I had a throbbing headache and an over-whelming desire to swallow the entire drinks cabinet, but settled instead for a beer in front of EastEnders *(true sign you are depressed when* EastEnders *constitutes light relief) – in which, I noticed enviously, the solution to clothes-shopping does not lie in traumatic excursions round half a city with an annoying friend and foul mood but instead in the ever-so convenient market stall from which everybody seems to find exactly what they are looking for straight away. Much preferred watching the good-looking vet hack away at Oscar's ingrowing claw on* Animal Hospital, *followed by a documentary about tadpoles turning into frogs, before phoning James, who would be a disappointing end result if the tadpole → frog → prince thing were to be true. He had instructed me not to call him until ten, up to which point he would be 'working very hard'.*

I'd been looking forward to telling him my good news, working out whether I would prefer my congratulations present to take the form of an embarrassingly large delivery from Interflora or a surprise weekend trip to Dublin. After much consideration I chose the Dublin trip on account of it taking more time and imagina-tion to organise. James, however, had chosen neither. He was in the middle of penalty time, shouted, 'You bloody idiot,' presumably at the telly and not me, and said he'd phone back in five minutes.

I waited by the phone for forty-five minutes, forming an impressively articulate argument in my head about how selfish he was (really satisfying, as I always win these arguments) until I discovered my brother had been hogging the line exchanging monosyllabic grunts with another delinquent. When James got through he was in an exceedingly chirpy mood. I have to admit I much prefer it when he's depressed. When he's all happy like this I get depressed because he's having a good time without me.

Anyway, he seemed pleased, though it was difficult to tell how much this had to do with the fact that Chelsea had just secured a 3–2 victory over Arsenal. He said he thought I would make a great office manager but couldn't imagine me being a businesswoman and thought it'd be much cuter if I worked in Tie Rack, to which I replied – cutely, 'OK, Wames, I wiwl wurk in Wie Wack.'

I wish I could stop doing this ridiculous pleasing-him thing but I have to say there is little point in getting pissed off with him for treating me like a shrew-woman when I cannot stop behaving like one. No matter how much I tell myself it is unattractive for a fully grown woman to speak like a two-year-old, I cannot seem to shake off the alarmingly subservient idea that it makes me more endearing.

What definitely did not, however, make me more endearing was the news that the job was taking me to London. I was unsure whether amid all my gooing he had grasped this so I pointed it out gently. 'Oh,' and then a very long silence was the reply.

This was not what I'd envisaged when skipping around fantasising about us in a one-bedroom flat with wooden floors and designer furniture somewhere in north London, snatching Prêt à Manger croissants together in the mornings and laughing over a bottle of Chardonnay in the evenings, me having just flown back from a day on location in George Clooney's garden, James having spent the day being jealous. Both of us happy and huggy.

Instead the image faded, like those happy scenes in scary films which you know are just there as precursors for something horrible to happen: James announced he was unsure of our relationship.

He thought it had got quite serious. Where he had dug up this negativity from (because 'serious' when it is used by a male to describe a relationship is, by definition, a negative term) eludes me, considering we see each other roughly one weekend in five.

If it hadn't been for (1) me pretending I had no plans for us living together, now or in the future, then (2) howling uncontrollably until he was mentally exhausted, I would now be single.

I feel emotionally drained. James makes me utterly miserable. Why can't we be a normal couple and whisper things like 'Me too,' down the phone and then when it's time to hang up play the 'No, you do it', 'No, you first', 'No, you' game. Tara phoned me the other day and went on and on about how she and Phil spend all their time laughing. She says they don't need alcohol or drugs because they get high on each other. Apparently he took her away in his dad's camper-van to the Isle of Mull to celebrate their year's anniversary and lit floating candles in the sea, one for each month they'd been together. James wouldn't have a clue. James doesn't have a clue. His numerical memory is stretched to its limit by football league tables and how many hours' sleep he is going to get. Oh, I am so depressed.

I am posting this to your forwarding address as instructed by your mother – not sure if Nanchang is the name of the town or the people you are staying with. She says she hasn't heard anything from you for a while either. That was not meant to be a hint. Miss you.

Lots of love,
Jess
xxx

PS James says I can stay with him and his aunt and uncle until I find somewhere to live but I must realise he's working very hard and will not have time for any of my traumas. He *is* my trauma.

PPS Apparently his uncle thinks I sound sweet. I think his uncle sounds sweet.

'Yes?' A tall man with a moustache had just opened the door looking irritated.

'It's Jess,' she said, trying to smile.

The tall man looked blank. She realised, appalled, that he had no idea who she was.

'Um . . . I've just . . . I'm here,' she began, trying to think of a polite way to phrase 'to live with you', when he suddenly shouted, 'Wendy!' and stormed off into the house.

She stood feeling dejected. Not only had James failed to show up at the airport despite her fantasies that, riddled with guilt and overpowering feelings of love, he might, he had now also failed to show at his house and, by all accounts, to tell anyone else that she would.

'Jess, hello.' A pretty middle-aged woman, presumably his aunt, had appeared. 'Sorry about David,' she said, tossing her head towards the hall. 'Memory like a sieve. Come on, let's get you in and sorted out.'

Jess bent down to pick up the first of her many bags then peered upwards smiling. A look of horror had just crossed Wendy's face. 'Good Lord, these aren't all yours, are they?'

'Um, well . . .' Jess giggled. There was no way of phrasing this one politely.

'David!' she shouted, and disappeared into the house.

When they had humped all six monstrosities up three storeys to a room that had clearly only become a guest one in the last half-hour, Jess felt about as wanted as a double-glazing salesman who, under the misguided impression that his services would be welcome, had just turned up with several windows, some wooden frames and an industrial glass-cutter. An anonymous B-and-B suddenly seemed appealing.

'I'm afraid James and Emma are out,' Wendy volunteered, as she puffed up a pillow, 'celebrating.'

Emma was James's nineteen-year-old cousin, whom he seemed to find attractive, intelligent and fun, qualities that Jess had not heard him bend over backwards to use when he talked about her. Nevertheless, she was not going to get jealous. Emma was obviously not all bad if she was prepared to celebrate the job of a cousin's girlfriend she had never met. And James, though not the most reliable luggage porter, had clearly been thinking about her. She smiled as she imagined the two of them raising their glasses to her success.

'They're both terribly pleased,' Wendy added, clutching the pillow and smiling into the distance.

'That's nice,' Jess replied modestly.

'Yes, we're all very proud.'

Jess paused. 'Thank you,' she said, smiling, 'that means a lot to me.' She had a feeling things were not going to be as bad as she'd anticipated.

'Of course, Emma's wanted this for ages,' Wendy inexplicably announced, 'but never dreamed she'd get into St Martin's.'

Jess flinched.

'You didn't know it was St Martin's, did you?' she said proudly.

'No . . . I—'

'So you can see why they're celebrating.' She grinned.

'Yes,' Jess replied sourly, 'I can now.'

Before there was time for the anger to sear uncontrollably through her veins, there was a scratching noise at the door and a little girl in a Buffy the Vampire Slayer nightie appeared.

'What's that, Mummy?' she squeaked, pointing at Jess, as if she'd just broken in through the skylight.

'That's James's friend,' Wendy replied, as Jess pretended to busy herself with a suitcase zip and tried not to get paranoid over 'friend'.

'Why is she here?'

'Hello,' Jess interjected, in an attempt to field the questioning. 'What's your name?'

The little girl looked terrified and fled to safety behind her mum. 'Mummy,' she whined, 'when is she going?'

'Very soon, darling,' Wendy said, stroking her hair lovingly. 'Very soon.'

When Jess had been left in peace she sat on the tentatively erected camp-bed sobbing pitifully, wishing for the first time ever that she was at home with her parents. Being in a strange place was one thing. Being in a strange place the night before the first day of a new job, patently unwanted by your hosts – including your boyfriend, who would rather go out and flirt with his cousin than meet you at the airport – was on a different plane of misery altogether. She decided to give up on the day and go to bed . . .

'Je-ess?'

She had gone to work but forgotten to wear any clothes and was trying to hide behind a fake cactus.

'Jessie baby?'

But someone had found her and was shining a very bright light in her face. They stank of smoke. They were also pissed.

'It's your boyfriend,' James bellowed, collapsing on top of her as the bed collapsed under her.

'You've just woken me up,' she murmured, resisting the urge to hug him as the evils of his recent behaviour came flooding back. 'I dreamed you were a cactus.'

'That's not a dream, baby,' he slobbered, insinuating something revolting with his groin.

'Jamie, you're disgusting,' a voice twittered from behind them.

'Jess,' he announced, lurching up, 'meet my fantastic Bohemian cousin, Twinkle.'

He was right, Jess thought. This wasn't a dream at all. It was a nightmare. 'Hi,' she said, as he pulled a tiny little person on to the bed to join them. She looked like a seal pup: sleek, shiny black bob, big, dark, intelligent eyes, cute little upturned nose. She would get whiskers in later life, Jess noted reassuringly.

'I was under the impression your name was Emma,' she said, flatly.

'It is,' Twinkle sparkled.

'I call her Twinkle,' James said, drunkenly flinging an arm over her shoulder, 'because she's such a star.'

It turned out, much to Jess's annoyance, that Twinkle had taken more than a bit of a shine to James, too, and at half past one in the morning decided to make this known with a pillow fight. Having pretended to find this amusing for approximately half a minute, Jess reminded them that her first day's work started in a few hours' time, at which point they descended downstairs to giggle over a whisky leaving her feeling like the head prefect and wishing that they'd tried at least once to persuade her to join them. After a series of squeals and conversation too quiet to make out but too intriguing to ignore, they had fallen asleep precisely at the moment Jess realised she couldn't.

'"When the red, red robin goes bob-bob-bobbin'"' – nine sevens are sixty-three, nine eights are . . . seventy-one, seventy-two, "The quick brown fox . . ." Oh, God.'

It was now 4.36 a.m. and her mind had started to go warped and peculiar. Maybe they hadn't offered her the job at all? What if she had misunderstood on the phone and they had told her they would *like* to give her the job but couldn't? They hadn't sent confirmation. Maybe she had been so delirious with depression she had *imagined* the phone call?

Suddenly she became aware of a strange rumbling noise. It sounded like a lorry being driven at speed over a series of cattle-grids, but unless they lived next door to a farm, it was James.

It wasn't enough for him, she thought angrily as she thrashed her head from side to side, to luxuriate in a bed the size of Brazil while she lay cramped on something a Lilliputian would have difficulty squeezing into, he had to show off this fact by doing loud snoring. It was an irritating reminder that he was blissfully asleep while she was not. She decided to wake him up and tell him this, but just as she got to her door, a small piece of paper caught her eye.

'Good luck. I love you,' it said. She read it again in stunned amazement. 'Good luck. I love you.' There was no mistaking it. As unlikely as the idea was, it had been written by James.

She grinned, marvelling at how such a tiny gesture could make everything she had ever hated about him vanish into thin air. He was always doing this: behaving like a wanker possessed then doing something sweet and endearing that cancelled out all his crimes and transformed him, albeit briefly, into the kind and loving boyfriend she had always hoped he might be.

She climbed back into bed in a haze of warm, fuzzy feelings, which were immediately cut short by the realisation that her ankle had caught round the flex of the lamp, which, after toppling dangerously around on the dresser, had just crashed noisily to the floor. It was a pink rabbit-shaped thing, which looked deceptively like something from a school tombola but was probably, she panicked, a cherished family heirloom.

She lay there, heart beating frantically, more awake than she ever normally was during the day. The birds outside had started doing happy chirping accompanied by a whirring milk float and distant miaow, as if this was not the middle of southwest London but somewhere on the set of *Postman Pat*. She listened as the busy world crept into action and slowly, gradually, felt her eyelids drooping . . . her head lolling . . . her mind drifting . . . peace . . . calm . . . then *brrring!* The alarm clock.

'For fuck's sake,' she screeched. She opened her eyes, reached over and slammed it off. Then closed her eyes and vowed to stay that way until the weekend.

The weekend – thank God. (I am now a work
  person who lives for the weekend rather than a
  student/unemployed person whose life is one
  long weekend)
Long to be a student/unemployed person
Soon to be a homeless person

Dear Alex,

  I hate my job.

  Being an office manager is not the exciting round of business meetings, film sets and George Clooney's garden but long, dull days in a cramped office, filing. Why didn't I listen to everyone who told me that working in TV is not glamorous?

  There are only three of us in the office – so much for my new work friends – so I don't even have the distraction of some fanciable male around to ease the boredom. (I resorted yesterday to the desperate measure of flirting with the courier. But he turned out to be foreign and just did manic nodding to everything I said.) There is no office gossip or in-jokes about Sandra from Accounts and my expensive tweed suit is redundant because everyone wears jeans. Oh, God. I hate my job.

  This is a typical day:

9.14 a.m. *I arrive at the office late, after an hour of tube trauma wedged under an undesirable man's armpit.*

9.30 a.m. *I open the mail: five identical copies of* Viking Direct *and one invoice.*

9.35 a.m. *I throw all the* Viking Directs *straight into the bin then spend half an hour searching for the right file to file the invoice.*

10.00 a.m. Brian arrives and talks at length about the new kittens' latest antics (is it just me or are other people's pet stories very dull?).

10.25 a.m. The phone rings. It is Aileen saying she will be late because a kitten has chewed her tube ticket. Brian thinks this is sweet.

10.30 a.m. Brian asks me to renumber in reverse order all invoices dating from 1975.

10.31 a.m. I go into the loo and swear at him.

10.33 a.m. I reappear and embark on file 1 of 38.

11.33 a.m. I am still on file 1 of 38.

11.34 a.m. I cleverly devise a new, faster system of numbering.

11.50 a.m. Aileen arrives with more kitten stories. Brian finds them funny and I get a sore jaw from lots of fake laughing.

12.30 p.m. I attempt to guard a hideously overpriced mozzarella sandwich from the marauding mangy pigeons in Soho Square. I eavesdrop on the juicy gossip of my bench companions while pretending to wait for friends by looking from the gate to my watch and back at the gate again with a perplexed expression.

1.30 p.m. I return to find the invoice file has bred in my absence: Brian has found an extra boxload.

2.10 p.m. I am momentarily relieved by a phone call from constantly cheery Jason at the photocopier company. He asks after my weekend as if we are long-term friends. An alarming thought that we might become so.

3.15 p.m. Highlight of the day! Brian asks me to send a fax to Channel 4.

3.40 p.m. I get a call from Channel 4 telling me they have just received twelve blank pages.

3.41 p.m. I re-fax correct side up with a note apologising for the dodgy fax machine.

4.10 p.m. I am nearing the end of file 1.

4.11 p.m. Horrific realisation that my new, faster system of numbering has resulted in five invoice no. 378s. The thought of re-renumbering is an insane one.

4.12 p.m. I hide four no. 378s in my bag.

5.20 p.m. I stand in a long queue at the post office with one letter.

6.00 p.m. Brian and Aileen leave planning their trip home via the catfood shop. They tell me I can go when I have finished file 1.

6.01 p.m. I go.

James is being distinctly unsympathetic about the whole thing and has started mentioning Tie Rack again. I think he must find something perversely sexual about the thought of me selling ties to balding men. For this and other reasons I am in a foul mood with him and am presently sulking in my room.

By the way, before I forget, thank you so much for your PC. Mum forwarded it to me along with a request from some alumni thing wanting cash from all graduates – yeah, sure, I'm three grand in debt but, hey, let me give you a couple more towards restoring the end gable of the philosophy building! Beijing sounds fun, though I must admit I had pictured you in a more rustic setting of the ploughing-barefoot-in-the-paddy-fields ilk, rather than getting sloshed on beer in a pub and tumbling into bed with whoever happens to be around. Isn't that what we went to uni for?

Anyway, I'm glad you are safe and well and not having to shut yourself up in a room to make your wanker boyfriend realise you are upset and angry! To be honest, I don't know why I'm bothering. Unless the person for whose benefit you are sulking is aware of it, there is little point in doing it. I have been here now for over three hours getting bored while he is downstairs doing merry laughing at the telly. However, I am being mature about it and refusing to let his happiness and disregard for my emotions annoy me.

To tell you the truth, I think half of my mood-from-Satan is a result of a prolonged hangover from last night. I had to go to one of James's scary fund-manager friend's parties full of successful, confident people, which just meant I got unattractively drunk, slurred a series of regrettably cringeful things and ended up with my head down the loo at 10 p.m.

I think the main problem was that I only knew two people, including James, and since I didn't want to appear a pathetic clingy girlfriend who couldn't talk to anyone, I spent a lot of time by myself gulping cheap white wine from a plastic cup, pretending I had chosen to be by myself by studying the backs of CD covers.

(According to Marie-Claire, *if this happens you are supposed to try frequent trips to the loo in the hope of meeting someone interesting on the way, but I just kept getting cornered by a weird man with a beard who seemed to have wandered in from the street, so I gave up.)*

I finally met the all-wonderful Zadia, though. James's description was useless. She has not got long blonde hair and blue eyes but shoulder-length light auburn hair and green eyes, although to be honest I was so pissed when I met her she could have had four heads and a Mohican. The minute we were introduced I started scrutinising her for possible flaws, which was harder than I had assumed it would be. She is one of those annoying girls who is pretty, friendly, bubbly, bright and interesting, but only when surrounded by blokes. When stranded with me she was both boring and bored.

I must say, I find these Jekyll-and-Hyde girls very irritating because they make all men love them by being flirty and fun and make all women seem bitter and cynical for noticing this. I have to admit, though, it is a clever trick.

Decided to try and copy her when I'd successfully ensnared a ginger-haired guy from Liverpool, but it was useless. He spent the duration of our conversation looking at someone – probably Zadia – over my left shoulder while I behaved like a demented cat watching a game of ping-pong in a desperate bid to make eye contact.

I soon realised, however, that all the fun people were, despite a magnificently large front room, squashed into the security of a matchbox-sized kitchen. Squeezed my way on to the only empty space – the fridge – and quickly realised why it was empty after splaying my legs for the tenth lad to retrieve a can of Foster's. I gave up and went to find James who, I was momentarily relieved to discover, was with a bloke. But the bloke turned out to be Tom. James seems to have developed a worrying schoolboy crush on Tom and I cannot see why. Tom is dull – the kind of person who reads the instructions to a microwavable meal – and only ever talks about his career at the Bar. I tried to lighten the tedious one-sided conversation we, or rather, he was having with a joke about improving his career by drinking more (he only drinks apple juice) but it lost its punch due to over-explanation.

(It's a bit embarrassing, really, because it was he who discovered me passed out on the loo – he was the only one left after everyone else in the queue had given up banging on the door and buggered off to wee in the next-door neighbour's flower-bed.)

By the time I'd staggered home with an equally pissed James I was seeing double, and as a result dropped a full pint of milk on the tiled kitchen floor. James's contribution to the situation was to slur repeatedly, 'Don't cry over spilt milk,' which, to a very drunk person at one in the morning, seemed hilarious, causing me to spend the following half-hour buckled over with hysterics as he attempted to Hoover up both glass and milk.

The fun ended, however, with the vacuum cleaner making strange smells, then strange noises, then evil growls, which turned out not to be the Hoover but James's uncle, red-faced and furious, swearing at high volume from the landing. The man has gone from finding me a mild nuisance to loathing the very sight of me.

As a result, I was relieved to escape the aftermath by getting up early this morning for a haircut – which, incidentally, is one of the other reasons I am so pissed off with James. It was he who made me have it done in the first place, saying it had got 'very long', which clearly decodes as 'very foul', and now it looks revolting and he doesn't even care.

Of course, I knew the minute I booked the appointment my hair would transform itself into a beautiful mane and look wonderful and so was not in the least bit surprised to wake up this morning to a Vidal Sassoon masterpiece.

Why does this always happen? For the previous three months I have attacked it with the entire Superdrug hair-care counter, including some ominous brown fudge stuff that I was duped into buying by the manufacturers, whose promises of 'adding volume overnight' led me to believe that at £18.50 a thimbleful they had to be telling the truth. And then I threaten it with a hairdresser and suddenly it does exactly what it should.

Anyway, it was a disaster. I should've predicted it, really. Anything that calls itself the Chop Shop is unlikely to specialise in subtlety. And I should know by now that it is always a good idea to take advice on hairdressers from someone whose hairstyle you like – rather than Aileen, who seems to model herself on a sculped weasel.

The minute I walked into the salon, which – another clue – was empty, six bleached hairdressers stopped gossiping and stared at me. In a pathetic voice I asked for Sammy, praying to the heavens above that she was not the grumpy-looking one in the corner. She was.

I was marched to the sink and, at the mercy of ten blue talons, given a nasty acupuncture-like scrubbing, which had the effect not just of cleaning my hair but of waking decades of dormant dandruff in the process. By the time she had finished my shoulders looked alarmingly as though they'd been caught in a brief Siberian snow flurry. She then ushered me into a seat and invited me to stare at my reflection in the mirror while she set to work demolishing what she described as 'unusually lifeless hair'. After smiling politely, I attempted to tell her I wanted to keep the length at the front and trim the rest but she just nodded then proceeded to do the reverse.

Having realised with a great deal of relief that we were not going to talk about boyfriends or holidays in Tenerife or, indeed, anything, I settled down to fixate upon my ugliness. I don't know *why, but I always look particularly vile in hairdresser's mirrors. I was shortly distracted from this self-loathing, however, by the discovery that my hair on one side was shorter than it was on the other, and hesitantly tried to point this out with lots of maybes, could-just-be-mes, not-sures. Sammy looked pissed off and continued to dry my hair in a bouffant. Then I found myself doing lots of sorrys, must-just-be-mes, thank-yous in a way that suggested she was the paying customer. Contrary to pre-cut visions of looking like Cameron Diaz with dark hair, I now resemble something out of* Prisoner: Cell Block H.

I decided to wait for James to notice before I said anything, which meant sitting through an entire rugby match with him stroking it affectionately, and me getting bored. Amused myself by imagining what a tribesman from the Kalahari would make of something that has men stampeding and mounting each other, pushing, grabbing, tripping up and wounding each other, but which purports, because it involves a ball, to be a game. I found the idea of legitimising such barbarity strangely comical and pointed this out to James, who looked at me crossly and accused me of taking a frivolous attitude to a highly skilful sport.

I got my own back, however, by faulting him for lack of obser-vation, i.e. my hair. He said he'd thought I looked different and, moving his head towards me in a token attempt at interest while keeping his eyes firmly fixed on the telly, said it was nice. I chal-lenged the meaninglessness of the word nice whereupon he suggested 'fine', followed swiftly, when he glimpsed my enraged expression, with the acceptable alternative 'chic'.

'Do you think it's more chic than before?' I asked him beadily.

'Yes,' he replied confidently.

'So you didn't like it before, then?'

The game ended with him telling me that I was obsessed with my appearance and me storming out melodramatically, shouting, 'Only because I am deeply insecure about the way you feel about me and am crying out for love,' which, though effective, turned out also to be embarrassing as his aunt was next door and heard all.

Anyway, I am now in an awkward situation because it's dinner-time and I refuse to talk to James, am still too mortified to face his aunt and live in fear of ever seeing his uncle again. Also, I don't think I can stand another night watching him piss himself laughing every time Emma opens her mouth. He insists she is a 'complete scream' and looks at me as though I am intrinsically evil if I so much as suggest that she isn't a fantastically amusing, entertaining and generous-spirited individual.

As a result I am now convinced he fancies her, which as well as being depressing causes a confusing problem in my head. Cousins, like other people's girlfriends, are supposed to be in the safe zone, not wandering around freely with the enemy.

On top of this I fear a repeat of last night's meal where his seven-year-old cousin, Lucy, took the opportunity of an assembled audience to announce she'd seen James and Jess 'doing something on the bed'. We were hugging, but this is difficult to justify in front of a pair of suspicious, disapproving relatives without turning puce in the process.

I can tell it's time to leave, so I will have to start looking in the sad and lonely column for flatmates soon, in the manner of a desperate person out of Shallow Grave. *Should this be my last letter to you, I hereby leave you my manicure set – as yet unused because I am still, despite ten years of trying, a neurotic nail-biter.*

Yours lovingly,
Jess
xxx

PS Bumped into arrogant Rupert from first-year Classical Culture lectures this afternoon. I was sweating along on Lucy's bike with my knees banging on my chin and almost cycled over him. He pretended not to see me until I shouted, 'Oi, Rupert Fotheringham-Bailey.' I hadn't noticed that he was with a stunning girl (who looked remarkably, come to think of it, like my pissed recollection of Zadia, but can't have been because she didn't seem to recognise me) and would certainly not have attempted confident name-shouting had I known. I stood feeling insecure as she stared at me and he did a crap attempt at being interested (still does annoying flicking of public-school floppy hair). He kept saying, 'Right, right,' whenever I said anything, then cut me off mid-sentence and said to the girl, 'Sorry, this is . . . Crikey, I've completely forgotten your name.' Double humiliation as I had obviously remembered all three of his.

'Three pints of lager, please,' Jess shouted, at a girl she could've sworn she'd seen somewhere before.

She had arranged to meet James and Toby in a place called the Bank of England, whose name had encouraged her to look for cash machines and mortgage posters, and when this had proved unsuccessful, to wait outside a neighbouring branch of Lloyds in the belief that James, the stupid prat, had got it wrong.

'How was I supposed to know it was a pub?' she whined, when an irate James found her half an hour later standing under a large sign appropriately titled 'Losing Interest'.

'Because how many banks do you know that serve alcohol?'

Weaving her way back through the thicket of pin-striped suits with a lager stain that didn't look immediately like lager marking her trousers, Jess marvelled at the hypocrisy of her fellow Londoners. They would make out it was living hell to be crammed into a tube carriage, squashed up against sweating strangers with no room to move and no air to breathe, then actively go and seek out those very conditions in a place where the only discernible difference lay in getting a pint of beer sploshed down you. As she got nearer, she could hear James and Toby talking.

'. . . and she's so kind and loving and always there for me. We have this kind of unconditional love thing, which is like, you know, so natural and . . . no one even comes close.' James was staring into his empty pint glass with the expression of a Channel 5 soap-opera actor about to cry. 'I just wish I could tell her this kind of stuff.'

'Yeah, I know mate, she's great. Not bad-looking either.' Toby grinned, blowing little haloes of smoke rings above both of them.

Jess felt a surge of happiness. Unconditional love. Kind and loving. No one even comes close. He loved her. Utterly loved her. And Toby, bless him, thought she was pretty.

Smiling coyly she handed them their drinks, making sure she kept the smallest one for herself. It was, after all, the sort of kind and loving thing she would do.

'So. What are you two gorgeous men talking about?' They had suddenly become unquestionably gorgeous, she decided.

'The love of James's life,' Toby replied, putting an arm around his friend. Jess tried hard not to grin before her compliment. 'His mother.'

There was a long-drawn-out pause while she tried to reassemble her expression.

'That's nice,' she said, then began doing manic machine-gun laughing.

James and Toby stared. 'What's so funny?' James asked, as if he was going to suggest she might like to 'share it with the rest of the class'.

'Nothing.'

'Wouldn't you agree she's a fairly amazing woman?' Toby slavered.

'Well, yeah, s'pose,' Jess mumbled. 'A bit neurotic about food, though.' She'd read somewhere there were two things you never criticised in a man: one was his manhood and the other she'd forgotten – until now.

'What d'you mean neurotic?' James snapped.

'Well, like the minute you say you're going out she starts preparing a little packed lunch.' She giggled, looking to Toby for support. Toby had suddenly developed an urge to study the inside of his pint glass. 'And if you tell her you missed breakfast last Tuesday she practically has a hernia.'

'Bollocks. Anyway, she's not neurotic.' He drained his glass and thumped it down on the bar. 'She just likes nurturing me.' Then, as if the fraught atmosphere had been detected by radio waves, his mobile rang.

39

'Hello,' he barked, and softened immediately. 'Hi, Mum.'

James's mum lived in Hong Kong but remained forever in touch with him. Jess had a feeling that the umbilical cord had not been properly severed at birth.

'Yes, I promise . . . yes' – jolly laughing – 'yes, Mum . . .' More jolly laughing.

'She's probably checking he's eaten dinner,' Jess said, smirking. Toby looked unimpressed.

'You too' – loving smile – 'love you lots, 'bye.' James grinned as he put away his phone. Jess tried not to feel second-best. The no-one-even-comes-close comment seemed more acute than ever, given that she was standing inches away from him and his mum was half-way round the globe. Then, just as she was working out what to say that would not sound bitter, petty or even vaguely jealous, he let out a little yelp of delight and threw open his arms in joy. 'Oh, my God, look who it is.'

Jess turned round to where the familiar-looking barmaid was standing carrying a turret of empty pint glasses and beaming enthusiastically at James.

'Look who it is indeed!' the barmaid squealed, jettisoning the glasses and giving him a hug that seemed to involve licking his neck. 'What are you doing here?'

'What are *you* doing here more like?' He looked ecstatic.

'Discovering that life as a freelance journalist doesn't pay the bills.' She laughed, gesturing to the glasses.

'Zadia's a writer,' James announced proudly, to what appeared to be Zadia.

Suddenly Jess made the connection. The girl at the party, the girl with Rupert, the girl behind the bar were all one and the same: irritating Zadia.

'James is a liar,' Zadia replied, laughing. 'Zadia's written two articles for the *Independent* and is having to scrape a living as a barmaid.'

Oh, God, Jess thought. She wasn't allowed to be attractive, nice, funny *and* modest.

'Jess, have you—'

'Yes, I can't believe it,' Zadia said brightly. 'We met the other day when I was with Rupert.'

'I'm sorry,' Jess replied coolly, feigning a blank expression and looking pointedly over Zadia's left shoulder, 'but I've completely forgotten your name.'

'You needn't have been so rude,' James hissed, when half an hour later they were hovering in Toby and Vanya's hallway.

'She was flirting.'

'She was being *friendly*.'

'So does that entitle me to stick my tongue in Toby's ear?'

Just at that moment Vanya wandered past with a stereo. She was Toby's long-term girlfriend with whom Jess was obliged to get on *because* she was Toby's long-term girlfriend.

'You wouldn't want to do that in a hurry, Jess,' she shouted, from the kitchen. 'He's got a wax build-up worse than an M25 traffic jam.'

'I'm not having this conversation,' James whispered, angrily.

'Because you know I'm right.'

'Because I know you're too immature to deal with the fact that someone might just want to be nice.'

'Do you fancy her?'

'Get lost, Jess.'

'Do you fancy her?'

'I'm not even going to answer that.'

'Food's up, you two,' Toby yelled cheerfully from next door.

'So you do.'

'For Christ's sake, Jess,' he exploded, kicking the skirting-board, 'what the fuck do you want me to say? Yes, I fancy her, and want to shag every little fibre out of her cute blonde tiny pores. Yes, I think she's got the most beautiful legs and I dream about them wrapped around my neck every night. Yes, I—'

'James, *sssh*,' Jess shouted, pointing tearfully at the kitchen

41

while trying to remember what Zadia's legs looked like and whether she would have described them as beautiful.

'Why?' James shouted, even louder. 'Eh? You embarrassed?'

'No . . . I . . . you,' she spluttered, unable to emit anything but a high-pitched squawk.

'You know what your problem is, Jess?' he continued, fiery-eyed.

She was tempted to say, 'You,' but had learnt, rather terrifyingly, the last time she'd done this that that had not been the answer he'd had in mind.

'You're so wrapped up in your own pathetic little world you can't think about anyone else. You can't stand the idea that I might enjoy the company of someone who isn't you. Well, here's news for you. I do. And if you've got a problem with that you either grow up or get out.' With that he kicked the skirting-board again, stormed through to the kitchen and left Jess crouched on top of Toby's football boots, sobbing pitifully.

By the time she'd toyed with the idea of marching home, rejected it on the grounds that it would be too depressing and lonely when she got there, imagined a series of accidents with oncoming cars that without being disfiguring or fatal would leave her wounded enough to make James feel guilty, then resolved to be mature about the whole situation by ignoring him for the rest of the evening, they had started eating without her. When she walked into the room, of course, everyone started speaking as though they were foreigners.

'James. How did you find work today?'

'I found it satisfactory, thank you, Toby. The pepper, could you pass it?'

'Certainly, James. Do you require the salt also?'

Jess looked round to where Vanya was chopping what appeared to be grass. She'd prepared a small Pakistani banquet, complete with funny-smelling candles and vulva-shaped napkins, and had tuned the radio to a station that played consecutive eighties love ballads of the sort listened to by late-night mini-cab drivers.

'Smells gorgeous, Vanya.' She hesitated, self-conscious.

'Oh, it's nothing special,' Vanya said, sieving yoghurt through a tea-strainer. She was one of those people who kept creamed coconut in the cupboard, just in case, and claimed that cooking was fun not function. But Jess had to concede that she did a marvellous job in pretending the recent screaming match had not taken place, and by the time dessert came along, had them all in stitches over a photograph in *OK!* magazine where Baby Brooklyn, strapped in a Manchester United baby sling, looked deceptively like a frog.

'Apparently Beckham's already got him signed up,' Toby said, jealously.

'Yeah but you read that in the *Sun*,' Vanya laughed, 'which also claimed that Posh is suing for half a million because someone said he'd inherited her Pinocchio nose.'

'Better that than her brains,' Toby said, guffawing.

'I like her nozhe,' James slurred.

But, once coffee arrived, Jess was less happy to discover Posh's nose had turned into Pamela Anderson's breasts, not literally – obviously – although in view of how little of Pamela's body was her own, Jess thought, it would not have been a surprising transformation.

'Yourzhe're nisher,' James slurped, having unashamedly ogled the topless Pam while everyone else felt obliged to wash up.

'No, they're not,' Jess replied, in a nun's voice. She wished it didn't take a scantily clad woman and a bottle and a half of wine for James to pay her a compliment.

'Zhay are,' he persisted, slipping a hand up her top to check.

The last time this had happened had been on the sofa in her parents' house when Sammy Palmer had lunged at her fourteen-year-old breasts, squished them around like Plasticene then tweaked a nipple until it bled. Had things really progressed since then, she wondered, removing James's hand and dashing to the loo to refasten her bra? Why were they still at the stage of behaving like sex-starved adolescents when Toby and Vanya were talking mortgages and mattress covers? Relationships, she decided, were like the London Marathon, and while everyone else was hurtling towards the finishing line, she and James were stuck at the start struggling to tie up their shoelaces.

'Who wants to know what the future holds?' Vanya chirped, dancing into the kitchen with a pack of Tarot cards. To Jess, the idea that this was something one undertook for enjoyment was baffling.

'Not that witchy crap,' James spluttered, re-evaluating his opinion when he noticed that some of the cards depicted bare-breasted maidens. 'Oh, *yes*.'

Vanya started shuffling the cards and talking in a voice she presumably thought made her seem mystic, then solemnly handed them to Jess, telling her to spread them only when she felt ready.

'Jessish alwaysh ready tershpreadem,' James chortled, causing Toby to look at Jess with renewed interest.

'Oh, shut up, James,' the girls chorused.

As Jess began carefully to lay out the cards, Vanya made encouraging groaning sounds, which, Jess thought, if she had been standing outside the room, would not necessarily be associated with a Tarot reading. Then just when things seemed to be looking promising, she turned over the Devil. 'Oh, no,' she moaned, suspecting, despite her Tarot ignorance, that a horned monster with a five-foot pronged fork was not a good thing. James and Toby, who had been unnaturally quiet, exploded with laughter.

'It's not funny,' she snapped.

'Yesh, tish,' James said, pointing at the card to indicate they were not laughing at her misfortunate future but at the Devil's microscopic penis.

44

'Look, if you two aren't going to take this seriously,' Vanya said, abandoning her spooky voice, 'go next door. The Tarot doesn't respect non-believers.'

Jess remembered someone saying the same thing about Ouija boards when she and some friends had thought it would be fun to do instead of double geography. Soon afterwards Freddy's perfectly healthy uncle had collapsed and died and they were convinced it was because they'd taken the piss out of the Ouija board. She decided to tell the story, substituting her own uncle as the victim to make it more frightening and dramatic, knowing that James was too drunk to remember she had never had an uncle.

'OK,' Vanya said slowly, peering at the cards with the concern of an *ER* doctor about to diagnose a pregnant woman with cancer.

'What? What is it?' Jess recognised Vanya's frown from the last time they'd done this.

'Well . . . the Devil's your immediate obstacle and this means . . . Hold on . . .' She picked up a book and began reading earnestly. 'This means that the questioner, that's you, must rid himself of a situation in which he feels trapped and oppressed. He is in a hopeless position,' she said, pointing to a weaselly chained creature in the foreground of the card. 'That's you – causing him misery and despair. The looming figure of the Devil behind,' she continued, looking pointedly at James, 'represents the problem the questioner feels is bearing down upon him, plaguing his whole existence.'

It didn't require a degree in Tarot reading to figure this one out, and while Jess wasn't sure she liked the ease with which Vanya had attributed to her the role of the shackled rodent, she took some degree of comfort from the pictorial representation of James, which had clearly left him lacking in a crucial department.

'But your future looks fantastic,' Vanya said enthusiastically, drawing this conclusion solely from a card that featured

45

what James described as a 'ponce in a skirt'. 'This card represents a sexy, attractive and charming young man, who would make a very exciting lover. It foretells a new relationship or change of sexual partner,' she exclaimed, as Jess, grinning insanely, began to plan how and where she might meet her Clooneyite hero.

''S'all bollocksh anyway,' James blurted, through his third cup of coffee, seemingly unfazed that having appeared as an inadequately genitalled devil he was now about to be upstaged by a Dale Winton lookalike in bonnet and slippers.

After a degree of unattractive begging from Jess, though, he agreed to have his cards read too, repeating to the point of absurdity that it was 'just for a laugh'. But when, after much reshuffling, the same two cards appeared in his spread also, prompting Jess and Vanya to gasp in the manner of a *Jerry Springer* audience, he didn't seem to find it quite so funny.

'What's wrong?' he said, flicking through the discarded *OK!* to show how little he cared. 'It's not like I believe in any of this shit, you know.'

'Well,' Vanya said, turning patronising, 'maybe not, but when two people draw identical cards it is usually a significant omen.'

'Like what?' Jess whispered, not sure she liked the smug expression now creeping into Vanya's face.

'Like a shared problem, perhaps with your' – Vanya tried hard to look as if she'd just thought of it – 'relationship?' Then, at pains to prefix everything with 'According to Tarot', she read out a chunk of text punctuated with the words 'flawed', 'pointless' and 'doomed', while all the time stroking Toby's arm in a not-all-couples-can-be-as-perfect-as-us kind of way.

By the time James and Jess made it on to the tube home their relationship seemed miraculously stronger than ever.

'Look out for your new lover,' James advised, gesturing to a group of pissed youths sprawled on the seats.

The last tube home was a bit like the end of a school disco, Jess thought. Bright lights, sleeping bodies and disgusting lechy blokes making last-ditch attempts to pull. 'I'm too shackled to my present one to look,' she replied, grinning.

'By all accounts he's a devil with a very small penis. What keeps you?'

A po-faced couple turned round and stared.

'I love him,' Jess said, then ruined the moment by lurching forward drunkenly as the tube shuddered to a stop.

'Clearly.' James laughed, and picked her up from a near-begging position. 'And I'll think you'll find he loves you too,' he said, then added coyly, 'Even though he doesn't always show it.'

Jess smiled affectionately. They could be quite loving, she thought, as long as they talked in the third person. As they stumbled towards the house, she reflected on how much their relationship was like trying to programme a video: sometimes she gave up all hope and sometimes she really thought it might work.

At work – see above
Not working – see below
Trying to calculate time zones so I can call Jenny
    in LA
Have just woken Jenny in LA

Dear Alex,
    I never thought the day would come when I would be pleased for the existence of the kittens. Arrived at work this morning to a message on the machine from Brian telling me they were at an emergency vet appointment because one of the kittens had been attacked by a blackbird. Have no idea how this inversion of nature can be possible, but to be honest I really don't care. I can now fart about all day doing nothing, though must remember to have an invoice file open on standby, should the grieving kitten-lovers return unexpectedly.
    Thanks for your letter which I've just reread out of boredom. No, God, I didn't mean it *was boring, rather,* I *am bored: there's not much to do once you've stolen a selection of the nice stationery and poked about in drawers you shouldn't.*
    It's nice of you to be so concerned about my shit job, though. Like you, I feel it must progress beyond invoices and kitten stories, but I'm afraid there's been little evidence of that so far. I feel about as productive now as I did aged twelve, tramping the streets with a bag the size and weight of my father to deliver those free newspapers that lie around the hall getting trampled on until someone can be arsed to chuck them away.
    In fact, I was despairing that I had the most unfulfilling job on the planet until I went shopping in Benetton the other day. I now know this is not true: Benetton staff have the most unfulfilling job on the planet. This is due to the division of labour as follows:

Job of customer *Pull out an immaculately folded jumper from the middle of an out-of-reach pile of similarly immaculately folded jumpers, unfold it, look at it for three seconds, discard it and move on to the next immaculately folded jumper. Repeat.*

Job of staff *Immaculately fold. Immaculately refold. Immaculately fold. Immaculately refold. Immaculately fold. Immaculately refold . . .*

It's got to the stage recently where I've even had to invent games as if I am not a fully grown adult coping with a tedious job, but a bored five-year-old in the back of a car. A favourite for a while was if-I-do-a-hundred-invoices-by-lunchtime-James-and-I-will-not-split-up, but this rapidly lost its appeal when I realised I wasn't particularly bothered if we did.

I can only assume it's because I am leaving (more later) but James has finally become the boyfriend I have wanted all along. Only now I'm not sure if I do. Extremely puzzling. He is doing strange things like getting out slushy videos with Céline Dion soundtracks and telling me I am special. Then last night – school night – he wanted to stay in my bed. (This is not a simple task with prowling uncles around. We had to devise a complex sequence of moves combining strategically timed loo-flushing with avoidance of a squeaky floorboard, but it was exciting and made James feel like Bond, which seems to be his ambition at the moment.)

Once ensconced, he became a needy, clingy person wanting little cuddles. This is just typical. I, as you know, have fought for this pre-sleep cuddling thing since the beginning and am for it on account of it being nice and cosy and a normal couple thing to do. James is against it for the same reasons. He claims it is uncomfortable, claustrophobic and the best way of achieving a sleepless night. In fact, the whole cuddling thing is just an extension of a football game for him where the bed becomes the pitch and we the opposing players. As a result, he has taught me to see all mattresses demarcated with half-way lines and respect his right to a free kick if I go offside.

Thus him suddenly wanting cuddles felt weird and wrong and definitely offside and meant we couldn't sleep. So we lay awake and reminisced about how we first got together – a conversation we never seem to tire of despite having it on a regular basis. I particularly like the bit about him thinking I wasn't keen because I played three games of pool with Toby, and he persists to marvel at such jealousy-inducing tactics even though I assure him it is a bog-standard female ploy to target the best friend.

Oh, Jesus, God! The phone has just rung and made me jump. There is no fun in doing no work if I'm going to be in constant fear of someone catching me. Anyway, it was Jenny. She couldn't get back to sleep so decided to call me for a chat, which was really an excuse to make me feel guilty for waking her up. I told her I thought I'd done well to get the eight hours bit, knew it was either + or – and just happened to go for the wrong one. But she didn't seem to agree. That's the thing with Jenny. The thought of calling her is nice until I actually do it and then I instantly remember it isn't.

Mind you, I seem to find everyone annoying at the moment, which I think is the result of the manic flat-hunting I am doing. I have got so used to seeing people in terms of 'Could I face them being a happy person in the morning?' and 'Would they leave their pubes on my soap?' that I can't be rational about anyone.

I had no idea looking for a house would turn me so insane. I have become obsessed with buying Loot *(a ridiculously expensive newspaper full of dodgy accommodation) but so, it appears, has most of London. By the time I have found a flat that sounds nice, so has everyone else. And because I don't know London very well, I get excited about a cheap flat in E18 and only understand why it's cheap after trekking twenty miles out of London to see it.*

I must be a mugger's delight, wandering aimlessly round dimly lit, deserted streets with my head stuck in an A–Z. I keep imagining watching myself featured on a Crimewatch *episode where an actress looking nothing like me walks down a dark alleyway as Nick Ross announces dramatically in the background, 'And this was the last time Jessica was seen alive.' It would be exactly the kind of thing I would watch and then do lots of ranting about how stupid the girl was to walk down a dark alleyway on her own.*

I went particularly bonkers yesterday, though, and started thinking everyone was a potential rapist including suspecting a little girl on a pink tricycle of being a murderer's decoy. As a precaution, I endeavoured to memorise all number-plates and hair colours, but even when I am consciously trying I cannot do it. I marvel at people who can remember that the normal-looking man in the Sainsbury's fish queue last Wednesday, subsequently wanted for three murders, six robberies and an attempted arson attack, had green eyes, hair in a side-parting and a freckle above his left nostril.

Anyway, here is a summary of potential flatmates so far.

Nightmare girls' flat

For some reason I got it into my head that it would be fun and sisterly to live with girls, so when I found an advert to live with three I immediately imagined myself in a cool Manhattan apartment with Monica, Rachel and Phoebe. Unfortunately, though, it was like walking into a hen night sober: the place was full of unexplained giggling.

Sample interview question:

ME: *I like to do housework at three in the morning with a feather duster clenched between my buttocks. How do you do your housework, and when? That question to girl number three.*

GIRL NO 3: *Tee-hee.*

ME: *Same question to girl number one.*

GIRL NO. 1: *Tee-hee.*

ME: *And finally, girl number two.*

GIRL NO. 2: *We don't because we're all just mad and crazy here. Tee-hee-hee-hee-hee-hee.*

I repeated this sequence with similarly fascinating topics ranging from phone-bill dividing to shower scheduling, to be told mid-giggles

*that they were 'all just mad and – tee-hee – crazy'. (Query: why
is it always the dullest people who claim to be mad and crazy?)*

Decided I would live with boys.

Nightmare boys' flat

*Found an ad saying, '3 professional men seek 4th person for shared
flat in N9', so phoned up immediately and made an appointment
to see it, congratulating myself on beating all the other fourteen
million* Loot *readers.*

*When I eventually found the correct flat (tend to get bored
listening to directions and think it will be easy to find until I try)
I was met by three pubescent boys with tiny brushed-forward fringes.
First thought: can you really, even in the very loosest sense of the
word, call yourselves men? Second thought: no.*

*They all did something with computers and were obsessed with
Harry Enfield. Unfortunately, though, I had timed my visit badly
to coincide with their own rerun of a particularly hilarious episode,
requiring only one of them to say, 'Remember that bit when he
goes, "Oi, give us your keys,"' to send all of them into uncontrol-
lable fits of hysteria. They seemed to have missed the point that
Harry is a comedian and they are not, and that no matter how
funny the original, something rather crucial gets lost in its regur-
gitation.*

Decided I would live with boys and *girls.*

Nightmare

*This was the worst option of all because it came via a friend of
James's mum and would therefore be embarrassing if we didn't get
on. We didn't.*

*They were a wanky bunch of barristers who'd decided to conduct
the interview as if we were in court, with me thinking each question was a trick one and trying to figure out the correct answer.
It reminded me of being back at school, aged twelve, when a new
sexual word was doing the rounds and everyone with older brothers
knew what it meant and I didn't. Lived in fear of being asked if*

I was bisexual/frigid/horny/lesbian, though quickly learned the safest answer to everything was no – until asked if I was a virgin and had to spend the rest of the day being laughed at because, in this particular case, no was not the right answer (until you became sixteen of course, when it was a very cool answer).

As the interview progressed I realised that they were doing what I am guilty of on the tube, i.e. classifying someone by the newspaper they read, and on the strength of that making wild assumptions about the kind of person they are. So I was struggling with the implications of a wrong answer to 'What music do you like?' when Lord Justice Wanker suddenly grabbed the TV volume control and drowned me out with Jeremy Paxman. I waited politely to be asked to continue but soon saw that I was flattering myself in assuming I could compete with Newsnight. Came away with the distinct impression that living here would be tantamount to playing a perpetual game of Trivial Pursuit.

The only consolation to be drawn from my hideous experiences to date is that the flats themselves have been quite nice. In fact, the quality of the accommodation seems to be inversely proportionate to the quality of the residents, with the exception of a disgusting hovel in Lambeth where a spooky Iranian bloke told me, while drawing the curtains and standing ominously in front of his bedroom door, that he wasn't so much looking for a flatmate as someone with whom he could share the rest of his life. Exit terrified female stage left.

I find it strange that in a city of seven million, I can't find one single person who is normal. I am beginning to think that maybe it's me who's – oh, shit, it's them. Bugger. Need to get invoice file . . .

Hi, back again. Sorry, didn't manage to finish this yesterday because Brian decided he was too traumatised by the near-death of a kitten to do any work, but not traumatised enough not to order me to do it for him. I am now sitting on a tube, extremely late for work, which is something the tube seems to know since it has just *got stuck in a tunnel. I am also nursing acute eyeball-strain from trying to read the girl beside me's* Hello! *and feeling ridiculously self-conscious and flustered because I can feel a woman opposite staring at me. All in all, a phenomenally shit day and it is only nine thirty.*

I hope you don't mind me writing to you on a tube. I have suddenly become panicked that I don't use time in a constructive manner: I watched this programme where a woman with five kids, three dogs, two Shetland ponies, one ailing grandparent and a demanding city job is setting up her own PR company on the side. Unfortunately, though, I've already fallen at the first hurdle – to read, understand, then be able to talk knowledgeably about the political pages of the Guardian.

Oh, God. The woman is still staring and I have just looked up at her. Now it's even more embarrassing because I keep catching her eye and have to keep pretending I'm intrigued by a Mars Bar wrapper on the floor. Why is it me who ends up looking neurotic when it's she who is doing neurotic staring, and why does this never happen with an attractive male?

The driver has now perceptively noticed that the train has stopped and is apologising for the delay. There is a person under a train at Upminster apparently. I don't blame them – think I'd throw myself overboard at the prospect of being twenty-nine tube stops away from civilisation – but I don't know why this means that we, thirty miles along the track, have to stop too. It would be nice to see it as a mark of respect for the poor dead person but given that everyone is now doing loud tutting noises this doesn't seem to be the case. I must say, I find it disgusting that the death of a human being becomes an incidental feature next to getting to work on time, although I have to admit I am quite pleased by its timing because I now have a legitimate excuse for my lateness.

For crying out loud, she's still staring! I think she must be a lesbian, though I realise it is big-headed to assume that just because I'm female she fancies me. I am tempted to ask her why she is staring but this would only lead to the whole tube staring because acknowledging the existence of a fellow passenger, even though I would say hello to her if I met her on a country walk, lie topless next to her if we were on a beach in Greece, is deemed, bizarrely enough, too forward.

It is now ten past ten, and I am tempted to skip work altogether. I will need to think of a convincing lie and stick to it because I have a tendency, in situations of lie-telling, to over-compensate and offer too many excuses – e.g. dog collapsed, kitchen flooded and Granny jumped off Eiffel Tower. I could take a sickie, I suppose, but I did that last week and had to spend the whole of the following day remembering to do fake coughing. By the end of the day I had a real cough.

And the prospect of being around James's aunt longer than is strictly necessary is an undesirable one at the moment. The Hoovering-of-the-milk episode rather blew up in our faces yesterday – well, not our faces exactly, James's aunt's face, when she was vacuuming the stair carpet. Apparently it just exploded. Huge bang. She went mad, and now James has got to cough up for a replacement as well as endure lengthy tutorials on the correct usage of domestic appliances.

Because I was to blame for encouraging the lazy option of Hoovering I feel obliged to pay half – frightening because I have no cash. I had done all my budgeting on an estimated salary of twenty grand – had even written a jolly letter to the student-loan people telling them I could pay back speedily due to my high-earning new job – and therefore was bitterly shocked when handed a cheque for £423.75 for my month's drudgery. For the first time Tie Rack is becoming appealing.

Great. A small oasis of joy when the tube started inching forward in jerks, only to find out it is just going to be inching to Earl's Court whereupon we will all have to get out and wait for another. The only consolation to be drawn from this tedium is that it is marginally better than invoicing. Will finish charting my miserable existence tonight . . .

Yippee! Yippee!! Yippee!!! I've just come back from the pub and everything is brilliant. Why did I think life is awful? Life is great. I've found a fab flat and am moving in this weekend. It's in Clapham. Totally love the people. They are brill. We have just gone to the pub together. Two girls and two guys. They are called Colin and Sam (he is a guy) and Jo and Sophie. And they want me to live with them. Yippee-yippee-yippee. One of the girls thinks I look like Winona Ryder and I told her she is very pretty. She is quite pretty. I think I might fancy Sam, though. He is a safari-tour organiser and has lovely hands and wears those boots we think are sexy and does palm reading and held my hand for a long time and said I had a strong love line. Did I tell you one of the girls thinks I look like Winona Ryder? Sam is very funny and made a funny joke about me, which was very funny. Oh dear, I think I'm a bit pissed. I don't fancy Sam, though. He's just a lovely person who happens to be good-looking. Well . . . quite good-looking. Not that good-looking, actually. Must go to sleep. The room has started to spin and everything in it has got a twin.

Love you for ever my bestest friend,
Jess xxxxxxxxxxxxxxxxxxxxxxxxx

PS Shitting Hell! It is four in the morning and I am now completely sober and, for some ludicrous reason, unable to sleep. I have just dragged myself downstairs for some water and found your PC lying on the kitchen table with 'Why is James being such a WANKER?' *about the only sentence not concealed by stamps or postmarks. While I agree this is a good question, I suspect it is not one that can be answered by James's family – though by now they will have had sixteen hours to try. Oh, God. Now I am never going to get to sleep.*

Jess was asleep dreaming that James had taken her on holiday to Greece. While this was perhaps a little over-hopeful, her imminent house-move had certainly had a positive effect on him. Having spent the duration of her stay keen to remind her that it was only temporary, he had now taken to moping around and staring with sad eyes at her belongings. In his less droopy moments, he was replenishing his sex reserves like a camel. Thus it was not surprising when, on the day she was due to leave, she was awoken by something that felt alarmingly like a penis poking enthusiastically into her lower back.

'You trying to tell me something?' she whispered, knowing of course that he was. She loved the way he could find her attractive splayed out asleep like a dead goldfish. Maybe she was more alluring when she wasn't trying to be, she thought, wishing she'd considered this before forking out £7.95 on L'Oréal's beauty-enhancing mascara.

Smiling sleepily, she stretched an arm behind her to find him and remind him that the back passage was Exit Only and that if he wanted to come in the Entrance was round at the front. She let out a high-pitched yelp. Unless he had undergone radical plastic surgery and a fairly major pubic hair spike, she had just made contact with her hairbrush. James was nowhere to be seen.

This had not been the plan at four o'clock the previous afternoon when he had phoned to tell her he would be coming straight home from work. The others were going out for beers but he just wanted to be with her.

'Really?' she'd asked, stunned by such an unlikely idea.

'Of course,' he'd replied, sweetly.

In anticipation of this she had fished out her lace camisole and a pair of suspenders, bought in a moment of confidence that had never returned long enough for her to put them on, and had waited in this high-class prostitute attire for James to come back and ravish her which, by the time she had fallen asleep, he had failed to do.

Switching on the light, she tugged at the hairbrush, whose presence was an irritating reminder that she'd spent a good part of the previous evening grooming herself for nothing. It had caught on her lace camisole and, in the way that necklaces mysteriously knot themselves together when left alone in the jewellery box, had now become entangled in a sea of pulled threads.

Suddenly she heard what sounded like an exotic mating call from a David Attenborough documentary so, too perturbed to sleep, she went to investigate, hairbrush flapping tail-like behind her.

The squawking turned out to be coming from James's room, where an unattractive representation of masculinity was sprawled fully clothed in a star shape on the bed. The room, lit by a lamp dangling dangerously close to the floor, smelt of beer and burned carpet.

Returning the lamp to its original position – on top of Melinda Messenger (who, along with the other pile of busty beauties keeping *Loaded* and *GQ* in circulation, was now servicing James as a table) – she walked over to the bed and peered at its occupant. Then, reminiscent of primary five's 'Autopsy on a Slug' project, amassed the following data:

Bodily Function	Evidence	% Deviancy from Normal
Breathing	Sporadic squawking with occasional pig-like grunts.	0%
Eating	Remains of McDonald's Double Whopper (possibly regurgitated – difficult to tell) congealing on chin and right side of jacket lapel. Bit of gherkin between front teeth.	0%
Urinating	Fresh urine splattered on shoes, socks, trousers, belt, sleeves and watch strap. Fly undone.	0%
Smelling	Urine. Also beer, and possibly vomit.	0%
Talking	None.	0%
Hearing	No response to 'Would you like a blow-job?'	100%

It occurred to Jess that little separated James from the slug, other than the ability to sound like a pig and that the slug would have had the decency to eat its own vomit. It was something to bear in mind, she decided, when cloning humans became the norm.

Once it became clear, however, that he was incapable of doing anything, she set about trying to undress him, tugging at his suit in an effort to prevent it from becoming any more of an origami masterpiece than it already was. But after subjecting his back to the kind of routine Russian gymnasts wouldn't attempt, and being told intermittently to get lost and piss off, she gave up and stormed back to her own room, wondering why she'd ever agreed with Tara, of perfect-boyfriend fame, that *Men Behaving Badly* was based on a stereotype that simply didn't exist.

With the dawning of a new day, however, she got her revenge. 'Morning, piss-pot.'

He was lying, ugly and rancid, in the same position in which she'd left him.

'Look! It's sunny,' she chirped, breezing into his room and throwing back the curtains in the way Julie Andrews might have done, had she not been singing her lungs out on the hillside.

'Urghhhh,' he moaned, emitting a high-pitched fart, the calibre of which confirmed that he had indeed visited McDonald's a few hours previously. 'You're hurting my eyes.'

Unconcerned, she scurried in and out of the room returning with wobbly piles of freshly ironed clothes, which she intended squashing into one of two remaining suitcases whose zips were still capable of zipping. Packing, she decided, was one of those things like putting on a duvet cover: hugely satisfying if you knew how to do it, and a pain in the arse if you didn't. She felt sure there was some kind of trick to both that somehow she had not been let in on and decided therefore to create her own system all over James's floor. As a result, the carpet, normally littered with boxer shorts and damp towels, now looked as though it had been given over to a family of moles, each of whom had unearthed its own little hill of jumpers, shoes, alarm clocks and shampoo bottles.

'Bollocks,' she yelped, as she stepped back on to the pronged adapter of her hairdryer.

'What in the name of arse are you doing?' Having tried unsuccessfully to hide under a pillow, James was now sitting upright looking furious.

'Packing,' she replied, emptying the suitcase for the third time that morning.

'Why?'

'Because I'm moving into my flat and if I don't get it all into this suitcase,' she said, concentrating on squeezing a trainer into a side-pocket designed for a notebook, 'then I won't be able to move anywhere and . . .' She stopped what she was doing and stared at him. 'You'd forgotten, hadn't you? You'd forgotten I was moving. I can't believe you'd forgotten.'

'No,' he replied, remembering.

'Then why did you ask why I was packing?'

'Ohhh, my head . . . owww.' James clearly thought it safer to divert the conversation at this stage and the sympathy option usually worked.

'I've got no sympathy for you,' Jess announced, returning to the trainer. She had two options for attack: the fact that he hadn't remembered she was leaving versus the fact that he'd got too *drunk* to remember. The drinking one, she reckoned, probably had more mileage.

'So. Where were you?'

'The pub.'

'Oh, right.' She tried to pretend she wasn't interested by studying the instructions of her electric shaver. 'Why?'

'Don't know, really. It's strange but apparently people go there to be sociable and drink and things and I—'

'No, James. I mean, why did you go to the pub when you said you'd come home to see me? You said you'd come straight home. I expressly remember you saying you—'

'OK, OK. Pleeeease, just shut up.'

Jess stared at him very hard.

'Look, Jess, can't we do this later? My head's very sore.' He was pressing his hand against his skull with the dramatic conviction of a *999* reconstruction. 'I think I might have ruptured something.'

'Don't be so pathetic,' she snapped, standing on a mole-hill. 'Anyway, why did you stay there so long?'

'I had to,' he said, after a pause.

'You had to! What kind of answer's that? You had to. Oh, sorry, I didn't come home last night, James, I *had* to shag Brian,' she squawked, before being forced off her molehill by a deflating tube of toothpaste.

'Yes, I had to. It was a work thing. Drinks for new starters.' He turned to face the wall with the logic of a child, who if he shuts his eyes can no longer be seen.

'Oh, for Christ's sake,' Jess shouted, on making the discovery that she'd walked Colgate Total over most of her underwear, 'I'm going to go mad in a minute.'

'Look, Jess,' he exploded, 'if you can't cope with me going out drinking with work friends on a Friday night then maybe we should think about—'

'James, I don't *care*,' she screeched, scraping at a globule of toothpaste that was oozing through the holes of her only lacy bra that didn't look as though it had had an unfortunate experience with a coloureds wash.

'Then why are you behaving like a crazy woman?'

'I'm not.'

There was a moment's silence while Jess scraped at the toothpaste and James remembered his head.

'So, who was there?' she resumed, trying to sound calm.

James continued to worry about his head.

'James? Who was there?'

'Oh, God, Jess, just the usual guys. Look, please you're really hurting my head.' He had got up and limped over to the mirror where he was peering at himself earnestly while massaging his temples in the manner of Uri Geller about to dupe the nation into believing they were all thinking of the colour red.

'So. No girls?'

'No.' He was pulling at an eyelid. 'Oh, yeah. One.'

'Who?'

'Sally. Look, d'you think I could've ruptured something?' He was now fixating on a mole above his right ear.

'Who's Sally?'

'The *new starter*, for God's sake. Jesus, Jess, what's wrong with you?'

'What's wrong with me? What d'you think's bloody wrong with me?' She'd started chucking clothes randomly across the room in the hope that some of them would land in the black bin-liner she'd upgraded to a suitcase. 'You go out all night, don't phone, don't tell me where you are, get me all worried that something awful might have happened to you and then I discover that you've been flirting with Sally all along.' She pronounced the word 'Sally' as if it were an infectious bowel disorder.

'I was not flirting with Sally. I was *talking* to her.'

Jess refused to make the distinction. 'Is she pretty, then?'

'She's all right.'

'So she *is* pretty, then.'

James had finally reached the diagnosis of severe internal brain rupturing and was pulling on his tracksuit bottoms as if they were going out of fashion – which, with yellow Day-Glo stripes, they clearly were.

'What are you doing?' Jess asked. The idea that she wasn't going to get the full analysis on Sally's appearance was disturbing.

'Going to the doctor's.'

'The doctor's?' she repeated, as if he'd just announced that he was off to masturbate in the library. 'Why on earth?'

'Because in case you hadn't noticed I've got something seriously wrong with my head.'

'I noticed that on day one, James,' she said sourly, sweeping the molehills into flimsy Tesco bags.

'My only hope is that if I die before I get there,' he said, without an ounce of sarcasm, 'you'll have the decency to attend my funeral.' He got up and hobbled out of the door.

'But . . . James?' she stuttered, following him out of the room. 'How am I going to get to my flat?'

His answer took the form of a particularly loud slam of the front door.

Three hours and a lecherous mini-cab driver later, Jess arrived at 37 Rose Street with several bulging bin-liners and a selection of cardboard boxes, looking less like a new resident and more as though she'd come to sell her wares. This was confirmed by the fact that no one seemed to want to let her in.

'Hello-ho,' she cooed, through the letterbox. She had given up on the doorbell, which just made a rude donging noise of the sort generated by a wrong answer in a Bruce Forsyth show. 'It's Jess,' she said, turning round in time to witness the stray dog that had been sniffing around her laundry bag lift its leg on what remained of her spider plant. 'Bugger off, you mutt!'

'Hello to you too,' came a voice from the doorway. She looked round to find an overall-clad workman clutching a spanner, covered from head to toe in a dark, greasy substance. It would've been sexy, she decided, had he borne more likeness to the Diet Coke Man and less to *EastEnders* Phil Mitchell.

'Colin!' she said joyfully, hoping that it was.

'You must excuse me but I've just reached a crucial stage with the suction chamber of the carburettor,' he said, 'but do come in and make yourself at home.'

Jess dumped her bags then trotted eagerly upstairs to find her room, which she was disappointed to discover was three times smaller than she'd remembered. The bed she had described to James as a luxury double was barely a single, and the mattress was decorated with enough stains to make up a comprehensive map of Asia. Whoever had been in the room before her had taken everything, including most of the wallpaper either side of the door.

Trying half-heartedly to convince herself that it would all look better with soft lighting and her ethnic candlesticks, she noticed something green sprouting from behind the curtain. Closer inspection revealed it to be a baby cactus with a note attached, saying, 'Please water and love me, Sam.'

Instantly, everything seemed better. The idea that a relative stranger could leave a welcoming gift was endearing. The idea that the relative stranger was Sam made it all the more exciting. In a moment of rogue self-confession, she caught herself hoping that not all of the 'me' referred to the plant.

Unable to face the thought of unpacking so soon after packing, she decided to familiarise herself with the rest of the house – the excuse she would use if she was caught.

Sophie's room, helpfully signposted 'Sophie's Room' courtesy of a Little Mermaid placard, was arranged in accordance with the towel sequence from *Sleeping with the Enemy*. It also seemed to be the cuddly-toy version of Battersea Dogs' Home with two anaemic teddy bears fronting the show. The rest was given over to photos of someone who looked uncannily like a male version of Sophie – blond, mousy-featured and weedy – and who, Jess supposed, was her brother until she found a picture of him with his tongue in Sophie's ear and decided that, unless they'd been inspired by *Brookside*, he was probably her boyfriend.

By contrast, Jo's room was what would have happened if Betty Blue had replaced Julia Roberts in the aforementioned film. Most of the flat's mugs, some of its plates, and all of its mess had assembled here. The wardrobe seemed to have emptied itself on to the floor, giving the rather exciting impression that a lot of people had suddenly got very naked, while the bookcase looked like a warehouse stacking unit for L'Oréal. The idea that Jo worked as a recruitment consultant seemed almost laughable, Jess thought, as she picked her way across the floor. She'd be hard pressed to find someone a place to sit, let alone a job.

Just as she was about to read a thank-you card addressed to 'Potato Head', which, from the photo above the bed wasn't a bad analogy, she heard a huge crash. It came from the kitchen, and was followed by whooping laughter. Terrified that she was about to be found out, she went down to investigate.

'Ha, ha, ha, ha.'

'Ho, ho, ho, ho.'

'Ha, ha, ha, ha.'

Sophie and Tongue Man were sitting on the floor wearing roller-blades.

'Hi,' Jess said, trying not to look jealous. The idea of blading with your boyfriend was up there with picnics in cornfields and horse rides at sunset.

'Hi,' they replied in unison.

'We've just been blading,' Sophie pointed out.

'Or trying to,' completed Tongue Man.

'I can't stop.' She laughed.

'And I can't start.' He chortled.

Jess wondered whether they could communicate independently or if everything was a joint effort.

'Sorry, Jess. This is Richard. Richard, Jess.'

'I would get up,' he began.

'But he'll fall over,' Sophie concluded.

A joint effort, Jess decided resignedly.

It transpired that it was Sophie's birthday and the roller-blades, along with a peculiarly shaped cardigan from Monsoon's fuchsia range, a Delia Smith cookbook and an enormous 'To My Girlfriend' card, had all been a 'joint' present. Jess looked on, doing plastic smiling, as they explained the benefits of sharing each other's belongings. She was intrigued to know to what occasion Richard might wear the cardigan.

Then Jo appeared. She was much taller than Jess remembered, with shiny dark shoulder-length hair shot through with streaks of red, which gave the impression that she had just sustained a rather nasty head gash. Clearly a high-street fashion enthusiast, she was sporting an eclectic mix of flowery hair-clips, cleavage-diving T-shirt and chunky Adidas trainers, exuding the kind of self-assurance Jess had been searching for since birth. 'Hiya, babes,' she shouted, bustling into the room with what appeared to be half of Warehouse and a large proportion of Oasis. It struck Jess that if Jo needed anything, it was not more clothes.

'Happy birthday,' she gushed, leaping on top of Sophie and using the opportunity to give everyone else in the room a semi-snog. 'And welcome!' she added, thrusting an arm in Jess's direction as if she were a GMTV presenter introducing a Hebridean folk-band. Jess fiddled with a fridge magnet and said, 'Thanks,' in a sheep's voice.

They had all planned to spend the evening at an Italian restaurant which, to Jess's paranoid ears, seemed to be called Tagalongs. It was only after a ridiculous pleading demonstration from Jo that she accepted the invitation to tag along too – which she wished she'd had the foresight to do a bit sooner since she missed her slot in the bathing rota and had to wait until SophienRichard appeared, red-faced and crinkly-toed. When it was her turn, the novelty of using someone else's Clarins body toner became of secondary importance to getting anything warm out of the tap, and soon she was reduced to the kind of shower she'd last had after being discovered with a cigarette at Girl Guide camp.

'Nice shower?' Richard enquired, as she emerged from the bathroom the colour of one of the less fortunate *Titanic* passengers.

'Ye-es,' she chittered, trying to fan away the Clarins evidence, lest the pink cardigan wasn't his only concession to effeminacy. 'Won't be long.'

'Take your time,' he said, calmly. 'We're all just chilling out downstairs.'

You're chilling, Jess thought, as she grabbed a jumper.

The restaurant turned out to be a collection of chequered-clothed tables and mushroom-shaped stools, which gave it an air of *Alice in Wonderland* innocence until you stepped inside and it became an asylum for sexually frustrated Italians. 'Ahhh, my beauteefool Eeenglish rose!'

'All right, babes,' Jo chirped, winking. She was one of those people who found it flattering to be wolf-whistled by workmen and beeped at by lorry-drivers.

'Table for sex?' he seemed to say, motioning towards something that looked incapable of supporting a couple of plates let alone anything raunchier.

'Yes, please,' Jo replied eagerly, unconcerned that his hand had now found its way to her bottom.

He led them round the corner to where a beaming Sam was already in place, hidden behind a present the size of a mini fridge. (It later transpired to *be* a mini fridge, which Sophie wanted for her organic vegetables, and was a gift from the rest of the flat. Jess smiled warmly at this generous gesture, until it was pointed out discreetly to her that she was now a member of the flat too and therefore owed £36.50.)

As everyone hovered around the table pretending to be indifferent to where they sat, she felt a rising sense of panic. The imminent seating arrangement looked destined to leave her stranded at the end talking car parts with Colin when she would rather, she decided, do some flirting with Sam. This wanting-to-sit-beside-your-best-friend syndrome was something she'd been unable to shake off since nursery school.

'Oh, no, whatever you do, don't make me sit next to her,' Sam implored, pointing at Jess and grinning. To her bitter disappointment, Colin took this literally and marched her off to the opposite end of the table.

'Red or white?' he said, loosening his collar to reveal a cluster of pimples.

'More blotchy, I'd say,' Jess replied, peering at his neck. 'Probably just a shaving rash.'

'The wine,' Colin said flatly. 'Which one?'

The food ordering proved just as complicated, mainly because the waiter was more interested in attending to his own appetite for Jo's cleavage rather than anyone's desire to eat.

'Can I have,' Sophie drawled laboriously, 'the Pizza Gorgonzola *without* the Gorgonzola. And – excuse me?' The waiter was winking lasciviously at Jo. 'No olives, unless they're green, in which case I'll have five.' She brought out a pen and started scribbling a series of numbers all over her napkin in the frantic way Einstein was reported to have done during the small hours of the morning.

'You can't tell she's an accountant, can you?' Sam joked, grabbing Colin's seat as he disappeared to attend to his acne.

'It's my fibre intake,' Sophie replied, pointing to the napkin.

'It looks tasty,' Sam said, laughing.

By the time the main course arrived, Jess and Sam had invented a game involving Sam's doughballs and Jess's mouth where the rules, although a little hazy, seemed to entail drinking lots of red wine. Colin, relegated to the corner, was tutoring a near paralytic Jo on the merits of working for Wandsworth Council and SophienRichard were spoon-feeding each other tomato juice.

'Ergh, yuk,' Jess squealed, as Sam threatened to dangle a piece of spaghetti down her top.

'Say, "I'm sorry, oh wonderful, sexy, Sam,"' he teased.

'I'm sorry, oh wonderful – *aahhhh*!!!' There was a loud crash as she slid off her stool and landed in a heap by his legs.

'No, I didn't say beg,' he said, lassoing the spaghetti around his finger. 'Kissing my feet will be sufficient.'

When it came to paying, however, things weren't quite so hilarious.

'That's 30 quid each, guys,' Colin announced, throwing a £20 note on to a saucer. 'I didn't have a coffee.'

'But we shared a starter,' Richard protested, 'so presumably we only pay for one.'

'You're not going to believe this, babes,' Jo said, 'but I've forgotten my wallet.'

Jess tried to feel happy as she signed away £78.50. She was a generous person, she told herself, calculating how many Oasis tops this would have got her, who loved giving.

As a token of their appreciation, Sam volunteered to piggyback her all the way home, which wasn't quite the self-sacrificing gesture he made it out to be: it gave him full licence to grope her inner thigh.

'There's a message for you from James,' Jo said, as they tumbled into the kitchen in the manner of a hearty couple from a dog-food commercial. 'Apparently you said you'd call him.'

'Did I?' Jess replied, distractedly, trying to chase Sam out of the room with the plant spray. Clearly she had more important matters to attend to and scampered off to find them.

Completely unable to find Sam anywhere
Resorting to sitting alone in a trendy Soho bar
   hoping people assume I am alone out of choice
   and not because I have no friends
Repeatedly telling myself I am mature enough not
   to care what other people think
As long as it doesn't look like I've been stood up

Dear Alex,

   I really wish Sam would turn up. I hate it when this kind of thing happens because instead of being angry that the other person is late I start thinking it's all my fault and I'm in the wrong place. I then go through torture trying to remember the arrangements and give up because every pub I think about suddenly seems the one we agreed to meet in.

   Hang on, I'm just going to buy a drink – the barman is looking at me as if this is McDonald's and I'm only here to use their loos, which admittedly I would if I could find them. I cannot understand why trendy bars think it's cool and sophisticated to hide their toilets.

   Hi, back again. Found the loos. No wonder I couldn't see them. I was searching for a little stick person wearing a triangular dress not some weird λ thing. How do people know what λ means? And how come they don't end up going into γ instead? I fail to see how they can term these 'public conveniences' when only people with degrees in Ancient Egyptian know they are toilets.

   Oooh, I can't wait for Sam to arrive, though. I have saved up all my stories from the day to tell him, which I love doing because he is always interested and does lots of laughing, which makes me feel like I am being very funny.

Anyway. How are you? Sam says that China was rated the seventh safest country to live in, so that's good. He once went to China. Erghhh, yuk, this wine is disgusting. I was under the impression that if it looked like a dehydrated person's urine sample it was a good thing – didn't realise that that meant it had to taste like it too. I cannot fathom my eagerness to hand over £3.50 for this, then go into Sainsbury's and think 94p for a loaf of wholesome granary bread is far too expensive. James says it's a problem with my understanding of cost versus value and once did a complicated sum to prove it. I see it more as an innate compulsion to get pissed at whatever cost or value.

Goodness. I've just noticed that this place is full *of good-looking men – doing that bloke thing of standing next to their mate with folded arms and chatting to them while looking around the room, as though they're not friends at all but strangers at a bus stop. I can't believe I've only just spotted them and now feel a bit insulted that no one has tried to chat me up – although admittedly if they did I would think they were desperate and slimy and query why they had to do it.*

The problem is I still remain hopeful about Vanya's Tarot reading, despite pretending to James I thought it was bollocks, and have become obsessed with thinking every good-looking man is my exciting new lover. The thing is – oh, phew, I've suddenly remembered why Sam's late. It's Wednesday night and he's looking after handicapped people. He does this every Wednesday and then all day on Saturday – even if he has a hangover or an attractive girl in his bed or both, although he says one is more frequent than the other and pulled a sad face when he said it which was incredibly cute. He claims that working with disadvantaged people makes him feel alive. That it's his duty to give something back to the world. I love this about him. Well, kind of love this about him. Actually, to be honest, I find it a bit annoying. It makes me seem a nasty person for wanting to spend my Saturdays shopping and having coffee with my friends.

But he's so funny. Did I tell you the other day he phoned me at work and pretended to be someone from the BBC? He made up this long story about how the chairman had this thing about garden hedges and asked whether we, as a company, would be interested in making a fifty-minute documentary on the history of hedges. I fell for it and faxed Brian straight away, rejoicing at being the chief negotiator for a company on the brink of a multi-national film deal.

Five minutes later I got a phone call from a furious Brian telling me that if I had time to compile comical faxes I had time to archive the invoices, and I had to spend the rest of the afternoon lugging boxes of files in and out of a dusty basement like a spotty youth on work experience.

The only good thing about the job at the moment is that Aileen is ill. Apparently she caught some funny flu thing from one of the kittens, which makes her have a perpetual period. I cannot think of anything worse than being trapped at home with a sickly pet and bumper box of Tampax but she seems perfectly content. She says it's nice to spend some time with the kittens while they're still young. I wouldn't be the least bit surprised if she claims maternity benefit for this.

Brian, meanwhile, is going totally loopy. He arrived at work yesterday with a Baby's First Year *book tucked under his arm and handed it to me with a grin out of Jack Nicholson's psychotic repertoire. I assumed it must belong to some distantly related nephew – given that Brian and Aileen don't seem sexual enough even to engage in the act for procreative reasons – and quite liked the prospect of thumbing through little fluffy baby pictures in prefer-ence to counting invoice duplicates from 1975, so I settled down intent on making the task stretch well beyond lunchtime.*

Then – horror! Sellotaped across page two under 'Baby's First Hair' was a huge clump of cat fur. It had gone all matted and smelt like wet school blazers and was completely repugnant. I can now only think of the kittens as spooky baby werewolves, which is unfair as it is clearly Brian who is the spooky one.

Other than this, though, work is still very boring but I have given up panicking that I'm stuck in a dead-end job because Sam says everything in life – even the bad things, e.g. my job – is meant to be and is there for a reason. I must say I love this idea of handing over all responsibility for my life to someone else. It means I can just relax since it is no longer my fault if I am a failure. Bollocks! I've just spilt wine on my top. It's actually Sophie's top, but if Sam is right, I must not get perturbed by this but instead assume it was meant to happen – although quite why whoever is organising my life should see a hefty dry-cleaning bill and a potentially irate Sophie as a necessary part of my existence is blissfully unclear.

I hope, however, this won't interfere with the clothes-swapping thing we seem to have going. This would be tragic as it is an excellent means of tripling outfits – like permanently living in Warehouse only more exciting because all the clothes are free. It certainly makes waking up in the morning more bearable since instead of rummaging around in the bottom of my wardrobe for the mangy pair of trousers that keep falling off the hanger I just go into Sophie's room and pick out a beautiful pair of suede ones from a nice see-through zipper case.

I wish I was like Sophie. Her wardrobe is all simple and calming, like a rail in Armani not the squashed-up hell of a changing-room reject rack in Miss Selfridge. I must learn to buy minimally and expensively like her and not frantically just because something is cheap/I am running out of time and need something to wear that evening/it is at a reduced price due to a wonky zip/there is only one left and I'm scared I will regret it later if I don't snap it up now/or other similar dilemma that has led to a wardrobe full of clothes I never wear.

Anyway, I am planning to start up a new regime where I will become a new and better person who does not do this sort of thing. I am really looking forward to this. It is Jo's idea because she says my whole sense of self is a reflection of how James sees me, i.e. weak and pathetic. She says the regime will be something positive I am doing just for me, and has offered to do it with me because *she wants Max to realise what he is missing out on and want her back. (Max is her ex. She dumped him three and a half years ago because, although he was good-looking and funny and generous and intelligent and sensitive and her best friend and always there when she needed him, she didn't think he was the one. But now she does, only he has a girlfriend and says it is too late.)*

Here is our new day:

6.30 a.m. *Rise free of a hangover and drink a pint of water while learning about exciting political developments from* Today *programme.*

6.55 a.m. *Jog to the swimming pool.*

7.10 a.m. *Do 50 lengths (30 breast/20 crawl) while reciting Chinese verbs (see Chinese night-class – in preparation for your return!).*

7.50 a.m. *Walk to the tube-station grabbing a juicy mango or similar healthy fruit from the street market. Give change to the homeless person and* ~~tell him to have a nice day~~ *(insulting and naïve to assume there could be anything nice about squatting on a damp pavement under a smelly blanket holding a cardboard sign).*

8.00 a.m. *Read* Condensed History of the World *on the tube.*

9.00–12.30 p.m. *File invoices.*

12.30 p.m. *Do step-aerobics class no longer feeling intimidated by those who are skinny/good at step-aerobics/both.*

1.00 p.m. *Have salad of pulses and beans with a glass of aloe vera juice while talking to any lonely old people.*

1.30–6.00 p.m. *File invoices.*

6.00 p.m. *Cycle to night-class, listening to classical music enjoyed for its own merits and not because it has been advertised on telly.*

6.30 p.m.	*Become known as the star pupil in Chinese night-class.*
7.30 p.m.	*Friendly cultural drink with new and interesting night-class friends.*
8.30 p.m.	*Cook tasty beansprout meal from recipe lent by new and interesting night-class friends. Eat, watching fascinating documentary on the Boer War.*
9.30 p.m.	*Do homework, reading all optional texts voraciously.*
10.30 p.m.	Newsnight.
11.15 p.m.	*Go to bed memorising ten previously unknown words from the dictionary.*
12.00 a.m.	*Say prayer for unfortunate people.*

We haven't started yet as it is always best to begin these things on a Monday. We were going to do it this coming Monday but, as Jo pointed out, the one following the one after that is the first of the month so we think it makes sense to wait until then. Come to think of it, the first of January is only three and a half months away. Perhaps it would be more sensible to become the new, better person right at the start of the year rather than two-thirds of the way through when you've got to start thinking about things like Christmas.

I cannot wait, though. I love imagining the new me in a beautiful handcrafted lace waistcoat (lace-making night-class on Saturday) with an athletic yet womanly body talking wisely about Russia's decaying economy in fluent Chinese.

In fact, the only bit of the schedule I think will be difficult to adjust to is the swimming. I find the mere idea of it mentally exhausting: remembering to take knickers if you're already wearing a swimsuit, dropping them in a puddle while squeezing everything into a locker, discovering the locker you have chosen doesn't lock, realising you haven't got 10p when you transfer all your clothes into a locker that does lock, dressing in a pygmy-sized cubicle without dangling your trouser legs in the mini swimming-pool on the floor, giving yourself pneumonia with wet hair on the way home, and generally encountering enough insurmountable hurdles to make the swimming part of the whole exercise seem a sensational joy.

Jo insists it's simply a case of throwing a towel and a hairbrush into a bag and zipping up and down a pool for a while – I think she's been exposed to too many panty-liner commercials – and dragged me along to prove her point, which only succeeded, as I knew it would, in further proving mine.

The hurdle on this particular occasion, however, reared its ugly head long before I'd even made it into the changing rooms. The night before, to be specific. I'd put on my swimsuit because I hadn't worn it for over a year and was scared it might have shrunk in the cupboard or something, only to find it had done the opposite and gone baggy, making me look like a malnourished African woman with droopy bosoms and sagging bum.

In an effort to counter this, I started trying to figure out the most flattering way of standing, which is when I discovered a new and altogether more horrific deformity – tufts of hair sprouting out at either side of my crotch and heading off down my thighs with the determination of a Day of the Triffids invasion.

(I wish I could control my body hair. It's like painting the Forth Bridge: by the time you've got to the end of the bloody thing, the bit you started at needs doing again. If I had any confidence at all, I would be walking around in a proud, feminist manner relishing my natural state as mini gorilla, not dashing for a razor with the rest of Marie-Claire at the sight of a microscopic wisp.)

After an unpleasant burning experience with a tube of out-of-date Immac and a Lady-shaver that looked as if it had scalped an Alsatian, I gave up and spent the following morning locating a beautician prepared to attack the foliage for my 7 p.m. dead-line. Eventually found a place claiming to specialise in 'unsightly hair problems', which I decided described my lower body fairly accurately, and trotted along to be cured.

I had been expecting to be greeted by a huge ape-woman with whiskers and furry nostrils, making me feel like a smooth hairless woman from a razor commercial, and was therefore horrified when a dainty blonde called Cheryl appeared, took one look at my inner thigh and went to fetch her colleague. Meanwhile, I was left helpless on the bench feeling like a specimen from the Neanderthal section of the Natural History Museum: 'The primate man and woman were almost indistinguishable during late Palaeolithic times. Above: a replica of a female whose pubic hair extends almost to the knees.'

Eventually she reappeared with a miniature version of herself and told me that Debbie was here to learn how to deal with problem cases. Debbie looked terrified and stared at my knickers. Cheryl told her there was no point in doing anything until the area was trimmed, at which point she produced a pair of enormous shears and advised her to 'hack off as much as possible'. Then she returned to stir her cauldron of scalding wax and inform me that most women in my 'predicament' trim themselves regularly. (I am sure this is bollocks. I tried it years ago and spent the next three weeks scratching ferociously at my crotch. Beauty is not worth this kind of pain.)

The hacking was followed by a sequence of tearing and ripping motions as Cheryl and Debbie between them reduced me to the state of a gibbering plucked chicken, occasionally telling me to relax when I started bleeding/perspiring unattractively/screaming. Then Cheryl led me out of the salon taking £2.50 extra to cover the shearing, assuring me that, if nothing else, I would at least be able to face the world. I have no idea how she expects me to do this when I can barely even face myself.

The notion that I was then expected to slog my guts out in a chlorinated swimming-pool seemed so hideous that I began plotting how to get out of it, working out what lie I could tell Jo, as if she were my no-nonsense PE teacher. I considered the overused period option but then remembered she knew I'd had it last week when she'd walked in on me crying at Pet Rescue. *Miserably, therefore, I realised I would have to go, and met a ridiculously hyper Jo outside Clapham leisure centre.*

Once we'd got changed and done lots of sneaking looks at each other's bodies, she went all weird and instead of wanting to splash around in the shallow end talking about boys, sped off to join the goggled brigade chasing each other in a manic fashion up and down the pool. I paddled after her half-heartedly, got a third of the way down one side then was whistled at by the lifeguard and ushered into the beginners' lane to be overtaken repeatedly by two five-year-olds wearing inflatable armbands.

I have subsequently decided that swimming is not the sport for me and am looking into replacing that particular slot on the schedule with something a little less strenuous, like an extra half-hour in bed. Jo is convinced she's going to convert me, though, so I will probably need to invent a chlorine allergy so that – Ooh, yippee, Sam's arrived. He's got a beautiful bunch of purple flowers, which must be because he's late. He's so thoughtful it's weird to think he's actually a man. Better go. Sam says hi.

Lots of love,
Jess
xxx

'They're beautiful,' Jess gushed, cradling the flowers to her chest as if they were the product of a nine-month pregnancy and not a twenty-four-hour Esso garage.

'I know,' Sam replied, returning to the table with a jug of something that looked alarmingly like sperm.

'But isn't purple supposed to mean hatred?'

'That's yellow,' he said, grinning.

'So what's purple?'

'A sort of bluish-red colour.'

Jess pretended to find him annoying.

'Don't know, you'd have to ask Mia. Anyway, thought it was time we started drinking sensibly,' he said, motioning to the sperm sample, 'so I bought a pint of *piña colada*.'

'Who's Mia?' She'd asked this in a tone that suggested she was far more interested in the answer than she should have been.

'The lovely lady who gave me the – oh, God.' Sam suddenly looked serious. 'Oh, no, you didn't . . . um, you didn't think the flowers were . . . for, well, were for . . . you?' he stammered.

'No, no, of course not,' Jess protested, waving her arms frantically in the air to indicate just what a ridiculous idea that would be. 'No, no, not at all. Of course not.'

'It's just that . . . well—'

'No, no, it's fine, Sam, really. So,' she hazarded, trying not to look crushed, 'Mia's an admirer, is she?'

Sam exploded into hysterics.

'What's so funny?'

'You,' he chortled. 'Of course the flowers are for you, you twat. What kind of guy would rock up forty-five minutes late with no word of an apology and a bunch of flowers that weren't for you?'

Jess could think of someone. 'I hate you,' she squealed, banging the flowers up and down on his head in an unconvincing display of anger. 'You're cruel and horrible and I hate you.'

'Help,' he pleaded, ducking out of reach. 'Someone save me from this wicked woman.'

A couple of girls looked round – enviously, Jess decided.

'So, who's this Mia, then?' she quizzed, once the flowers had ceased to be a viable means of attack and had begun doing what all petrol-station flowers do an hour after purchase – wilt rapidly, then die.

'The woman I bought them from,' he said, still cowering, 'so I suppose indirectly they *are* from her.'

By the time the third jug of *piña colada* had arrived, Sam was converting the sugar bowl into a beach with cocktail umbrellas, matchstick men and a sea of melted ice-cubes. Jess, meanwhile, was engaged in the productive enterprise of feeding hardened bits of rolled-up wax back into the candle. '. . . and then I think I'd spend huge amounts of money in Joseph or somewhere and then . . .' She looked troubled as she plotted the next instalment to her fantasy day. 'Oh, yeah, I know, meet lots of friends for lunch in Harvey Nicks, then spend *all* afternoon having massages and stuff and then get taken out for a lavish romantic dinner by . . . umm . . . by . . . Am I allowed famous people?'

'Yes, but remember I might not be available,' he cautioned, grinning.

'Damn. Well, then, I suppose I'd have to settle for George Clooney and go somewhere posh for cocktails, but we'd probably have the cocktails *before* the lavish dinner, then go to some amazing hotel where they have things like water-beds and drink the whole mini-bar, because I've always wanted to do that, and then have the most mind-boggling sex all night on the veranda because it would be hot because George would've flown us out to some remote island in the Bahamas, only they don't have Harvey Nicks in the Bahamas, do they? I suppose I'd have to forgo that bit and settle for an afternoon swimming in the Caribbean with Brad Pitt, just for a bit of variation. Yes,' she said conclusively, 'I think that would just about do it. OK, your turn.'

'Well,' Sam said, rescuing the leg of a drowning matchstick man and chewing it thoughtfully, 'I'm not sure I'd be up for the veranda stuff with George' – he smiled – 'but if he wanted to fly me to the Bahamas . . .'

'So you'd go to the Bahamas too?' Jess said excitedly.

He shook his head and had suddenly gone all serious again. 'Do you know what I'd really want to do?'

'Win the lottery,' she said, annoyed she'd forgotten to include that option herself.

'See little Jimmy walk.'

There was a stunned silence. Jess felt as though she'd just devoured a delicious three-course meal in front of a documentary on starving Romanians. It hadn't even begun to cross her mind that someone's fantasy day might involve the happiness of another.

'Not miles,' he said, 'just to the end of the garden and back.' He picked up the dismembered matchstick man and stared at it solemnly.

'Do you think he will?' she whispered, fighting back an overwhelming desire to laugh. It was always the same: she could sit through numerous comedians on the telly without so much as cracking a smile, but give her tragic news and she practically doubled over in hysterics.

'Probably not,' he said resignedly, giving the man a ceremonial burial among the cigarette ash. 'Let's go.'

Finding a taxi willing to drive to Clapham was like trying to feed a juicy fillet steak to a vegan. 'Sorry, mate, not going that way,' was the standard reply before they zoomed off in the direction of – unless there had been a serious editorial oversight in Jess's *A–Z* – Clapham.

'You need to get into the near-side lane, mate,' Sam instructed, once they'd finally located a driver who'd take them, only because, as they were all in the process of discovering, he hadn't a clue where he was going. 'Then right at the next junction,' he continued, as they swung round spectacularly to the left.

'What you thinking?' he said, turning to Jess, whose suggestion that they look for a tall building with a funny roof then search for the A3 from there had let her off navigating duty for the time being.

'Oh, you know, just things,' she replied, deliberately obtuse, lest he realise that what had been occupying her mind for the previous five minutes were not altruistic thoughts about handicapped people but rather whether or not Jo's beige top would go with her grey trousers and if so, whether she would need a belt.

'Yup.' Sam nodded, so wisely that she wondered if he was going through similar anguish over one of Colin's outfits. Probably not, she concluded, given Colin's wardrobe.

'Fourteen, mate,' the driver shouted, once they'd arrived at Rose Street, after a fascinating tour of a local rubbish depot.

'Does the fourteen refer to the price or the number of attempts it took to get here?'

The driver looked unimpressed.

As they entered the house, Jess's first instinct was not to saunter in the manner of a relaxed person towards the kettle/fridge/loo, but to turn into a frenzied bull and charge hell for leather at the flashing red button on the answer-machine. It was by far and away her favourite piece of machinery, and although often the bearer of the dismal 'no messages' disappointment, she treated it as a constant monitor of her popularity. Sam had referred to it jokingly as her lifeline and hummed the *ER* theme music when one day it had ceased to flash. She had pretended to find this funny until, after several unsuccessful attempts at resuscitation, they were forced to spend almost a week and a half waiting for a replacement.

'You have five messages,' the robot stated, sounding peculiarly Californian, given that it had spent most of its life in a Taiwanese factory.

Yippee, Jess thought, five messages.

'Jo, you piss-head. It's Pooch. Call me.' All Jo's friends had names like bottled alco-pops.

'Mummy here,' the next one began. It was Sophie's mummy, who never seemed to feel the need to say so. She habitually sounded as if she'd swallowed the sugar bowl and only ever talked about food. 'Just to say that Auntie Ellie's sending on that yellow-pea soup recipe so you're not to panic. Apparently you shouldn't use a whole lemon – makes it too zingy. Anyway, sweetheart, hope the snuffle's gone. Hot honey and some early nights,' she advised, presumably, Jess thought, in relation to the flu and not as a rather ingenious means of spicing up Sophie's sex life. 'Daddy sends his love. 'Bye, darling.'

'Hi, Jess, it's James.' In contrast, James always felt the need to say who he was. 'Where are you? I thought you said you'd be back at seven. I've had an awful day.' He left a short silence to elicit sympathy, then continued, 'I won't go into it here but . . .' – and then did precisely that, relaying the events of his day in all their microscopic and tedious detail: 'gilt switch from the 03s . . . 05s rallying . . . 05s at market . . .' Jess pressed the fast-forward button. 'Up ten ticks . . . and wiped out three days P and L.' He left such a dramatic pause here that she thought perhaps he might have blown up a ferry – until she remembered that P&O owned the ferries and that whatever he had so ruthlessly wiped out it wasn't a cargoload of innocent people.

'Hi, Jess, just James again. It's nearly nine. I thought you said you'd be back at seven. I'm not fussed or anything, it's just that I thought . . . well . . . I thought we were going to do something nice tonight and, anyway, just give me a call when you get back, OK? Thanks.'

'Shit,' Jess said, suddenly recalling from the recesses of her *piña colada*ed memory a vague association with James and a Wednesday night.

'James again,' a plaintive Bambi voice squeaked from the machine. 'You've obviously gone out. Please call me when you get back. 'Bye. Even if it's late.'

'Oh, God,' Jess moaned, checking her watch and trying to work out whether twelve eighteen would be deemed late.

'What seems to be troublin' me lady?' Sam had just bounded into the room in a pair of Mickey Mouse boxer shorts, which would possibly have been a better fit on Minnie.

'Would you be pissed off if someone called you now?' Jess asked.

'Depends if that someone had blonde hair, ample breasts and wanted to sleep with me,' he replied, sinking his teeth into one of Sophie's organic bananas.

'And if they were flat-chested and frigid?' she said, instantly regretting the suggestion as his eyes wandered unashamedly over her body.

'I'd tell them to get a boob job and a dildo and see me in the morning. Night,' he chirped, scampering off to bed leaving Jess slightly miffed that he hadn't felt inclined to disagree with the flat-chested bit.

'. . . and I didn't think you'd want a mad woman waking you up in the middle of the night,' Jess said, sitting at her desk the following morning drawing little triangles on an invoice.

'You're not a mad woman,' James replied, contradicting a lifetime of telling her that she was, 'and, anyway, I wouldn't have minded.'

She found it deeply disturbing when he said things like

this. It was wrong and suspect, and reminded her of the time when Gilly Saunders at primary school, after excluding her from all gang activities for several months, had suddenly elected her supreme gang leader.

'So when am I going to see you?' he continued, in his disarming new role as Normal Boyfriend.

'The weekend?' she suggested, wondering why, after spending the best part of their relationship training him to behave like this, she suddenly didn't think she liked it. It was as if she'd invested six years in a veterinary-science degree only to qualify and discover that she hated animals.

'The weekend! But that's ages away.'

'James, it's the day after tomorrow.'

'Why don't we do something tonight?' he volunteered eagerly.

'Can't I'm afraid. Said I'd watch *The Full Monty* with Sam.'

'*Do* the full monty, more like.'

'What's that supposed to mean?'

'Oh, wonderful, hilarious Sam,' he mimicked.

'No. Just nice, funny Sam,' she corrected, hoping she sounded as infuriatingly reasonable as he always did when she accused him of thinking Sally was pretty. 'You can come if you like,' she added, with about as much enthusiasm as a Burger King attendant.

'OK,' he bleated.

There was a prolonged silence.

'So. What have you been up to?'

'Ummm . . . not much. Actually, James, I'm going to have to go – the other line's flashing. I'll call you later, OK?'

'When?'

'When I can, James,' she barked, before cutting him off mid-bleat. 'Good morning, Green Fingers.'

'Yes, good morning,' trilled a ridiculously camp voice, which could only, Jess decided, belong to Sam. 'Could I speak with one of your producers?'

'No, I'm afraid that won't be possible today, sir,' she said, pleased to have cottoned on to him so early this time, 'but we do have a full range of first-rate prostitutes available for one- or three-hour hire, all of whom will be happy to do three-somes at just a minimum surcharge.'

There was a short silence. He was trying to think of a witty comeback, she thought gleefully.

'Perhaps you can help, then,' he replied, somewhat lamely, she decided, given the obvious gag to be made about classing herself as a *first*-rate prostitute.

'I can certainly try, sir,' she purred, 'but I think you'll find I'm a bit out of your league.'

'It's Ben Clarke from Walters and Co. I'm phoning regarding—'

'Yes, I know what you're regarding, Benny-boy,' she hissed. She could tell that Sam was trying not to laugh.

'Great. Well, we've got the go-ahead from the client *vis-à-vis* the copy so it's now a case of setting up a pre-production meeting. It's looking like the gnome thing will work but we're still waiting for clearance from the client *vis-à-vis* the animated weeds – could be a problem with the NSPCC, weeds strangling gnomes suggesting a stifling of children's imaginations.'

Jess erupted into hysterics. '*Vis-à-vis* you're a complete prat and should've been strangled by a weed at birth,' she hooted. 'And, by the way, your camp accent's crap.'

'Excuse me?' Sam said, refusing to give up.

'I suggest you take one of your gnomes and stick it up your – Hello? Sam? Hah! – can't take it, eh?' She couldn't help grinning as she replaced the handset.

'Who was that?' Brian asked, bumbling through the door with a large Dunkin' Donuts box.

'Oh, just my flatmate being annoying,' she replied, eyeing the box with delight.

'Right, well, we need to keep the lines free,' he said, placing the box, much to her disappointment, in the fridge. 'I'm expecting a call from the agency. It's a big job, this one, if we get it, so we need to make sure . . .'

A sudden and extremely unattractive vision started forming itself in Jess's mind.

'Um, which agency would this be?' she squawked, praying to Mary, Mother of Jesus, that the situation, despite overwhelming evidence to the contrary, was salvageable. That it was just some hideous nightmare out of which she would shortly awaken into a sun-dappled room full of baskets of pot-pourri and gently flapping muslin curtains, clutching Wilbur, her little fuzzy duck.

'Walters and Co. Now, how about some coffee?'

Oh, God, she wailed, her head in her hands. Oh, God. Oh, God. Oh, sweet Lord God.

Enduring a fortnight from the depths of hell's inferno
Hoping to die and be reincarnated as an African
hippo or similar sedentary beast who does not
have to cope with hellish career crises but merely
spends life wallowing in mud and grunting

Dear Alex,

I have lost a kitten. My life is in turmoil and I have lost a kitten. Ordinarily I would not care only I am supposed to be baby-sitting the little buggers and, much like you cannot tell a parent that while they were out having a wonderful time at the theatre you mislaid their child, I cannot inform Brian and Aileen that I have lost their kitten. Oh, God.

I would not be here at all if I wasn't feeling so crippled with guilt about last week's hideous cock-up where I did not so much make a meal of things as a three-course dinner with coffee and After Eights. Having assumed, wrongly as it turned out, that the person on the phone to whom I was making a series of lewd sugges-tions was Sam, I then discovered rather too late that it was the ad exec of a company offering us – until I offered him, among other things, a prostitute – a lucrative commercial. Since I cannot bring myself to tell Brian, I must endure the equivalent of a mini heart seizure every time the phone rings. I do not know what to do and now, in some horrible twist of the Devil's fork, I have lost a kitten. I am ruined. I am over. I am doomed to a career in Tie Rack. I must have one last hunt . . .

Alas, no kitten, but instead a yummy green liqueur in their drinks cabinet. I feel much calmer now. I'm sure the kitten will just pop up somewhere – it's probably having a little sleep in a sock or something. I must say, I love snooping round other people's houses. I can sort of see the appeal of being a burglar, only burglars

89

have to do everything in a hurry and wouldn't have time to look through photo albums, read private letters or peer inside bedside tables for evidence of sexual things.

Talking of which, thanks for your letter. I have a query, though – who is sexy Greek yoghurt model? That Swede from the youth hostel in Beijing who did all that good kissing stuff, perhaps? A word of warning, however. If you are going to continue to perform exciting sexual acts, and by all accounts that would be a highly advisable course of action, please send all descriptions to my new address: *37 Rose Street, Clapham, London* (can't remember postcode). Mum insists she would never read my mail but said, in her forwarding letter, 'Looks like Alex is writing Chinese already.' I can only assume she is referring to the 'MO' bit, and while I do realise that the term *multiple orgasm* will doubtless be unfamiliar to my mother, I am anxious she does not inhibit in any way your graphic detailing of multi-cultural sexual practices.

And, secondly, I wish you hadn't said that thing about fancying Sam. Obviously I don't because, well, for starters it would be like fancying my brother – yuk – and, anyway, he's my flatmate and no one finds their flatmate attractive, which is precisely the reason they are your flatmate. But now you've said it, all I can think is that I *do* fancy him. And now I keep going all shy and peculiar and can't be normal with him. For example:

How I used to be	How I am now
Eating honey straight from the jar with my forefinger.	Not eating honey at all.
Watching TV avidly while slumped in an unattractive heap on the sofa, unconcerned whether Sam is in the room or not.	Watching TV but really concentrating on whether I look more seductive lying down or sitting up, while being constantly aware of where and how Sam is sitting.

Leaving clogged-up razors, Jolen hair-bleach and dandruff shampoo on the bathroom ledge.	*Hiding anything that alludes to the fact that I am not naturally clean, shaven and blemish-free.*
Going to breakfast in flip-flops and an Alice band.	*Skipping breakfast entirely to concentrate on plastering body in cosmetics.*
Taking phone messages from girls who are clearly his friends and sound nice.	*Suspecting any female who phones.*
Pointing out my pimple.	*Covering up my pimple.*
Uninterested in and oblivious to anything Sam wears.	*Able to distinguish between Sam's navy blue V-necked T-shirt from Next and his navy blue V-necked but with a slightly deeper V T-shirt from French Connection.*
Never running out of things to say.	

It was only when I started checking his horoscope in the news-paper that I knew I must like him in a way that wasn't purely friendship, because if he was just a friend I would not find the fact that Venus was in his rising sun of any interest whatsoever. As it is, any tiny morsel about his life, e.g. that he hates it when the loo-roll holder is squint, intrigues me and makes me want to tell someone.

But now the whole thing has got totally out of hand and I leap at any excuse to talk about him, irrespective of whether anyone is interested. For example, I managed, with an alarming degree of ease, to steer a conversation Jo and I were having about Jo's work friend's garage round to why Sam's allergic to Sugar Puffs. I know

I will have to start rationing this otherwise people will suspect but I find it much more fun than, say, eating a chocolate bar or watching Friends.

However, I am now going through a horrible maths-multiple-choice-exam agony, trying to figure out whether he likes me too. One minute I think it is (a) definitely me, the next (b) Nancy from work, occasionally (c) both of us, then suddenly I think I have got entirely the wrong end of the stick and it is (d) he is a homosexual. It is really difficult to tell because he is so friendly to everyone that you could just as easily put forward a case for him fancying the window-cleaner as you could the beautiful Spanish girl in the bakery at the end of the road (who I have no brain-space left to get paranoid about, incidentally).

I tried to fish it out of Jo by telling her, in an isn't-it-just-so-ridiculous voice, that the woman in the cinema had thought he was my boyfriend (slight stretching of truth, the word she actually used was 'brother') and waited for her to look at me in a knowing manner and say something like 'He wishes,' or 'In his dreams.' Instead she just smiled and said, 'Oh, Sam, he's such a flirt.'

Why does this always happen to me? A bloke chats me up and pays me lots of nice attention, leading me to believe that I am being singled out because he finds me unbelievably irresistible and a beautiful sexual temptress, only to discover several days later, having decided I might like him too, that he finds all girls beautiful temptresses and I just happened to be a handy one.

I am now so confused about it all that I am going bonkers. I've compiled the following list of ambiguous things Sam has done to show you what I mean:

(1) Left his bedroom door ajar for two nights in a row despite usually closing it completely.

(2) Said, 'It's lovely to see you again,' when he'd only been away for one night.

(3) Let his knee touch mine without pulling it away when we were on the tube.

(4) Came into my bedroom just as I was getting changed for bed to ask me whether I'd seen his tent poles.

(5) Asked if I wouldn't mind sharing a whites wash.

See what I mean? I suppose this must be the type of thing lawyers face all the time but at least they're entitled to interrogate their subject openly and don't have to bottle it all up so that it becomes inflated in their head like a large Mr Blobby.

The only person I've allowed myself to discuss it with is Drippy Moira, who says I am analysing far too much and should just relax and enjoy it, which is all very well for her to say but she is not the one trapped in a web of foggy uncertainty. She also pointed out that I have a boyfriend, which although true is not relevant – like saying I have a Marks & Spencer's anorak when I'm trying on a Nicole Farhi coat.

The thing is, James is being really pathetic at the moment and has turned into one of those limpet things you try to scrape off rocks during biology field trips. Whenever I suggest we do something normal for young, dynamic people of our age, i.e. get drunk, he makes a peculiar face and says, 'Nah, let's just get a Chinese and watch Casualty,' as if we have been catapulted into middle-age and have lost the urge to socialise with anyone, even each other.

And recently he's started talking about what we should do at New Year, which feels very odd because normally if I book us for dinner with friends past the end of the week he goes all funny in a way that suggests I am really ensnaring him in a trap of church fêtes and weekly trips to Asda.

I haven't seen him much recently. He keeps phoning and suggesting we do stuff together and then when I tell him I'm busy he says he thinks I've gone off him. This isn't really true, but the more he says it the more I think it might be.

I tried asking Sophie if Richard had ever just suddenly gone all weird and gaggy like James is being, but she looked puzzled and said she didn't know what I meant. She says I might have *this syndrome she read about where you are only ever attracted to men who abuse you and hit you and stuff and that if a man is nice to you you push them away because they don't have the capacity to make you feel inferior and useless. Now I'm worried that I'm suffering from a premature form of this disease and will end up married to a wife-batterer, reduced to cowering behind frying-pans with black eyes.*

I wish I had a relationship like Sophie's. It's always so constant and stable, like the straight-line bit on a heart monitor, whereas James and I are the frantic zigzaggy bit going crazy in the middle. She claims relationships are all about teamwork and knowing how to play each other, and made the whole thing sound like a game of hockey which, come to think of it, is probably a large reason why I am having such difficulty.

I really like Sophie, even though she has a perfect life. I mean, it's not her fault that everything always goes well for her. And she's so nice to me. Like the other day when I burst into tears because I couldn't get my duvet cover on (it seemed traumatic at the time), she just did it like she was a nurse, and made me a soothing cup of camomile tea. And this morning she came into my room and found me hurling myself at my wardrobe – I was trying to close it – and showed me this brilliant way of dealing with excess clothes.

Basically, you get two empty bin-liners, one for clothes you are going to keep and the other for those you are going to give away to needy people. Every time you put an item in the 'me' bag you put something in the 'needy people' one as well. Sometimes it's quite hard, like when you want to keep all four pairs of jeans for your-self, but Sophie pinned a photo of a naked African baby on my noticeboard with 'I have nothing' written underneath it to remind me of who I would be depriving by my selfishness. (I'm not sure how much a little baby in Kenya would use a pair of size twelve Levi's but I'm assuming they can be made into something really useful, like a quarter of a curtain.)

I loved doing this, imagining semicircles of little African and Filipino kids all wearing my cast-offs, holding hands and singing

'We Are The World' with Bob Geldof. I also rather enjoyed the exciting Narnia-style discovery of lots of clothes I didn't know I had, scrumpled up at the back like used tissues. In the end I managed to get two full bag-loads, then Sophie kindly took the 'needy' one down to the charity shop for me because I'd promised to go clothes shopping with Jo.

Now I can't wait to get home and put the other half of my clothes back into the wardrobe and watch them dangle around in all their nice new space. Oh, God, but I won't be going home. I'll be busy scouring Primrose Hill with a heavy-duty flashlight and sniffer-dogs for a kitten. Misery.

Must go and have one final hunt and attempt to mop up the kitten poop I walked into the carpet earlier. I keep trying to think of lies I could tell to get myself out of this shit – as it were: like the ginger one upstairs went berserk, ate its brother then shat him out all over the hall, but this rather loses its credibility the minute you set eyes on the ginger one – a little fluffy Walt Disney creation clearly incapable of miaowing at a mouse.

Shit. That's their car. Here goes . . .

Jess

xxx

PS Apparently James has a surprise for me. I hate surprises. They're invariably something you either know already or something you don't want but must pretend you do because someone has gone to the effort of making it a surprise. Right now the only surprise I want, ironically enough, is a kitten.

'Aaaaarghh! *Fucking hell!*' It was half past one in the morning and Jess was standing in the middle of her bedroom screaming at a Marks & Spencer bag that, she could've sworn, had just moved.

'What's wrong?' Sam asked, appearing in the doorway with a hairstyle that looked as if *he* had suffered the shock.

'That!' she squealed, pointing at the bag.

'Jess, it's a bag. If I'm going to be woken at dead of night by a hysterical female I expect it at least to be because she's suffering from a sudden incurable desire to sleep with me and not because' – he threw himself on to the bed – 'she's bought something from Marks & Spencer's that doesn't fit.'

'There's something in it,' she whispered, taking full advantage of the fact that she could now grab hold of his upper torso under the guise of terror.

'Shall we see what it is?' he suggested, as if he were presenting *Play School* and it was time to choose the window. But just as he said it, the bag lurched forward, teetered on the edge of the bed, lurched a little more, then toppled to the floor. Had this been a horror film it would now have entered the realms of the implausible.

'Jesus Christ!' he yelped.

'See?' she said, rather pleased that the poltergeist had performed on cue.

'What on earth are you two doing?' Sophie was standing in a Little Mermaid nightie, staring in disbelief as they clambered frantically on to Jess's desk.

'Keep away from the bag!' Sam shouted, like something out of a *Lethal Weapon* film.

'Why? What'll it do? Explode?'

'That's a possibility,' Jess said.

'Sam, have you and Jess been smoking something?' Sophie seemed to think Sam lived off a diet of pasta and hash, which wasn't, as Jess was finding out, entirely off the mark.

'What's going on?' Now Colin had appeared with a torch, as if he were not in a fully electrically powered house but camping in a deserted field somewhere near the Lake District.

'Jess and Sam are hallucinating,' Sophie said flatly.

'I see,' he replied wisely. Colin was always claiming to 'see' but rarely seemed to get the gist of anything. 'What about?'

'The bag has moved,' Jess said. 'It was on the bed and now it's on the floor.'

'And did you put it on the floor?' he asked, spotlighting it with his torch.

'Colin, if we'd put it on the floor we wouldn't be standing shitting ourselves on my desk.'

'I thought Sophie said you were hallucinating.'

'Look, why doesn't someone just pick it up?' Sam said, looking directly at Colin. 'Like Colin, for example.'

Suddenly there was a funny scuffling movement from within the bag and a furry rodent sped out and scuttled madly across the floor.

'Help!' Sophie shrieked, diving on to the bed with an urgency, Jess suspected, that she wasn't in the habit of employing in the bedroom. 'It's a rat!'

'No, it's not,' Jess said, matter-of-factly, jumping down from her safety raft. 'It's the kitten. It's the fucking kitten.'

Once they'd all established why Jess should be relieved to discover someone else's pet among her M&S purchases, the task of how to return it to its owners began to cause problems. Sam's suggestion, that they wrap it up in newspaper and send it down the chimney, was voted a no-no by Sophie, who cited a number of humane reasons why this would be cruel. Colin came up with the brainwave of waiting until Monday and taking it into work then, by which time, Jess informed him, she would have *no* work. Eventually it was decided that Jess and Sam would return to the house, look for any open windows and, if none was accessible, try to ram it through the letterbox.

'It's not working,' she whispered, thrusting the kitten towards the door while Sam waved a tin of skipjack tuna tantalisingly out of reach through the letter-flap. 'Maybe it's a vegetarian?'

'Maybe it's two thirty in the morning and I'm freezing my bollocks off,' he replied. 'Look, just . . . I don't know . . . Push its head through or something.'

'Sam! It's not a puppet. You try.'

'Fine,' he said, yanking at his arm. 'Oh, great. This is just great.'

'What?'

'My bloody arm's stuck.'

Jess felt alarmingly as though she might laugh. 'Here, let me try,' she offered, tucking the kitten under her arm as if it were a newspaper, and taking hold of Sam's upper arm ready to pull. 'OK, after three. One, two—'

'*Shiiiiiit!*' Sam yelled, as he catapulted backwards, dropping the tuna on the wrong side of the door in the process, and landing on top of a slightly dazed Jess. The kitten, which up until now had shown only fleeting signs of life, leapt to safety through the very hole they'd been trying, for the last half-hour, to coax it into.

'Bingo!' she shouted, throwing her arms around Sam in elation.

'Will you promise me one thing?' he said, as they picked themselves off the pathway and scurried out of sight. Jess wondered whether this might be the moment for something dubiously sexual to happen. 'That if I ever have kids, you will *never ever* go near them.'

The next morning she was still in bed recovering when Jo, who seemed to think Sundays were all about charging up and down the King's Road with sunglasses on your head looking at little blue glass bowls in Habitat, returned to disturb her.

'Je-ess. You awake?'

'No,' Jess mumbled, pulling the duvet over her head.

'Jess babes, it's twelve thirty,' she said, scratching at the door.

'Don't care,' Jess replied.

'And I've got something really cool to show you.'

Suddenly the door burst open and Jo appeared in the middle of the room wearing a Wonderbra and a pair of ridiculously tight black suede trousers.

'Da-dah! What d'you think?'

She looked like someone who hovered outside illuminated 'Girls!Girls!Girls!' signs in Soho.

'Yeah,' Jess muttered, wondering exactly which part of the ensemble Jo was proud of.

'Three fifty. Can you believe it, babes? Three quid fifty.'

'Wow.' Jess yawned, then blinked. There was something strangely familiar about the trousers. 'Where from?'

'This little shop down the road. You should go. They've got heaps of your kind of stuff,' she chirped, strutting towards the bed like an ostrich. 'Sort of nice and not too trendy.'

'Gee, thanks, Jo,' Jess grumbled, staring at the trousers – they weren't overly trendy themselves. 'Well, at least those might stop you borrowing mine, I suppose.'

'Which reminds me,' Jo said, marching over to the wardrobe, 'that blue top of yours.'

'Is gone,' Jess said proudly. 'In fact, it is probably winging its way to a little African girl as we speak.'

Jo looked bewildered.

'As are the majority of my other clothes which I have pointlessly kept for years.'

Jo looked even more bewildered. The idea that one should do anything with clothes other than leave them lying all over the carpet was a bizarre one indeed.

'Sophie,' Jess continued smugly, 'has totally revolutionised my clothing dilemma. From now on I will have a minimal yet totally functioning wardrobe.'

'Very minimal,' Jo said, staring at the empty rail. 'So is this little African girl getting *all* your clothes?'

'No, you uncharitable one.' Jess smiled, motioning towards a black bin-liner in the corner. 'Not my favourite ones.'

Jo waltzed over to the bin-liner and peered inside it. 'And this is a favourite for what reason exactly?' she enquired, delving into the bag and holding up a zebra-patterned sweatshirt.

'Yes, well, it's obviously been put in the wrong bag, hasn't it?' Jess said, condescendingly.

'And would the same be said for these?' she continued, brandishing a pair of bright green leggings.

Jess stared in horror as it dawned on her what had happened. 'Oh, no. No, don't tell me,' she shrieked.

'It's OK,' Jo laughed, 'it'll go with this,' she said, pulling out a sequinned felt waistcoat, 'which I'm sure will all come in handy should you ever become a Peruvian goat-herder.' She was beside herself with hilarity.

'It's not funny,' Jess cried, bolting out of bed and frantically tipping the rest of the contents on to the floor. 'She's taken the wrong bag. Sophie's taken the wrong bloody bag.'

'Where are you going?' Jo shouted, as Jess sprang to her feet and fled out of the door.

'To get my clothes before the fucking Africans do!'

'Who's being uncharitable now?' Jo retorted, as she tried on a floral headscarf.

'Excuse me,' Jess panted, bursting through the doors of the Salvation Army charity shop, as if she were not one lone soldier but an entire regiment.

A small woman in a yellow cardigan writing 5p on a porcelain vase looked up. 'Can I help you, dear?' she asked, placing it among a host of other ceramic misfits.

'Yes,' Jess announced purposefully. 'Yesterday a friend of mine dropped off a bag for your Aid to Africa appeal.'

'That was kind of her.' The woman smiled.

'Yes, but the thing is, it was the *wrong bag*,' Jess said, as if by being old, the woman was also deaf and stupid. 'You see, the bag she was meant to give you was full of . . . well, you know, stuff Africans might need,' she said, 'only she gave you *my* bag instead, which was full of stuff *I* need, and I really want it back.'

The woman pursed her lips, making them disappear into the folds of her chin like a turtle.

'Oh, God,' Jess said, alarmed, 'it hasn't already gone to Africa, has it? I mean, obviously I'm keen to help in any way I can.' She laughed nervously. 'It's just that, well, if there was any way of salvaging, say, my Joseph jumper, perhaps, and I had a pair of rather nice—'

'We didn't send it to Africa, dear,' the woman replied, stroking her arm comfortingly.

'Oh, thank heavens above.'

'No, dear, we didn't think it was quite the right *quality*,' she said, guiding Jess across the shop, 'so we decided to try to get rid of it here.'

'Get rid of it? What – sell it?'

'Yes, dear,' the woman replied, motioning towards a rail headed up by a crop of yellowing fur coats.

'Oh, my God . . .' Jess scanned a selection of her most treasured clothes sandwiched between turquoise Crimplene skirts and nylon floral blouses.

'Well, can't I just take them back again?' she said, pulling out her Joseph jumper and discovering to her horror that it was now worth £2.95.

'That's not really within the moral conduct of our organisation,' the woman said, glancing pointedly at a picture of an emaciated Ethiopian captioned 'Please Give Generously'.

'So I'm going to have to buy back my own clothes?' Jess

said furiously, as two girls pointed to one of her dresses and exchanged mutual throwing-up signs.

'Well, someone's going to have to, dear.'

Half an hour and £54.50 later, Jess was struggling into the house carting as many clothes as she had been able to rescue plus a few extras she'd been unable to resist.

'So you found the shop, then?' Jo exclaimed, pointing at the bulging Salvation Army bags. 'Told you it was your thing, babes,' she said, contorting her body into a minuscule leather jacket. 'Oh, by the way, James rang. Said he needs to talk to you urgently about your surprise.'

'Oh, God,' Jess moaned, slumping down on the stairs in the manner of a heavily pregnant woman, 'I've had enough surprises to last me a lifetime.'

'Don't worry, I think this is a good one,' Jo trilled, tapping her nose, winking and flouncing towards the front door. 'See ya, babes.'

Jess watched as Jo's sleek suede bottom vanished out of sight.

'Oh, my God,' she shouted, in sudden realisation, 'those are my trousers!'

Whatever James had in store, she decided, as she sloped her way to the telephone, would have to be better than this.

Unable to contemplate a worse surprise
Unable to contemplate how James, who can know
  me so intimately in some respects, can fail so
  hopelessly to know me in others
Unable, let's face it, to contemplate James

Dear Alex,

As you can see from the mangy rain-sodden Highland cow on the front of this PC, I am not lying under swaying palm trees on a secluded Caribbean beach, but in my bedroom in Inverness intrigued to know which particular bit of this hideous bank-holiday weekend James thought I might like. Disappointed does not even touch on how I feel.

When someone tells you to pack something smart and be prepared to see people you haven't seen for a while, you expect it's because they have organised a huge party or similar where everyone will get very drunk and write complimentary sentimental things about you in a gigantic card (which you will then bring out and admire at moments in your future life when you are feeling in need of a good ego boost). Not because you will be spending the weekend with your parents, driving for twelve hours up the M1 to do so, eating chewy Little Chef burgers on the way, and playing 'I Spy' with someone who claims to have spotted something beginning with the letter Z on the outskirts of Doncaster. I feel as though I've been an innocent baby duped into eating puréed broccoli by believing the loaded spoon is really a choo-choo train. Hold on – no room left on this shitty PC . . .

On top of all this I am suffering from the nagging conviction that while we are marooned up here with bad local television and a smattering of sheep, everyone else is in London at one enormous party getting drunk and snogging. It comes from the same paranoia family as the one where you are out having a lovely post-work drink and suddenly decide you are missing out on something more exciting at home in the form of juicy letters, millions of answer-machine messages and all your flatmates waiting eagerly to see you (which, of course, only means you get home to no letters, no messages and a spookily dark, empty hallway). I wish I could just relax and enjoy my surroundings rather than suffer this mild internal panic that something a whole lot better is happening somewhere else.

I think a large part of my problem at the moment, though, is not so much missing out as missing Sam. I know it's pathetic as it's only been a matter of hours, but we've been getting on so well. He's been fabulous, solving my work crisis by phoning up Walters and Co. pretending to be Brian and blaming my horrendous phone-call blunder on a phantom work-experience girl called Sadie. As a result, the weed-killer commercial is now back on, I'm getting to help with the filming, Brian is ecstatic and everything is hunky-dory.

Well, not totally hunky-dory. I have finally admitted to myself that I do fancy Sam, which although liberating in one sense is problematic in another, i.e. James. It seems cruel and rather ironic that after months of nagging him to meet my parents (not because I had any interest in him doing so but to stop my mother referring to him as 'The Phantom James' every time I mentioned him) he has finally done it, precisely at the moment I have decided I don't want him.

I say 'decided' and obviously I really want to dump him, it's just that every time I plan to do it something happens. For example, I will be on the verge of revving myself up and someone will say he's a really cool bloke or a random girl will flirt with him and I will be thrown off course and start thinking maybe he's all right after all, and I should hang on to him. I've tried to compile a list to help me with this confusion.

Pros of Dumping James	Cons of Dumping James
Would become a wonderful free spirit able to roam the world at will, unshackled by feelings of unhealthy dependence towards another human being.	*Would be single.*
Would no longer need to shave my underarms regularly.	
Would resume contact with all my friends who I have completely neglected for my boyfriend and cook them big delicious reconciliatory dinner parties.	
Would be able to devote time to me, my career and other important things rather than perpetually obsess over the relationship.	
Would be able to wear my purple cardigan again.	
Would take up interesting new hobbies and visit places of cultural and historical interest with all the time I would formerly have spent massaging James's ego.	

> *Would go to parties, not as a*
> *boring couple who leave at*
> *midnight sober, but as an*
> *exciting single person, flirting*
> *with hordes of attentive men*
> *and waking up in a hand-*
> *some stranger's bed after a*
> *night of animal-crazed*
> *passion.*

I know there are probably other drawbacks but I just can't –
oh, yeah, I wouldn't be able to borrow his grey Jigsaw jumper.
See, this is the thing. On the surface, splitting up with someone
seems simple, like chucking out a pair of old boots that have big
gaping holes in the soles and are no longer fashionable. But the
minute you're on your way to the bin, you realise:

- *You are too sentimentally attached to your boots/boyfriend.*
- *The holes in the boots/boyfriend might potentially be fixable.*
- *The boots/boyfriend might come in useful at a later date, e.g.*
  fancy-dress party/dinner function where everyone is in happy
  couples.
- *You might never find any better boots/boyfriend again.*

Anyway, I am not going to rush into a decision as I am too
traumatised by the recent Inverness-and-not-Caribbean disap-
pointment to think straight. And I don't think now is the time to
upset someone who is presently having a jovial time downstairs
with my mother watching a pre-recorded University Challenge
(yes, my mum records this) and playing Who Can Guess the Correct
Medical Term for an Inflamed Nostril Bone with a selection of
bespectacled computer nerds from Reading.

It seems ludicrous now to think I ever worried about them getting
on, it's just that I hate it when I am the connecting link between

two sets of people who have never met before. It makes me get all panicky that they are not going to say/do the correct thing, as though they are not capable socialised adults, but performing seals in a circus, which an expectant audience of ten-year-olds is waiting to watch me coax through blazing hoops with balls on their noses.

But, as it is, everyone has behaved spectacularly and so far the only embarrassing things have been:

(1) Dad shouting, 'Bollocks', when he dropped his knife.
(2) Mum producing a photo of me, aged eight, looking insanely ugly with no front teeth, crouched in a washing-up bowl with a helium balloon attached hoping to fly.
(3) Dad referring to Manchester United as a bunch of spineless wankers.
(4) James wearing his Manchester United top at the time.
(5) Mum calling the radio a wireless.

James says he thinks my parents are lovely and they, particularly Mum, think he is lovely too. In fact, everyone thinks everyone is lovely and we have all transformed into one big Sunday-lunch-eating Walton family.

I love this warm fuzzy duvet feeling, although I'm annoyed with James for seeming like a normal nice boyfriend. Mum keeps saying she doesn't know why I complain about him and when he's like this, neither do I. It is as though he is a screaming sickly child who, when its mother calls the doctor out in the middle of the night, stops screaming and turns into a contented little bundle gurgling at the ceiling.

The whole thing has now got fairly ludicrous with Mum doing funny little giggles every time James says anything, following him around the house in a manner alarmingly reminiscent of Mrs Robinson. Then last night a mysterious camp-bed appeared in the middle of my room, complete with hand-towel and small hexagon-shaped bar of soap. I was perturbed by the resemblance my bedroom now bore to a swirly-carpeted boarding house in Clacton-on-Sea until James appeared, looking for his pyjamas, which we found placed discreetly under the camp-bed pillow.

We are assuming this is my mother's way of letting us sleep together but as she has failed to mention it we think it best also to creep under the blanket of denial – or, in this case, slightly embarrassing Holly Hobbie duvet – and behave as if nothing has happened. I cannot help being suspicious of her motives, though. Why, half-way through the weekend, uproot James from a comfy double to a little piece of foam on springs that if you happen so much as to breathe in the wrong direction buckles up and sends you hurtling head first towards the skirting-board? It is the equivalent of having a fridgeful of chilled Chardonnay and offering your dinner-party guests warm Lucozade.

James claims it is because she can tell how crazy we are about each other and doesn't want to separate us in a cruel Miss Hannigan-depriving-Annie-of-a-father way. But this is James's solution to everything at the moment. The hire car we have got doesn't seem to be working any more, and when I enquired how we might get back to London, he said, completely seriously, 'Love will find a way.' It's as though he has suddenly become the lyric writer for Mariah Carey and now sees life in soft-focus shots of deserted beaches at sunset.

Personally, I am concerned that the bed move has more to do with Poppy the dog, who waited until we had all sat down for dinner before she presented us with a used condom. Sometimes I think she is not a dog at all but some fanged relation of Beelzebub sent to persecute me.

To be honest, I'm relieved she only found one. James and I seem to have turned into rampant rabbits, copulating all over the place as if it is our mission to create the entire cast of Watership Down by sunset. I don't know why when we have a nice private bedroom in London we have to behave like lust-induced maniacs here, where there are things like patrolling parents, thin walls and sniffer-dogs.

I think it might have something to do with the fact that I am perpetually imagining life without him, which makes him seem *more attractive and desirable. And he is so keen to do anything for me that, well . . . Thinking about it, I might just see what he's up to . . .*

Bollocks. What a stupid, stupid idea. In a euphoric state of bunny mania, and because, when you're lying semi-naked on the precipice of paralytic pleasure condoms seem little faraway unimportant things, James and I decided it would be fine to have unprotected . . . well, anyway. Very, very bad idea. James did not perform according to plan and, like Napoleon at Waterloo, did not retreat his troops in time, with the result that at four in the morning, while he is in blissful post-coital slumber, I am sitting in a neurotic sweat calculating the odds of being pregnant. Half an hour ago I felt sure I could feel a sperm head-butting one of my eggs and decided that the risk of becoming a single mother on unemployment benefit was an unwise one to take.

In a blind panic, I have just phoned the family-planning clinic (tragically inappropriate name, given that planning a family is clearly the reverse of our objectives) and endured a pre-recorded Samaritan woman telling me that, due to the bank holiday Monday, free and confidential advice would not be available until Tuesday. It is Sunday. I have to sit around for two days while a human life – well, semi-human, given its parenting – forms itself in my womb. By Tuesday it will probably have little toes. I am not going to think about this, but return to bed, go to sleep and hope that in the process of doing so all child-making facilities in my body will sleep also, killing any potentially baby-filled eggs and ensuring that I will not have to do it for them by forking out £14.95 for the hideous morning-after pill.

Urgh, urgh. Feeling like eight different flavours of shit. It's now Wednesday afternoon, we're on our way back to London and have just stopped off at something that calls itself the Happy Eater. James is looking suicidal with a burger while I am trying to distract myself from what is going on inside my body by writing to you on the back of a Happy Sausage Sizzler flyer. Despite feeling violently nauseous I am endeavouring not to chuck up the pill I have just

taken because, contrary to a normal illness when puking is a beneficial act, if I throw up now I will have to start all over again and
personally I would rather give birth to a selection of six-headed
triplets. I have no idea what they put in these things but whatever
it is feels as though it is not so much preventing pregnancy as
dissolving my entire womb.

James, as part of his Devoted Boyfriend repertoire, is taking the
whole thing very seriously. He keeps rubbing my shoulders and
telling me I need to be 'looked after and protected' until I pointed
out that I could've done with the protection bit three and a half
days earlier, which shut him . . . Oh, hold on, he's trying to read
this, having finished studying the car-radio manual. Apparently
there is a way of tuning it so that it will randomly hop from one
station to the other. I don't really know why we should want this
but he has become obsessed with the idea that we do and if it will
stop him prodding the dashboard every five minutes when he is
supposed to be concentrating on ensuring we don't crash, then
frankly I'm all for it. I'd better go.

Lots of love,
Jess
xxx

PS Crisis! James has just stormed off to get petrol and I am in
shock. He wants us to move in together! I can't think of a worse
plan, and in a less direct way told him so. He has now gone all
mad-eyed and is looking as if he might douse the car in petrol and
set light to it. I am refusing to be manipulated by this kind of
behaviour. I love my flatmates and will not be forced to leave them
for a cantankerous pyromaniac.

'Malteser?' Jess said, proffering the bag when they were a safe enough distance away from the petrol station for her to assume that, for the time being at least, she was not about to perish in a flaming Ford Fiesta. 'Chocolate-coated raisin?' she continued, holding up something that looked as if it would be more at home in a cat-litter tray. 'Flat Irn-Bru?'

James stared stormily ahead, as though he were auditioning for a role as an Armani menswear model.

'Look, James, I'm sorry, it's just that . . .' She scrabbled around in her memory for the kind of thing he used to say to her during times of rejection. 'I just don't think it would be healthy for us.'

'I thought you loved me.'

'I do.'

'Then why are you being like this?'

'Like what?'

'Like . . . like . . .' She watched, stunned, as a tear rolled down his face and plopped on to his lap. 'Like you don't care about me any more.'

Just at that moment a discussion on mollusc-farming off the coast of Wales flicked to a chirpy DJ, who seemed to be performing the dual role of presenter-cum-lovers'-messaging-service: '. . . and this next one's for Dave from Kelly in East Croydon. Dave, if you're listening, Kelly wants you to know that she loves you very, very much, and can't wait until you move in together in two weeks' time.'

Jess stared in horror at the radio. 'Oh, look, it's started to rain,' she said, but the DJ continued to prattle.

'Ah, isn't that sweet? Let's hope it all goes well for the happy couple, and to start them off,' he chirped, clearly unaware of the unsuitability of his choice, 'here's Rose Royce with "Love Don't Live Here Any More" . . .'

James, overwhelmed by the poignancy of the moment, started to sob. 'I l-l-love you,' he spluttered, blowing his nose in a loud hooting manner on his sleeve.

'Here.' Jess handed him a McDonald's napkin.

'Why? Why? Why?' he wailed, banging his fist on the steering-wheel and inadvertently beeping the horn, triggering a series of counter-beeps from the car in front, the car behind and an approaching lorry-driver.

'Because your nose is running.' She laughed, then stopped when she realised that he wasn't. 'Look, it's not as if we won't still see each other and, anyway, you wouldn't want to live with me.' She smiled. 'My alarm clock's too annoying.'

But, rather than consoling him, this made things worse. The alarm clock, usually the cause of frequent arguments on account of its tendency to go off erratically in the middle of the night, had suddenly become a little love object, encompassing in its broken plastic frame everything James felt about his girlfriend.

'It's not annoying,' he blubbed, 'it's cute.'

By the time they'd got to the outskirts of London, Jess had exhausted her supply of cheerful subject-changers of the 'That's a pretty sheep, isn't it?' and 'I wonder if they know their back windscreen-wiper doesn't work?' variety. She was now embroiled in the much harder task of navigating their route home.

'You need to get on to the . . . yellow road, I think,' she said, rotating the gigantic map 180 degrees, and searching the surrounding industrial estate for signs of what the key termed 'a small kirk'.

'It's so sweet the way you do that,' he said suddenly, looking at her as if they were in a fabric-softener commercial.

'Do what?' she asked, stunned that she was map-reading and he wasn't screaming at her.

'That,' he said, motioning towards the upturned atlas.

'Oh,' she replied, realising she had just been directing them into Glasgow. 'Actually, it's the green road you want . . . the A1, I think.'

After a series of wrong turns and dead-ends, they arrived at her flat, and she left James to drive home alone under the pretext that she needed a good night's sleep before the weed-killer commercial.

The minute she walked in, though, she had a spooky sixth sense that something was up. The place was dark and unusually quiet, but something about it suggested there were people around. She knew immediately what it was, of course. Her flatmates were hiding. They were waiting for her to turn up and they were going to surprise her. She decided to play along. She loved her flatmates.

'Hello? Anyone here?' she sing-songed, switching on the kitchen light. 'Anyone hiding in a . . . cupboard perhaps?' she said, theatrically flinging open the doors to the utility room, causing an avalanche of chequered boxer shorts and, more seriously for her right shoulder, the ironing-board. Just at that moment there was a noise behind her.

'What on earth are you doing?' Colin was standing in the doorway wearing green wellington boots and Sophie's Little Mermaid bathrobe, making it not immediately obvious why it should be him that was asking the question. Jess noticed he was carrying a torch. Did he ever, she wondered, not carry a torch?

'*There* you are.' She fought off the ironing-board and removed a pair of boxer shorts from her hair.

'Did you think I was in there?' he suggested, in a rare moment of perceptiveness.

'Well,' she stammered, glancing round the room for any likelier explanation and spotting, propped up against a mug and a fork with a grain of rice on it, a note. 'Oh, goody,' she squealed, 'a letter.'

'Jess,' it began, 'I believe these are yours.' There was a little arrow after the word 'yours', which seemed, though Jess couldn't see why, to be pointing to the fork. As far as she knew all the cutlery belonged to the flat. 'Dishes, in case you didn't know, don't wash themselves,' it continued, causing Jess to glance to her right where a neatly stacked pile of dripping plates, pans and glasses seemed to suggest that they did. 'Could you please clean them? Richard is allergic to mould. Sophie.' ☺

''S a bit pathetic, isn't it?' she said, turning to Colin for support. But Colin was fiddling with the dressing-gown cord, exposing as he did so bits of his anatomy that she would rather not have seen. 'And petty. What kind of person does all that washing-up and leaves out two measly things?' she ranted. Colin had started shuffling uncomfortably from one wellie to the other.

'Actually it was me,' he said, after she'd solved the dilemma by throwing the offending objects defiantly into the bin. 'Sophie told me to.'

Sophie, Jess decided, the all-things-organic-and-African-baby-lover, had suddenly metamorphosed into a mallet-wielding Stephen King creation capable of holding hostage anything from a couple of dishes to, it would now seem, Colin. A suspect thought started germinating inside her head. 'Is that why you're wearing her dressing-gown?' she asked.

'No,' he muttered, then added illogically, 'There was a power-cut.'

Sometimes Jess feared for Colin. He seemed so incapable of doing anything that she wondered how he had ever got through a day, let alone made it into his twenties. But as he launched into a blow-by-blow account – literally – of how he had single-handedly tried to restore the power by taking a spanner to the fuse-box, short-circuiting the system so that there was no electricity, except in the kitchen, she began to fear for everybody.

'Perhaps we should call a plumber or something,' she said, casting an anxious glance into the darkened hallway.

Colin burst out laughing.

'What?' she snapped.

'A plumber!' he said, guffawing. 'I think you mean an electrician,' and then, as if it were the funniest thing he had ever heard, disappeared into the blackness snorting repeatedly, 'A plumber, ho, ho, ho, a plumber, ho, ho, ho.'

Eager to milk as much as she could from their enforced state of darkness, Jess went off to find Sam. She had been looking forward to seeing him again, playing through a number of fantasy scenarios in her head, none of which had had the romantic element of a power failure.

A warm, inviting glow was coming from his room, accompanied by the tinkling sort of music normally heard in ethnic-cushion shops.

'I've missed you so hopelessly, desperately,' she declared, from behind the door in a breathy 1950s love-movie voice, sliding a leg around the frame and running her hand seductively up and down it. 'Please . . . tell me you feel the same.' There was a moment's silence and then, to her horror, a high-pitched giggle. Poking her head round the door, she felt suddenly like a worm who, after spending a lifetime wriggling its way to the surface, had popped up in an aviary. There, swathed in Sam's patchwork quilt, was a girl.

'Hi, Jess,' Sam said, rising from a position she deemed too close to be platonic, and giving her the kind of hug one normally reserves for animals and small children, 'this is Petra.'

Jess watched, crushed, as the quilt parted and a tall, pig-tailed beauty rose phoenix-like towards her. 'Jess, at last, how lovely to meet you,' she said sweetly. Jess noticed she was wearing Sam's jumper.

'Petra's been teaching blind children in Thailand,' Sam said, grasping her from behind and pressing his face against hers as if they were part of a photo campaign for Dateline, 'but had to come back because she was so in love with me.' Petra pretended to find this untrue.

Erghh, puke, Jess thought, trying to maintain her fixed grin without looking as though she had a jaw disfigurement. 'Well, I'm sure you've got a lot to catch up on, so I'll just . . .' she bleated, backing awkwardly out of the room, 'go and unpack.'

'Here, take this,' the goddess offered, handing her one of the candles circling their love-nest. 'It's got ylang-ylang in it, which supposedly enhances your sexuality,' she said, smiling coquettishly up at Sam.

'Thanks,' Jess snapped, grabbing it and resisting the urge to set fire to the pigtails.

Once alone in her bedroom, she flung herself dramatically on to the bed where she lay staring at the ceiling and inter-mittently bursting into tears. Eventually, shattered by her efforts at self-pity, she fell asleep, leaving a soggy Wilbur to extinguish the candle by means of a deftly executed head-butt.

'Jesus, what the f—' she yelled. Her dream, in which Petra was about to be mangled by a ferocious baby goat in the middle of the yoghurt aisle in Asda, had been cut short by a painful noise. Squinting into the room, she tried to work out why all the lights were blazing, her alarm clock was imitating a fire engine and someone was watching the test-card at high volume.

'Shut up,' she groaned, blindly flailing an arm at the clock, trying to return to watch Petra being devoured by the goat. But the siren continued in its mission to wake up anyone still asleep in Uzbekistan, forcing her to turn over and switch it off. It was then that she discovered it was flashing 8.17.

'Fuck and buggerations!' she shrieked, leaping out of bed and hopping round the room like a lunatic. 'I'm late, I'm late, I'm fucking late.'

Suddenly she was aware of a figure standing in the doorway. A slightly stunned-looking Jo was lurching from side to side watching her in disbelief as she fled around picking things up and putting them down again. She was wearing a top that looked as though it had been made during a material shortage crisis and a pair of flared trousers that evidently hadn't. Her hair was doing wild things with kirby-grips and her makeup, what was left of it, appeared to have been applied with a spoon. 'Thank God you're still awake, babes,' she muttered, stumbling into the room and collapsing in a heap on Jess's bed.

'Awake? Awake?' Jess screamed, yanking indiscriminately at pairs of knickers. 'No thanks to you. Why didn't someone get me? I'm supposed to be sitting behind a camera directing people and things and instead I'm—' She stopped rummaging and turned round. Jo was crying. 'Jo? What on earth's the matter?'

'I'm . . . I'm . . . I'm a failure,' she sobbed, burying her head in Jess's pillow and wailing.

'Oh, God.' Jess sighed, dumped the pile of knickers she had accumulated and went over to the bed to comfort her. 'You're not a failure,' she said, unconvincingly.

'I am,' Jo protested into the pillow.

'No, you're not,' Jess replied, wondering how long this charade was going to last.

'I am,' she choked, surfacing for air and breathing clouds of alcohol fumes directly into Jess's face. 'Colin screamed at me *because* I woke him up, you're screaming at me because I *didn't* and . . . and . . . and Max doesn't love me,' she wailed, bursting into fresh torrents of sploshy tears.

Jess glanced anxiously at the clock. 'I'm sure Max does still love you,' she suggested gingerly, 'it's just that, well, he probably feels bad saying it, what with his girlfriend and stuff. Anyway,' she continued brightly, giving Jo a hearty, little punch, 'you've got plenty of other guys, you don't need Max.'

'I need Max,' Jo wailed.

'Look,' Jess said, trying to disguise the mounting panic in her voice, 'I don't mean to sound insensitive here but I'm in a bit of a rush. I was supposed to be at the studio an hour and a half ago and if I don't get there soon I'm likely to spend the remainder of my days jigging at the back of a dole queue with the rest of the Full Monty.'

Jo did a large sniff. 'What time is it?'

'Eight twenty-three,' Jess replied, jumping up with renewed panic at this discovery and resuming her fumblings with the knicker drawer.

'Colin said it was two thirty,' Jo said, as if she were a six-year-old and Mummy had just contradicted Daddy over bedtime rules.

'Yeah, well, Colin wouldn't know if it was Christmas and Santa had just leapt down the – Two thirty?'

'I think that's what he said,' Jo sniffed pitifully. 'He was shouting so much I could barely hear.'

Just at that moment, Jess spotted her watch in a plant pot into which, in a fit of Petra-disgust, she had previously thrown it.

'Fucking great,' she said, as it dawned slowly on her what had happened. 'Just fucking great.'

'Jess,' Jo stammered, clutching her stomach, 'I think I'm going to be sick.'

Five and a half hours later: 8.17

'Je-ess? Jess?' Colin was standing outside her bedroom, scratching at the door like an anxious rodent. 'I think you need to wake up.'

'Wha'?'

'It's about eight seventeen,' he shouted through the door. 'Time to get up.'

'No, it's not,' she groaned. 'Wrong time 's power-cut,' then turned over and fell back into a deep, happy slumber.

'I see,' he said. 'Sleep well, then.'

And she did. For hours. She had another dream about Petra, while Jo, who'd passed out mopping up a pool of vomit, lay snoring contentedly on the floor. It wasn't until an ambulance screeched past outside that either of them stirred.

'Ohhh, my head,' Jo murmured, rolling over and narrowly missing the regurgitated remnants of an onion bhaji. 'Jess?' she groaned. 'Got any Nurofen, babes?'

'Mmm?' Jess grumbled. 'Whassatime?'

Jo stretched out an arm limply and patted the surrounding carpet for the watch. 'Two thirty.'

'That was last night,' Jess said sleepily, propping herself up on one elbow and looking at the vomit. 'The real time?'

''Tis,' Jo replied, throwing the watch at the bed. 'We've slept the day away, babes.'

Jess stared at the watch in horror. 'I can't fucking believe this!' she yelled, and bolted for the door.

When she eventually made it to Shepperton Studios she was disappointed to discover it was not some kind of idyllic mini-Hollywood set among the hills of southern England where Jude Law and Sadie Frost wandered round hand in hand and directors sat in canvas chairs shouting, 'Action!' at a smiling Gwyneth Paltrow, but a collection of gigantic warehouses on the outskirts of Twickenham.

After wandering round the complex several times in a pair of ludicrously inappropriate high-heeled sandals, searching vainly for stage D which didn't seem to be connected in any way to stages C or E, she went to seek help in a building that was obviously in use because a bright red light was shining outside it. The minute she opened the door, however, she realised she'd made a grave mistake.

'What the fuck was that?' yelled a voice from the corner. 'Cut.'

Forty people dressed as pecan nuts turned round and stared at her.

'Whatever the fuck that is, get rid of it,' the unidentified Satan boomed again, and several boys carrying rolls of masking tape charged out of the darkness towards her.

'Oh, God,' she squealed, 'I'm sorry, I didn't—'

'Ever heard of the red light?' one snapped. She couldn't work out if this was some kind of oblique insinuation that she was a prostitute, or a television term for knocking.

'Um – I just—' she stuttered, wondering whether to say 'thought this was the toilet'/'need to borrow some masking tape'/'want to die' when her sentence was abruptly finished for her by one of Satan's spawn.

'Better get out.'

'Yes.' She nodded assertively, and tripped over a cable.

Twenty minutes later she had located stage D and was standing patiently outside it when a familiar voice hailed her. She turned round to see Brian struggling towards her carrying the kittens in a cage labelled 'Celebrity Cats'. He was probably hoping they would be spotted by a talent scout, she thought derisively.

'What in the blue blazes do you think you're doing?' he shouted. Brian never shouted.

'Waiting for the red light to go off,' she replied confidently, glad that she had at least learnt something from her brush-with-death experience.

'Jess,' he shrieked, 'it is five past four! You were supposed to be here almost *twelve hours ago*. And now,' he yelled, 'you're telling me you've been standing outside staring' – he looked as though he was going to combust with fury – 'at a light-bulb!'

Luckily just then a couple of bearded men in jeans appeared carrying a gigantic pot plant.

'Couldn't give us a hand with this, could you, darlin'?' one asked, leering at her legs.

She looked anxiously at Brian, who was doing ostentatious loud breathing. 'Um, OK,' she squeaked, grasping a branch somewhat ineffectively and following them into the studio.

Having imagined the place to look like a bigger version of *Richard and Judy*, with a few more bouquets of chrysanthemums and perhaps the odd fruit bowl, she was slightly disappointed to be confronted with something that looked as though it was still being built. Burly men were standing on scaffolding hammering things into walls and shouting, 'Tilt her more to the right, Bob,' at weedy-looking men in glasses below, and the floor was covered in thick black cabling, as though it had just been invaded by a colony of eels. At the far end of this enormous workshed, several huge lights with tinted Cellophane pinned across them were shining down on something, and lots of people were standing around looking concerned. She was beginning to think she had walked into a vast B&Q.

'Can we have Jess on set now? Jess on set now, please,' Brian shouted, as if he were the store manager requiring assistance with a delivery of wheelbarrows.

'That's me!' she shrieked excitedly to a group of workmen eating biscuits. 'I can't believe it!'

Until now she'd been rather unclear as to what she would be doing. Brian had mentioned things about coffee percolators not working properly and the surprising amount of sandwiches set designers tended to go through, but she couldn't really see the connection between this and her role in the commercial. It had now, however, become clear. She was to be in it.

She skipped towards the set, which seemed to be the entire *Blue Peter* garden plus pond erected on a stage. Two gnomes were standing on a piece of convincing grass out of which some Triffid-looking weeds were sprouting and making straight for the gnomes' genitals.

'Here,' Jess cooed, flailing her arms madly in the air.

'OK, doll, what's your name?' a rather handsome man with a ponytail asked.

'My name's Jess,' she replied proudly, as if it were *Blind*

Date and she was going on to add, 'and I'm a sales rep from Birmingham, Cilla.'

'Right, doll,' the handsome man continued, 'you just pop up there,' he said, gesturing to a mock rock garden, 'and look pretty,' then added – quite flirtily, Jess decided, 'which shouldn't be too difficult.'

She clambered eagerly up on to a mossy boulder and perched there grinning inanely. This was what working in television was all about, she thought, relishing the fact that every single light, person, lens, cable and biscuit seemed to be pointing in her direction.

'OK, doll, let's see them.'

'Um . . . OK,' she said, giggling modestly and hitching up her skirt. In the distance a cameraman gave an appreciative whistle.

'Your legs are lovely, doll, but that's not what we're after here.' He smirked suggestively.

'Oh, right,' she stammered, glancing down at her bosoms.

'Whenever you're ready,' he said, as she pushed out her chest provocatively, 'we'll have the kittens.'

Having kittens
In Waitrose
One hour before my dinner party

Dear Alex,

My life has just reached meteoric proportions of hideosity. I was simply standing innocently in the queue with my basket (I always take a basket rather than a trolley, thinking I will only be getting a couple of potatoes and some Jaffa cakes and then, before I know it, the basket is brimming over and I have to shuffle it along the floor with my feet while everyone else sails past looking smug and sensible with half-empty trolleys) when the woman at the checkout told me my credit card wasn't valid.

I hate it when this happens because instead of saying, 'Well, it worked perfectly well an hour ago,' and making out it is their fault, I go all sheepish and guilty-looking as if I have just been caught trying to embezzle half a ton of cocaine out of Mexico.

The whole thing turned into an almighty fiasco with women ringing buzzers and keying complicated number sequences into tills and the entire queue giving me death stares. Eventually Cassandra, from Customer Services, told me they were awaiting authorisation from my bank and promptly escorted me, minus my shopping, into the poky little room I am now in.

It is all horrendous. Everyone in the shop thinks I am a criminal, I am supposed to be cooking broccoli and cream cheese tartlets for eleven and the bank has refused to acknowledge me unless I can tell them either my pin number or my mother's maiden name, neither of which I can remember. Now my bank too is going to think I'm a criminal. Shitting hell. Right, must think . . .

~~4751~~
~~4571~~
4157

The thing is I am not entirely convinced this isn't my bicycle-padlock number.

~~3983~~
~~3893~~

Oh, this is just useless. If Sophie hadn't made me chuck out the piece of paper it was written on in my wallet I would be fine. As it is, she has made me memorise it in such a complicated way, involving Richard's brother's birthday and the calorie content of an organic raspberry or something, that it is now impossible to remember.

I feel as though I am fifteen again trying to do my chemistry Standard Grade on the strength of remembering sulphuric acid is **H**arry's **2 S**exually **O**rganed **4** **J**ess (easy to memorise because I fancied Harry at the time and therefore had a limitless capacity for retaining any information about him, however irrelevant and, with regard to this particular mnemonic, doubtless untrue).

Oh, God, it's half past six. In less than an hour a horde of ravenous guests will be descending on my doorstep expecting food, which has all been confiscated in the manner of a Boy Scout camp. I still need to buy the main course (stupid fish thing – Sophie's idea), think of a pudding and wash my hair. And I haven't even contemplated what I might wear.

Why, oh, why do I leave everything till the last minute? It's like Christmas. I tell myself each year I will not charge around town on Christmas Eve, getting trampled on by three billion shopping-crazed maniacs while trying to grab the last bottle of Body Shop raspberry ripple bubble bath and what's left of Thornton's orange creams, which no one will like anyway, but will instead be a calm, organised person who buys reduced wrapping paper in January, presents in August and sends Help the Blind cards in November.

I can't cope with this. Perhaps I should do something relaxing like assemble the seating-plan. That's always a fun job. OK . . .

```
         Me      Sam      Jo     Richard
       ┌─────────────────────────────────┐
       │                                 │  Helen
Sophie │                                 │
       │                                 │  Colin
       └─────────────────────────────────┘
        James    Pooch    Max     Petra
```

No, that won't work because:
(1) Petra is beside Max, and Jo doesn't want him sitting near anyone pretty.
(2) I could swap places with Petra so that I am beside Max – which Jo seems to want and I find slightly insulting – but that would mean Petra is beside Sam which is a definite no-no.
(3) Uncertainty over whether Max will come anyway, as he still hasn't replied to three phone calls.
(4) Helen (tedious work friend of Colin's) is near Richard, which Sophie won't have because they once had a drunken snog at Colin's work's party, which Helen took as the beginning of a relationship and told everyone they were going out with each other.
(5) Also, who to put next to Colin who he won't bore other than Helen?

I'm going to try again. Right . . .

```
        Richard  Petra   Colin    Jo
       ┌─────────────────────────────────┐
       │                                 │  Max
Helen  │                                 │
       │                                 │  Me
       └─────────────────────────────────┘
         Pooch    Sam    Sophie   James
```

Oh God, this is even worse:

125

(1) *I am miles away from Sam and Sam is opposite Petra (though still undecided whether optimal flirting can be achieved beside or opposite).*

(2) *Richard is still too near Helen.*

(3) *Colin will monopolise Jo and want to talk about Wandsworth Council so that she won't be able to flirt with Max. (Although I must say I quite like the idea of him and Richard sandwiching Petra – possibly cocooning her from the rest of the table?)*

(4) *Pooch will intimidate Helen and might flirt with Sam.*

This is impossible. It's like trying to do one of those hideous aptitude tests at school. I know there is probably some logical way of attacking it, like making all the people who can't sit together an X and all the people who fancy each other a Y and then doing a complicated sum involving Pythagoras to get the answer, but I just can't do it. That's the thing, though, isn't it? It's all very well going to school and learning about algebra and how to divide fractions but what's the point if, at the end of the day, you can't apply it to important everyday things like dinner-party seating plans?

What's the point anyway? I will most likely be spending the night in this Customer Services cell drinking water and eating gruel before being handcuffed by the Fraud Squad and marched off to prison.

James would be keen on the prison option. He's pissed off with me because I forgot I was supposed to be meeting him for dinner. Apparently he waited for an hour and a half in Caffè Uno, which I pointed out must have seemed spookily relevant, i.e. uno = one, but he just shouted and said it wasn't spooky or relevant just very fucking annoying.

Anyway, it all turned out fine because he went into a pub and bumped into Toby, who was also alone having just discovered his girlfriend Vanya was a lesbian. He is distraught about it and never wants to see her again, which James cannot comprehend at all. As far as he is concerned, having a girlfriend who is also a lesbian is like having a television that is simultaneously a football, a beer-dispenser and a liberally minded Swedish masseuse.

They decided, however, in the ensuing beer-swilling, women-hating bonding session, that they would be better off living together – though not, I assume, in a homosexual sense – and have just moved into a flat in Notting Hill with some guy called Richard. They seem very happy there, so happy in fact that I have barely heard from or seen James since. Obviously this means he has stopped the ridiculous sobbing and pitiful pleading stuff, which is certainly a good thing, although in a bizarre way I quite liked it. There is something rather nice about knowing that someone is so desperately in love with you they need perpetually to cry about it.

Anyway, I am not going to worry about this as I have got more important things to deal with at the moment, re *the inexplicable arrival of Petra. I have no idea where she has sprung from but I would be grateful if she would just spring right back and leave me and Sam to resume our flirting undisturbed. I feel like a hyena who, after doggedly pursuing a baby monkey, has managed to grapple it to the ground only to watch, helpless, as a passing vulture swoops down and snatches it from under me.*

If only Petra were a vulture. She is so sickeningly nice I just want to hit her. The other day there was this French bloke who was obviously lost as he was wandering round in circles with an A–Z and a gigantic rucksack looking bewildered. Instead of walking past him, which is what I did, Pukey Petra stopped and asked him if he needed any help. It turned out he was trying to get to St Paul's but had somehow wound up in Covent Garden, so Petra walked him to the tube station carrying *his rucksack. See? Sam is never going to want me when he can have a younger version of Mother Teresa with beautiful skin and a natural desire to help others.*

The thing is, I am not entirely sure what is going on between them. One minute I think they're old work colleagues, the next I'm convinced they're lovers. Maybe they are just really good friends who happen to hug a lot. It's at times like this I wish we were not living in an era where there is no longer any clear line between romance and friendship and everybody just jumps wishy-washily in and out of bed with everyone else, but were instead back in the fifties courting in the cinema and going to civilised dances with men called Giles.

Oh, God, I wish I knew what was happening. I know I should just ask someone, but because it is so blindingly obvious to me that I fancy Sam I assume it is going to be equally blinding to them. Thus the simple question, 'What's the story with Sam and Petra?' becomes tantamount to shouting, 'I am totally infatuated with Sam and need to know whether he and Petra are going out with each other because if they aren't I would like to start a relationship with him with a view to marriage and possibly, thereafter, kids.'

In fact, the only occasion I plucked up courage to mention it I got so worked up about making it sound offhand and casual that I ended up gibbering into my glass like a gin-sodden bag-lady. Thus I have resorted to obsessing internally about it which, although not very good for my sanity, means at least I appear cool and together to everyone else.

Oh, hold on . . . Cassandra has come back and is saying they will accept my card if I can just give them my mother's maiden name. For crying out loud I don't know it!!!! They are giving me three tries, as though I'm on some horrendous ITV game-show and can either leave off where I am and go home with £100 and a microwave oven or forfeit it all for the chance of a holiday for two in Barbados. Quite frankly I would settle for my shopping and the sudden but temporary affliction of flu on all ten guests. Anyway, I have gone for Robertson, Robinson and Rowlinson. One of them is bound to be right. Must go.

Jess

xxx

PS Shit. I've just remembered. It's Peters.

'It's Peters, isn't it?' Jess said, as a chirpy Cassandra waltzed back into the room.

'They're not at liberty to tell me,' she replied, doing something horribly Jeremy Paxman-like with her lips, 'but I'm afraid your previous choice was unsuccessful.'

'So that's it, then, is it?' Jess snarled, grabbing the card and hurling it across the room. 'You normally put your customers through this kind of' – she was tugging frantically at her coat, which had wound itself round the chair leg, causing her to behave like a jack-in-the-box every time she attempted to stand up – 'this kind of torture?'

Cassandra remained calm. 'I'm sorry,' she replied softly, 'but unless we get authorisation from your bank that your overdraft limit's been approved there really is nothing we can do.'

'But I suppose it's perfectly all right for you to go snooping into my finances in the meantime!' Jess snapped, yanking her coat free and lurching forward as she did so. 'For all I know,' she added, 'you could've embezzled a fortune.'

Cassandra's lips thinned into a condescending smile. 'Given why we're here,' she said, 'I don't think that would be possible.'

By the time Jess had stormed her way home, she remembered with fury that her keys, along with her credit card and most of the evening's dinner, were still at Waitrose.

'For Christ's sake!' she shouted, bashing at the doorbell until all it could manage was a painful twanging then nothing. 'Let me in!' she shrieked, fist in the air like a madwoman. Suddenly the door gave way and a ghoulish creature appeared with cucumber eyes and a turban.

'Hi, Jess,' the ghoul said pleasantly, removing its eyes. Jess peered in horror at something that would not have been out of place in the penultimate scene of *The Exorcist*. It was Sophie. 'I'm just relaxing.' She laughed. 'It feels divine.'

'That's nice.' Jess stomped upstairs.

'Jess,' Sophie twittered, tripping gaily behind her, 'did you tell the guests seven for seven thirty or seven thirty for eight? It's just that Rich wants to have a bath with my geranium oil but he's not sure whether he'll have—'

'Tell Richard he can have a bath all fucking night if he wants. And while you're at it,' Jess screeched, kicking open her bedroom door while Sophie stood paralysed in shock, 'you can tell the guests to go fuck themselves.' She marched into her room and slammed the door.

Minutes later there was a funny scrapy noise, and Sophie appeared at Jess's bedside like an animated cherub from a Woolworth's Christmas card. 'Here,' she said sweetly, handing her a cup of camomile tea, 'sip this.' Sophie seemed to think the solution to all the world's problems lay within the three-by-three inch diameter of a camomile teabag. 'Entertaining can be stressful, Jess,' she said. 'You mustn't get yourself so worked up. Remember,' she continued, smiling kindly, 'they've come to see you, not the food.'

Jess wondered whether this was the moment to inform her there *was* no food. 'Thanks,' she said, with a self-pitying sniff as Sophie tiptoed out. She quite liked being traumatised when there was someone to be traumatised to. Kicking doors and screeching was all rather pointless if there wasn't an audience.

Suddenly she was snatched back into reality by the doorbell.

'Jess!' Colin's eager shiny forehead was poking round the door. 'Your first guest's here.'

There was something about his bulbous face that immediately irritated her. 'Can't you deal with them?' she snapped, shoving an aerosol up her jumper and spraying wildly.

'Deal with them,' Colin repeated.

'Yes,' she said. 'You know, offer them a drink or something.'

Colin looked confused. 'I see, OK.' He proceeded to stay exactly where he was and stare at her.

'Is there something else?' she barked, grabbing things off hangers, holding them up then hurling them at the floor.

'Well, yes, actually,' he stammered, rustling something behind his back. 'But it's maybe not a very good time.'

'No, Colin, it probably isn't,' she said, rummaging around on the carpet for the first top she'd discarded and ducking behind the wardrobe to put it on.

'I'm just . . . well, we've got the red phone bill, you see,' he said, nervously, 'and . . . the thing is . . . well . . . most of the calls seem to be . . . well, yours.'

'*Fuck!*' Jess yelled. Streaks of white deodorant had appeared down her front. It was an unexplained mystery of getting dressed that, however she put on a top, this unfailingly happened.

'It's not very much,' Colin battled on hopefully, 'I mean, once you take into account the line rental and—'

'Colin,' she howled, 'I am *trying* to prepare for a dinner party.' Colin looked slightly surprised – understandably, given that so far she'd gone nowhere remotely in the vicinity of the kitchen. 'Very shortly there will not be just one guest downstairs but ten. Ten guests!' she exclaimed, waggling all her fingers in the air as if she was about to embark on a rendition of 'Ten Green Bottles' with Floella Benjamin. 'They are coming here for food. I have no food. I have no means of getting any food. And if I did, I have no means of *paying* for any food.' Her voice had started to squawk unattractively. 'Be assured that a letter from BT concerns me very, very minimally at this stage.'

Colin backed away, gnawing at a nail.

'Sorry,' she said crossly. 'Tell them I'll be down in a minute.'

Half an hour later Jess appeared. Having worked through a number of visions based around the theme of trying to coax everyone out of the house and into the expensive restaurant round the corner, persuading, in the midst of it, someone to pay her portion of the bill, she was overjoyed to discover a set of happy faces seated round the table chatting animatedly and munching salmon tartlets. She felt an overwhelming urge to hug them all. Including Petra.

'Oh. Gosh. Thank you,' she choked, as if Michael Aspel had just brought in her entire fifth-form common room.

'It's nothing,' Sophie said, fluttering past her with a tray of piping hot anchovy canapés.

Immediately aware that someone was missing, she wandered into the kitchen where, through billowing clouds of steam, she could see Sam draining a cauldron of pasta tubes into what appeared to be the washing-up bowl.

'Don't tell Soph,' he said conspiratorially.

'You realise that's a health hazard?' Jess mimicked. They both laughed. This was all turning out rather well.

'Thanks, Sam,' she said, gazing up at him. A man who was attractive and fun was one thing. A man who was attractive, fun and could cook was something altogether different.

'You're welcome,' he said, picking out a tube of pasta and pretending to smoke it. 'But ya owe me one, honey,' he drawled. They laughed again.

Suddenly Jess was aware of a figure entering the kitchen. 'So, what's Master Chef cooking, then?' It was Petra.

'Something to delight your eyes and tantalise your taste-buds, fair lady,' he said, taking his pasta cigarette and tapping it delicately on Petra's little snub nose.

Jess looked at her in fury. 'Here.' She grabbed the nearest thing to hand and thrust it at Petra's chest. 'I think someone wanted water.'

Petra looked perplexed. 'But this is the milk jug.'

By the time they had all devoured a case of wine and a

plateful of what Sam called his Pasta Tuber-Culosis, which was not, given its method of preparation, an entirely reassuring title, the barriers of social convention had all but crumbled: Helen was snoring on the sofa clutching a dangerously full glass of claret at a forty-five-degree angle, Petra was in the kitchen showing Sam and Sophie how to do a weird Thai dance, involving entwined torsos, mostly Petra and Sam's, and Pooch announced that she fancied Colin. 'I think he's sweet.'

'Go for it, babes,' Jo slurped. 'Just get me Max.'

'And I bet he's great in bed.'

Jess looked over to where Colin, still shiny-faced, was sitting absent-mindedly picking his nose.

'Where's Max?' Jo shouted, thumping the table.

The whereabouts of both Max and James were a mystery. Having spent the first part of the evening reassuring Jo that they would probably turn up fashionably late, Jess had to concede that at a quarter to eleven they were stretching the fashionable a bit far. 'Perhaps he didn't get your message,' she offered optimistically.

'I left four,' Jo replied, burping.

'Maybe his answer-phone doesn't work,' Pooch suggested. 'Or maybe he tried to call but couldn't get through.'

Jess loved girls. Their ability to extract the positive from the clearly hopeless was never-ending.

'James has probably got stuck in traffic,' she said. 'I might just give him a call.'

'Hello?' A girl's voice answered the phone.

'Who's that?' Jess snarled.

The girl giggled. Jess could hear the sound of people chatting in the background. Then muffled laughter.

'But that's what's-his-name from *Casualty*, isn't it? Hello?'

'Who's that?' she snapped.

'It's me, your boyfriend,' James said, laughing.

'No. The girl.'

'What girl?'

'The girl who answered the phone.'

'Oh, *her*,' James said, laughing again. 'Zadia.'

'What's Zadia doing there?'

'Right at the moment,' he said, 'she's cooking us a stir-fry, and then,' he continued, shouting into the room, *'she's going to get us some beers!'* Jess could hear Zadia shrieking in mock-protest followed by a loud crash.

'Arghhh! Get off! Tobes, save me.'

Jess waited for the flirting-fight to end.

'Jess? You still there?'

'Of course I bloody well am.'

'What's wrong?'

'Does the fact that you're supposed to be at my dinner party mean *anything* to you?' she shrieked.

There was a long silence.

'Or would you rather stay and eat beansprouts with Zadia?'

James hooted with laughter.

'James! This isn't funny.'

'Calm down,' he cooed.

'I am *perfectly* calm.'

'Listen, I was going to come, I promise, but the thing is—'

'The thing is what?'

'The thing is that . . . well' – he lowered his voice to a confiding whisper – 'I can't leave Toby.'

Jess exploded. 'For Christ's sake, James, Toby's not a dog, he can look after himself!'

'He's upset, Jess,' he replied, in a tender tone she'd never heard before. 'Vanya really hurt him.'

'So I suppose the fact that I'm upset doesn't matter,' she replied sulkily.

'Of course it matters,' he said, irritatingly reasonably, 'but right now Toby needs me.'

Jess could tell that no matter what card she played, Toby held the trump because at the end of the day he was (a)

James's best friend and (b) the one who had spent three and a half years going out with a lesbian. She decided to cut her losses and seek solace in a bottle with a worm at the bottom . . .

'I ashully love him. Really love him.' What had originally started off as a game of Truth or Dare had degenerated into some kind of debauched end-of-sixth-form disco massacre with bodies slumped in various stages of consciousness around the room. Jess, it would seem, was the only one still playing the game.

'I ashully love him. I do.' She was propped up on her elbow, slurping at the remains of someone else's wine.

'But I thought you had a boyfriend,' Richard replied, looking horrified.

'Well . . . yesh . . . sort of,' she giggled, 'but norreally.'

'And do you think this chap knows you like him?'

She hiccuped, then attempted to shrug her shoulders. 'Dunno.'

'You should tell him. He might like you back,' Richard said, running his hand contemplatively up and down the stem of the wine-glass in a way that, even though she could hardly focus, Jess registered as rather sexual.

'Nah,' she blurted, 'he lovzhe shomeone elshe. Anywaysh, who do you love?'

'Well, I'm afraid it's rather boring,' he said, in an apologetic Hugh Grant voice, 'but, well, Sophie, really.'

'Sophiesh not boring,' Jess exclaimed, 'she jush sometimesh annoying.'

Minutes later, Pooch staggered to the table. She had been trying unsuccessfully to seduce Colin. 'So, Rich, got any good-looking single friends for me?' This seemed to be her standard opening line, whether she was talking to a friend, a colleague or, as had happened earlier that evening, Sophie's father.

'Good-looking, yes. Single, no.'

'Any brothers?'

'Yes. One. But I don't think he'd be your type.' He smiled.

'Why not?' Pooch asked, which Jess had to admit was a good question. If Pooch had been able to find Colin attractive, she was evidently not in the habit of restricting herself to any particular set of conditions.

'He's gay.'

It dawned on Jess then that she had been so busy seeing Richard as some kind of appendage to Sophie, she had forgotten he was a person in his own right. In a drunken attack of guilt she started firing questions at him. It was only, however, when they'd come round to discussing his new flatmates – male – that Pooch, who'd sat with a bored expression throughout, regained interest. 'Single?'

'One of them, yeah. But only recently,' he replied, then looked serious and added, 'traumatic split-up.'

'Nah,' said Pooch, swiping an arm wildly in the air, 'don't want emotional baggage. Just sex.'

'Whass about thother one?' Jess slurred. 'He sounz nice.'

'Girlfriend, I'm afraid,' Richard replied, then, in a hushed, furtive voice, added, 'although, between you and me, not for long.'

Pooch looked like she'd just stumbled upon a stash of fifties poking out of a cash machine. 'Really? Why?'

'Relationship's just run its course,' Richard replied. 'Time for pastures new.'

Suddenly, in the only moment of lucidity Jess had experienced all evening, she sat bolt upright. 'Whass his name?'

'Who?'

'The bloke in crap relashionship.'

'James. Why?'

'Oh, Jeeshush,' Jess wailed. Richard looked confused. Pooch grinned. 'Thass me. My crap relashionshit.'

Sobbing my heart out
Completely miserable
Cold, damp and in danger of blowing my nose off
*   my face*

Dear Alex,

I have come to the conclusion there is no point in trying to come between two people in love. I realise this was what Rick Astley was singing about way back when I was trying to snog Stuart Kelly on the stairwell of Pricklewood Church Hall's community disco. If only I had heeded his wise lyrics I would not now be sitting nurturing suicidal thoughts in some God-forsaken shed on Tooting Common.

It is bonfire night and in a desperate and unattractively begging manner I have offered to help Sam ensure that nineteen handicapped children don't sit on, leap-frog over, or eat, a firework.

I had spent all week in dreamy fantasies of the two of us huddled round rosy-cheeked little disabled people, eyes wide with wonder pointing and ahhing as if in a Disneyland commercial as tiny specks of glitter cascaded out of the velvet sky. Or laughing coyly as Sam, holding a defenceless infant in his arms, got everybody to write 'I Love You' in the air with their sparklers.

I was not, therefore, prepared for the fact that it would pee solidly for the entire evening, that most of the kids would run screeching at my groin with every tiny bang, and that Petra, who had spent all week expressing her regret at not being able to come, would turn up wearing a beautiful hand-made knee-length leather coat looking like a taller version of Marilyn Monroe.

Because I did not have the foresight to bring either a raincoat or a torch (essential to retrieve traumatised runaways from underneath nearby bushes) I am being forced to sit in a windowless warehouse with eleven bored children, while everyone else is outside whizzing and pooping and swinging gaily from Petra's pigtails. The only thought that is keeping me from nailing myself to a catherine wheel right now is of Petra metamorphosing into Guy Fawkes.

I suppose this is all a punishment because I did not come here out of any desire to be charitable and kind to handicapped people but merely to flirt with Sam. Obviously I would not normally be this shallow and uncaring if it wasn't for Petra. She has taken to hogging Sam in a greedy manner as if he is our child – which, in many ways, I wish he were. At least when you are a divorced parent you can demand weekend visiting rights and half the summer holidays and do not, presumably, have to resort to rushing to charity bonfires in a miniskirt.

If only she would fuck off. Surely there are lots of other attractive men she could seduce. Why does it have to be mine? That is the problem, though. In so many ways men are just like university library books: there may well be thousands of them to choose from but inevitably the one you want is always on loan to someone else. Oh, for Christ's sake, two of the kids are crying . . .

I have had enough. I was just trying to ascertain why Penelope had found it necessary to steal Rosalin's hat, while grabbing Bernard round the neck to prevent him from pulverising a boy with no left arm, when Sam and bloody Petra pranced in, swinging between them, as if in a Hollywood feel-good movie, a tiny autistic girl. They stared in horror at what, I admit, must not have looked good. Sam took me to the corner, still dragging Bernard, and told me patronisingly that the best way to deal with children when they are upset is to show them how much you love them. 'Violence,' he said, as I tried to relinquish my grip round Bernard's neck, 'leads to emotional scarring.' Now he has put Petra in charge and all the kids are doing the 'Singing Kettle' song and looking as though they have never been happier.

I hope you can read this. These invoices are all I've got in my bag to write on, excluding a crushed Tampax and a flyer for the fast, effective removal of blackheads, which the guy seemed particularly insistent on giving to me rather than to any of the other half-million shoppers milling around.

I seem to have amassed an alarming amount of invoices – a mixture of a rather erratic renumbering system and sheer laziness, i.e. easier to stuff one little invoice stealthily into my bag than clamber on top of the gigantic shelving unit, torture myself with frequent renditions of the alphabet song to find the file for T, then discover, once I have heaved it down from the highest shelf, that the invoice is from Tateman's, who are the lawyers and hence belong to a different filing family altogether entitled, 'Still to Pay'.

Recently the filing has got much easier because everything seems to go straight into the 'Still to Pay' file, including my pay slip. I was going to say something to Brian about this, but the day I'd planned to do it his accountant turned up and whisked him into a little room. He came out two hours later looking as though he might throw himself head first into the Thames. So in a monstrous act of lunacy, I suggested he postpone payment of my salary. It was one of those things that when you say it makes you feel all warm and happy inside but thereafter cripples you with regret.

Anyway, instead of being grateful and praising me for my kindness, he swatted the air with his hand and said, 'Pah!' as if I'd just offered to pay 24p towards the National Debt. It may be pah! to him but presumably he does not have to eke out £423.75 over insanely just-because-it's-London priced rent, inexplicable council tax demands for £1508.30 and nagging red telephone bills. Which reminds me – I still need to post the last one. In fact, it's a miracle it is ready for posting at all. I don't know what it is with phone bills but they seem to turn normal balanced perfectly generous people into mean nasty Scrooges who fight over 0.042p and deny ever dialling 192.

Out of a total bill for £132.17, I ended up paying £67.84 because: Sophie claimed she only called her mum; Jo claimed she made all her calls at work; Sam claimed he was so popular everyone just called him; and Colin claimed he never used a phone.

I asked James if he had the same thing in his flat but he said, no, not at all, because he, 'Tobes' and 'Rich' (new irritating abbreviations he has taken to using as a result of, presumably, a slight crush) just share everything. Oh, my God. I forgot to tell you. Rich is Richard – i.e. Sophie's Richard. It turns out he and Toby were at school together. I can't get over how one minute London is a big, anonymous, fierce, hostile metropolis, and the next a wee friendly village in the Highlands – although obviously without the sheep, and, I suppose, quite so much rain.

Anyway, it was at my dinner party I discovered that the Richard who James described as 'a great bloke' and the Richard who used up all the hot water in the morning, even though he was a guest, were in fact the same Richard. It was when he said that one of his flatmates was about to chuck his girlfriend and I was thinking how juicy it is to get other people's gossip that realisation struck: (1) his flatmate was James and (2) the soon-to-be chucked girlfriend was me.

So now I have gone all paranoid again, waiting in for his phonecall and stalling any offers of weekend activities until I find out what he is doing (which is usually something with 'Tobes' but he will only tell me this late on Friday by which time all weekend plans have been arranged and I am excluded from everything).

And recently, because he keeps finding limp excuses for not coming to stay at mine (he still hasn't been to my flat or met my flatmates), e.g. he needs to renew his tube ticket and for some complicated reason can only do this at his tube station, or the zip on his suit-carrier has broken and therefore he will have nothing to wear – plastic bags and wearing the same suit the next day apparently not viable solutions – I end up trooping over to his. But this is not simply a case of chucking a toothbrush in a bag and hopping on to a tube, but instead a torturous exam in packing-planning. Where before my mornings were just chaotic, they are now bedlam.

These are just a few of the issues that must be addressed at the ungodly hour of 7.15 a.m.:

- *Knickers. How many pairs? I may only be staying for one night but will one be enough? What if my period comes three weeks early? It is probably best to take eight, just in case.*
- *Toiletries. Deodorant. But it is nearly finished. Could I risk borrowing James's? No, because he is a man and I would smell butch all day. Take the almost empty aerosol and the body spray, just in case.*
- *Outfit for the following day. Can I risk wearing the same thing twice in a row? No, people might notice. What should I wear? V-necked black top? But it is slightly see-through so I would also need to take a black bra. Maybe the grey polo would be better – all-purpose and doesn't need ironing. But what if we go out that evening? Will the grey polo be posh enough? And what if it were a freak sunny day? The grey polo makes me do funny sweating and stinks after five minutes. Perhaps it would be easier to wear the same top for two days running and take a change of trousers instead? No. Take the black top and the grey polo plus the useful white T-shirt and the blue shirt and perhaps a skirt, just in case.*

Then just as I am about to leave, it hits me:

- *The pork chop in the fridge! Today is the last day it can be eaten and I was going to do something clever with it and the leftover soup. Maybe I should stay here tonight, eat the chop and go to James's tomorrow night?*

Dilemma.
No, it is silly to put a pork chop before your boyfriend. I will go to James's.
I then spend the duration of the walk to the tube trying to work out the least pain-inducing way of carrying something that has turned into a small caravan, while doing mad listing in my head, convinced I have forgotten something. Then just when I've managed to talk myself into believing I haven't, I step on to the tube and remember:

- *Shitting hell – my house-keys!*

I have to confess I find the whole thing very stressful. James says I am making a fuss about nothing but he isn't the one who has to trek between Notting Hill and Clapham like some kind of knicker nomad. Anyway, he's promised to stay at mine tomorrow night so I'm not going to have a go at him. Better go – Barnaby's wet himself.

Lots of love,
Jess
xxx

'But you promised,' Jess whined. She was sitting at her desk with the phone tucked under her chin, punching holes in invoices.

'Ye-es,' James said, slowly, 'but that was before Tobes reminded me about footie.'

'And?' she snapped. 'The problem being?'

'The problem being that I don't have my kit with me and I—'

'No, James, the problem being' – she bashed her fist on the hole-punch – 'you haven't *once* been to my flat.'

James let out an exaggerated sigh. 'Oh, God, not this again. Look, Jess, I—'

'Well, I'm not going to come to yours, if that's what you're thinking.'

'I don't expect you to,' he said, with infuriating under-standing.

There was a protracted silence.

'So don't you care that you're not going to see me?'

'I think I can last a couple of nights without—'

'Fine. See you never,' she spat, and slammed down the phone.

Ten minutes later it rang again. Convinced it was going to be a reconciliatory James pleading to come and stay with her for a week, she put on a suitably wounded voice and picked it up. 'Hello?'

'Hi, it's me.'

Disappointment kicked her in the stomach. It was Brian, informing her that neither he nor Aileen would be coming in because they'd caught a group of 'yobs' trying to stick a rocket up the backside of one of the kittens. It would seem, Jess thought, that the entire male population had turned irrevocably evil.

When she arrived home that evening, however, this didn't seem to be something that concerned Jo, who was sitting at the kitchen table holding two bananas suggestively in front of Sam. 'OK. So, like this?' she said, moving the bananas closer together.

'Which one's me again?' Sam queried.

'This one,' Jo said, gesturing to the bigger of the two.

'Yup,' Sam nodded, grinning, 'I'd be happy with that association.'

'Sam,' Jo snapped, 'stop pissing about. Concentrate.'

'If it's not a stupid question' – Jess slumped down at the table to join them – 'what are you two doing?'

Jo beamed. 'Sam saw Max today.'

Jess stared blankly. 'And?'

'And I'm trying to find out things,' Jo replied, grinning somewhat psychotically.

Several minutes later, it transpired that she had found out rather a lot. Based on the fact that Sam, while grabbing a sandwich in Tesco's, had spotted someone by the microwave meals section that looked like Max, she had managed, with the bananas as props, to construct the kind of detailed profile that would make Miss Marple seem amateur.

'So if he was this close he must have seen you,' she continued, looking intently from one banana to the other.

'Did he speak to you?' Jess interjected.

'No,' Jo said, dramatically, 'he didn't.'

'I wonder what that means,' Jess said thoughtfully. 'Maybe he was nervous.'

'Or maybe he didn't want to seem over-keen.'

'Or maybe he was just getting his lunch,' Sam implored, laughing. 'For God's sake, you two. Give the bloke a break.'

'She did that three and a half years ago,' Jess warned.

'And look where that's got me,' Jo added.

'Half-way to the loony asylum by the looks of things,' Sam said, chortling.

'OK, so if it was Tesco's in Hammersmith,' Jo continued, choosing to ignore him, 'he must still have the same job.'

'And you're positive it was the microwave section?' Jess said.

Sam nodded and yawned.

'Which can only mean one thing,' Jo concluded, sticking her tongue inside the bottom of her right cheek and smirking.

'He's single!' they announced in unison.

Sam exploded with laughter. 'You guys are nuts! You'd analyse a hair follicle if it was male.'

'And you miss out on the richness of life,' Jo retorted, 'because you're incapable of recognising hidden agendas and implicit meanings.'

'And you two just miss the *point* of life' – he rocked back on his chair, chewing on a matchstick – 'that blokes are simple.'

'We know that,' Jo sneered.

'They don't have agendas. They work on a no-mess, up-front policy. If they want something they ask for it.'

'And?' Jo said.

'If Max *is* single and *does* want you,' he said, biting the top off one of the bananas, 'believe me, he'll let you know.'

The room fell into a hushed silence. This was undisputedly the wrong thing to say. Not only had it clearly thwarted the point of the last half-hour's discussion, it had also shattered every single one of Jess's hopes that really, underneath it all, irrespective of appearances, comments and, of course, Petra, Sam fancied her.

'What's up, guys?' Colin had just come in. He was wearing his boiler-suit and a baseball cap back to front and presumably, Jess decided, thought he was American.

'The girls are building psychological profiles on hair follicles.'

'Neat.'

'Ignore him,' Jess said. 'We just think Max *might*' – she looked pointedly at Sam – 'be single.'

'So what's with the might, guys? Why not find out for sure?' he said, still in the phoney drawl. He pointed to the thing he claimed never to use. 'Call him.' This, Jess realised, was the only thing of worth Colin had ever said.

Twenty minutes later, giggling somewhat manically, Jo picked up the phone. 'I can't,' she squealed, throwing down the handset as if it were the handle of a very hot pan. 'What if a girl answers?'

'Jo, we've gone through that,' Jess said, pacing the room in shared excitement. 'You just sound all cool and ask for Max.'

'OK, OK, right, I'm going to do it.' She began shakily to dial the number, then stopped. 'Hold on. I've forgotten what I do if it's an answer-machine.'

'You hang up.'

'That's right. OK.' She was taking deep, slow breaths as if she were about to go into labour. 'Right.'

Suddenly, the phone rang.

'*Oh, my God!*' Jo shrieked.

'*Jesus Christ!*' Jess yelled.

'What should I do?'

'Pick it up!'

'I can't!'

'You can!'

'What do I say?'

'Anything!'

'Like what?'

'I don't know!'

'You do it!'

'No, you!'

'I can't!'

'Oh, for God's sake, hello?' Jess had grabbed the receiver, then pulled it away from her ear, looked at it as if it were a newfangled piece of machinery she'd never seen before, and put it down again. 'He's gone.'

'Oh, no,' Jo groaned, banging a fist against her head. 'Why? Why didn't I get it?'

Then it rang again.

'Argh!' She sprang to her feet.

'Go on,' Jess shrieked.

'Ohhh, God,' she said, reaching for the handset and closing her eyes in anticipation. 'Hello?'

A look of disappointment engulfed her face. 'It's for you.'

Loud thumping music was coming from the receiver and Jess could barely hear a thing. 'Hello?'

'Jess, it's me.'

'Hi, me,' she said pleasantly. It was James. He was speaking in a weird stilted voice as if aboard a spaceship. 'Don't tell me – you're coming to stay at mine,' she said, laughing.

The music stopped. There was a long-drawn-out silence. She could tell immediately that something was wrong. Something she couldn't put her finger on until he asked, in the suspiciously caring tone he only ever used when something terrible was about to happen: 'How are you?'

Indescribably miserable
Catastrophically distraught
Tragically heartbroken

Dear Alex,

   Just when I thought it wasn't possible for my life to sink any further into the abyss of hopelessness, it has just got up, walked over and driven a stainless-steel carving knife into my soul.

   James has chucked me. I now know what Scary Spice meant when she told Hello! *her heart was nothing but a mangled carcass.*

   Oh, God . . . I cannot believe this has happened to me. When you read about it happening to other people, it is actually quite juicy and fun, and even though you pretend not to be, you are fascinated by all the horrid details, but when it happens to you it . . . it isn't fun or fascinating at all. Just hideous.

   Everything has gone. A year and a half of love, support, closeness. Of shared toothbrushes and shaved legs. Of watching Football Focus *on the sofa with a duvet. Of buying joke presents and calling each other Twerpy. Of laughing at Jimmy Hill's chin and Tie Rack arguments. Of late-night phone calls. Cuddle-rationing. Jumper borrowing. Sex. All for what? To be thrown heartlessly and ruthlessly on to the scrap heap of inhumanity, to fester with heartache and die of loneliness. Oh, God. I am so depressed.*

   Sophie has just come into my room to empty my bin. It seems a bitter irony indeed that tonight is also bin night. Oh, Jesus, how could he have been so cruel? He just phoned up and said it. 'It's finished,' he said, like we were a packet of Rice Krispies. Oh, God I hate him.

Why did he have to do this? He says I am overcrowding him and becoming needy – that I am a hungry person and he has no more food to give me. I asked him if that was because he was giving his food to someone else – Zadia, for example – but he just went all cross and said I'd missed the point. What is *the point, though? Oh, I am so miserable. I even resorted to unattractive pleading but he wouldn't change his mind. He said he preferred me when I was confident and even though I said I could become confident again I know it's useless, because one of the hideous things about confidence is that no matter how good you are at pretending to be so, it is only truly effective when it is 100 per cent genuine.*

The only thing this act of cruelty has taught me is that the human body is capable of howling for two hours and twenty-three minutes without rest. Twenty-four now. I would not be the least bit surprised if, in the process of achieving this feat, my tear ducts have burst their banks and flooded all over my brain. I keep imagining little people inside my head in yellow rubber dinghies desperately clinging on to wobbly brain cells as torrents of tears gush past them in the manner of hurricane aftermath footage. It certainly feels as if something is up there causing me to feel like a psychopath.

Sophie has told me that, in extreme distress, people do odd things – one man carved off his penis (I am assuming this is what she meant by 'Peter Pecker') and tried to eat it when he found out his wife was having an affair, so she has made me do this graph to monitor my emotions. I suspect, however, that if I had a Peter Pecker I would be eating it too by now.

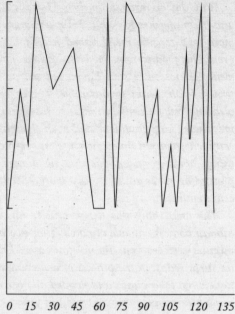

Wishing to carve
off his Peter Pecker

Staring crazily at
the wall

Wishing he would
call and say it was
all just a silly joke

Thinking about all
our good times
(brain too awash to
remember specifics)

Kicking the wall
screaming,
'Bastard!'

Convincing myself it
will be fun and
exciting being single

0   15   30   45   60   75   90   105   120   135

Trauma time elapsed in minutes

This is supposed to make me feel better but I think, judging from the last bit, I am going a bit madder. I fear it is only a matter of time before I turn into Jo's friend Mule – dumped three months ago and still bursts into tears every time she has to press the 'single' button for a tube ticket or fill out a marketing questionnaire on what shampoo her partner uses.

Oh, God. I need to do something calming – listen to some classical music perhaps, or lie out on the pavement and look at the stars. Actually, I think Jo's idea is the best. Pints of raw vodka. She keeps coming into my room and filling up my mug like those waiters at posh parties who skulk around with wine bottles and succeed, in an alarmingly short time, in getting you utterly wasted without you ever having emptied your glass.

She is being so brilliant. As are all my other lovely flatmates. Only Colin is being annoying, telling me to 'Chill, man,' and 'Take a mellow pill,' as if he is a dreadlocked rap artist. Apparently this always happens when he talks to his American cousin Buzby but it doesn't last more than a couple of days.

Ooh, Jo's just come in again. Yippee! More vodka. And Sophie wants to know if I feel up to a couple of venison medallions in yoghurt and juniper sauce. I am so lucky to be surrounded by such caring people. They have all been wonderful, agreeing with all the vile things I have said about James and often joining in. Jo confessed that even though only Sophie had met him, they all thought he sounded a complete prick – apparently they have wanted to tell me this for ages but felt they couldn't: they thought that because he was my boyfriend I loved him. 'Not any more,' I yelled, and we all cheered as if we were on the set of Friends.

Actually, if I'm being honest, I'm rather enjoying being traumatised. Beside the fact that you can do whatever you want because, well . . . you're traumatised, it also means you become the centre of attention because whatever problems anyone else has, being chucked by a boyfriend can rarely be beaten. Thus I have been phoning up all my friends, some of whom I haven't spoken to since James and I first got together, and they have all been great, letting me talk about myself for ages and saying, 'Poof! That's hardly important,' whenever I ask about them.

Mmmm . . . I think I might have one of Sophie's medal things after all. I must keep my energy levels up – not only is howling mentally exhausting, it also makes you rather peckish. Right, off I pop. Sorry about all that misery stuff before. I don't know what was wrong with me, I mean, James is only a person. It's not such a big deal.

I hope you are happy. Remember – you don't need James.

Bye-bye.

Jess

xxx

PS I've just remembered – Drippy Moira! I forgot to phone her, plus another schoolfriend and my old recorder teacher. Now I will be able to spend all tomorrow on the phone too. Yippee!

'BT, Jonathan speaking, how can I help?'

'My phone doesn't work.'

'OK, madam, what seems to be the problem?'

'If I knew that,' Jess snarled, 'I wouldn't be calling you.' She was slouched on the sofa the following morning in jogging bottoms and a dressing-gown trying to open a tin of Sam's grapefruit segments.

'OK, madam, if you'll just bear with me, I'll transfer you to our technical faults depart—'

'I am *not* a technical fault.' She struggled with the complexities of the tin-opener. 'And if I have to do another of your numerical multiple choices I'll go insane.'

There was a short silence while Jonathan clearly wondered where that put her current mental state. 'Very well, madam,' he said, patiently. 'If you can give me your account number I can—'

'I don't know it.'

'It's the number on your bill to the top right of—'

'I don't have a bill.'

'A name, perhaps, then?'

Jess paused. 'Colin.'

Jonathan paused. 'Rrrright, and your surname, Colin?'

'Ummm . . . ohhh, God, I can't remember. Philips, I think, maybe.'

There was a further protracted silence, then Jonathan's voice returned, softer, sympathetic and more understanding. 'Is Mummy there, Colin?'

Jess stared in horror at the phone.

'Or Daddy maybe?'

She couldn't quite believe this was happening.

'Colin – you there, son? Can you go and get Mummy for me?'

'My Mummy and Daddy,' she hissed, 'are in Inverness. My name is Jess and I am a capable adult living independently in London. Colin,' she snapped, 'is the name on the bill.'

By the time Jonathan had enlisted the help of several colleagues, located the correct account and pretended he had never mistaken her for a five-year-old boy, Jess had cut her finger trying to gouge a grapefruit chunk out of the half-open can.

'Bollocks,' she muttered, delving into the depths of her bag for a tissue.

'Right,' he said, 'your line's been temporarily suspended.'

'Oh, for Christ's sake!' she shouted, just as she unearthed, along with the tissue, a crumpled-up envelope addressed to BT.

'It appears we're still awaiting payment of £132.17.'

'But I . . . you see, it—'

'This amount's been outstanding for rather a long time,' he continued, 'and we can't do anything until it's settled. I suggest you get that boyfriend of yours,' he added, jovially, 'to pay up.'

'He is not my boyfriend,' Jess said. Then as the horrors of the previous night kicked in again, she broke down. 'I don't have a boyfriend.'

'I'm sorry, madam, but until we receive payment, your line will remain suspended.'

Jess paused. 'Have you any idea how lonely I feel?' she howled. 'How isolated and marooned? The phone is all I've got in the world. It's my lifeline. My friend. My umbilical cord to civilisation. My . . . my . . .'

There was a funny clicking noise.

'You're reconnected,' he said, then added, 'I'll expect a cheque by tomorrow,' and, in a way that would not have made him BT's Customer Carer of the Year, hung up.

The minute she replaced the handset, the phone rang.

'James?'

'Where in the name of arse are you?'

Brian. In all the chaos of the last twelve hours, she had forgotten to go to work.

'Oh, hi, Brian, I'm . . . umm, you see—'

'No,' he yelled, 'I don't have time. Get yourself down here *now.*'

'But I—'

'I've got a furiously important meeting in less than an hour and I can't find a bloody thing.' Brian was always claiming to have furious meetings – lately, though, Jess had noticed, he'd been spending more time on the furious part.

'Are you looking for anything in particular?' she hazarded.

'A completed file of invoices would be a start.'

She gulped as a sick feeling began to adhere itself to the lining of her stomach.

'I thought you said you'd numbered them,' he ranted.

'I did.'

'So why the hell are half of them missing? *Where are they?*'

Jess could think of a few answers she might offer him. On a plane bound for China, however, wasn't one of them. 'Umm . . . in a file perhaps?' she squeaked.

'No, they are not "in a file perhaps", Jess,' he snapped, 'because I have ransacked the place.'

This, it turned out, when she panted into the office three-quarters of an hour later, was by no means an exaggeration. Lever-arch files were strewn everywhere; on the floor, hanging off desks, on tops of radiators, propped up on coffee mugs, suspended from computer cabling, and one had even, she discovered, wound up in the toilet bowl. The only solace to be drawn from this scene of carnage was that Brian wasn't in it.

Collapsing at her desk, she let out a strangulated bleat.

Short of a miracle or the timely appearance of Jim'll Fix It, she was doomed. Brian would sack her, warn everyone else not to employ her and she would be reduced to spending the rest of her life claiming unemployment benefit in a building that smelt of urine.

Then a thought struck her. If she could forget to post the phone bill, it might be possible she could also forget to post the letter she'd written to Alex on the back of the invoices.

Wildly, she shook her bag. Lipsticks and cheque books, hairbrushes and tampons, wallets and keys cascaded on to the desk in front of her. But no letter. Then, poking out from underneath the frayed lining she was intending one day to sew up, she saw it. A pleasingly crisp envelope. She yanked it out, then stared in a bewildering mixture of deep disappointment and utter excitement. It was addressed to her:

Dear Jess,

I think you're great. I think you're beautiful. I think you're fun.

I also think you'll: think I'm a weirdo for writing this/be too upset to care/probably be back together with James before the day's out.

If none of the above apply, however, I have a ~~prostitute~~ *proposition for you! Petra told me to be patient and wait, but I can't. I know if I turn my back for a second you will be snatched up. So I am humbly asking to do the snatching. If you'd like to be snatched, there's a party tonight at eight. If not, I'll settle for staring fondly at your little blue toothbrush with a broken heart.*

From the man with no hidden agendas, no implicit meanings and no shame,

Sam

Jess sat paralysed, not knowing whether to sing from the heavens, shout from the rooftops or run round the office with no clothes on. Her dilemma, however, was solved for her: the phone was ringing.

'Sam?'

Pitiful yelps were coming from the receiver. 'It's me.'

She froze. It was James.

'Where have you been?' he spluttered. 'I've been calling and calling. I tried you at home and couldn't get through, I tried you here and no one knew where you were, I tried . . . tried everywhere I could think of and . . . and . . .' he snivelled, 'I thought you were dead.'

Jess gulped. She was beginning to wonder whether this all wasn't a weird, warped, self-delusional dream out of which she would wake to discover she was still as miserable as ever and, on top of it all, hopelessly late for work.

'I love you,' he whined, 'really, really love you. Jess, please . . . I've made a horrible mistake. Last night . . . I didn't know what I was doing. It was mad. Toby's fault. Football fever. Please, Jess, can't we just forget about it? Please . . . I want you back more than anything.'

'I thought you didn't have any more food to give me,' she said curtly, then, as if he had just been trying to sell her a cut-price stereo, added, coolly, and in a way that surprised even her, 'I'll think about it.'

Then she picked up her pen and scrawled . . .

Urgent Fax

Dear Alex,

Help!

I know you gave me this number for emergencies but this is a crisis. Please ignore everything I have just sent you (except the invoice letter, which you must return immediately).

It turns out I am not a romantic reject after all, but a beautiful damsel sought after by many men. James, after all the needy and I-am-too-hungry business, is seemingly not out of food at all. In fact, he has replenished his larder and in a freakish eleventh-hour turn-around, similar to Saddam and the UN weapons inspectors, is now welcoming me into it. He wants me back!

But Sam has just announced he rather fancies a piece of me too. Yippee! He is not in love with Petra, the pigtailed goddess, but with me! *Me, me, everyone wants* me!!!!

I cannot believe that having fantasised about this for ages, delighting in images of James and Sam as deadly jousters charging at each other with lances while I jostle and jeer on the sidelines with the rest of the villagers, it has now happened – although without, obviously, the lance bit. Only instead of wanting to swig from tankards of ale and jig the merry night away in a rustic barn with sawdust on the floor and little piglets trotting around, I am tense, overwhelmed and, quite frankly, confused.

I do not feel like a woman of desire and sexual beauty but like an old, dilapidated house that having lain empty and unwanted for years has, by some divine intervention from God or a very clever estate agent, received two extremely attractive bids at once. But which to choose?

Please help. Make my decision for me – tick the relevant box below and fax back immediately.

Many thanks,

Jess

xxx

Sam ✓

Should Jess choose Sam?
Read the left-hand pages . . .

James

Should Jess choose James?
Read the right-hand pages . . .

What Goes Up . . .

Ooh, happy, happy me
Happy, happy us
Happy, happy world (with the exclusion –
     obviously – of things like starvation, civil war,
     natural disasters, etc.)

Dear Alex,
     You were right. This is most definitely, beyond any shadow of a doubt, the right decision. Sam and I have got together. And it is all marvellous. James, however sexy, is not right for me – I know that now. Sam and I are in love.
     I had forgotten how wonderful the first flush of romance can be. When you've been holed up for so long in a tiresome half-dead relationship it's like slopping round in a dank muddy quagmire all day in leaking wellie-boots, then leaping over a stile and finding yourself dazzled by sunlight in a magnificent luscious meadow where wild poppies sway in the breeze and little lambs caper and frolic.
     It all started at the fabulous party last weekend. Actually, the party wasn't at all fabulous. In fact, it was rather shit and had it not been the catalyst for Sam and I to snog, I would have gone home pissed, in a foul mood, suffering from the traumatised belief – because no one seemed in the least bit interested in talking to me – that I had become irrevocably boring. (I must say this is a frightening road to go down because the minute you think about it, the more everything you say sounds boring, making you so preoccupied with not being boring that, in the process, you actually become boring.)
     As it was I spent most of the evening doing frenzied flirting with Sam – made much more enjoyable because a girl called Emily

Ooh, happy, happy me
Happy, happy us
Happy, happy world (with the exclusion –
    obviously – of things like starvation, civil war,
    natural disasters, etc.)

Dear Alex,

You were right. This is most definitely, beyond any shadow of a doubt, the right decision. James and I are back together. And it is all marvellous. Sam, however lovely, is not right for me – I know that now. James and I are in love.

I can't believe I never realised that all you need to do if a relationship is going badly is end it then restart it. I suppose it makes sense – a bit like a car engine on a frosty morning: no good in pumping away furiously on the accelerator, just turn off the ignition, wait a wee while then try it again and vroom!

And we are certainly vrooming. Even though we weren't apart for that long we both agreed how odd it is that when you love someone the way we do, every second you aren't with them is an eternity. Well, I said the eternity bit and James said odd, but it amounts to the same thing. Apparently the minute he'd ended it he instantly forgot all the reasons why and could only remember all the lovely things about me, which I thought was really sweet, though when I asked him what these lovely things were, he had forgotten them again.

Anyway, there is certainly no denying it – we sampled life without each other and decided it wasn't possible. We are meant to be together. Like a bacon sarnie and tomato ketchup, according to James.

Oh, it is bliss being in a happy relationship. And to be honest, was trying to do the same but Sam didn't fancy her and kept wanting to stick with me. It has certainly made me realise that the trick to enjoying a party lies not in meeting new people, having interesting chats or getting sloshed with your friends, but merely in having someone to flirt with.

Ooh, it was so exciting, but also peculiar because although we have flirted in the past there has always been the annoying nuisance of my boyfriend. It felt strange knowing we were allowed to flirt – like turning eighteen and going into a pub when you've been underage drinking for four and a half years already.

The minute we were alone, though, rather than lunging at each other panting with lust and ripping at clothes, we went shy and retarded, started talking politely about coffee, playing with matches, fiddling with fridge magnets, hovering round door frames, pretending to be interested in the second half of a terrible film with subtitles and finally, when it became impossible to stall bed-time any longer, having a little snog beside the toastie machine in the kitchen.

Fraught as it was with awkwardness and, of course, underlying panic that he might at any moment do as he'd been threatening for most of the evening and go to bed, I loved it. There is something indescribably exciting about the will-we-won't-we bit of getting together. I've come to the conclusion it is by far and away the best bit of any relationship, which creates a rather confusing situation logic-wise. The reason it is so thrilling to begin with is precisely because of the anticipation of being with them but if it is never going to be as good from then on, what is the point in continuing with it?

Anyway, I am too joyful to worry about this now. Indeed, I am so deliriously happy I can scarcely remember what I'm like when I'm normal, i.e. miserable. Perhaps this is what happens when you've found true happiness. I have certainly given up on all efforts to concentrate on anything that isn't in some way related to Sam. In fact, all I feel equipped to cope with at the moment is staring moonily out of the window imagining our wonderful new life even though it hasn't been a week yet, I have a feeling, probably because I am a woman and therefore intuitive about such things, that this is it. In fact, I wouldn't be surprised if he wants us to move in together soon. He is certainly cured of all the space and overcrowding stuff and has reformed into the kind of all-perfect boyfriend Cosmo *claims is achievable in ten easy steps.*

Indeed, ever since I took him back we have hardly seen or spoken to a soul, happy just to be together, alone. Like two little pupae in one cocoon; cosy and snug and oblivious to the rest of the world. Oh, tra-la-la-la-la.

Actually, I suppose I'm a wee bit scared of seeing other people. It's just that I had told practically everyone I knew that James and I had split up, expanding at length about what a wanker he was and how I would never go near him again, even if he begged me, and now, well . . . it's a bit embarrassing. It reminds me of the time I went round weeping on everybody because I was convinced I'd failed a history test and them being all nice and sympathetic and saying they were sure I hadn't, and then having to tell them a week later that, due to what I'm still convinced must have been a cock-up in marking, actually I got 98 per cent.

Anyhow, my flatmates have been cool, even Sam who didn't seem particularly jealous or upset, which I was a bit pissed off about. Sophie says I should be careful. That we are in the honeymoon phase but very soon reality will kick in. She is missing the point that we are not boring accountants like her and Richard, who think a relationship is all about meeting after work at Tesco Metro's fresh pasta counter.

No!

We are a young, fiery couple where reality means shagging all through the night, hosting wild mad parties and going on spontaneous romantic trips to the Lake District. (We haven't done these things specifically but it is only a matter of time.) And yesterday we booked a holiday. James had been insistent that he wanted to take me away somewhere nice ever since I'd agreed to take him back. I kept saying, 'No, no, don't be silly,' whenever he mentioned together. Heavenly images of the two of us blading hand in hand through Hyde Park, renovating little cottages in Cornwall, and trekking bareback across Nepal.

It's startling how quickly one can turn what is really just a couple of snogs and the odd mumbled arrangement to spend Saturday night together into a wedding, babies and twice-yearly summer holidays in Brighton. I know it's not healthy to form an entire life-plan on the basis of the first six days of a relationship, but I can't help it. Indeed, only last night my meticulous plotting was thrown into disarray by him casually mentioning he might go travelling in two years' time. Rather than being relaxed and cool and asking him which countries he wanted to visit, I started thinking frantically, Oh, my God, what will happen? Will I go travelling with him? Does he see me going with him? Do I want to go travelling with him? Do I want to go travelling? Is he assuming we'll have split up by then? Will we have split up by then? Oh, my God.

The thing is, I'm not terribly sure we're even going out yet. One of the peculiar things about snogging your flatmate is that you bypass all the initial formalities of conventional dating etiquette (psychotic waiting by the phone, cringeful weekly dates at the cinema) and catapult into an informal arrangement that is hopelessly unclear. If we didn't happen to live together I suppose it would be described as 'seeing' each other – a term to which I am strongly opposed on the grounds that for blokes it seems to mean a way of shagging someone without the hassles of a relationship, and for girls, just a painfully long time wondering whether it's too early to use the word boyfriend yet.

As it is, we have passed all that and are at the stage of being happy and secure with each other – the stage that most couples achieve months into the relationship. In fact, we seem to be doing the whole thing backwards – like sitting down to dinner and starting with the apple crumble. Perhaps we'll end up like a couple I read about who got together as a result of being flatmates and six months later were so happy together that as confirmation of their growing commitment to each other moved out into separate houses.

it until he conceded that if I was that uncomfortable with the idea of him paying, he'd let me pay for myself. Hmph . . .

Anyway, we are going to a little Greek island called Syphilos for a week in April. We've got this fantastic deal with a new package company called BlueSky – £99 for everything, including a full English breakfast every morning, free tickets to a 'Drink Till Yer Drop' Competition and the unlimited use of a snorkel for Wednesday afternoon. Apparently they're just starting up, hence £99, hence weird month April, hence nowhere-to-be-seen-on-a-map Greek island, but I'm sure it will be fine.

James has never been on a package holiday before – shunning the post-finals bucket deal to Lanzarote in preference to wandering round archaeological sites in Athens with half of Japan – so he is worried that it will be full of fat people from Manchester eating hot dogs. He is also concerned because Sandra, the orange woman who booked it for us, described the accommodation as basic, but I assured him they always say that so that you don't expect fluffy thick-pile carpets and shoe-shine sachets.

Anyway, I'm sure it'll be lovely – probably a little apartment nestled among olive groves or a villa on a picturesque hillside over-looking the Aegean Sea. I'm trying to convince him it'll be romantic staying somewhere a bit rustic and off-the-beaten track, but to be honest, I think he's yearning for the shoe-shining facility.

I can't wait, though. I keep imagining us in a series of snap-shot frames: hand in hand running through the waves, me tanned and stunning with a lithe, enviable body, head tossed back in laughter, him, also laughing, wet and sexy; me in a flowing sarong watching lovingly as he plays volleyball with a selection of cute kids in sun-hats; him and all the cute kids trying to throw me in the sea; both of us sitting in a little taverna, moon shimmering on the water, me feeding him freshly picked olives from the overhanging olive tree bough, him wearing a pale yellow jumper tied casually round his shoulders, pointing at a lone yacht.

The thing is, I really wish it was sooner than April. I worked out it is still four and a half months away, which feels like an

Sam

Anyway, I must remember that, despite all this, we are still only in the blossom of our love. I must not let the relationship run before it can walk. Just the other day, for example, I caught myself staring longingly at the most satisfying yellow-head I have ever seen protruding like bubble-wrap out of his back and had physically to restrain myself from reaching over and squeezing it there and then because, as everyone knows, squeezing spots, along with weeing and farting, are not things you are supposed to do in front of someone you have just got into bed with, but rather to be preserved for the more intimate moments of the future.

But that's the problem. It is so easy to get carried away with how natural everything seems, allowing things like spots, personal hygiene and nice underwear to slip entirely by the wayside. I discovered this, to my utter mortification, last night when, after I had failed to brush my teeth, Sam announced that my breath smelt. Erghh – horror. There is nothing worse than someone telling you this. I have now got completely paranoid, swallowing whole tubes of Polos at a time, speaking like a ventriloquist at the slightest whiff of a suspect odour and thanking the Lord above that we do not live in ancient Jewish times when, apparently, it was within the legal rights of a man to divorce his wife for this very reason.

Ooh, yippee – I think that's him at the front door. He's taking me to the dry ski slope tonight – he's always thinking up wacky things to do – and then we'll probably catch a snack at a trendy bistro in Notting Hill.

We've decided to keep it secret – to avoid anyone in the house feeling as though they ought to be leaving the room just because we happen to be watching Newsroom Southeast *together – so time to ourselves is special and precious. The problem is, one of the magical things about the beginning of a happy relationship like ours is the overwhelming and deeply exciting urge to touch each other constantly. It's as though we are one of those circuit-board things from fourth-year physics, where the bulb will only light/we are only happy, if the circuit is unbroken/a limb, hand or small toe* awfully long time, especially once you've started imagining how wonderful it will be. Mind you, as Jo astutely pointed out, the fact that it is so far in the future says a lot about how committed James must be. And Sandra did say that April is a popular month for honeymooners. Not that we're honeymooners yet, of course.

Oooh, I've had such a marvellous week – meeting him for cosy drinks, doing secret giggling, walking arm in arm, phoning up just to tell him I love him, doing passionate showing-off snogging on the tube platform. That's the thing, though, when you have a boyfriend who is nice, the rest of life becomes superfluous and all you really care about is when you are next going to see your nice boyfriend.

This weekend should be great too. Tomorrow he is taking me shopping, though I pray not to the King's Road. I went there with Jo the other day and felt as if I'd turned up uninvited at a casting session for Storm model agency without the correct brief – which seemed to be sunglasses (despite encroaching rain clouds), minuscule mobile phone, Gucci handbag, and the ability to look as if you are related to Kate Moss.

I expect we'll just go and trample on some slow-moving Americans in Oxford Street or hang out with trendy people in Notting Hill. We'll need to go somewhere with a branch of Morgan, however, because I think he's planning to buy me this lovely V-necked tight-fitting top I saw there and was going to buy until I discovered it was £65. (How can it be possible to charge £65 for a piece of shiny material with four sequins on it?) At least, I think it's that one because he asked me what it was like, which is peculiar considering normally if I even mention anything to do with clothes, he looks all vacant and switches on the telly.

And then we will probably spend the rest of the weekend relaxing, possibly going for a long country walk and staying overnight in a quaint little converted stables B-and-B with mock thatched roof and minuscule dolls'-house-sized windows. Can't wait.

Anyway, I must go – said I'd be at James's by nine. I'm going *is touching. Clearly, though, we are unable to create this electrically charged field of passion in company, hence we are reduced to grabbing odd bolts of lightning, as it were, whenever we're alone.*

That's definitely him. Help – must hurry and get ready. Toothbrushing is of obvious importance after the halitosis scare, then outfit selection. I have to say, the evening's events pose a severe problem re underwear. Clearly I do not want to spend the night in BhS swaddling, yet the tantalising lacy affairs are sure to ride directly up my bottom the minute I attempt to ski. Hope you are as happy as me.

Lots of love,
Jess
xxx

PS The knicker quandary above is the result of a sneaking suspicion that tonight we might actually have sex, having so far followed the bizarre logic of sexual etiquette that deems the withholding of intercourse a positive reflection of the relationship and the performing of all manner of far more intimate acts in the meantime perfectly acceptable. Must go. Delicious night of passion ahead.

to cook him fillet steak and baby mushrooms – his favourite. I figure it is only fair, especially in view of the fantastic shopping extravaganza tomorrow.

Lots of love,
Jess
xxx

Sam

. . . Must Come Down

'Ug . . . ugaw . . . ug . . . aww . . .' Sam grunted, his reddened face turning almost bulbous with fervour. He'd been boinging up and down for some time now, making such extraordinary noises that it wasn't clear whether he was having fun or a minor epileptic fit.

Jess, meanwhile, was having neither, unable to concentrate on anything but the prong of a belt buckle digging so sharply into her lower spine that it was as if, in his enthusiasm to shag her, he'd popped out the other side and skewered her to the bed as though she were a shish-kebab.

'Urghurghhhhh,' he continued, snorting into the pillow as she tried to wiggle off the buckle, passing off the movement as a writhe of passion. This was largely unsuccessful and resulted in him depositing her back into position, growling, 'I want you,' which, she decided, given the circumstances, was rather stating the obvious.

Having concocted a vast array of finely detailed fantasies where Sam, sensuous, sexy and selfless, carried her awestruck by the splendid beauty of her nakedness, to a bed made of white silk to lick, rub, massage, kiss, stroke and suck, leaving her in no doubt that paralytic sexual fulfilment was not just something invented by Jilly Cooper, she was now perturbed to discover that the only thing she was enjoying was that it would soon be over. To say that the experience was a disappointment was an understatement. She felt like a pork fillet being tenderised by a hammer.

'Wow,' Sam said, in a long, satisfied sigh, removing the condom and holding it up proudly, as if he belonged to a remote African tribe where identity and leadership qualities were measured solely on the ability to produce a lot of sperm.

Fantastic Shopping Extravaganza

'D'you not think it makes me look fat?'

'Nope.'

'What about the jacket?'

''S fine.'

'Not too big over the shoulders?'

'Doesn't look it.'

'What about when the buttons are done?'

''S fine.'

'Maybe it's the trousers, then?'

'Mmm.'

'They're quite long, aren't they?'

'Not really.'

'I just think the whole thing does something funny to my waist.'

'Mmm.'

'D'you think the colour's OK?'

'Yup.'

'You don't think a lighter one would look better?'

'Nup.'

'So you think this colour's better than the other one?'

'Yup.'

'You know, I still think it makes me look fat.'

James peered again at his reflection. He had been doing this now for most of the morning, pulling his shoulders back, sticking his chin out and pursing his lips into a semi-pout, in a way that he presumably thought represented how he would look, should he choose to buy the suit.

Why, Jess wondered, did mirrors do this to people? Everyone looked fine until they went up to a mirror to check, and then

Sam

He looked all glowing and contented, and seemed unconcerned that Jess was neither. She felt cheated. It was as if they'd sat down together to play a fruit machine, fed it 15 quid's worth of joint cash and, through an ingenious sequence of nudges and hold buttons, won the jackpot, all of which he had just walked off with.

Jess lay there listening to his post-coital grunts fade into a rhythmic snore and felt horribly alone. Sex with Sam was supposed to have verged on the otherworldly, a confirmation of their intense friendship and undeniable compatibility. A climactic, earth-moving culmination of weeks of highly charged forbidden flirting. A tender, intimate sealing of the unbreakable bond between them. It was not supposed to leave her feeling alone. It was not supposed to leave her feeling empty. And it was certainly not supposed to leave her feeling that the only person she really wanted to be lying next to, the only person she really wanted to be intimate with, was James.

When they awoke the following morning it was to what sounded like a firing squad conducting an early-morning drill directly above them. But it turned out to be Jo, preprogrammed to rise at seven even at a weekend and resentful of anyone born without this in-built system of torture.

'Sam, have you seen Jess?' she shouted, from the hallway, causing Jess to dive under the duvet, hyperventilating, as if she were five and this an exciting game of hide and seek.

'All of her,' Sam whispered, delving beneath the duvet and unashamedly fondling his balls.

'I don't understand it. All her stuff's still here, but she hasn't slept in her bed,' she continued, as Jess took in the absurdity of her situation. It was eight in the morning: she was lying sweating and suffocating under the duvet of her flatmate's bed, face to face with his genitals, hiding from another flatmate who had no idea that just a few hours previously they had been engaged in a frenetic rogering session that had

– wham – out came an expression so far removed from how they normally looked that they might as well be staring at a Salvador Dali.

'Just get it, James,' she said, yawning, slouching further into the velvet armchair, clumping the front of her hair into a baby pony-tail and examining it for split-ends. Having rejoiced in images of spending the day looking beautiful in an array of expensive clothes with a dazzling gold card that wasn't hers, she was more than a little pissed off to discover that her Richard Gere had suffered a generosity crisis and was incapable of looking at anything he couldn't buy for himself.

'I don't know . . .' he said, with the pained expression he normally reserved for when he thought he was ill.

'Come on, it looks *fine*.'

'Nope,' he said assertively, disappearing into the changing room. 'I'm going to get that first one we saw in Selfridges – that way we can pick up the shoes *en route*.' He poked his head round the cubicle door. 'You OK?'

'Fine.'

'What's wrong?'

'Nothing.'

'Sure?'

'Yup.'

He shut the door and started to whistle.

Jess stared in fury. He had deliberately flouted the rules. He knew he was supposed to ask her what was wrong many, many times, that she would say lots of 'I'm fine's and 'Nothing's, that he would then have gently and sensitively to tease it out of her with thoughtful, perceptive guesswork, and that only after he'd shown a great deal of genuine concern would he be allowed to know, at which point he had to make it clear how sorry he felt and how determined he was to make amends. At no point during this game was anyone supposed to whistle.

'I'm going,' she shouted, dramatically, as if she were in a

Sam

left her sore and bored, and him with an enormous erection.

'She's probably porking a hunk,' Sam replied, laughing.

While the idea that anyone could refer in such a way to the act of making love repulsed her, Jess refrained from chewing off his porking instrument there and then because she knew that any suspicion Jo might have harboured as to her whereabouts would now have been quashed: 'hunk' was the last term she would associate with Sam.

'You're gorgeous, you know that?' he said, once the coast was clear and Jess had resurfaced like something out of a *Carry On* film with red face and mad hair. She softened a little, trying to remember the last time James had said something nice like that. He tended to issue compliments when he was either drunk and didn't mean them, or when he wanted something, she recollected bitterly, looking fondly at Sam, who suddenly manoeuvred himself on top of her and asked, in a voice that he presumably thought made him endearing, 'Permission to enter, ma'am.'

'Permission refused,' she said, in a slightly cross hockey-teacher manner. If he wasn't prepared to do the warm-ups he wasn't allowed to play the game. After a couple more determined stabs, he gave up and lay looking wounded and feeble as if he'd just been deprived of urgent medical treatment.

'So, come on, then,' he volunteered, after a pause, reaching over and trying his luck with her right nipple. 'What number am I?'

For an awful moment Jess thought this was an invitation to rank him on sexual performance, a vile, confidence-wrecking concept dreamt up by cruel Gavin Turner who she had believed could be tamed from his bastard ways by a little tender loving and who, after she had had sex with him for the first time, announced without irony, and in a way that suggested she should feel very proud, that he had just given her six and a half out of ten.

At the time she had been appalled to find herself, rather

Tennessee Williams play rather than the menswear department of Jigsaw.

A few shoppers looked round. James continued to whistle.

'James,' she shouted louder, 'I'm going.'

'OK, Twerpy, see you in Selfridges.'

'Whatever,' she yelled, and marched out of the shop.

Back in the mayhem of Oxford Street, she began to hate everyone on sight. Sophie had told her it wasn't possible to hate strangers. She had obviously never been to Oxford Street.

After battling valiantly against the tide of oncoming faces, she decided that the torture of walking like a snail and having her bag knocked off her shoulder in the process was worth the risk of being mowed over by a motorcyclist and stepped into the bus lane to continue her journey unobstructed. It was then that she spotted James, who had somehow managed to get ahead of her, looking earnestly into the window of Morgan. A wave of affection gushed through her.

Approaching him lovingly, she wondered how she could have been so wrong about him. He wasn't selfish, mean and incapable of doing anything nice, but kind and thoughtful and about to buy her a very expensive top.

'It's not there any more.' She smiled, taking his arm and stroking it.

James continued to gawp.

'The top,' she repeated. 'They've changed the display.'

James remained silent, puffed out his cheeks and exhaled in satisfaction. 'Cor,' he drooled, 'Toby's right – these mannequins have great tits!'

Whether it had been an ingenious plan of escape or simply his predisposition to behave like an arse, James successfully got out of the rest of the day's shopping. His moment of dismissal came somewhere between developing a suspected brain tumour in Oasis and refusing to move from the window of a pub showing football, unless the alternative involved than disgusted by his arrogance, disappointed not to have scored a bit higher. But he'd assured her that six and a half was perfectly acceptable, given that eight was only issued when two women were involved, nine when the two women were lesbians, and ten could never be achieved by any woman, however attractive, talented or desperate to please. Ten was the real thing. Unsurpassable, exhilarating and incomparable. Ten was masturbation.

'Ninth? Two hundred and forty-second? . . . First?' he added hopefully.

She realised, only marginally relieved, that he was talking quantity rather than quality. The how-many-people-have-you-slept-with conversation, she'd discovered over the years, was one of those slightly terrifying rites of passage in a relationship that seemed to take place *after* you had slept with the person, at which point if you had just come in at four hundred and ninety-third there was little you could do.

It was even more terrifying, she thought, as she racked her brains for a possible number, when you had to go first. Confidence and a substantial talent for being psychic were definite prerequisites since there was no way of telling where your partner might draw the line between sexually normal and a shag-happy slapper.

'Guess,' she said, stalling the torture.

'OK. We talking high or low?'

'That depends,' she mumbled, then took the safe option. 'Low probably.'

Sam looked serious, as if trying to do a long-division sum in his head. 'Eighteen?'

She gave a high-pitched yelp. Clearly she had just shagged Don Juan.

'Lower?'

'Umm . . . a bit. Yeah.'

'Thirteen?'

It was no good. Even if she made it up he would find out

quarter-hourly visits to Burger King. Therefore when Jess turned up six hours later and laid out her purchases on the floor she hoped he would feel obliged to feign interest.

'Mmm, that's nice.'

'Which one?' she asked excitedly.

'That top thing.'

'This?' she said, holding a strappy black item against her shoulders and laughing. 'It's a dress, Twerpy.'

'How silly of me,' he said, raising an eye at the hemline.

'So which one's your favourite, then?'

'Hmm . . .' he mumbled, scanning the floor. 'That,' he concluded, pointing to a light blue cardigan in the corner.

'James,' Jess replied flatly, 'that's my old one.'

By the time she had completed the tutorial, he was lying on the sofa looking stunned. Little did he know, however, that the trick question was still to come.

'So which should I wear tonight?' She was now standing in front of him dangling two identical pairs of black trousers.

He looked at them thoughtfully – experience had taught him not to rush in. 'Either,' he said confidently, 'because they're both the same.'

'The same?' Jess said, incredulously. 'James, they are not remotely the same! These ones are hipsters and have Lycra in them and these' – waggling their twin in the air – 'are *completely* different. Look at the seams, for starters.'

James did as he was told, moving his eyes suspiciously from one to the other, as Toby walked in.

'What's this? Hypnosis?'

'Something like that, mate.'

'I'm showing James my new trousers.'

'And I take it you do realise,' Toby said, treading on the dress, 'that you've bought two identical pairs.'

Jess decided to give up and went off to do her fashion-advising unaided. When she reappeared half an hour later wearing, as it happened, neither pair of trousers, James and eventually, since one of the unfortunate things about lying was that it was always so bloody hard to remember what you had said.

'Five and a half,' she said flatly.

Sam, having lain perfectly quietly all morning, suddenly burst into manic laughter.

'What? What's so funny?'

'Five and a half,' he spluttered, crumpling into ever more raucous laughter.

'So,' she snapped defensively, 'sex is special for me. I don't want to go around shagging every Tom, Dick and Harry.'

'Presumably, though,' he roared, now beside himself, 'you have at one stage shagged a dick.'

It wasn't until he'd rolled around clutching his sides for a good ten minutes more that she discovered he wasn't laughing at the inadequacy of her sexual past.

'How can you possibly shag half a person?'

'It was a long time ago,' she said crossly, 'and he was a whole person.'

'OK,' he said, still sniggering, 'talk me through how you half shag a whole person.'

By the time Jess had finished she'd got so tangled up in defending what did and did not constitute intercourse, which was really her way of denying she had ever gone near Stuart Henderson, let alone allowed him, albeit momentarily, to 'pork' her, the issue of how many people had had the good fortune to end up in bed with Sam had been overlooked.

'Well, it's a whole number.' He grinned, then looked all shy, fiddled with the corner of the duvet and announced meekly, 'Two.'

Jess did her best not to look dumbfounded. It was as if she'd gone into a very expensive shop, eyed up an attractive leather jacket and, in the process of trying it on, discovered it was only £7.99.

'Two?'

Toby were sitting exactly where she had left them with six opened cans of Kronenbourg.

'You going like that?' she said, in the tone her mother used whenever Jess left the house in anything that couldn't conceivably have been bought in Laura Ashley.

James looked confused. 'Going where?'

'Sophie's comedy-club thing.'

'Ah,' he said awkwardly, glancing sideways at Toby. 'The thing is—'

'What?'

'Well, the thing is . . .'

Toby was trying to sidle out of the door unnoticed.

'The thing is—'

'The thing is what, James?'

'Well, we were sort of planning on doing this lads' thing and—'

'And what? You'd rather do that than come out with me?'

'Yes. No. Look, what I mean is—'

'What you mean is, whenever I arrange for us to do something with my friends you always let me down.'

'Jesus Christ, Jess!' he exploded. 'Why does everything always have to come down to you? You, you, you!' He was thumping the armrest of the sofa, causing the TV remote control to bounce up and down in protest.

'So now you're saying I'm selfish, is that it?'

Suddenly James was scrabbling to his feet, hurling a cushion at the telly.

'I simply cannot deal with you when you're like this,' he yelled, marching towards the door.

'Like what?' Jess screeched.

'Irrational!' He walked out of the room and slammed the door.

Jess kicked the cushion. It was always the same. They would both scream and yell obscenities then James would claim he was maturely discussing the issue at hand while she was being

Sam nodded. Suddenly everything had changed. He was not some indiscriminating callous-hearted porking maniac but a sensitive and naïve little soul, caught up in a world where sexual diffidence had no place.

Two explained everything: the bad sex – clearly only a lack of practice; the slightly too-enthusiastic laughing at her own number of sexual partners – a thin disguise for a deep sense of inadequacy; the relentless need to make jokes of a sexual nature – his way of dealing with this inadequacy. She smiled and looked at him with renewed tenderness.

'The second one *was* seven until last night,' he announced, suddenly and inexplicably.

She looked at him blankly. She hadn't the faintest clue what he was talking about.

'The second one *was* seven until last night,' he repeated, looking at her expectantly, as if he'd just told a joke and was waiting for her to get it.

A horrifying image flashed across her mind. Surely he couldn't be suggesting that the second of the two had been . . . No, that would just be . . . that couldn't be . . . or was he saying that *he* was seven when . . .

'D'you want to guess the first one or shall I tell you?' He was now grinning. He looked repulsive.

'Sam, I don't think—'

'Three,' he said, smiling. 'The first whole number's three and the second whole number's eight. Three eight. Thirty-eight. Congratulations, my gorgeous,' he said, giving her a big hug, 'you are number thirty-eight.'

Monday morning came round, as Jess noted it all too frequently had a habit of doing, much faster than any other day of the week. Rather than quiver in dread under the duvet, fighting back waves of nausea and the desire to sleep for a fortnight, she got up early, determined to tackle once and for all her increasing inability to get anywhere on time.

irrational. She decided there was no point in trying to reason with him and left angry, late and alone to meet the others.

'Oh, my God. Jess babes, are you OK?' Jo was looking at her as if she had just turned up with a knife through her neck.

'Ye-ye-yes,' she stammered, fighting off tears. Nothing was more guaranteed to make her cry than someone asking her, when she was trying to be brave, if she was OK.

Jo looked around suspiciously. 'Where's James?'

'He's . . . he's . . .'

'He's where?'

'I . . . he—'

'The bastard!' Jo spat. 'He's done it again, hasn't he?'

Just then Sam bounded through the entrance sucking a lolly. 'Hey, there! Who's died?'

'James, with any luck,' Jo muttered.

Sam sidled up to Jess and laid an arm around her waist. 'Apparently this,' he said, reaching into his pocket and whipping out another lolly, 'is the cure to all men problems.'

Jess tried to stop herself breaking into a smile.

'You pop it into your mouth, pretend it's something else, give it a good crunch and, hey – problem solved.'

She grinned up at him, eyes watery, feeling, for the first time since she'd got back together with James, a twinge of something that smacked horribly of regret. He tore off the wrapper and, unashamedly flirty, moved the sweet towards her. As she parted her lips to receive it, she began to suspect it wasn't a lollipop that could solve her problems with James. It was Sam.

'Guys, it's start – oh, my God, Jess, what's wrong?' Sophie had just come out to find them.

Like a baby that had been distracted momentarily from its bawling, Jess resumed crying. 'It's, it's—' she blubbed, removing the lolly as a dollop of saliva inched its way down her chin.

'It's James,' Jo said, rolling her eyes to the ceiling. 'The bastard's gone and dumped her. Again!'

Sam

After clattering around the house showing off, she got ready in the luxury of a calm she imagined non-late people took for granted, and was just about to leave, feeling as though she ought to be grinning into the camera on a Special K advert, when the phone rang. It was Brian telling her she needn't come in until lunchtime.

'For fuck's sake,' she muttered, banging down the receiver.

'What's wrong?' Colin had just lolloped into the kitchen.

'I've just been told I've got the morning off.'

'That's nice.' He waddled over to the fridge.

'No, it's not. I got up specially and now I'm going to have to drip around feeling exhausted all day and not get any praise for being at work on time.'

The idea was alien to Colin. His life was run by a watch set ten minutes early. 'Well, you know what they say,' he offered, tucking into a mountain of cornflakes. 'The early bird catches the worm.'

Right now, Jess thought, the only worm she'd caught was Colin – it wasn't a desperately large incentive to get up at all, let alone early. She decided to retreat to bed, whereupon she fell instantly asleep, had various traumatised dreams featuring Colin as a gigantic pigeon and arrived at work hot, panting, flustered and, despite all attempts to the contrary, late.

''Scuse me,' she mumbled, fleeing past a timid-looking girl tripping daintily down the stairs towards her. She looked exactly, Jess thought, as the girl gave her a meek almost idolatrous smile, like one of those poor buggers reduced to traipsing brightly coloured CVs round production companies in the hopes of getting a few weeks' unpaid work as a tea-maker.

'Sorry,' she shouted, diving into the office and knocking over the coatstand in an attempt to be efficient by picking up a vomiting fax.

'Not to worry,' Brian said, disarmingly pleasantly, gesturing her over to his desk where a laminated lurid green CV entitled

'Oh, no,' Sophie said, fishing in her bag for a tissue. There were two things Sophie seemed to have been born with: one was the inability to swear; the other was a mini pack of tissues. 'Here you go, you poor lamb.'

'I tell you,' Jo ranted, 'if I ever meet that selfish, good-for-nothing piece of shit, I'll give him what for.'

'But . . . but . . .' Jess snivelled hopelessly.

'Who does he think he is, for God's sake?'

'But he—'

'Someone needs to tell him he can't go round treating people like dirt whenever he feels like a change of scenery.'

'He—'

'Bloody self-indulgent wanker.'

'He hasn't bloody dumped me!'

Just then an almighty roar of laughter erupted from the room next to them. It wasn't until they walked in moments later that Jess discovered, to her horror, she had been the cause of it.

'Nice of you to join us,' a balding comedian shouted, as everyone turned round to stare. Jess, red and flustered, tried to shuffle inconspicuously into a chair.

'He hasn't bloody dumped you, eh?' the comedian exclaimed, to more hoots of hilarity. 'Well, how's about that, eh?' More hooting. 'You know, it's no bloody wonder us guys don't understand women. I mean, there you are doing your hardest to please her – flowers, chocolates, multiple orgasms . . .' A couple of revolting-looking women jeered, presumably, Jess thought, at the idea of an orgasm. 'And then what happens? You get someone like – what's your name, love?'

Again, all eyes were on her. 'Jess,' she squeaked, wondering why, even in situations of extreme mortification, she felt compelled to tell the truth.

'Someone like Jess here who complains not because of the flowers, oh, no, she likes those, not because of the chocolates, heaven forbid, certainly not because of the multiple orgasms

Sam

Amanda Drain confirmed the sad, hopeless mission of the timid girl's visit.

'If I can just get you to stuff these,' he said, handing Jess a pile of letters, 'then frank them, that would be great. And then,' he smiled, 'I want to have a little chat.'

'OK,' she replied, grinning. She could tell by the tone of his voice that this was positive. Brian never 'chatted' when something was bad.

Returning to her desk she embarked upon the laborious task of matching the correct envelope with the corresponding letter, a task of such phenomenally dull and simple proportions it was frighteningly easy to get it wrong. Just as she was running through a fantasy selection of what Brian might have in store for her – 150 per cent pay rise, small acting role in fantastic forthcoming LA-based commercial, destruction of all invoice files – the answer, like a miracle from above, appeared in front of her: 'Dear Amanda . . . Thank you for coming in to see us . . . pleased to offer you the position of office junior . . . look forward to having you on board our team . . .'

So that was it, she thought, barely able to contain her excitement. A promotion. Amanda Drain was to be the new office junior and she was to be the new office . . . Senior? Producer? Director, maybe.

No more invoices, she rejoiced. No more filing. No more numbering, photocopying, faxing. No more making milky tea. No more ordering packs of paper-clips. No more licking envelopes, stamps or bottoms. No more wonderful *nothing*!

It was remarkable, she reflected folding up the letter and grinning happily, how it was always the wonderful things in life that were thrown at you when you least expected them.

– oh, no, no, no – she complains, ladies and gentlemen, because you haven't *dumped* her!'

The entire audience turned round, looked at her and dissolved into uproarious, bellyaching laughter.

By the time Monday morning came round Jess was feeling like throwing herself in the path of a high-speed train. Having spent the weekend being shouted at, laughed at, then humiliated, she was relieved to discover when she walked into the office, characteristically late, that something at least was going well for her. As if by a cute Tinkerbell figure, her desk had been tidied and reorganised. The usual higgledy-piggledy mess of invoices, fluorescent Post-it notes, and chewed pen lids had been condensed into a nice, neat, shiny blue tray labelled in large and deeply satisfying letters, 'Outstanding Work'.

She smiled, recalling all the times she'd assumed Brian thought she was useless. How could she have been so mistaken? Not just 'very good' or 'well done', but 'outstanding'! She was clearly very talented.

Just as she began wondering whether she shouldn't be applying for something a little more in keeping with her capabilities – the civil service maybe, or a high-powered executive-type role – Brian came in.

'Oh, hello, Jess,' he said pleasantly, in a way he hadn't done before. 'You'll notice I've put your stuff together,' he continued, gesturing to the tray of joy, 'and I'd like it sorted by the end of the week.'

'OK,' she gushed, nodding eagerly.

'I expect by now you've realised why this is,' he said, peering down at her with furrowed brow as if she were a dog who'd just peed on the carpet.

'Um . . . well . . .' Jess giggled.

She clearly hadn't. 'I'm sorry to say we've gone hopelessly over budget. As from next week,' he said, looking rather embarrassed, 'I'm afraid you will be out of a job.'

Sam

In the Dole-drums

Sacked
Shortly to be dumped on a 'Where are they now?'
    tape, sandwiched between Andrew Ridgley and
    Mr Blobby
Looking, come to think about it, remarkably like
    Mr Blobby – fat and spotty due to perpetual
    unemployment-eating

Dear Alex,
    According to last month's Marie-Claire, *everyone's life is made up of high and low points, and if you feel stuck in a low one and cannot see how it will ever get any better all you need to do to get a sense of perspective is gaze calmly at a mountain range (not very helpful if you happen to live in Holland, or Clapham for that matter). 'As the eye scans from summit to valley up to summit again,' the article reads, 'one comes to understand the relationship of mutual dependence that exists between life's ups and downs. To know hot we must also know cold; the mountain is only high because the valley is low.' Assuming this is true, I am presently staring directly at Death Valley.*
    Oh, God, I am so depressed. Unemployment is not, as I fondly recalled when I was employed, a case of doing all the things you never had time for when you had a job, sitting around feeling relaxed, smoking dope, reading improving literature and evaluating where you really belong in life, but rather one long-drawn-out reason never to get dressed. Indeed, if it wasn't for the fact that I have to eat and occasionally defecate, I might never make it out of bed at all.
    As it is, I have developed an unhealthy interest in the fridge, staring psychotically inside it every five minutes as if it contains

Out of a job
Seriously doubting my chances of ever being in
  a job
Slightly wondering how much I really want a job

Dear Alex,
  I sometimes suspect I might have spent a previous life as a vicious crocodile. That I am only on this planet to do penance for eating a boatload of kayaking holiday-makers. It would certainly explain why every aspect of my present life is going so diabolically wrong.
  Jo says she thinks it might be because I didn't respond to a chain letter. I am strongly against this idea since everyone knows that chain letters are only a means by which very sad people bully others into copying out the same thing twenty-five times with promises of extremely bad luck if they don't comply. The thing is, if I'm being honest, I think she might be right – after all, what is losing a job if not extremely bad luck?
  Anyway, Jo is being really kind and said that because she works in recruitment she knows how to fiddle really crap CVs like mine so that they look good. She has done a terrific job and it is now unrecognisable. I am at her offices at the moment, waiting in the lobby for her to print it out then photocopy it fifty-five times. Just look at the fantastic transformation.

Sam

a dazzling array of promising job offers, rather than half a tomato, some out-of-date eggs and a tub of Flora. But instead of closing it again, returning upstairs and doing something useful with my life, I start thinking that maybe I need to eat something – like an omelette, perhaps. I then spend ages ferreting around for something to put in it, contemplate being creative with a packet soup, decide the whole thing's too much hassle and end up trying to disguise the fact that I have just eaten eight biscuits out of someone else's food cupboard. If I do not get a job soon I will be whisked away on a reintegration-to-society programme sporting festering bedsores and a body the size of a tank.

In trepidation at this idea, I am now sitting in the offices of a rather mad film-location company awaiting the second half of an interview for a job I neither want nor stand any chance of being offered. I am recoiling in horror at what a hideous mess I have made of things so far and surreptitiously pulling at a skirt that seems to think it would rather be the hem of my jacket, while all the time keeping a crazed eye on my bike which, because I have no idea what the number might be, is pretend padlocked to a lamp post. If it wasn't peeing with rain I would leave right away.

The reason I am here at all is down to Brian, who apparently (presumably in a fit of guilt for having given my job away to someone mad enough to think numbering invoices and filing were rewarding enough tasks in themselves not to require being paid for doing them) suggested me as someone whom Find It Productions might like to employ. This, however, is now unlikely, given that I was incapable of locating the street, let alone their office – No. 5 being followed bizarrely by No. 17 – and had the lack of foresight to tell them this, thus scuppering right from the start my chances of a job at which being able to find things is presumably a fairly integral part.

I have to admit, though, when Brian mentioned it I got rather excited about the prospect of scouting for film locations, imagining myself as a female Indiana Jones trekking through Brazilian rainforests with binoculars round my neck, stopping occasionally by scenic waterfalls to sketch my vision of the film's action.

What it should be:

CURRICULUM VITAE

Education

Inverness Grammar School: Higher Grades – History B, Geography B, English C (wrote essay on Shakespeare's use of irony in Wuthering Heights*), Maths C, French E (lowest mark in year).*

University of Edinburgh: MA Honours in English; (scraped) 2.1

Jobs

Paper-round; Sausage factory worker (1 day); Series of low-paid waitressing jobs, mistakenly given up for: Burger King toilet attendant

Relevant Experience

Bugger all.

Tenuous Experience

Collected song requests from ward of dying geriatrics with intention of doing weekly stint at hospital radio. Never went back.

Pot-scrubber for kitchen of local television studio.

Wrote a 200-word article for student newspaper entitled 'Student Apathy', in moment of panic that I was not making the best of my student days, preferring to spend them in pub or bed.

Sacked from unimaginably dull job filing invoices for kitten-obsessed maniac.

Skills

Being late. Chatting to friends on telephone. Playing the beginning of Für Elise on the piano.

Hobbies

Drinking. Lying on hot beaches. Watching telly.

For a large part of the interview I was led to believe that this might indeed be the case. I was shown exotic photo after exotic photo until the whole thing became less like an interview and more like a post-holiday slide show delivered by the kind of person who thinks it is perfectly all right to invite all their friends round for dinner then bore them rigid with eighty-four shots of a camel.

Indeed, by the end of it I had said so many lovelies and how-beautifuls that I was beginning to wonder whether it wasn't a test to see how long I could remain polite, and that at any moment the interviewer might start hurling abuse at me to see how I handled stress. Instead she asked me, quite calmly, if I had any questions. I hate this question. The only thing I can ever think of asking is how much money I am going to get or how few hours I can get away with working, neither of which you are supposed to be concerned about if you want to work in television. I know the trick is simply to prepare three enquiries beforehand, relating to the history and future plans of the company, then ask them in a way that suggests you are interested in the answers, but I tend to become so consumed by what I am going to wear and how I will get there that the interview bit sort of passes me by.

So I ummed and ahhed and behaved as if I'd been born with one brain cell, then muttered something about looking forward to getting out on location, at which point she told me I would be based entirely in the office. The tantalising photos and references to exotic Caribbean islands were to show me what everyone else would be doing.

Bugger this stupid skirt. Without visibly moving it has swivelled round so that the split is resting over my crotch. I wish I'd just worn a sensible pair of trousers and not listened to Jo's claims that women who wear skirts to interviews are 67 per cent more likely to get the job. As this clearly relies both on the interviewer being male and the skirt fitting, neither of which applies here, this has been a useless piece of advice.

Admittedly, though, I am not entirely blameless for my prosti-tute appearance. I now realise that I was insane to believe anything

What it is now:

CURRICULUM VITAE

Education

Inverness Grammar School: Higher Grades – History A, Geography A, English A(*) (awarded national prize), Maths A, French A

University of Edinburgh: MA Honours in English; First

Jobs

Knowledge Administrator: *Chief Distributor of valuable information to widespread communities.*

Meat Standards Regulator: *Invaluable member of team responsible for the detection of BSE.*

Catering Manager: *Duties included: customer care, sustenance co-ordinator, high-level financial transactions, rota supervising.*

Fast Food Disposal Officer

Relevant Experience

Presenter of hospital radio. Tripled listening figures and revolutionised output format. Given own show with guest appearances on local radio.

House Manager for national television studio.

Regular contributor to student newspaper. Elected Deputy Editor – responsible for bringing newspaper to national recognition with double awards: 'Best Student Newspaper of the Year' and 'Promising Young Editor of the Year'.

Producer for Green Fingers Productions. Responsible for directing and producing major commercials aired nationwide.

Skills

Punctuality. Forming, developing and sustaining a network of social relationships. Grade 8 Piano.

Hobbies

Viniculture. Travelling. Sport – tennis, hockey, hill-walking, running, badminton, skiing, pole-vaulting.

Sam

positive could be gained from cycling to an interview in a suit. It is so long since I've actually got on a bike that I had a rather outdated notion of what it would be like – in the same way that old ladies assume you are always twelve because that was how old you were last time they saw you. I believed it would be a marvellous way of freshening my mind for the interview, envisaging myself pedalling merrily through deserted hedge-lined country lanes, a little wicker basket in the front full of freshly picked apples and a tinkly bell that I would ring if a bunny happened to lollop into my path. I was, as a result, hideously unprepared for the reality.

Riding a bicycle in London is the equivalent of swimming in an ocean full of sharks without a snorkel: freezing cold, impossible to breathe, and in constant fear of being cut up. Thus the happy-tootling-through-the-blossom image suddenly became hurtling-breathlessly-along-the-A205 in an absurdly unsuitable Wallis two-piece, covered from head to toe in grime, with excruciating thigh pain, carbon monoxide poisoning, numb fingers and a sweaty groin.

Naturally my bike, which had looked perfectly fine and gleaming in the garage, only worked in third gear and, as I was to discover at various crucial points along the way, had a habit of disconnecting the chain if any pressure was applied to the brakes. When I was not skimming the ground with my legs splayed open like some kind of insane comic book character, I was scrabbling around in the gutter with a minute piece of loo paper and a Bic pen trying to hook an oily chain back on to rusting cog wheels without getting sliced in two by an oncoming lorry in the process. The idea that this was a relaxing way in which to start my day was one of lunacy. I arrived looking and smelling like a near-dead sea bird hauled to safety after an oil spill.

Jesus's balls. The guy who has now walked in and to whom I have just given a dirty look – chiefly because I thought he was the runner and looked far too young and cocky to be so – turns out to be both the company director and my second interviewer. He is chewing gum and will see me when he's had a 'slash'. I

175

I cannot really see how I can go wrong with this. Even I would be keen to employ me. I hope it works because I'm sure the novelty of slobbing around in PJs all day watching daytime telly and eating things out of jars with your fingers can't last for ever. And obviously I am keen to press ahead with my career. And not have to do unattractive begging with the bank every time I need to use my card.

The money thing's getting a bit desperate so I've started doing the lottery on Wednesdays as well as Saturdays. Why is it that when you are at your poorest like this, you start throwing money at things that are clearly a waste *of money? Like lottery tickets, for example. Is it that you become so delusional with poverty that the idea of sustaining yourself via the normal route, i.e. a job, seems so impossibly unattainable as to make winning thirteen million in the lottery seem more likely?*

I certainly think being poor turns you slightly insane. Like the other day when I decided to answer an advert in the paper saying, in temptingly vague terms, 'Do you want to earn £50 for half an hour's work?' I should have known this would be a mistake – like entering a Reader's Digest *competition and coming away, not with the prize draw of £40,000 or even a kettle, but with a decade's worth of Cellophane-wrapped junk mail containing fake brass keys and pictures of Mrs Burnley from Wolverhampton holding a gigantic cheque for, surprisingly, £40,000.*

When I phoned the number on the ad, it all sounded fine. They said that it was for a new car lot that was opening and they needed people for its ad campaign. It would be 'a couple of shots with a car'. Unable to see past the big juicy £50 flashing in my head like a fruit-machine jackpot, I skipped off to my fate – which transpired to be a God-forsaken gravel pit in the Docklands, two Ford Escorts and some overweight housewives from Essex.

Of course I should have turned away there and then, but I sort of forgot that I could – in the same way that it still comes as a startling revelation when, bored at a dreary social occasion, I suddenly remember I don't have to stay and suffer but can get up cannot believe I have spent the last twenty minutes pretending I am taking notes from a tedious magazine devoted to lighting equipment in an attempt to look impressive when the boss walks in, when the 'boss' looks as though he would rather be taking Ecstasy tablets in an underage nightclub. Back soon . . .

You are not going to believe what has now happened. I have just got home to discover, among some mail for a stranger and eight identical flyers for Dial-a-Pizza (what in the name of flying arses is the point in that?), a letter for me.

When you are unemployed mail is like UN grain deliveries to the starving: rare and unpredictable but a sheer delight when it comes. I was euphoric. I was also aware that the handwriting on the front was James's.

With a degree of excitement, and perhaps a little more enthusiasm than should be attributed to a fragment of a past one professes to have left behind, I ripped it open and nearly jumped out of my skin. James, for whom the idea of merely writing his name is stretching creativity to its limit, had written me a poem.

I have no idea what to make of it, other than to feel slightly miffed that it has taken the relationship to end for him to do what I would have died and gone to heaven for when we were together – which I think, in his primary-school way, is what he is trying to say:

When love is there inside your heart
It is an anchor in the dark,
And lonely nights are few and rare
For in my world I have you there.

But then day dawns and with it too
A feeling that I don't need you,
That what is right and should be done
Is leaving you and having fun.

and leave. Unfortunately, a similarly dazzling realisation did not hit me in the Docklands gravel pit. Instead I followed a sleazy-looking photographer into a warehouse and agreed to don a revolting orange and lime striped leotard with frizzy tutu and toy-shop plastic wand. Half an hour later he had us draped over the bonnet of a blue Ford Escort, pointing our plastic wands at a banner overhead saying, 'Magical Prices for Ordinary People' (clearly a copywriting gaffe from the outset because whatever else I and six fat women from Essex wearing tutus looked like, it was not, with any stretch of the imagination, ordinary).

I think I could just about have survived this humiliation and written it off as something never to be resorted to again when what should bloody happen? Jo comes back from work the following day pissing herself laughing and pointing at page eight of the Daily Mirror. Horror.

Then, in what I took to be a stroke of much-needed luck, I got a phone call. It was Bobby from Model Mania who'd seen my photo and wanted to know which modelling agency I was signed up to. Naturally I assumed he was (a) a pervert (b) mistaken or (c) joking. But he seemed so adamant he was none of these that I told him, getting really rather excited, that I didn't belong to any agency. He said he was astonished by this and then asked if I would be interested in getting a portfolio together as I had this season's 'look' – which I assumed must be not very tall, not very thin and not very attractive. Anyway, I got so carried away with the idea that I agreed to meet him the next evening at a trendy Soho brasserie of the sort frequented by famous people, models and, as I now imagined, me.

Spent the next twenty-four hours in frenzied excitement, replanning the rest of my life on the basis of my burgeoning new career as a model. Then I started having paranoid delusions of grandeur. If I had the potential to be a model, perhaps I had other hidden talents I wasn't aware of? A natural gift for the cello, maybe? Or fly-fishing? What if I was a bowls genius? The trouble with this kind of thinking, though, is that it makes you rather depressed, because unless your parents were both psychic and pushy when you were

Sam

And for a while this sort of works
I drink a lot and act a jerk,
I tell myself that I am fine
Being on my own time after time.

But very soon a hole appears
The size to fill a hundred tears,
And then I see but all too late
That I have made a grave mistake.

While this is clearly not going to make him Poet Laureate, I can't help wishing he had never written it. There is something unsettling about someone you had dismissed from your life as an emotionally stunted, freedom-obsessed moron creeping back into it and challenging the foundations of your reason for dismissing him in the first place. James is supposed to remain vile, arrogant, soulless, mean and irrevocably selfish to the end of his wretched life. He is not supposed to write poems about love and wanting me back.

Oh, God, though. What if I have made a grave mistake too? What if all he needed was time and now he is ready to be a normal human being with emotions and things? Maybe right at this moment we would be blissfully happy somewhere, by the banks of a rivulet perhaps, or on a snow-capped hilltop, talking, sharing and analysing the depth of our feelings in a heart-searching communion of minds?

No. I'm just being silly. I have been fooled by something which was, no doubt, copied out of his cousin's homework jotter. James is a bastard. Like chameleons, bastards have the cunning ability to appear as they are not, but when all is said and done both bastards and chameleons will never be able to change what essentially they are and always will be: unattractive overgrown lizards. I will not give the poem another thought.

La-dee-la. I wonder what I'll do today. I suppose I could make another omelette. I wish I was still working at Green Fingers. I two, however destined you might have been for the World Bowls Championships, you're sure as hell not going to make it now.

So, by the time it came round to meeting Bobby I was so determined to make a go of it, and so excited about the prospect of doing so, that what happened next will possibly go down as the most disappointing moment in my life. Bobby had turned up all right. And Bobby was glad I had come. In fact, Bobby thought I had a lot of potential. Because Bobby, the little piece of conniving shit, was Sam.

The worst thing about it all, obviously excluding that I was no longer going to be a model, was that I had told so many people I was. They were now going to think I believed I could be – which, to be honest, I had. Anyway, I decided to treat the whole thing as it was intended to be treated, i.e. as a hilarious joke, rather than how it actually felt – i.e. humiliating.

I must say, though, part of me likes being at the centre of jokes like this. It makes you feel rather special and popular. James would never be this funny. I mean, it's not that he's not witty, but he just doesn't make me laugh the way Sam does. Oh, hold on, Jo wants me to make a decision about the font . . .

Oh, my sweet heavens above. Guess what has happened. I can't believe it. I was trying to decide whether I wanted my CV in Times New Roman or Arial when Jo had to take a phone call, so I thought I may as well take advantage of the free computers and check my e-mails. And, oh, my Lord. Sam has sent me a message. I know it's wrong to get even slightly excited by this but I just can't stop my heart going into trampolining mode whenever I see his name on my screen. The association it triggers off in my mind of uncontrollably exciting flirting has turned me, quite literally, into Pavlov's salivating dog. This is what it says:

> Subject: Bobby says sorry
> You put the sunshine into my day and the moonshine into my dreams. Does Kate Moss want to go for dinner?

Yippee! But what do you think it means? Obviously, a dinner invite is not to be taken lightly, is it? Although – oh, God – I've *had a purpose then. A sense of direction. Oh, God. Why do both my ex-job and my ex-boyfriend now seem appealing when all I did when I had them was wish I didn't?*

Bugger James. Why did he have to send that poem? I was doing perfectly well until he decided to turn all John Donnean on me. Now I can't stop thinking about him, which is wrong. I have a lovely boyfriend now. Sweet, funny, kind Sam. We have a great relationship. We laugh, we joke, we get on superbly. I mean, it's not amazingly sexual but that's not everything, is it? Much better to have someone who's going to be your friend and care for you than eight orgasms a day and constant paranoia.

I just wish I could fancy *him a bit more. I mean, it's probably just an adjustment thing, like when your car breaks down and the garage give you a little Nissan thing with the indicators on the wrong side and a funny gearstick. For a while you grind around trying to find third and put the windscreen wipers on every time you turn left but then you get used to it, and when you get your old car back again it feels wrong. Not that I'm thinking of taking James back, you understand. Nor do I own a car.*

Anyway, I do fancy Sam most of the time – like when he's just washed his hair and looks all fluffy and clean. Or when he wears his nice beige jumper. And just because every time I see him I don't want to rip all his clothes off doesn't mean we can't be happy. After all, if James and I had done a bit less of the bodice-ripping and more of the friends-talking thing we might still be . . . Anyway, it's of no consequence to me where James and I might be. I'm going to make an omelette. . .

Yippee-doodle-dandy. Marie-Claire *is a wise and wonderful publication. The mountain thing was right. Entirely. I am now out of Death Valley and sitting admiring the view from Mount Kilimanjaro.*

I have a job. Well, not exactly *a job, but darned near one. Sophie has a dad's brother's friend of a second-cousin neighbour's son-in-law who works at the BBC as a script editor. She encouraged me to send him this thing I'd been dabbling in. I didn't tell you about*

*just thought, what if it is meant to be taken lightly, like the first
bit about the sunshine? What if the whole thing is a joke – after
all he has called himself Bobby and me Kate? Maybe it's just
another extension of the model thing. Oh, God. This is the problem
with e-mail – the pressure to be amusing is virtually overbearing,
yet it's so bloody hard to get any intonation across that you end
up producing something open to at least seven different interpre-
tations, none of them amusing. I don't know why people rave about
how fantastic it is at easing communication when in my experience it seems to do the opposite – as evidenced by the fact I have
spent the last half-hour trying to compose a reply. Have managed
to whittle it down to five possibilities:*

Reply	For	Against
'Kate would love to have dinner. Please choose restaurant special-ising in lettuce.'	Suggests dinner invite has been taken in the casual, light-hearted manner in which it was issued.	Ignores flirting mileage to be got from naughty acceptance of datey-dinner invite when already have a boyfriend.
'Kate regrets that she already has dinner partner in form of long-term boyfriend.'	Mentioning boyfriend is the only right and proper thing to do.	Mentioning boyfriend is the only way to guarantee he will lose interest immediately.
'Dinner sounds lovely. When?'	Straightforward and honest.	Straightforward and honest.
Wait three days before sending reply.	Suggests dinner invite is just another event in busy un-employed life.	Will not be able to keep up façade of busyness when slobbing round flat cooking omelettes.
No reply.	Will not have to overstretch brain trying to think up witty replies.	He will assume I have not received it and entire reply-strategy will be pointless.

it before because, well, to tell you the truth I didn't think it was particularly good – it's amazing how your whole sense of self-belief can change with a single compliment. It's nothing special, really, just a few thoughts I'd jotted down on the back of an envelope the way we writers tend to do, about a film called Barking Mad *based on a man trapped in a dog's body who falls in love with his female owner.*

Anyway, he's just called me up – sounds a very nice man indeed – and said how impressed he was with it. Actually, I'm being a bit modest here, the word he used was 'tremendously' impressed, going on to say – I can't believe it, I keep replaying this over and over in my head – 'I particularly liked the way you dealt with the psychosexual tension, something most screenwriters have extreme difficulty with.' I am a screenwriter! He wants to meet tonight at eight to discuss plot development. I wonder if he'll be attractive.

Lots of love,
Jess
xxx

PS Just had a creative miracle brainwave. If I make the owner male not female, then the dog will be gay. And who better to play a gay dog than George Clooney? I am a genius. Not only am I to become a famous film-writer but I will be directing George Clooney into the bargain. Must remember to get his agent's number though, before ER *nab him again.*

One minute I am strongly in favour of the first because obviously I am keen to encourage all flirting opportunities with Sam, then the next I think, What am I doing? I shouldn't be interested in encouraging anything with Sam and resolve to give him the perfectly-happy-with-boyfriend-thanks-all-the-same line. But I don't know if I am happy. Three weeks ago I was so sure James and I were completely right for each other, that all our problems were solved, that we had the kind of rare love found only in Whitney Houston songs and Thomas Cook brochures for the Caribbean. But now I am not so sure. A bit like self-professed reformed alcoholics, we have started going off the rails again but have not yet reached the point where we are honest enough to acknowledge this. Thus while we are screaming, yelling and clearly not getting on, we are pretending that everything is fine.

Oh, God, what if I have chosen the wrong bloke, after all? That's the problem with choice: it's so confusing. The idea of it is always so appealing and liberating, but in reality you end up relentlessly wondering about the life you didn't choose. Maybe the answer is not to have a choice at all? Maybe I should have married Brad MacCormack in the milk queue?

I had better go. Jo is motioning at me from behind a glass screen, presumably because she has accomplished the secret photocopying. I can't wait to see the finished product. There is something triumphant about seeing your life condensed on to one side of A4 with all your achievements (or, in my case, amended achievements) flowing one after the other down the page and everything that has ever gone wrong in your life nowhere to be seen.

Lots of love,

Jess

xxx

PS For fuck's sake! Jo has just handed me fifty-five copies of a CV for Jeccisa, born 28/11/00.

Girl Talk

'George Clooney?' Sophie said, raising her eyebrows and smiling as if she were a teacher and Jess had just said something sweet but very stupid.

They were sitting on Jo's bed acting as fashion consultants for an insanely over-excited Jo, who had finally secured what had been turning into a rather tragic lifetime's ambition: a date with Max.

'You never know,' Jess mumbled, feeling a bit of a berk for having said anything.

'Exactly,' Jo exclaimed. 'I bet Ben Affleck didn't think he'd be shagging Gwyneth when he sat down to write the opening scene of *Good Will Hunting.*'

This was presumably meant to make Jess feel better but the comparison with beautiful, talented, multi-billionaire residents of Hollywood had the opposite effect. She began to wonder whether she hadn't perhaps been a bit premature with her plans for canapé lunches and pavement-café drinks with George. It was a bit like arranging the seating-plan for the wedding of a daughter she had not yet conceived.

'Phwoarr, Ben Affleck,' Sophie growled suddenly, in a most unlikely display of carnal desire. Jess and Jo looked at her, stunned. Sophie was like a parent: she wasn't supposed to be sexual. 'What?' she protested.

'Nothing,' Jo said, smiling. 'I just didn't know you were such a fan.'

'I'm not,' she snapped defensively. 'I just think he's attractive. He's probably a complete jerk.' Sophie was one of those people who assume that good looks and a nice personality are mutually exclusive. Given that she was going out with Richard, this was probably, Jess decided, a good thing.

'Sorry, babes,' Jo said, unperturbed, 'but look on the bright side. At least they'll realise you're ambitious.'

'Why?' Jess replied, drily. 'Because someone who can't spell their own name suggests someone determined to get ahead?'

'Because, going by my watch' – Jo checked the time – 'you've achieved a hell of a lot for someone born this morning.' She laughed, looked at her watch again and shouted, 'Shit, is that the time? We need to go.'

It became apparent, at about the same moment as Jess realised she'd missed *Ricki Lake*, that Jo's cock-up with the CV had nothing to do with speed, carelessness, or the pressures of a prowling boss, but was merely the result of an impending drink with Max. She was incapable, Jess was about to discover, of thinking about anything else.

'Oh, my God, oh, my God, only two hours and seventeen minutes to go,' she squealed, as if it wasn't so much a trip to the pub but a two-week all-expenses-paid holiday to the Bahamas.

'Café Rouge seems a weird place for a date,' Jess said, staring despondently at her pile of ruined CVs. 'Kind of a meeting-Mum-for-lunch place.'

'Don't say "date"!' Jo shrieked. 'It's not a date. It's just a casual drink thing. Completely informal. Nothing big.'

'Oh,' Jess said, rather confused. Jo had spent the best part of the week grooming herself for this non-date.

'It's just that if you say "date", it makes it into this huge thing,' Jo explained, 'which it isn't. Well, at least, it might be, but if you say it is then it invariably isn't because you've made it into this thing before it's actually turned into this thing itself. D'you see what I mean?'

'Max is good-looking and isn't a jerk,' Jo offered, pulling her hair up, admiring herself from a number of different angles, then letting it down again.

Max, Jess thought, was in danger of becoming one of those all-perfect wonder-stars, the tales of whose infallibility her parents would have inflicted upon her at regular intervals during her childhood, and whose name she would spend the rest of her life loathing. 'OK, here's a question for you,' she volunteered, keen never to let the conversation stray too far from her own interests. 'Who would you rather end up with? A sexy wanker or an ugly soulmate?'

'That depends,' Jo said, rubbing L'Oréal foundation lavishly into her face. 'Is the ugly soulmate rich?' The idea that she might be without the means to spend vast quantities of money regularly seemed to take precedence over love or attraction.

'It shouldn't be important,' Sophie said, self-righteously.

'They're both as rich as each other.'

Jo pouted at herself in the mirror. 'Is the ugly one ugly-ugly or sexy-ugly?'

'Ugly, as in you-don't-fancy-him-ugly.'

'In that case it would have to be the sexy wanker,' she concluded. 'I'd get the soulmate stuff from my dog.'

'Your dog?' Sophie giggled.

'Yeah, well, blokes are crap at it anyway. My dog understands me.'

It was clear that Sophie, for all her attempts otherwise, did not.

'I'd go for the ugly soulmate every time,' she said, looking all smug and pleased with herself, as if she'd just got something right in class.

'So you're saying you wouldn't mind getting into bed every night with something that resembles a turnip?'

Sophie shook her head. After all, Jess thought, she wasn't a million miles away from doing that already.

Jess nodded obediently.

'Anyway. He's probably got a girlfriend or something.'

But this, it transpired half an hour later, wasn't something that seemed to be troubling her. Having spent an unnaturally long time in the bathroom, she was now standing in front of her selected committee – Jess, Sophie and occasionally a wandering Colin – in a very peculiar assortment of clothes. The only possible explanation was that half-way through getting dressed she'd suffered an identity crisis, which had left one side of her body thinking it was Cilla Black, and the other, Ronan Keating.

'Good heavens, Jo,' Sophie exclaimed, 'are you planning on pulling in that?'

'She's not pulling anyone,' Colin said stiffly, then parroted, with no hint of irony, 'It's just a casual drink.'

To prove the point, Jo was going through the agonising process of trying to choose the less formal of the two outfits.

'OK, babes,' she said, straddling the door frame so that only Cilla was in view. 'This? Or . . .' She deftly manoeuvred round and hitched up her skirt, revealing a pair of black shiny trousers underneath. 'This?'

'Definitely the first,' Colin said, just as Jess and Sophie pointed unanimously at the second.

'Oh, God, this is useless,' she sulked, 'I may as well go in my nightie.'

'Well, that would certainly be casual,' Jess said, laughing.

'Look, Jo, just wear what you feel comfiest in,' Sophie said.

'My nightie.'

Just then Colin turned round and cast a wary eye in the direction of a floral nylon number poking out from under the pillow. 'I'd wear the skirt,' he said.

Jess looked round to where he was sitting legs apart on the bed. The idea was mildly abhorrent.

'Yeah, but Jess and Sophie said the trousers,' Jo continued, too preoccupied to entertain visions of Colin in a skirt,

Sam

'You can't build a relationship on sexual attraction alone,' Sophie said, with the look of someone who had never tried. 'It runs out. You've got to have the foundations of friendship otherwise it'll never work.'

'So let me get this straight.' Jo had her hands on her hips in a way that she clearly thought lent authority to her point. 'You'd rather compromise thirty, forty even, years of passion for the knowledge that at sixty-five you'll still be able to have a friendly chinwag over the Ovaltine.'

'All I'm saying' – Sophie was getting irritated – 'is that finding someone attractive isn't the be-all and end-all. So what if they're not going to make your heart miss a beat? They love you. That's what counts. And if you love *them*' – she'd started to go all high-pitched and get unattractive nervous blotchy marks across her chest – '*really* love them, love their soul, love what's on the *inside*, then you can grow to love what's on the outside too.'

Jo looked as though she'd just walked into a wall. '*Grow to love?*'

'Yes.'

'Sorry, babes, I don't mean to be rude' – Jo often began her sentences with this disclaimer before going on to be extremely rude. It was along similar lines to people who use the casual and offhand opener 'by the way' before delivering an earth-shattering piece of news – 'but I think that's bollocks. It's either there or it's not. It's like saying if I really love Zingu, which I do – a lot – then it's only a matter of time before I can make myself fancy him too. I don't think so, babes.'

'Zingu's a dog,' Sophie said flatly.

'Exactly. My point. No matter how much I love his insides I'm never going to want to shag him.'

Sophie looked unimpressed.

'Unless of course I'm into bestiality.' She laughed.

'Oh, just forget it.'

'and the skirt looks like I've got dressed up specially.'

'But you have,' he replied, confused.

After a great deal more consulting, it was decided she would wear the trousers and trainers as a way of looking as though she hadn't made any effort, the pale yellow shirt because Max had once said he liked it two and a half years ago, hair down unless it started going lank and greasy and lots of makeup cleverly applied to look as if she wasn't wearing any.

'So, babes, you seeing James tonight?' She was pouting into a powder-compact mirror working out the most desirable angle at which to approach a kissing scene, should one arise.

'Nah, he's got some work thing,' Jess mumbled.

'James has always got some work thing,' Sophie said, laughing in a way Jess found slightly evil.

'Yeah . . . well . . .'

'Is everything all right between you two?' She was wearing her concerned face, which had a tendency, Jess thought, to make her look like a frog.

'Yeah, fine. Why?'

'Oh, nothing, it's . . . you just don't seem very, well, happy, that's all.'

'James never makes her happy,' Jo volunteered chirpily, smearing what looked like runny tomato ketchup over her lips. 'Is this too bright?'

'He does,' Jess replied defensively, then added, 'sometimes.'

'You should chuck him, babes.' This was always Jo's solution to the problem but Jess didn't think it was the moment to point out that Jo had spent the best part of three and a half years regretting doing exactly that. 'Come and have fun being single with me.' She smiled, then pointed at the ketchup. 'On or off?'

'Maybe,' Jess mused. Certainly what Jo had shown her so far of the single life wasn't exactly a huge incentive.

'On or off?' Jo persisted.

'D'you think he loves you?' Sophie enquired, doing the frog thing again. 'Off.'

'Come on, babes, don't take everything so seriously. All I'm getting at is that if you can't look at him and go, "Phwoaarrrr, I want you on the floor now," then what's the point?'

'Comfort and security,' Sophie said, punctuating her words in a manner reminiscent of Tony Blair addressing the People. 'Companionship and laughter.'

'But don't you see?' Jo persisted, unwilling to give up. 'That's like saying . . . that's like saying Jess should go out with . . . with Sam, for God's sake!'

Suddenly Jess, who'd been enjoying hearing her own love dilemma ping-ponged back and forth across the room, froze rigid. She knew this would not be the moment to blush but the very fact that she knew she mustn't meant, of course, that she did.

'They get on, they have a laugh, but she's hardly going to want to do him at the end of the night, eh, Jess?'

'I think Jess should answer that,' Sophie said, sounding alarmingly like a tutor who was all too aware of who had done the tutorial preparation and who had not.

'Answer what?' she gulped, pulling at her hair to disguise her now purple face.

'Would you go out with someone like Sam who's a great friend and a good laugh and all that, even though you don't . . . well, you know—'

'Don't what?' she snapped, more defensively than she'd meant to.

'Well, who isn't a Ben Affleck, shall we say?'

So now even Sophie didn't think he was attractive. Jess shrugged.

'Of course maybe you *do* think he's a Ben Affleck,' Sophie suggested, with a little sideways laugh at Jo.

'Hardly.'

'So?'

'So what? Yes. No. No, probably not. I don't know. Who

'Well, he says he does.'

'Jess? On or off?'

'On. I mean, I guess he must, if he says he does.'

'And d'you love *him*?' Jo asked, dabbing her mouth.

'Yeah, s'pose.'

'You suppose,' Sophie repeated. 'That doesn't sound like love to me.'

Jess bit back the inclination to suggest that since love for Sophie consisted of organic meals for two, elderberry and geranium oil baths, and pairing Richard's socks, she was more than happy not to have made the grade. Instead she smiled meekly. 'Really?'

'Believe me, you know when you love someone. You know when it's right.'

Jess looked at Sophie with her long flaxen hair, her fuchsia cardigan and her little clog-like shoes and wondered whether she wasn't right. Not about love, but her approach to love. She was so sure, so unquestioning, so contented. Was Richard, with his receding hairline and enthusiasm for accountancy, so right for her that she never wanted something different? Better? More? Someone with a sense of humour, perhaps? Or even just a full head of hair?

And as she sat feeling smugly superior for not being so willing to compromise, a strange and unwelcome realisation came over her. Sophie wasn't the one in a relationship that made her miserable. Sophie wasn't the one running obsessively after an ex she dumped too long ago to remember. Sophie wasn't the one in any of these messes. Sophie was the one, the only one, who could truly claim to be happy with what she had. What, then, Jess wondered, did that say about being unquestioning?

'I think that's bollocks,' Jo said, mid-application of a third layer of mascara. 'I mean, I didn't think I loved Max. I didn't think he was the one. And now look at me.'

'Exactly,' Jess said.

cares?' They were now looking at Jess intently, as if trying to read something in tiny print on her forehead. 'I'm going to get ready. So whatever, really. Probably not, come to think of it, but . . . so . . . I'm . . . um, late, yeah.' She stumbled to her feet, flashed a fake smile at her bemused audience and disappeared out of the room.

'No Ben Affleck, eh?'

Jess screamed. Sam had just appeared from behind her bedroom door.

'Jesus, Sam! You gave me the fright of a lifetime.'

'Clearly,' he said. 'So? Anything else I should know?'

He looked serious. Sam never looked serious. He was supposed to be pulling moonies at passing grannies and doing rude things with the fruit bowl, not looking serious. But that was the trouble with constantly funny people, she conceded: no one ever gave them licence to be anything but. 'What d'you mean?' she said, in a light, airy voice, resisting the urge to run out of the room, panic, rewind the last five minutes and chuck a pint of vodka down her throat.

'Well, you obviously don't find me attractive,' he said, looking small and shrivelled, as if all the stuffing had been vacuumed out of him by a heavy-duty Hoover. 'I just wondered if there was anything else you wanted to say. My back's a bit spotty, maybe? Could do with a few more sessions at the gym?'

Jess stared. It was never a good idea to do this. Bodily insecurities should be kept locked away and obsessed about internally, not shared with your partner. After all, she had learnt, if a flabby bottom and squint nipples could escape unnoticed, what on earth was to be gained from giving them unwanted publicity by pointing them out?

'May as well get it all off your chest now,' he continued. 'No good in bottling these things up.'

'What on earth are you talking about?'

'Jess, don't pretend.'

It was alarming, she thought, as she stood trying to look

'So what are you saying?' Sophie said, going all twitchy and impatient.

'That it's just the same as buying . . . I don't know, a pair of shoes.'

Sophie looked at Jess blankly.

'Well, put it this way. You might find a pair in Clapham that you like, that fit you, that seem fine. And that's great. You buy them and they're great. OK? So, let's say they're Richard.'

'What's Richard?' Sophie said flatly.

'The shoes.'

Jess watched as Sophie tried to recast Richard in the form of a pair of slip-ons from Jones.

'The point being?'

'The point being,' Jess said, not sure if there was a point, 'that there may be another pair of shoes that you like *more* than the ones you bought, that fit you just that little bit better, that are that bit nicer. And they could be in Holloway or Switzerland or Africa, even, and you'd never know about them. D'you see what I'm saying?'

She didn't.

'Oh, my God, I get it!' Jo screeched, always being able to relate to a shopping analogy. 'God, babes, we'd better start travelling,' she said, laughing.

'I think both of you are missing the point,' Sophie said, after a long, reflective pause. 'That when you've found what you want, you stop looking.'

Just as she said this, Jess glanced down at her clogs and as she did so she caught Jo doing the same. Suddenly, Sophie's little wooden clodhoppers seemed to say it all.

'Jesus's arse!' Jess yelled, when several hours later she was woken by something that sounded like a hyena.

'I'm going to kill myself,' Jo cried, as she collapsed on the bed and belched.

Sam

confused, how much someone's attractiveness rested on their own *belief* in it.

'Look, Sam, I had to say that, otherwise they'd have suspected.'

'It didn't sound like that from where I was standing.'

'Well, then, you shouldn't have been standing there.' She waited for the artillery bombardment of 'You are an imbecile' insults to come hurtling towards her through the air, the usual format in her experience of an argument with a man – more specifically, James.

Nothing. Not even a little squeak. He was looking shrivelled again.

'Sam, I'm sorry, OK? I shouldn't have said anything. I panicked. Anyway, you should be pleased,' she said, approaching him the way she'd seen mastered so effectively in films, which had, of course, looked uncannily natural and sexy when accomplished by an attractive actress, and clumsy, verging on the ridiculous, when attempted by her. 'I managed cunningly to foil them.'

Sam looked at her blankly. 'I don't see why we have to *foil* them at all.'

'Sam, we've been through all this,' she said, moving away and staring despondently inside her wardrobe. 'We don't want to make anyone feel uncomfortable.'

'You mean we don't want to make *you* feel uncomfortable.'

Jess felt uncomfortable. 'What's that supposed to mean?'

'That this whole secretive thing is because you're embarrassed to admit we're together.' There was an extended silence. Had a nail been lying around, Sam had just got up, walked over and hit it square on its minuscule head.

'Don't be ridiculous, Sam,' she said, hauling out a skirt. 'Now. Skirt or trousers?'

Sam stared.

'Trousers?' she offered, picking up a crumpled linen item and dancing it around in the air.

'Jo, it's the middle of the night,' Jess remonstrated. 'Can't you do it in the morning?'

There was an ominous silence.

'No,' she squeaked, and burst into tears.

It turned out that the 'casual' approach to the evening had been taken one step further by Max who, after failing to show for the first part of it, had appeared in his football kit with three friends, one of whom was female.

'So you're not one hundred per cent sure he's actually going out with her?' Jess was trying her best to extrapolate something positive.

'Well,' Jo snivelled, brightening at the prospect, 'not one hundred per cent.'

'OK, so can you think of anything, any sign he might have given, to suggest she might just have been a friend, or the girlfriend of one of the other guys maybe?'

Jo stared at her tissue, concentrated hard, then burst into a fresh round of tears. 'No.'

'Well. Girlfriend or no girlfriend, I certainly think he was flirting. I mean, pointing out your shirt. That's a very good sign.'

Jo looked up at her. '*I* pointed it out!'

The whole thing, Jess decided, as she fed Jo the remainder of the loo roll, was becoming a bit like the lottery: having missed the jackpot, they had now got to the fifth ball and with it the realisation that they weren't even going to win a tenner.

'Well, what was he doing inviting you out in the first place? I mean, what does he expect, for God's sake?'

'He said he was just being friendly.'

'I hope you told him being friendly doesn't involve arranging a date and then bringing along your girlfriend,' Jess ranted.

'Well, I tried to, but then Sam started—'

'*Sam?*' Jess hoped the violent explosion his name had just

185

Sam

'Am I?'

'Are you what?'

'Being ridiculous.'

'Of course you are. You know you are. You're also being useless. Skirt or trousers?'

He looked at her and gave a weak smile. She knew that feeling: the desperately-wanting-to-believe-something-was-true mixed with the haven't-an-ounce-of-courage-to-push-it-and-find-out dilemma. And as she pranced around trying to cheer him up, as if he were not a fully grown man but a toddler in an indeterminate moment between laughter and tears, she reflected on how all relationships were just like a game of cricket – though generally, she conceded, not quite so dull. There were batters and there were fielders. Until now she'd always been a fielder, scrabbling around after a ball she could never catch. Now she was clearly a batter. And she wasn't sure that she liked the responsibility.

'Skirt,' he said, smiling. 'You know I think you look gorgeous in the skirt.'

Jess smiled back. The whole thing was becoming a bit like a Colgate commercial.

'Now go,' he said. 'I've got important business to attend to.'

She gave him a querying look.

'By the time you get back, me and Ben? Pah! You won't be able to tell the difference.'

By the time Jess got back, however, she would have been hard pushed to tell the difference between Sam, Ben and a dancing doorknob, which was not something she might have predicted when she had walked into the Cross and Dagger five hours previously.

'Hi, I'm Jess,' she had said confidently, leaning across the bar and offering her hand to a good-looking olive-skinned man earnestly reading the sports section of the *Guardian* and straddling a bar stool, she couldn't help noticing, in a very desirable way. She'd been in the bar for ten minutes before caused in her stomach wasn't quite so apparent on her face. 'What? Sam was there?'

'Yeah. The thing is, Max made it sound like *I* was the one being—'

'But? What was Sam doing there?'

'Drinking, I suppose. To be honest, I don't think it was him who arranged the—'

'What? On his own?'

'I don't know. No, with a girl I think. Anyway, what do you care?'

'Oh, no. No, I don't care at all,' Jess protested, instantly regretting her decision to play it cool by a delayed response to the dinner e-mail. 'No, no, it's just,' she stuttered, resisting the urge to shout, '*what girl?*' 'Well, it's just I thought he was going to the cinema, that's all.'

Jo looked straight at her. 'I know, you know.'

Suddenly, Jess felt every embarrassed little nerve in her body beaming out like neon signs through her eyes. 'Know what?'

'And I know you're just not saying it,' she continued, beady-eyed.

'No, I'm not,' Jess snapped.

'Yes, you are.'

'I am not.' She had now gone red.

'He doesn't love me any more, does he?'

'Oh, *right.*' Jess breathed a huge sigh of relief. 'No. I mean, yes. No, what I mean is I'm sure he might.'

'I know it's ridiculous, that it shouldn't matter, that I should just forget about him and move on, but I can't. I just can't.' She started kicking the wall, at which point Colin, who had been asleep next door, kicked back.

'You just need to meet someone new,' Jess soothed, unable to stop her mind floating back to Sam, 'and fall in love with *them.*'

Jo looked as if she'd just been asked to gun down half of

she'd spotted him, getting anxious she mightn't recognise him or that he'd be some unappealing beer-bellied chain-smoker. But she knew immediately it was him. He had BBC written all over him. He also had a body to die for. This was better than anything she could have imagined.

'Hi,' he said throatily, smiling tentatively at her outstretched hand. He looked faintly as if he knew her.

'*Barking Mad*?' she prompted, grinning expectantly.

'I hope not.' He laughed.

'No, I mean me. The dog. Well, not me,' she giggled, 'I'm not the dog. Obviously.'

'I . . . er . . . I'm sorry?'

'It's Jess,' she said, waiting excitedly for him to make the connection. Then, throwing open her arms like a game-show host, 'Dah-dah!'

'I don't . . . I . . . um, I think . . . wrong bloke.'

The evening headed off on a somewhat downward spiral after that. The right bloke, when he eventually appeared, was the kind of person no one ever picked for their rounders team: he was small, rotund and neckless, and gave the impression that breathing did not come naturally. After plying her with a gigantic goblet of Chardonnay, he launched into explaining how misunderstood he was as a writer, finding it necessary to emphasise his point by caressing her left hand.

It took a further bottle and a half, however, before Jess reached the enlightened discovery that, while her own mission for the evening had been to make inroads into screenwriting, the BBC and ultimately Hollywood, his had been to make inroads into her. In one of his less steady exits to the gents', therefore, she seized her opportunity and fled.

Sam might not be Ben Affleck, she reflected, once she'd made it to the sanctuary of a black cab, but he could have been a hell of a lot worse. Just before passing out, she made a determined promise to be more positive about him in the future.

Clapham. 'I don't want to meet anyone new!' She kicked again. 'I want to meet Max. I want to fall in love with Max.'

Jess stared despondently at the floor. Reasoning with Jo was as possible as having an interesting conversation with Colin.

'You don't understand, babes,' Jo sniffed, 'you can't control love. You can't dictate its terms. *It* dictates to *you*.' She paused and let out an anguished sigh, then added, 'Only I didn't know that,' and threw herself across the bed.

'I see,' Jess murmured, wondering whether Jo wasn't right. It certainly felt like outside forces were controlling her feelings for Sam: it was just difficult to tell whether those feelings were related to love or to the prospect of an exciting alternative to James.

'D'you know what the worst thing is?' she sobbed, smearing her nose on her sleeve.

'That you've got mascara on your shirt?' Jess hazarded.

'That it's all my fault. If I hadn't dumped him in the first place we'd probably be . . . be . . . be married!'

Jess gave up, reached over and engulfed her in a big, motherly hug. She had no idea that Jo had been living with such regret. If ever there was an argument for hanging on to James, she decided, this was it.

Over and Out

Doubting the foundations of my relationship with Sam
No longer able to hide under our safe little duvet
 of mystique and exciting secrecy
Sophie's discovered a condom

Dear Alex,

You'd think we were living in wartime Britain and had just been caught with a stash of powdered banana – or whatever it was they considered a luxury. Everyone has gone mad. Totally berserk.

It started two hours ago when I got home perfectly jolly to find Sophie sitting at the kitchen table with a face like a grapefruit. This is not uncommon. Sophie, I have discovered, will go into strops over the most bizarre things, like if someone puts her mayonnaise back in the wrong compartment of the fridge or there is a curly pube in the bath. She doesn't shout or anything, just goes all silent and broody, which is much more annoying because she will refuse to utter a single word until you have asked at least twenty times what is wrong. And even then you have to suggest what it might be, giving her several other hitherto unthought-of reasons to be pissed off.

Richard's marvellous with her, teasing it out with such ease you wonder if he isn't wasted in accountancy. He says, in a stoic, caring-saint manner, that it is just her plea for attention, a hangover from a childhood spent being overshadowed by a precocious elder sister.

I find this kind of reasoning unbelievably irritating. It's like those people who get away with being boring mutes at parties under the guise of being 'shy', which allows them to stand aloofly sipping wine looking alluringly mysterious while you make a prat

No longer with James
Technically no longer with James
To be honest – still with James

Dear Alex,
     I often think life would have been a whole lot easier if I had
just been born a lesbian. I would probably be shacked up by now
in a meaningful relationship with someone who really understands
me.
     Sophie says I should relax, that life is only as complicated as
you make it, which is fine if your boyfriend thinks you're the next
best thing to non-iron shirts, but irrelevant if he is a dysfunctional
lunatic. James, after asking me round here, buttering me up with
a lovely meal then taking me to bed and performing all kinds of
extra-curricular activities, has just announced he thinks we should
have a trial separation.
     What the hell is going on? One minute he is chucking me, the
next he cannot be without me, then he is screaming blue murder
at me and now? Now he is treating me like a month's free trial
no-obligation-to-buy electrolysis home-kit from the back of Marie-
Claire.
     The thing is, to tell you the truth, while obviously I shouldn't
let him steer the relationship in any direction he desires, this trial
thing seems to be having quite a favourable effect. We haven't offi-
cially started it yet, as it makes more sense for me to stay here
tonight, but since it was conceived – two hours and forty minutes
ago – we have been laughing, chatting, joking, hugging and having,
I must say, incredibly amazing sex.
     But now he has gone to get cigarettes and I'm not sure what
is happening. We are getting on extremely well but we are also

of yourself, knocking back booze and uttering whatever garbage comes into your head just to keep alive a conversation they are not expected to, and cannot be in the slightest bit arsed to be part of.

So I decided to ignore her – much the most annoying thing if you are in a mood – and started humming merrily asking about her day and being so chirpy that she was forced to tell me.

She'd found a condom. She hadn't been prying but had just happened to wander into my room, glance casually into my bin, always the first thing one thinks of doing when going into someone else's bedroom, and see it. She knew I'd gone to bed alone and that she'd emptied the bins the day before so it had to have got there during the night. This therefore begged the obvious question: was I sleeping with Colin?

For someone who claims almost to have got a first, Sophie can be remarkably thick at times. I didn't know what to be pissed off most about: that she'd been snooping in my bedroom, that she had assumed that what I did in my bedroom was any of her business, or the disturbing – and on reflection, insulting – fact that she thought me capable of having sexual intercourse with Colin.

'No,' I said indignantly, preparing myself for the full explanation, which I was then prevented from delivering by the hugely mistimed arrival of Sam.

And then all hell broke loose.

Sophie, using the part of her brain that had worked such wonders for her finals, put two and two together then collapsed into a chair, mumbling, 'I knew it, I knew it,' which, given what she had just accused me of minutes before, seemed rather untrue. Jo appeared twenty minutes later and started pissing herself laughing, then out of nowhere burst into floods of tears, claiming she was hurt and mortally offended that we hadn't told her before. Colin isn't back yet but is insignificant in most respects anyway. And Sam is so deliriously happy that we finally are a publicly recognised couple that he has gone roller-blading in Regent's Park to celebrate.

The thing is, now that the exciting episode-of-Dynasty drama splitting up. We are not going to see each other for a month but we are going to a dinner party next week. We will not be having any sex but have just done it three times. I am confused.

James says that is why we need rules. I find the whole idea of regulating our relationship in this way unnatural and wrong, as if it is nothing more than a complicated game of Monopoly. But James says all human relationships are constrained by rules and that our relationship is more like Monopoly than I think since I am always owing him money and never win any beauty contests. Hmmm.

Anyway, we have compiled a list, which has proved quite tricky. This is what we've agreed on so far:

We will NOT	We WILL
See each other.	Go to Richard's dinner party together. Go to the New Year's Eve party together (a waste to spend £60 on tickets and not go). Also go to the other drinks party.
Phone each other.	Phone each other if we are feeling miserable, lonely or just want to talk.
Snog or shag anyone, including each other.	Tell the other person if we snog, shag or fancy anyone.

James is adamant that we stick to this, otherwise it will just be chaotic and we will end up back together before the month is out. To be perfectly honest, I can't see what has changed except that he has become a lot nicer. He says that although it may look as if he has died down I realise, with a sinking sense of defeat, that the reason our relationship has been so much fun is because nobody was supposed to know about it. There is nothing more thrilling than having to scuttle around at dead of night just to grab a few stolen moments with your secret lover. But now that it's out in the open it doesn't seem nearly so magical. Apart from a few rants from Sophie about upsetting the 'flat dynamics' (total bollocks and extremely unfair, considering she spends her entire time Velcroed to Richard's hipbone) everyone says they are happy for us. We have not so much been offered the forbidden fruit but been handed it in a gold-rimmed casket with a tag attached, saying, 'Eat me.' So why, I ask you, does it now seem unappealing?

Some of the problem is that I have started thinking about James's poem again. In fact, I am doing more than thinking about it: I have read it so many times that I have memorised it (wish I had possessed this skill for Shakespeare's sonnets). I keep seeing him sitting at his desk staring in a melancholy way out of a rain-spattered window with tears plopping down his cheeks, and can't help feeling that the least I owe him is a reply. This is what I've got so far:

When you left me all alone, I shed a tear for what we shared.
When you left me all alone, I shed a tear for I felt scared.
When you left me all alone, I shed a tear for (something that rhymes with 'ared')
So why do you now tell me, James, that for me only you still care?

Will probably need to think of a more upbeat second verse – after all, I don't want him thinking I'm a suicidal wreck – but I quite like the way I have carried over the crying theme from his poem thereby depicting us as two lovelorn suitors separated by an ocean of tears. Mmm, might use that line, actually. Just going to see if Shakespeare can offer me anything pithy . . .

Crikey. Sorry. I started this letter half a week ago then forgot about it. I keep doing this at the moment. The other day I bought is having his cake and eating it, this is far from the truth as his mind is in torment.

I can't say I've noticed this, although he does seem to be getting ridiculously uptight about what we are now going to call ourselves – the dating lexicon does not have a term for in-a-relationship-but-pretending-not-to-be.

Anyhow, I am not going to obsess about this when I have got much more important things to concentrate on like my career, or at least my job. I'm not too sure whether it is my *job as, strictly speaking, I am replacing someone who is ill. Jo got it for me because she said I was in danger of turning into a very sad person who never got dressed. This is only partly true as sometimes I did put on my jogging bottoms.*

At first I wasn't very keen. That is one of the problems with being unemployed. You moan to the point of tedium about not having a job, then the minute one comes your way you panic and start thinking that maybe you don't want one after all. This feeling was compounded by the fact that Richard *and* Judy *were doing a phone-in on infidelity and I had a trip to the corner shop planned for the afternoon. When I told Jo this she said that was entirely why I needed a job.*

It's with a company called FunFilms – a misnomer if ever I've heard one – and I am filling in for a girl called Belinda, who I am assuming has three heads as I am incapable of doing even a fraction of her workload.

The office, open-plan up millions of stairs, is completely manic, with about ten phones ringing at any one time. It is crammed with long tables swamped with bits of paper and computers, at which terminally stressed people sit shouting obscenities. A large telly programmed only to MTV blares in one corner and a whiny fridge gyrates in another. I think it'd be more relaxing working in a chicken factory.

My first day was hideous, made worse by the fact that when I walked in nobody noticed I was there. I hung around the door feeling like a berk until someone eventually asked me whether I thirty Save the Children Christmas cards – hideous sombre things with bearded men in capes riding horse-drawn carts through bleak landscapes (have absolutely no idea what this has to do with Christmas). I only bought them because they were reduced, which, thinking about it, negates the charitable gesture. Anyway, I'd written a few bland Happy Christmases on some of them, then just ambled away and forgot about them. They're sitting under a pile of junk on my desk, staring up at me like an unfinished essay.

I did, however, manage to finish that poem. Would give you the rest of it, only I was so petrified of Sam finding it that I hid the only copy in such an obscure place that now even I can't find it. I sent the original inside a Christmas card – the only Christmas card I have actually sent. I hate Christmas cards, but I'm still trapped in that school thing where they act as a popularity monitor only, unlike schooldays, without the enthusiasm to send any myself. This is the worst possible combination because it means you get a decreasing number each year, convince yourself it's a result of no longer having any friends and end up, depressed and miserable, idolising the person you were aged eight when, popular, attractive and fun-loving, you got 124.

That's not to say, however, that I didn't love getting your Christmas card. I'm glad everything's going well, despite the hideous money-belt-down-the-train-toilet-hole fiasco. What a pisser – so to speak. Were you actually doing the business when it fell down? And couldn't you have got the train to stop? I guess you've updated my granny's euphemism for peeing, though, but I'm not sure whether 'I'm off to spend a penny' doesn't lose something of its immediacy when it becomes 'I'm off to spend 6000 yuans and 500 quid's worth of traveller's cheques.'

If it's any consolation, I'm having a similarly dismal festive season. Indeed, the only thing of joy to be extracted from any of it is that I have, albeit temporarily, got a job. Jo got it for me after discovering I had spent an entire day plucking my bikini line. It's with a mad production company called FunFilms. I'm not sure what they do but it involves a large amount of running around

*was the courier. When I said I wasn't he shouted, 'Fuck,' and
walked away.*

*Just as I was contemplating the attractive prospect of sneaking
out and catching the last of* Richard and Judy, *a kind man who
I* think *is called Steve rescued me. (I really must find out if that
is his name as I have been there for a week now and it is getting
quite embarrassing. Also he is the only person I feel able to ask for
help and it is becoming increasingly difficult to get his attention
without using his name.)*

*He immediately set me the task of retrieving a whole lot of lost
U-matics for a director whose name I couldn't pronounce. The
trouble was, I didn't know what a U-matic was, nor when they
had got lost, nor really why we needed them back, so the telephone
calls were largely a waste of time. I kept getting terrifying women
from Polygram asking me all sorts of questions to which I didn't
have an answer, but instead of admitting this and thanking them
for their time, I started saying things like 'I don't have that information to hand at the present moment,' and 'Can I get back to
you at a later date regarding this matter?' as if by speaking as
though I was reading from a legal document could disguise my
ignorance. There is nothing worse than trying to pretend you know
something when clearly you don't.*

*By lunchtime I hadn't located a single U-matic, so Steve –
Simon maybe? – suggested I photocopy a 200-page script instead.
Relieved finally to have been given something I could do, I trotted
off to the photocopier which, for some inexplicable reason, had been
placed in the lobby next to the loos.*

*He wanted it all on headed paper, which shouldn't ordinarily
have been a problem but I just couldn't get the stupid machine to
do it. Every time I thought I'd cracked it, the heading, the text or
both would appear upside-down, the opposite way round or back
to front. The more flustered I got the more it kept spitting out the
wrong thing.*

*Eventually I had to ask some bloke who'd passed me three
times on his way to the loo. I'm sure he thought I was completely*

the office with a phone attached to an ear, opening and slamming filing cabinet drawers while repeatedly amending gigantic time-tables on whiteboards and swearing at the fax machine. Someone recently described it as the only office in London where you have to book a day's holiday just to go to the loo. Have a feeling this wasn't entirely a joke.

When Jo told me they did commercials – still no evidence of this, mind you – I imagined myself in little tight pink T-shirts and dungarees slouched around glass offices smoking dope with trendy Bohemian Soho-ites, also in dungarees, complete with Liam Gallagher hair and Mancunian accent. I did not for one second assume I would be the only one who hadn't gone to Eton.

The women – all two of them – are hearty Germaine Greer types, who give the impression they were reading Nietzsche before nursery school, only eat bean salads and never seem to be out of Timberlands, while the men stride around in pastel-coloured shirts open at the neck and say things like 'Bugger' and 'Blast', with the exception of one guy from Jamaica who has a perpetual smile and only ever says, 'Be 'appy, man,' which I am assuming is his attempt at irony since it is about as absurd as me turning up in a kilt and shouting, 'Och, aye, the noo,' at everyone.

I don't seem to have done anything much yet – that being one of the problems with being temporary. No one seems to think you're their responsibility and every time I try to ask if there's anything I can do, which clearly, given that I am the only one who does not look as though they have just stuck their finger in an electric socket, there is, they just stare at me blankly, glance vaguely around the room, then say something idiotic like 'Not unless you can build an edit suite in an hour.'

So I just bumble around trying to look as if I'm doing things and drawing attention to myself only when I do do something, e.g. send a courier off with the wrong package, arrange pick-up cars from the wrong location.

But there's only so long you can go on playing the new-girl card

*thick since everyone knows that photocopying, like stuffing
envelopes and making tea, is something even the most retarded
moron can do. I therefore found myself making feeble allusions to
'the photocopier at university' and 'when I had to photocopy my
thesis' in a pathetic attempt to prove I was not the incompetent
halfwit I seemed to be.*

*Possibly the worst moment of the day came at three thirty
when I realised I hadn't had any lunch. Planning to rush out
and grab a sandwich, I'd just got to the door when a voice
exploded from behind a shelving unit: 'And where do you think
you're going?'*

'To get some lunch,' I squeaked, turning red.

'Lunch, my dear,' he hollered into the room, 'is a luxury.'

*I don't know whether I'm going to be able to stand this. Jo says
the first week of any job is hellish and I should stick at it as it is
better than moping around the house eating muesli with a fork.
I'm not so sure. Anyway, I expect enormously capable Belinda will
return soon and I can go and find something less hernia-inducing
to do, like stuffing envelopes, perhaps.*

*The trouble is, Christmas is coming up and my friends who are
being successful – which is all of them – will want to buy expensive presents to show off this fact. I will feel obliged to compete and
end up tripling my overdraft, wishing I had not been so quick to
run away from any form of paid employment in favour of* Richard
and Judy.

*Thank you, by the way, for the lovely Chinese coin necklace.
Jo says they are selling identical ones for £6.99 in Accessorize,
which, given that you tell me the coin is the Chinese equivalent of
a quarter of a penny, would appear to give the 'margin' element
of the term 'profit margin' an entirely new meaning.*

*And thanks, too, for your advice on the Sam e-mailing dilemma.
I wish it had reached me sooner because I opted for the play-it-
cool-and-don't-respond-for-a-few-days strategy, known to work
such wonders on the phone-call-returning routine. Unfortunately*

before people get pissed off. The first few days, though obviously trau-matic, were at least bearable because no one really expects you to be any good, especially if you're only there as a stopgap. But, then, before you know it you've been there over a week and it no longer becomes acceptable to take three hours to put in a new fax roll.

I keep hoping secretly that the assignment will come to an end and wonderful Belinda – the girl I'm replacing who is supposedly ill but I suspect is just off doing a spot of Christmas shopping – will come back and restore the peace. But then I get haunted by visions of long empty days spent plucking, compounded with the urgent no-money trauma and resolve to stick at it.

Sam's been super. Really fantastic. He lets me moan and moan for ages then says something sweet like, 'They don't deserve you,' or, 'Let's sod the lot of them and run away.' James would never be this nice. He'd sit there with a glazed expression, making me feel as though I was being exceedingly tedious, then interrupt mid-sentence and say, 'If it's that bad just get another job,' thus failing spectacularly to get the point that I do not want *to be offered a sensible solution like this, wishing instead to spend hours on end in a state of unrelenting self-pity with someone who is going to be nothing but wholeheartedly sympathetic. Like Sam.*

Recently, though, he's been getting a bit gaggy and last night told me he loved me. At least, I think *that's what he said. He was stroking my hair at the time and whispered it so softly that I didn't fully catch it, and the trouble with not quite hearing things like this is that you can't then ask them to repeat it because not only does it ruin the moment it also sounds suspiciously as though you're fishing.*

So I lay pretending to be asleep while constructing an intellec-tual Jeremy Paxman-style argument for and against him having said it, followed by a detailed analysis of the repercussions thereof. Caught myself in a less intense moment feeling chuffed that I had so effortlessly earned such an accolade, then remembered, horrified, that it was someone else's feelings we were talking about, not Jo telling me she liked my shoes.

*with e-mail it translates rather literally, with the undesirable result
that he seems to have assumed I didn't get it and took someone
else out instead. Predictably this sent me into a frenzied state of
regret, culminating in a panicked early-morning dash to work to
send the following:*

> *Kate Moss has found a size 6 gap in her diary. Would the
> dinner date still like to squeeze in?*

*Waited excitedly all day for a flirty follow-up, jumping at any
excuse to be near the computers and becoming so obsessed with the
'inbox' icon that when '1 new message' flashed up I thought I was
going to collapse in rapture. But it turned out to be from a Polygram
woman saying she had no idea what I had been talking about
and could someone feed her some sense. And that was it.*

*Sam has mentioned nothing of the incident and now he seems
to have some sort of girlfriend and I feel I have not so much missed
the boat as been left marooned on a desert island. I know it is
unfair as I have a boyfriend – or whatever James wants to call
himself – but I can't help feeling that if Sam really liked me he
would not be interested in anyone else. I've not met her yet but
have already started entertaining images of Claudia Schiffer.
Apparently he met her at that party he invited me to when he
wrote that cute note telling me he liked me and I chose – insanely
as it would now increasingly appear – to go back out with James.
Seemingly she's fancied him ever since, phoning him until he gave
in. I must say I find the idea of bombarding someone into submis-
sion like this mildly abhorrent – war-crimes tribunals have punished
for less.*

*Anyway, he hasn't breathed a word about her to me, so I've
had to resort to snuffling around for details in the manner of a
gutter journalist. In fact, it's a bit like all those celebrity magazines: everyone concurs on the girlfriend bit, but each gives a
slightly different version. I've tried asking Jo but she's so caught
up with the whole getting-Max-back enterprise that she just gives
me vague, distracted answers. There is nothing worse than trying*

Anyway, I suspect he won't say it again. It's a bit like lending someone 50 quid – there's an unspoken agreement that they will return it and until they do you're unlikely to lend them any more. Which reminds me – Jo owes me £34.80 for the electricity bill. I must go and prepare a casual off-hand way of asking her for it without seeming mean and stingy. I hate doing this. Best to get it out of the way now, though, before it becomes too obsolete to mention.

Lots of love,

Jess

xxx

to get information out of someone about a topic in which they clearly have no interest.

Ooh, yippee! James has just come back with fags and toffee fudge ice-cream, with which he is intimating doing naughty things. What fun! I'd better go. Oh, I love being on trial separation – wish we were on it permanently.

Lots of love,

Jess

xxx

Sam
Kiss and Tell

'Um, Jo, I was just wondering, you know that electricity bill
. . . Jo, I'm on the scrounge, you couldn't just . . . Look, Jo,
I know this sounds really petty but do you think you could
possibly . . . Jo, no rush, but do you remember that electricity
bill?'

The following day, putting in a hair-clip: 'Oh, by the way,
Jo, you still owe me for that electricity bill . . . I think you've
forgotten you still owe me . . . Have you forgotten you still
owe me? . . . You've forgotten you still owe me . . .'

Two days later, trying to get to sleep: 'Jo. Electricity bill.
Pay up now, you miser . . . Oi, Jo, you owe me cash . . . Hey,
skinflint, ever going to give me that dosh? . . . Time's up,
dude, give us your money . . . Look, Jo, hand it over . . . FOR
CHRIST'S SAKE, JO, WILL YOU FUCKING GIVE ME THE SODDING
£34.80 FOR THE BLOODY ELECTRICITY BILL!'

One week later: 'Hi, Jo.'
Jess had just got back from work to find her flatmate
stretched out luxuriously on the sofa in a soft pink satin
dressing-gown, her head, swathed in a fluffy towelling turban,
propped up on one hand, and a plate of olives on the cushion
beside her, looking smug, contented and every bit as though
she were the rich wife of a twenty-two-year-old footballer
being paid an absurd sum of money to do an 'At Home'
photo shoot for *Hello!*.

'Hiya, babes. Good day?'
'Not really,' Jess grunted, collapsing into the armchair, then
scanning the room. 'Any mail?'
'Not unless you want Colin.'

'And then we woke up in a pool of melted ice-cream.' Jess laughed, grabbed the empty wine bottle and shook it upside down over her glass.

'Max and I once did that with shaving foam,' Jo said, lighting a fag, 'but it gave me thrush so we changed to yoghurt.'

'I think I might call him,' Jess said, walking over to the fridge, opening it, staring inside it, then closing it again.

'Max?' Jo asked, brightening.

'James.'

'But isn't that against the rules?'

'Fuck it.' Jess gave a roguish smile, picked up the phone and dialled. 'Hi, it's me.'

'Who?' James sounded slightly cross.

'Me. Your girlfriend. Well, not officially your girlfriend,' she laughed, 'but sort of your girlfriend. Your official *non*-girl-friend.' Then, when it started to seem as though he really didn't know who she was, she added, 'It's Jess.'

'Oh.'

'Hi. So. How are you?'

'Look, Jess, I thought we agreed—'

'Yes, I *know*,' she said, chirpily, 'I'm breaking the rules and I'm very naughty but I just wanted to, well . . . wish you a happy Christmas, I suppose.'

'Yes, well, happy Christmas.'

'So. Doing anything special?'

As he began to talk politely about a family trip to Cornwall, Jess wondered why it was that having been officially apart for six and a half days they were now behaving as though they were talking to a petrol-station attendant.

'Actually,' he said, after a pause, 'I've broken a rule too.'

'I'd hesitate to give Colin a gender,' she said, scrabbling around on the newspaper-strewn floor, picking up an un-opened bank statement and staring at it despondently, 'but I suppose he's marginally better-suited to the term than *this*.' She sighed loudly and threw the letter, still unopened, back into the chaos.

'So why was your day so bad, then, babes?'

'When you spend most of it photocopying a bee, yours would be too.'

Jo grinned expectantly. 'And why were you photocopying a bee?'

'Fuck knows. Nobody tells you. They just scream they need an A3 picture of a bee by three o'clock.'

'So what did you do?'

'Nothing for quite a lot of the time. Then panicked, bolted up and down Oxford Street like a lunatic, managed to get hold of a bee-keeping manual in Waterstone's then got back to the office to discover it was a wasp they wanted, after all, not a bee.'

Jo hooted with laughter. She had taken to treating Jess's life as a kind of stand-up comedy routine on permanent stand-by for whenever she fancied a laugh. While trying not to be offended by this, Jess couldn't help wishing for the kind of best-friend set-up she'd seen working so marvellously well in romantic comedies. Here, she noted with envy, the lead woman was blessed with a friend who did not appear to have a job, a partner, a problem of her own or, indeed, any concern in her life other than to cater for, pander to, talk about, listen to and dedicate all her efforts towards the happiness, success and ultimate fulfilment of the life led by her one and only best friend. Jo fitted this description in precisely no capacity at all.

'But by then it was too late,' she continued, 'so I had to try to get the arsing photocopier to enlarge a minuscule photo of some anorexic African bee-thing that *looked* like a wasp,

Jess laughed. 'Oh, good, so we're quits. Which one did you break?'

'Well . . . completely unintentionally,' he said, giving a nervous little laugh, 'the one about snogging.'

It took Jo the remainder of a bottle of whisky to convince Jess that leaning out of the window shouting, 'Wanker', while beneficial for many psychological reasons might not be quite so productive for the more practical ones, in particular the neighbours. They were currently in their bad books, having received a threat only last week because Sophie had decided to Hoover the lounge at midnight. Apparently the guy had come round in his boxer shorts and been cross but rather sexy with it and Jo, eager to see him similarly inadequately dressed again, wanted to make sure that when she did so, it was for reasons unrelated to complaint.

'Wanker!' Jess shouted, hurling herself at the sofa.

'Wanker,' Jo echoed, closing the window.

'Wanker,' a familiar voice suddenly blurted from the doorway. They both looked round to where Sam was standing chuckling and munching on a cheeseburger.

'You know it's rude to talk about me behind my back,' he said, staggering into the kitchen, followed meekly by a shrew-like girl who was nibbling feverishly at a chip.

'Jess, this is Emily, Emily, this is Jess.'

The two girls exchanged feeble smiles – a limp disguise, Jess knew, for the frantic sizing-up operation that was going on behind both of them. A bit like the Thames on a sunny day; they could give the impression of being pleasant and welcoming, but underneath all sorts of nasty things were lurking.

Emily, Jess came to the conclusion, was someone who thought it attractive to dress like her mother. She was wearing a long floral skirt, a shapeless cream jumper of the sort more normally found in home-shopping catalogues, and a pair of sensible court shoes, the replica of which Jess had spent her which was a complete fuck-up anyway because when I managed to get the whole thing on one bit of paper – kept getting half a wing on a separate sheet – some fucker came up and demanded to use the copier urgently, reset the bloody machine and forced me to start all over again.'

Jo was chortling away happily. 'Why didn't you just set the memory button, babes?'

Jess looked at her. There was nothing more infuriating than finding out *after* you had sweated and cursed your way through a technical trauma that the whole hideous nightmare could have been averted by the simple pressing of a button. She decided to ignore this discovery and helped herself to some wine. 'And do you know the most ridiculous thing about it?'

Jo gave an eager little shake of her head in anticipation of a hilarious showdown.

'I thought it mattered that I didn't have the bee photo. There I was with a fucking honours degree and I actually thought it mattered.' She drained the glass melodramatically. 'What the fuck am I doing?'

Jo had moved towards her, sitting upright, looking grave and concerned. Instead of trying to disagree, Jess realised, horrified, that she was, by her funereal silence, *admitting* the job sounded crap. It struck her that an alarmingly large reason why she was working in television at all was that it was a relatively cool thing to tell people about at parties. Stripped of its prestige like this, it seemed rather pointless.

'Drinking my booze by the look of things,' Jo said, searching around for a change of subject and finding it in the remote control and, more especially, another bottle of wine.

It didn't take long, therefore, for the dead-end-job dilemma to become slightly pissed laughing at a man in a docu-soap who'd just got a parking ticket and was trying, as was the universal human tendency in such a predicament, to squirm his way out of it.

childhood trying to avoid. She did, however, have a pretty face and, if it wasn't swathed in the manner of Anne-of-Green-Gables-attending-Sunday-worship, a nice figure. She disliked her straight away.

'Much as we'd like to join you,' Sam slurred, a piece of gherkin lolloping out of the corner of his mouth, 'we're going to bed.' Then he tripped over the bin, pretended to scold it, bumped into the table and stumbled out of the door. Emily, giggling nervously, trooped after him.

Jess sat slumped in the sofa like a very fat person unable to get up. It wasn't bad enough that her semi-boyfriend had just snogged someone else, her only alternative, it would seem, was about to do the same.

'I can't believe that's the same girl who did all that desperate forceful phoning,' she said, trying to encourage Jo to join in with a similar nasty remark. 'She looks as though she'd get a fright if the toast popped up.'

Jo laughed. 'Appearances can be deceptive, babes. She's a lot stronger than you'd think.'

Jess sighed, wondering whether people would say the same about her in her absence. 'I need to phone him.'

Jo looked at her sternly. 'I don't think that's a good idea, babes. You didn't exactly leave things very positively.'

This was a large understatement. Without having given James a chance to explain, she'd told him in no uncertain terms to go fuck himself in a tree, before bursting into tears and slamming down the phone.

Unfortunately, though, she was rarely ever able to leave things be, preferring instead to ruin any chance of salvaging the situation by doing it completely to death. Fuelled by whisky and, more specifically, the knowledge that Sam was no longer available, she convinced herself she could make amends.

'Just be really cool and casual, then,' Jo advised, when it became clear that Jess wasn't going to back down. 'You've got to make out like you don't care.'

'He's practically crying,' Jess hooted.

'He *is* crying,' Jo squealed.

'Oh, look, sweet, he's phoning his girlfriend.'

'Like she's going to be able to get him off,' Jo guffawed. 'Oh, my God, babes.' She'd stopped laughing suddenly and had her hand over her mouth. 'I forgot.' She pushed her front teeth over her lower lip and winced. 'James rang.'

'Oh, really?' Jess said, in a splendidly prepared, composed manner. Jo had a habit of dropping bombshells like this without any warning, and was about as efficient at doing so as Nato air troops. 'What did he want?'

'Don't know, really,' she mumbled. 'Oh, my God, I don't believe it, she's going to give him another one.'

How, Jess thought, could she even begin to be interested in the telly at such a moment of crisis? 'Jo? What did he say?'

'I don't know, babes. I can't remember.'

'Did he say anything about a poem?'

'What poem?' Jo looked at her suspiciously. 'Oh, no, babes. Tell me you didn't write him a poem.'

'Of course I didn't write him a poem.' Jess hoped that Jo would be too entranced with the parking-ticket fiasco to probe further. Luckily, she was.

'Sorry, babes, he didn't really say anything, to tell you the truth. Just said to say happy Christmas and . . .' She stalled, keeping a firm eye on the screen. 'Oh, yeah, if you wanted to call tonight not to bother because he wouldn't be in. She's given him *another* one. I don't believe it.'

Jess gulped. This was the first time he'd phoned since they'd split up. She'd assumed he was dead. Or existing in another world with famous people and the Royal Family. Not out and about doing normal things, being fine, carrying on with life, using the telephone.

'You OK, babes?'

'Me?' Jess said, as if it were perfectly possible that Jo had

'But he knows I do,' she moaned.

'Well, just say you've changed your mind, that you think it's a good idea to see other people.'

'But I don't.'

'And be cheery, like you're having a really fun time without him.'

'But . . . well, isn't that a bit deceitful?'

'Babes,' Jo said, lighting another cigarette and exhaling in a long, slow way as if she were Joan Collins in *Dynasty*, '*he*'s the one being deceitful.'

Just as she was about to pick up the phone Sophie came in and started scuttling round the room, opening all the windows and ostentatiously emptying the coffee mug Jo was using as an ashtray into the bin Sam had left up-ended on the floor. Without her, Jess had often thought, they would all be lying dead from dysentery.

'Is something wrong?' She was writing 'Sophie's' on a tag and tying it round a bunch of organic grapes.

'James is snogging someone else and she wants to call him,' Jo said, stubbing out the butt end of her fag on the side of the table. 'We're planning what she should say.'

'Well, isn't it rather obvious?' Sophie replied, arranging the grapes in the fruit bowl as if they were about to become part of a still-life oil painting. 'You just tell him the truth – that it's making you miserable and unhappy and you don't like it.'

It was hardly surprising, therefore, that the resultant phone call was a disaster:

'Hi, James, it's Jess again.'

'Look, Jess—'

'No, no, I'm just phoning to say that I'm fine. Couldn't be happier, in fact. Having a fantastic time – out every night, parties, hectic, boozy-booze, that sort of thing. You are so right, by the way. It's a fabulous idea for us to see other people, really great – wish I'd thought of it. Well done, you, though, eh? And so . . . yeah.'

been addressing the radiator. 'Fine. Yes. Couldn't care less, to be honest. I'm not going to call him back, though. No point.'

'No, I wouldn't,' Jo advised, still fixating on the telly. 'He probably only did it to gloat about that babe.'

Jess froze. Then lurched in horror as a siren started wailing inside her head, accompanied elsewhere by the urgent need to do diarrhoea. 'What babe?'

Jo turned round and when she saw Jess's face, she immediately looked horrified. 'Oh, God, didn't you . . . Well, I mean it's . . . I don't think . . . umm.'

Jess felt crushed. The thought of James with someone else was bad enough to stomach. Hearing it from someone who'd never met him was altogether vomit-inducing – like getting your finals results from a neighbour, or a pregnancy-test outcome from your brother.

'Jo? What babe?'

'Look, I don't know. Sophie mentioned he was snogging some bimbo but that's all I know. I'm sure it's nothing. Anyway,' she said, in a bright, jolly voice as if she were a primary-school teacher and no one would take him as their partner, 'you've got lovely Sam.'

Just then the front door crashed open and SophienRichard appeared. Sophie was dressed in a dark olive heavy velvet dress with her hair tied back in an insubstantial bun and looked as though she should be wandering around Elizabethan mansions saying things like 'Hark' and 'Alas, thou dost weep'. Richard, meanwhile, had gone for a more contemporary feel with a lurid orange shirt, and a tie that appeared to have copulating dolphins swimming up it. Both of them were pissed.

'Hi, everyone,' they chorused, waltzing unsteadily into the room and depositing themselves on top of each other on the sofa.

'Richard's *very* drunk,' Sophie announced, in the slow, patronising tone that only very drunk people tend to use.

There was a long pause.

'Oh, God, what's the point?' she wailed. 'I'm not cool and casual, I'm miserable, totally miserable. I don't want us to see other people . . . It's horrible . . . I want us to . . . to see each other,' she howled. The rest of the call, such as it was, was engulfed in tears.

A few days later, however, she was in the shower rejoicing. She'd managed to last a whole twenty-four hours without sobbing at the sight of James's Oasis CD, the house was peaceful because everyone but her had left to go home for Christmas – which, due to her chaotic sense of organisation, she was still sorting out – and she'd just received a rather flirty card from Brad MacCormack of milk-duty fame. She had the distinct impression that things were on the up – which was exactly when it happened: a loud, scary, ominous bang.

Heart beating furiously, she switched off the shower and got out, then made her way gingerly across the floor expecting at any moment to come face to face with a masked gunman. Slightly disappointingly, no such terrorist appeared, and by the time she got to her door she was beginning to think she'd made the whole thing up.

And then the horror struck. She had gone into the shower with her bedroom door open. She had come back from the shower with her bedroom door closed. In the meantime, she had left her window wide open and the door's Chubb lock on, because, ironically, she had feared the night-visit of a masked gunman. She had now, cleverly and effectively, locked herself out of her room.

'Shit! Shit! Shit!' she yelled, dripping wet and hurling herself at the door in the way she'd seen accomplished so effortlessly in films. Clearly, though, it wasn't going to achieve the desired result for her.

'Oh, God.' She slumped to the floor and banged her head against the locked door. 'Help.'

Sam

'So's Sophie,' Richard said, giggling.

'Sophie shnot.'

Jess forced out a few fake grins, wondering why other people's lives always seemed so much more fun and sorted than her own. She imagined them in years to come, still blissfully happy together, Sophie hunched up under a little tartan blanket knitting socks, Richard in green wellies and a cap teaching his grandson fly-fishing, all of them around the fireplace sucking Werther's Originals.

'You OK, Jess?' Sophie was looking at her with spirally eyes. 'James was ashking after you.'

Suddenly Jess, who had shown only minimal interest in the conversation so far, sat bolt upright like a startled rabbit. 'James?'

'YOUR EX-BOYFRIEND,' Richard seemed to feel it necessary to shout.

'Thank you, Richard, yes, I do know who he is,' she said, then added, hoping it would be hotly denied, 'I gather he's got a new girlfriend.'

'I don't think she's actually a girlfriend, is she?' Jo interjected tactfully.

'No, she's not ashully a girlfriend,' Sophie repeated.

'Nah. She's not a girlfriend,' Richard confirmed, in a pleasingly dismissive fashion. 'Just some bird he's shagging for a bit.'

Jess tried hard to look as though she didn't care. In the space of an evening James had gone from floating around somewhere in Never-Never Land to thrusting himself upon her, and now, by all accounts, though less metaphorically, upon somebody else as well.

Although she knew she wasn't supposed to be jealous, angry or, indeed, even interested, she felt an alarming mixture of all three. It was one thing to imagine he might be with someone else. It was quite another to *know*.

Morbid fascination forced her to discover that Sophie had

When it became clear that help was not available, she decided that the only solution was to get some clothes from Jo's room and rethink the dilemma when she was warm and dressed. Scurrying across the hallway, she pressed down on the door handle. Nothing. She tried again and pushed. Still nothing. Frantically, she moved to Sophie's door. The same. She tried Sam's and even, in total desperation, Colin's. Every single bugger, in a manner totally out of keeping with the Yuletide spirit of generosity, had bloody well locked their door.

'Jesus,' she wailed, collapsing on the stairs and contemplating Christmas spent alone in her towel.

Then she hit on an idea. Right outside her window was a thin ledge with wrought-iron railings, which an estate agent might have described as a balcony, but which anyone trying to get on to it would realise it was not. It ran right the way across the houses and could be clambered on to, at least if you were Houdini, from the window. That was it, she decided. She would simply pop next door, nip through their window and inch across to hers. Simple.

Thrilled with her ingenious solution, she leapt up and skipped downstairs. It wasn't until she was almost out of the front door, however, that she realised she had overlooked one major problem. She was wearing a towel.

Searching the kitchen, she considered oven-gloves and tea-towels, and when that proved insubstantial wandered through to the lounge where, instead of the usual selection of drying underpants and discarded clothing, there was nothing but a single dust-covered sock down the back of one of the radiators.

In desperation she thought about wrapping the U-shaped mat from the base of the toilet around her neck and pretending it was a scarf, but it smelt strongly of urine and looked exactly like the U-shaped mat from the base of the toilet. In the end, she decided, she would look marginally less mad in the towel.

not met the girl, which was, she was learning, a severe tragedy, since it meant relying on Richard for the kind of information that, being a bloke, he was useless at providing.

'Long – Sophie's long, or long as in down to the shoulders?' she said, doing a sawing motion against her left shoulder.

Richard turned round and squinted at his girlfriend. 'I think it's short.'

'So she's got *short* hair,' Jess confirmed, feeling as though she was getting somewhere.

'Yes,' he said emphatically, then looked back at Sophie and added, 'Actually, come to think of it, it might just have been up.'

She decided to try a different tack. 'OK. Can you think of someone she looks like who we all might know?'

Richard looked blank.

'One of our friends perhaps? Or someone from the telly?'

Richard still looked blank, then contemplative, then vague, bored, then suddenly enlightened, almost aroused. 'Ulrika Jonsson,' he said, and flashed an enormous grin.

By the time Jess had assembled the kind of e-fit image that would have had the entire male population of the nation's police force clambering over their truncheons to arrest, she realised that whatever this girl's shortcomings, eager though she was to know, Richard was not going to be the one to expound on them. There seemed little point in carrying on. 'I'm off to bed, guys.'

'Night,' the merry couple cooed.

'Night,' Jo echoed.

'Night,' she managed.

Then, just as she had got to the door, congratulating herself on remaining so buoyant in the face of such adversity, Jo shouted in alarm, 'Oh, my God, babes. I forgot.'

She spun round in horror. Not again. She'd had enough bombshells for one day.

'I still owe you for that electricity bill, don't I?'

'I'm terribly sorry to bother you,' she began, to a fresh-faced public-schoolboy figure who, she decided somewhat excitedly, must be the boxer-shorts man of the Hoovering complaint. He was rather attractive, she noticed, even though he was wearing a pink shirt and corduroy trousers the same colour as the walls of a public toilet. 'This is all terribly embarrassing but, you see, I was having a shower and, well, I'd left my bedroom window open and stupidly hadn't thought the wind would . . .' She looked up mid-sentence to find the attractive man grinning.

'Would make it rather cold, I should imagine,' he said.

She gave a coquettish giggle. 'Yes, well, no, I wasn't having the shower actually *in* my bedroom but . . . anyway,' she continued, realising from his expression that he had never assumed she was, 'I've locked myself out and was wondering whether I could climb through your bedroom window so that I can walk along and into mine – if you see what I mean,' she added, giving a little isn't-this-just-so-ridiculous laugh. Clearly he thought she was trying to seduce him.

Two minutes later, though, she practically had.

'Only legs as svelte as those would get through that gap,' he said, chivalrously, passing her stubbly ankle through the window, while she tried simultaneously not to land in a pot-plant, look unattractively contorted or flash unnecessary bits of calf, crotch or cleavage as she did so.

'Thank you ever so much,' she gushed, when she made it.

'It's been a pleasure,' he said, with a flirtatious laugh. 'We must do it again.'

'Only next time I might put on a few more clothes.' She giggled, looked down at the towel and discovered to her horror that she'd been standing with her left nipple on full display.

'Not too many, I hope,' he said, gesturing to the disappearing breast.

By the time she'd scurried, giggling and frozen, across the precipice and in through her own bedroom window, the seed

Sam

Miracles, she reflected, as she left the room and climbed the stairs, if small ones, did occasionally happen. She threw herself on to the bed and fell asleep, hoping a few more might come her way.

of a satisfying idea had sprouted. Pulling on some clothes she marched to the telephone.

'James, Tobes and Rich aren't in at the moment. Leave us a message and we'll get back to you. Cheers.'

'Hi, James. Jess here. Just to say not to worry about breaking the rules. I'm seeing someone myself at the moment. Nothing serious – my next-door neighbour, would you believe? But, like you say, it's healthy for us to see other people. Hope you're well – and oh, yeah, happy Christmas.'

Sam

New Year's Eve

Wondering why nothing seems to go my way
Sitting on a train going painstakingly slowly out
of my way
Composing an angry letter to Richard Branson
  that I will spend the next twenty-four hours
  furiously believing I will actually write, then
  not think about again
Which is probably precisely why Virgin trains can
  get away with running two and a half hours
  behind schedule

Dear Alex,

  I feel as though I've been on this train since I was four. I am supposed to be at a New Year's Eve party·in London in less than five hours' time and am sitting staring out at a field of cows somewhere on the outskirts of Edinburgh.

  Everyone around me has started doing loud, dramatic sighs, looking at their watches then glaring stormily out of the window, with the exception of a horsy-faced woman to my left, who finds it necessary to bleat a running commentary on our tortoise-progress into her phone – 'Frightful shambles . . . Oh, some God-forsaken Scottish wasteland . . . No, I quite agree . . . Fearfully inefficient.' A group of terrifying teenage boys with earrings are slouched in the aisle across from me drinking Special Brew and playing a stereo in need of fresh batteries, a large woman with eight children all called Kylie is restricting access to the toilets – one of which is blocked with green paper hand-towel things, the other swilling with urine – and a man doing lots of desperate sweating is ambushing anyone brave enough to enter our carriage in a uniform. To top it all, no one seems interested in telling us

Hideous Christmas
Hideous New Year
Hideous realisation they are both now over and I
    have nothing to look forward to except three
    months of sleet and wearing five jumpers

Dear Alex,

   *Erghhh. The thought of going to work tomorrow is making me
feel almost suicidal. It's that horrible back-to-school feeling that
makes you think you ought to be looking out a clean shirt and
sharpening all your HB pencils.*

   *I always forget this about holidays. They are really, when you
think about it, just a disguised form of mental torture, building
you up until you are happy and relaxed then shattering it all on
the last day, which is so contaminated with feelings of doom and
misery as to make the whole thing utterly pointless, verging on evil.
A bit like alcohol and a hangover, I suppose – the latter is so
horrific it annihilates any enjoyment you might have had of the
former.*

   *I think the problem with Christmas in particular, though, is
that it is so closely followed by New Year, creating a kind of wine-
sodden oasis in the middle of an otherwise bleak and dismal desert,
i.e. the rest of the year. Surely if Jesus was such a self-sacrificial
miracle worker he could have engineered it so that he was born in
July, thus allowing for a big party half-way through the year as
well as at the end of it, rather than meanly cramming both into
the same week.*

   *Mind you, I can see His point. A hot sunny Christmas would
be all wrong. We'd become like the Ozzies, singing carols around
the barbie, glugging chilled mulled wine from the cool box and*

what's going on unless it's taking place in the buffet car.

I know I should be using this opportunity to write my Christmas thank-yous but the thought of it is making me feel ill – strings of insincere superlatives about ceramic soap dishes. It's the same every year. If I could just get myself motivated I'd get them all done on Boxing Day rather than putting them off until they become an impossibly colossal chore that I go to ridiculous lengths to avoid. (It's startling how normally tedious things like washing-up or Songs of Praise Christmas Special *suddenly become joyous activities when you are supposed to be doing something else.)*

The stupid thing about it all is that they only take about six minutes to do, especially Christmas ones where you just write your standard 'Thank you for the lovely ——. It is the prettiest —— I have ever seen. It will come in very useful when I ——.' then copy it out eighteen times using sausagy primary-school-teacher handwriting so that it looks as though you've written more.

Instead, all I have done is stare blankly out of the window trying intermittently to read my book, which is one of those ones with lots of complicated foreign names that I find a bit of a fag to follow.

In fact, I don't seem to have done anything at all, come to think of it. But that's the thing with travelling. It's one of those unexplained mysteries that you can spend an entire journey just sitting, sleeping, eating and staring, yet arrive at your destination so exhausted that it's all you can do not to collapse on the platform in a comatose heap.

I think I'm still recovering from Christmas. It's a bit like travelling too in many ways – trundling unsteadily from sofa to kitchen to toilet back to sofa again, staring mindlessly at the telly, dozing off at odd times in the middle of the day and stuffing all sorts of sugar-coated rubbish into your mouth out of boredom rather than anything touching on genuine need.

It was the usual hideous family gathering with the addition of my dad's aunt, who is fat, bossy and says things like 'Of course, in my day we didn't have: fancy tree decorations/Christmas hanging baubles off the magnolia. It would totally destroy the essence of Christmas, which is, after all, about fluffy snowmen, twinkly fairy-lights, and consuming vast quantities of food in a centrally heated house.

Anyway, I don't know where I get the idea that New Year's Eve is a 'big party': from as far back as I can remember it has been a miserable experience. Every year is exactly the same: everyone starts talking about it some time in August when I am still at the stage of trying to find someone to come on a last-minute holiday with me. I blithely assume the event will sort itself out of its own accord and that a splendid invitation to a ball or country-manor dinner dance will plop through my letterbox. I therefore cease to give the matter another thought and take it for granted that I will spend the evening eating, drinking, laughing, dancing and slurring an approximation of 'Auld Lang Syne' with 150 friends.

But then December arrives and my splendid invitation has not arrived and New Year's Eve has become this colossal social extravaganza to which everyone but me is invited. I get panicky, phoning up anybody I can think of while trying to convince myself that just because everyone else will be getting sloshed at a wild party doesn't mean I have to, and that just as good a time, if not better, can be had sipping sherry with my parents in front of the telly in the living room.

Unfortunately, though, my desperation for social inclusion at any cost always quashes any plans to be mature and individual, and before I know it I am spending another New Year's Eve getting increasingly sober trooping round overcrowded pubs trying to get a drink.

I really thought this year was going to be different, though. For once I did not feel like a leper or social outcast but instead a rather cool person, having managed to get all my flatmates (except Jo, who had already said yes to six other offers) to buy tickets for the party I was going to – never an easy task because instead of being one of those confident people who are natural social leaders, I go all meek and timid and assume no one will crackers/presents, we just: made them from seaweed/played tug-o'-war with old socks/packed everything we owned into a thimble, put on our hair-shirts and went to live in a concentration camp for a fortnight.'

In stark contrast my brother, who has only ever known the privileges of a Coca-Cola culture, felt obliged perpetually to remind us that he has joined the Anti-Consumerism Club at school, which seems to entail drinking filtered rainwater, chucking out a selection of perfectly good clothes and standing every Saturday morning outside M&S with a banner saying, 'Do you really need it?'

As part of this caring, sharing, do-gooding, self-sacrificial we'll-wear-white-socks-sandals-and-no-deodorant policy, he informed us that he would not be buying a single Christmas present for anyone this year, then proceeded to spend the day hogging the telly with his – a spanking new up-to-the-minute Nintendo Playstation.

In fact, the whole day was doomed from the start when we woke to find that the dog had knocked over the tree. It was lying felled in the middle of the living-room floor alongside a sickly looking Poppy who, having eaten all the edible Santas, some gold tinsel, a couple of plastic baubles, and made a commendable start on a selection of the more interesting-smelling presents, had then thrown up the whole lot on the antique rug.

Naturally this caused everyone to flap around arguing about the best way to get vomit stains out of Persian goat's wool, with the exception of Dad who, after opening his presents and telling us all to lighten up and enjoy the festive spirit, went into a furious rage because someone had thrown out, along with the wrapping paper and 15 quid's worth of Boots vouchers, the instructions to his automatic Point'n'Shoot camera.

I tried hard this year, but I just don't know what gets into me when I go home. I seem to revert to being a stroppy, out-of-control, foul-mouthed teenager slamming doors, going into hour-long sulks and refusing to tell anyone – because to tell you the truth I don't know myself – what on earth is wrong with me.

want to come, apologising for the thing before it's even happened and spending the duration of it feeling nerve-rackingly responsible for anyone kind enough to have joined me, asking them every five minutes whether they're having a crap time and whether or not they wouldn't rather, all things considered, just go home.

Typically, of course, it was me who ended up having the crap time. I should have predicted it. If there is one thing I learnt at university it is that the success of a social occasion is directly disproportionate to the amount of time spent preparing for it. Thus the fact that I shelled out a £30 supplement to come back from Inverness early, strategically booked a haircut to allow a week's growth in case of emergency and had my outfit, down to the colour of nail varnish, planned several weeks in advance should have told me the evening wasn't going to be a winner.

Indeed, this became obvious fairly near the beginning – at the moment I walked in. Everyone, as far as the eye could stretch, was in jeans.

I froze, unable to speak, imploding with humiliation, feeling as though I had just walked on to the Trisha *show with the accompanying caption, 'Jess says she will do anything for attention.' I was wearing a full-length sequin-embroidered gold silk dress. In situations like these I know it is best simply to smile and make out it was always your intention to wear something a little special, but instead I headed straight for the nearest loos where I burst into tears and sat on the exposed rim of the toilet seat. I spent the rest of the evening trying to hide inside one of Sophie's cardigans with a circle of dried urine imprinted on my backside.*

I have to say, I hold James responsible for this sartorial misjudgement. He had all the tickets, having bought them on his never-in-use-when-we-go-shopping credit card, and was useless when I asked him what I should wear. 'Whatever,' he said vaguely. Then, when pushed, he added, 'Something nice.'

I suppose I was willing him to say the dress because, despite living in what purports to be the most exciting city in the world, I never seem to have an opportunity to get it out of my wardrobe.

Sam

I must say, though, I did a sterling job in disguising my disappointment at the discovery that Dad's aunt, who only ever seems to give presents she would like to receive herself, had given me three pairs of sensible pants and an electric juicer. I have never in my life come across a more useless piece of machinery. Contrary to the accompanying images of a jolly woman tossing in a couple of oranges, pressing a button and receiving, three seconds later, a nice cool glass of Robinson's fruit and barley drink, I toiled with six apples, eleven bananas and an orchard of satsumas, to discover, after a horrible rumbling noise, it had just spat out something that looked suspiciously like a malnourished person's attempt at a sperm sample.

Oh, Christ. The men across from me have started swapping train-delay stories, as if, when you are stuck in a potentially dire situation that is entirely out of your control, you want to hear horrifying tales of eighteen hours in bus depots and 4 a.m. stop-overs in Grimsby.

What on earth makes them do this? Is it that they assume you want to be prepared for what may lie in store ahead of you? Or do they think it will somehow make you feel better to know that there exists a fate worse than spending New Year's Eve trapped four hundred miles from London in a carriage full of lunatics?

I hope we get there. I've invested so many fantasies in this evening – me looking ravishing, James collapsing with desire, me doing joyful laughing, James pleading to take me back, me calmly explaining I have a new boyfriend now, James committing suicide – that I think I'll combust with unfulfilled nervous anticipation if we don't.

At least, I hope James will be there otherwise it will be a fruitless waste of time, not to mention exceedingly pissing off as I have had to turn down a juicy party offer of Jo's to go to this – which, I am in the process of discovering, is becoming a common theme in my life. I seem to exist in a total party-vacuum for months and then two will come crashing along together causing a furious decision-making agony. After constructing lengthy balance sheets

I was going to check this with Sophie and Jo beforehand but it would have meant phoning them over Christmas specially, thus appearing both excited and keen, which would not have been good because everyone knows that it is uncool to make a big deal of a party.

Anyway, as I had clearly done precisely that, I decided, after an extensive but futile search for anyone I knew, to hide in the corner and drink my £60 worth of alcohol alone. But just as I had found a free plastic chair, sat down and started staring out into the room pretending I was enjoying watching everyone else have fun, I felt a tap on my shoulder. 'It's Jess, isn't it?' a sweet, kind voice said. I looked round to discover the horribly unwelcome sight of Zadia. She was six times more attractive than I remembered.

Although I would rather have remained in the corner in my ball dress, glugging wine like a frenzied alcoholic, she insisted on dragging me over to join the 'others'. They transpired to be an unattractive male friend of hers called Stew who, despite fancying the pants off her and clearly standing no hope in hell of achieving this, seemed more than content with, if not slightly oblivious to, his role as her personal ego masseur, and, to my sheer and utter horror, James.

The idea that he had been there all along and failed to notice me was a punch in the stomach. The idea that this was because he was too busy flirting with Zadia was several rounds with Mike Tyson.

I smiled insipidly and began jigging self-consciously on the side-lines, fighting back an overwhelming desire for the overhead lighting unit to collapse on top of an insanely confident Zadia and a similarly powerful yet clearly inappropriate one to throw myself on top of an uncannily sexy James. Instead I went to look for Sam under the pretext of getting a drink. He has a way of making me feel special that James, after a year and a half, still hasn't mastered. But after wandering round the place several times, looking increasingly as though I had no friends, I gave up and was forced to join in my head, either I plump for one option, arrive and immediately realise I should have gone for the other, or – and this is the more common scenario – I get so desperate and plagued by the missing-out syndrome that I say yes to both, decide it is perfectly possible to split the evening in two and make mad plans to flee across London in the middle of the night. This is always a disaster. I spend the first party unable to relax and worrying that I should be leaving for the second party, then when I get to the second party I have missed the best bit and everyone else is going home.

Anyway, I'm sure tonight won't be nearly as traumatic. To be honest, I'm more concerned about what Sam is going to wear than anything else. He's threatening to put on his hideous black shirt and matching crocodile shoes, which he seems to think make him look attractive and look so tragically unattractive it defies belief. I keep trying gently to coax him into something different, saying things like 'What about that lovely beige jumper?' or 'You could always wear those nice boots, of course,' as if it is just something that's popped into my head, rather than something I have been obsessing about for days.

I know it's stupid, that it shouldn't matter if he looks like a middle-aged reptile, that I shouldn't give an arse what anyone else thinks, but that's entirely it. I am so undecided myself that other people's opinions are everything. I'm not used to this. I was so pathetically besotted with James that I never considered that anyone else might not be. But that's the thing with really wanting something – you just assume everyone else does too.

The thing is, I keep thinking that if Sam and I could just get on with it inside a hermetically sealed container it would be fine. When it is just the two of us I start to believe I do fancy him, that I am falling in love, that we are going to get married, buy a semi-detached and have little squidgy babies called Jack and Rosie. And then we go out and there are other people and they are accepting us as a couple and I want to go round shouting, 'No, no, please don't accept us. Please don't think I'm 100 per cent certain about this. I agree with you. I also think he is quite ugly/too *the warped love triangle on the dance floor, having to make that awkward transition from walking to dancing, which is embarrassing enough at the best of times without the added set-back of looking like a gigantic pumpkin.*

Then half an hour later I was standing in the queue to the ladies', relieved to have escaped what had degenerated into a kind of vicious competition with Zadia and me jostling for James's attention, as if he were a Swaziland king looking for a wife and we were young girls in straw skirts and brightly coloured necklaces hoping to be the one, when a dishevelled and bleary-eyed James appeared.

'Jesh,' he slurred, while everyone in the toilet ran around shrieking, 'It's a man, it's a man,' like something out of a Jane Austen novel, 'I've been shnogging Zadia.' Then, without any hint of remorse, shame or sense of wrongdoing, he embarked on trying to do the same thing to me.

Of course, now I realise it was a stupid, stupid thing to kiss him back. I'm positive I only did it because I was feeling insecure about the dress, which was pointless, because a tiny snog in a toilet is hardly compensation for an entire evening looking like a prat. Anyway, I am just going to forget it ever happened, be mature and sensible and ignore James for a very long – oooh, that's the phone. I wonder if it's him? I'll just check and go to the loo . . .

Erghh. It was Emily asking for 'Sammy' in a cute childlike voice. I cannot stand the idea of them having a cosy, happy relationship on top of everything else. And, to finish things off, there was no loo paper.

Oh, God, my stomach has just done an involuntary lurch at the sight of my alarm clock. I have to be at work in less than nine hours' time. I keep catching myself wishing for ever more drastic scenarios to prevent me from going in at all – e.g. freak flood, all computers stolen, suspect bomb peeking out of rubbish bin at the end of the street. Surely it's not normal to see one's career in terms of strategies of avoidance?

The thing is, I know I would be fine if it wasn't so frantic. It's gangly/is currently wearing disgusting crocodile shoes.' But, of course, the minute someone insinuates something even mildly nega-tive, I go on the defensive, prattling on about just how wonderful I think he is.

The ridiculous thing about it all is that no one gives a shit. I mean, if I meet someone's boyfriend I don't suddenly think, Shame, if he'd just worn a pair of chinos . . . or, Hmmm, his bottom lip sticks out a bit too far. You just acknowledge they're someone's boyfriend and get on with it. Which is what I am now going to do.

Oh, tedium – my Christmas thank-yous. I think I'll just stare vacantly for a bit then get down to them . . . Wish the Tannoy would shut up, though. It keeps clicking on and everyone looks eagerly up at the ceiling – peculiar logic: you will hear better if you actually look at the sound – then a Glaswegian bloke, who has clearly only recently learnt to read, starts listing what's on offer in the buffette car with so little attempt at enticement you'd rather be eating the six-year-old ingrained chewing-gum remains on your seat-cover. Right. Thank-you letters. Hope you had a nice Christmas – or whatever it is they do in China.

Lots of love,
Jess
xxx

PS For crying out loud! The train has now ground to a halt and an announcement has just been made, and this is not a joke: 'Ladies and gentlemen, on behalf of Virgin Trains I would like to apolo-gise for the delay in your journey today. We will be on our way as soon as we can locate a driver' – which begs the rather obvious question: HOW THE HELL HAVE WE GOT THIS FAR? I am going to get drunk. One thing's for sure, I'm never going to make it to the party now.

like working on the ward of ER without the excitement of Dr Ross walking past. I still haven't a clue what I should be doing most of the time, which is fine if I can just hide in the corner pretending to do important things with bits of paper, but terrifying the minute anyone asks me to do something, which happens quite a lot with as many as six people shouting orders at me at any one time.

I live in constant fear of the phone. It rings every second with people I have no recollection of having phoned who claim to be returning my call. After stalling them with hold buttons and imaginary 'other callers', I find myself thrown into a petrifying guessing game, which has me bumbling around grappling for clues as to why I might have called until I resort to the embarrassing and cripplingly unprofessional measure of asking them.

Recently I have gone one step further than this – picking up the phone and forgetting who I am calling, as happened the other day when I tried to order fifteen rolls of fax paper from the British Film Council.

Oh, God – I simply cannot cope with the thought of any of this. I am going to have a beer. Everything is always so much better with alcohol inside you.

Lots of love,

Jess

xxx

Who's Been Sleeping in Jo's Bed?

'Yes, you are,' Sophie said insistently. 'Of course you are.'

She was pointing at something that looked a bit like a large radish and claiming, convincingly, that it was Jess. It was the third photo from the New Year's Eve party that Jess had no recollection of having posed for.

'Well, why am I wearing that revolting pink thing, then?' she protested, peering at a vast piece of cerise material forming the body of the radish.

Sophie looked hurt. 'Don't you remember? You were upset and sat on the toilet in your dress, only the seat was up and you got a wet circle on your . . . behind,' she whispered. Sophie used euphemisms for most parts of the anatomy.

Jess looked blank.

'So I lent you that . . . revolting pink thing,' she said, pointing to her treasured cardigan, 'to cover up. Remember?'

Jess wasn't sure she did. Being drunk and having the evening pieced together for you by someone else was a bit like being reminded about something you'd done when you were two. She *felt* she remembered it, but couldn't be 100 per cent certain how much was genuine memory and how much an assembled collage of photos and repeated accounts strung together with a large dose of imagination.

'Oh, my *God*!' Jo and Sophie had started shrieking and pointing frantically at a misfit photo that had appeared in the middle of the pack, clearly unrelated to any of the others because it had been taken six months previously, the last time Sophie had remembered to use her camera.

'Look at my *hair*,' Jo squealed.

'Look at mine,' Sophie protested.

'Look at mine,' Richard echoed, rather pointlessly, Jess

Who's Been Sleeping in Jo's Bed?

Never drinking again
Really mean it this time
From now on I'm going to force myself to drink
  water not just when I am hung-over and it
  tastes delicious but at all other times when it is
  bland and boring

Dear Alex,
  I wish I could empty the contents of my head into the gutter
and start all over again. I could almost cope with feeling as if a
mangled cat had been deposited inside my body, if last night had
been at all worth it. But it wasn't. It was one of those horror nights
that are so dire you think that by the law of averages something
amazing must be about to happen, so you take the gamble, miss
the last tube home and stick around. But it just gets even more
dire and you end up sloshed and exhausted at two in the morning
forking out a fortune for a taxi you wouldn't have needed if you'd
just left at twenty past eleven when you first wanted to.
  Added to this run-of-the-mill catastrophe was that I managed
to lose my wallet, find it again and in the meantime end up in
bed with someone who wears a gold medallion. Eghh, and the worst
thing of all is that he's still here. In my bed looking all ugly –
which, strangely enough, I don't remember him looking last
night.
  I don't know how all this happened. It was one of those drunk
things where one minute you are with a whole group of people and
the next you are romping around on the sofa fumbling with belt
buckles.
  I'd forgotten how cringeful the whole undressing thing is when
you're with someone new. It's murderous enough trying to make

realised, since not only did Richard not have any hair, but they all seemed to be conforming to the universal human condition that, when faced with a group photo, you search immediately and only for yourself.

She picked up a stray shot taken before the unfortunate swaddling in Sophie's Monsoon monstrosity and admired it secretly. It was rare to find a photo of herself she didn't instantly want to deny the existence of, or alternatively put into a photo album, that being, in her experience, the safest way of all to ensure no one ever saw it. She continued to glance sneakily at it, as if it were a mirror in a public place, wondering how to ask Sophie for a copy without having to admit why.

'Wow, she's a bit of a babe, who's she?' Jo had been shuffling through the photos as though they were playing-cards and had just flicked one across the table with the dexterity of a croupier.

Jess thought for a fleeting second it was her she was referring to, and looked up, grinning expectantly, until a familiar pretty face came spinning through the air towards her. Zadia.

'Fuck-face,' she said flatly, picking up the picture and glowering at the human version of the figurines that people with thick-pile carpets and frosted-glass doors display on mantelpieces.

'Worth a squirt,' Sam said, leering over.

'Let's see,' Richard said, suddenly eager.

'Sam!' Jess scolded. 'That is a disgusting thing to say about a woman.' She was appalled, but more especially jealous. While it was acceptable for *her* to cavort around fancying and flirting with whomever she felt like, it was forbidden, verging on criminal, for Sam to suggest that anyone other than her and, at a push, his sister could be in the slightest bit attractive.

'Anyway, she's really quite thick when you talk to her,' she lied, realising the minute she said it that this concern was far from their minds.

struggling out of a pair of trousers and tugging a tight top over your head look sexy without having to remember to suck in your stomach and refrain from showing excess pubic hair in the process. And he kept insisting on whispering things to me every five minutes, as if we were not two unattractive drunkards, bare bums to the ceiling, rest of limbs cricked at peculiar angles on a sofa with crusting food-stains, but two lithe beauties surrounded by billowing dry ice on a film set in Malibu.

The problem was, I was totally unprepared for the evening – i.e. spiky legs and underarms, disgusting, spotty, unwashed body, greasy hair – because the last thing in the world I expected to do was pull. It's always the bloody same. I attend diligently to the maintenance of my body then let go for a fraction of a second and what happens? It sprouts all over the place, looks utterly revolting and I end up with a man – or approximation of – in my bed.

It didn't seem to put him off, though. Mind you, I don't think anything short of a tornado would have done that. He was like a dog with a bone – in more ways than one – and seemed to work on the basis of first come, first served, which, not surprisingly, turned out to be him.

Anyway, then a really exciting thing happened. I'd been passed out for about an hour when I woke up with a mouth so dry and stuck together it did not so much feel as though I had dehydrated myself with alcohol as swallowed a tub of peanut butter. I dragged myself, still wearing half a bra and one sock, down to the kitchen for some water and was just scrabbling around in the sink for a glass when I heard a scuffling noise behind me on the sofa, followed by a sharp intake of breath, a little snigger and the unmistakably cheeky voice of Sam calling 'Cute butt!'

I know the cool thing would have been to turn round slowly and sexily, strut confidently hands-on-hips towards him, take a long, seductive sip of water and say something like 'Cute dick!' but unfortunately one only ever thinks up such dignified comebacks after one has turned bright red, made a stumbling lunge at the

'That's what people said about Melinda Messenger until they discovered she had nine O Levels.' He grinned.

'Eight, I think you'll find.'

'Let's see.' Richard was practically dribbling.

Jess handed him the photo grudgingly.

'*That*'s her,' he said, pointing in disbelief.

'Yes, exactly, Richard, thank you. *See*, Sam?' she shouted, turning and smiling triumphantly. 'Not everyone's attracted to plastic.'

Sam was chuckling. 'I never said I—'

'No,' Richard protested, 'that's *her*. That's the girl I meant. The one I was telling you about.'

Jess looked puzzled. 'What girl?'

'The girl James is shagging.'

Later that evening Jess was still reeling in horror, lying on her bed staring at the ceiling, torturing herself with images of a delirious James giggling under the duvet with Zadia, when Sam walked in.

'You're much prettier than her, you know.'

'Than who?' Jess snapped, irritated to have been disturbed from her self-pity.

'Fuck-face,' he said, moving to join her on the bed.

Despite herself Jess smiled. 'No, I'm not.'

'Of course you are,' he said, planting a kiss on her forehead. 'You'd get at least . . . oh, let's see . . . three squirts.'

Jess pretended to thump him with a pillow. 'Sam! I *hate* that expression,' she squealed, as he raised his arms in mock-defence. 'Anyway, you wouldn't say that if all you'd seen was a photo of me. I look hideous in photos.'

'I bet I could find a squirt-worthy one, though.'

'I bet you couldn't.'

'Deal,' he said, leaping up. 'Right, where d'you keep them?'

Jess pointed to her wardrobe. 'But you're not going to find anything nice.'

light switch, contemplated making use of the walk-in freezer and fallen, crippled with embarrassment, to the floor. The only saving grace was that he felt sorry enough for me to throw me his sleeping-bag which, given that he too was dressed on the economical side of decency, felt a bit like receiving my bus fare from a homeless person.

It turned out that he'd been sleeping on the sofa because Emily was snoring. Love the idea of her being horribly masculine in bed. Since I had no desire to return to Medallion Man upstairs, especially when there was some tasty forbidden fruit downstairs, I decided the only right thing to do was take my water, return the sleeping-bag to the sofa and join him. And this indeed proved to be very right. We ended up having the most intriguing, flirtatious, revealing and altogether exciting conversation I have had in a long time.

It transpires he is not blissfully happy with Emily, after all, describing her as sweet but sometimes a little dull (love 'sweet' – so deliciously devoid of anything sexual). He wouldn't say anything too damning, despite my attempts at probing, but certainly doesn't seem as keen as I'd assumed. This, I have to say, sheds a new light on things. It is like going from being told you have to run a race against Linford Christie (and therefore giving up on the spot), to being told Linford's injured and realising you are now – as it were – in the running.

But then things got even more exciting because Sam moved his foot so that it was touching mine under the sleeping-bag and said, 'Does Kate Moss want to go for dinner?' I told him that Kate had already replied in the affirmative and, through a process of talking at cross-purposes for a while, we discovered, that thanks to my general technological ineptitude, I had somehow managed not to send him the e-mail. Hence him not replying, hence him giving up, hence Emily.

So we agreed, after a great deal more foot-touching, to go for dinner next Thursday. Then we heard a noise upstairs, had a brief, furtive and tantalisingly intimate hug, and scurried off to

Sam

As Sam began to haul down two large red albums, Jess wished again that she could feel the right things for him. That a surge of powerful desire would rush through her system whenever she was with him. A sense of uncontrollability. It was as if their relationship was a portable radio. It had all the correct components, was tuned to the right wavelength, was great company and could be taken anywhere, and yet it lacked the one thing to make it work: the battery.

'A-ha!' Sam exclaimed, crouched by the wardrobe flicking through the album with his back to her. 'Like the belt-over-the-blouse combo, Jess.'

'I'll have you know belts with blouses were very trendy when I was fourteen,' she laughed, tossing her duck up and down in the air. 'So, not worth a squirt, then?'

Sam didn't reply.

'Sam?'

Still no reply. He was obviously transfixed by another fashion flop.

'Hey!' she continued, throwing her duck at the back of his neck. 'What's happened to my squirt-machine?'

Suddenly Sam's voice cut through the silence. '"When you left me all alone, I shed a tear for what we shared."'

Jess lurched in horror.

'"When you left me all alone, I shed a tear for I felt scared."'

'That's personal.' She jumped up and tried to snatch the poem from him.

'"I still have feelings I know are wrong,"' he continued, as she tore it out of his hand. '"So tell me, James, where do we belong?"' He stared up at her coldly. 'So. Where do you and James belong, then?'

'Nowhere,' she said, ripping it up into tiny pieces.

'I think you're wrong there, Jess,' he said, getting to his feet. 'You see, I think you do belong somewhere. I think you belong together. I think you deserve each other.'

'No,' Jess pleaded, 'look, I—'

our respective rooms. I think I might be falling in love with Sam.

Oh, God, Medallion Man is snoring now too. I really wish he'd go. Maybe he's hoping for more action. Or maybe, even though only a few hours ago he was tumbling around confidently naked, he is now too shy for me to see his body and is waiting for me to leave the room before dashing like a thunderbolt for his clothes. No. That's the kind of thing I would do after shuffling around wearing a duvet trying to find my pants. Oh, no – horror. My pants! I've just remembered I was wearing disgusting florally ones with bits of jaggy elastic. He took one look at them and said – this is so cringeful, 'You obviously weren't expecting me tonight.'

Why does this keep happening? I will be quietly getting on with my hangover when suddenly out of nowhere – wham – another hitherto forgotten incident floods back on me, like those sick burps you do three hours after eating a meal that hasn't agreed with you.

Oh, God, my head is throbbing. Suspect it's less to do with the hangover per se *and more the fault of the awful radio. I realised I'd been listening to the local station far too long when I could recite their breast-enlargement ad word for word (cannot see why they feel the need to preface it with 'Sarah is not an actress', though, when Sarah is obviously still mastering the basics of reading: 'I used to. Have small and. Saggy. Breasts but now . . .'). So I've switched to Radio 1 to escape low-budget mania only to get a cocky DJ taking the length of a commercial break to adver-tise that they have* no *commercial breaks.*

Right, that's it. I'm going to make a point of going to the loo very loudly and if he still doesn't wake up I will simply sit on top of him until he does. Won't be a sec . . .

I'm going to scream in a minute. I was just on my way to the bathroom when I heard a giggle, followed by the deep rumble of a man's voice, coming from Jo's room. I stood in the hallway feeling jealous, trying to see if I could hear anything more, when

'And there I was worried about you. Worried I'd upset you by making a comment about another girl. But none of this was about me, was it? None of it. It was all about *him*.' He got up and slammed his way out of her room.

The following morning Jess was lying in bed, alone and miserable, wondering how to make it up with Sam when Jo burst in. She was flapping an envelope and wearing something Miss Selfridge would pass off as an evening dress, which meant it was light pink, extremely short and see-through.

'Pssst. Babes. You awake?'

Fleetingly it crossed her mind not to be but the intriguing envelope got the better of her. 'I am now,' she mumbled.

Jo skipped joyfully across the room to join her. 'You are going to *so* wish you came out last night, babes.' Jo, along with half the world, had started talking like Chandler.

'Really?' Jess replied flatly. It was alarming, she realised, how quickly one's enthusiasm for socialising, getting hammered and, when she thought about it, being young and fun diminished so drastically when you lived with your boyfriend. It was a bit like becoming American: you turned lazy and over-sentimental and stayed in wearing baggy clothes, eating disgusting amounts of junk food and watching undemanding television on the sofa.

'So what did I miss?'

'Everything.' Jo grinned so hard she looked crazed.

Then it dawned on Jess. One only ever described an evening in such ludicrous terms of hyperbole for one reason: 'You pulled.'

Jo closed her eyes for a very long time and inhaled a slow, satisfied breath. 'Oh, yes,' she exhaled dramatically, 'very much so.'

It turned out that after downing several pints in the manner of a football hooligan, she had stumbled along to a nightclub with a crowd of Richard's friends, one of whom she had *her door opened and she slipped out looking all glowing and shiny-eyed, mouthed the word 'lush' and scampered down the stairs, reappearing seconds later with two mugs of tea. From what I can gather from our rushed whispering session on the stairs she is with an utter Adonis – some guy a friend of Richard's introduced her to. She said he oozes sex appeal from every pore but will tell me all later, then scurried back into her room doing annoying smug grinning.*

It's not fair. Why can't I be with someone like that? I know it's horrible but I can't help preferring it when she's miserable. There's something quite unbearable about your friends being happy when you're not.

Then I had horrible remnants-of-alcohol-eroding-the-body diarrhoea only to discover there was no loo paper. Sophie has been waging a flat war over loo paper for several weeks now, claiming she is the only one who ever buys it. Everyone said this was crap and each named an occasion on which they remembered purchasing a pack. Sophie said she refused to buy a single roll again, with the result that for the last week and a half there has been no loo paper.

In fact, the only good thing to have emerged from the last five minutes is that Jo, in a quite unnatural fit of domesticity – clearly only to impress her new-found sex maestro – has offered to cook the four of us brunch. At last I have an excuse to get this disgusting object out of my bed. Yippee! Back soon.

Jesus Christ almighty. You are not going to believe what I have just been through. It goes down as very possibly the most horrific moment in my entire life.

I was standing in the kitchen picking baked beans out of the pan, listening to Jo sizzle with lust over the fried bacon and occasionally glancing over to where slobbery-chops was tackling a sandwich the size of his head. In fact, it was just when I witnessed egg yolk dribbling down his chin and was wondering why, when you don't fancy someone, something as harmless as a bit of stray food on their face can fill you with almost violent revulsion, when escorted back later for coffee, which had been less of the instant kind and more of the why-don't-we-do-some-grinding-along-with-the-beans variety. After a steaming night of frothy passion, he was now lying fully percolated in all his resplendent and virile nakedness under her Winnie-the-Pooh duvet, while she, far too excited to sleep, had nipped next door for a bit of half-time commentary.

'So then he started undoing my bra, only he couldn't get the—'

'Hang on, hang on, was this before or after you told him you had your period?'

'Way before, babes. No point scaring him off until I had to.'

'And?'

'And by the time he'd found out' – she grinned, looking unbelievably pleased with herself – 'well, put it this way, the Red Sea wouldn't have stopped him.'

As she proceeded to document every minute detail of her night of lust with the sex-god, Jess rejoiced at the pleasures of being born a girl. One of the best things about going to bed with a new bloke was the knowledge that you could spend the following day talking about it. What must it be like, she wondered, to be a guy and not be able to do this? To get back and not have the urge to tell someone who did what to whom with what, where and how often. James had once caught her on the phone to a friend asking who had orgasmed first. He had been shocked. He hadn't known the half of it.

'I'm telling you, babes. This guy is lush. And his kisses . . .' She was arching her back and doing something revolting with her tongue.

'It's OK, Jo, I think I can imagine.'

'No, babes, you can't. Unless you've actually *felt* it,' she whispered, throatily, 'you can't possibly imagine.' Jo had obviously been a lot more sexually starved than she'd given her credit for, Jess thought.

I heard a peculiar scraping at the kitchen door and Sophie appeared. She was being very weird and kept doing strange winking at me as if we were in the midst of plotting a hilarious joke. She then went over to her organic fridge and started raking around, asking me if I'd had a good night in such loaded terms that I felt sure she'd discovered I'd eaten her asparagus tips and was just softening me up before turning round to thwack the living daylights out of me (not, I have to admit in hindsight, something she is in the habit of doing). Then she fished out a peach, gave it a more scrupulous wash than I have had in weeks, and tripped out, tilting her head in a final, conspiratorial wink.

I looked round the room suspiciously for clues, peering at myself in the oven window in case I'd been walking about with a bogey dangling from my nose, then turned around and studied Jo for signs of collusion. But she was happily dicing onions and seemed oblivious to Sophie's antics. Whatever it was, I decided, Jo clearly wasn't in on it. So I set about stabbing some sausages and hearing ever-juicier tales of her night with the sex-god, so much so that by the time I heard the footsteps of a stranger descending the hall stairs, I was practically falling over myself to meet him.

Obviously, though, I did not make any attempt to show this enthusiasm because if he was the multi-talented sexual beast he seemed to be, I did not want to give him the satisfaction of thinking I'd been waiting eagerly to ogle him. So I carried on slicing mushrooms wondering whether I should have been quite so hasty to bung on my stained-because-I-never-remember-to-wash-it dressing-gown.

And then it happened: a distinct, almost spooky change in the atmosphere. At first I thought I'd imagined it until I noticed Jo had gone all giggly and girlish and was fussing around someone standing in the doorway. I couldn't see him right away because I was behind the door doing my not-particularly-interested act with the mushrooms, so it wasn't until he'd walked right into the middle of the kitchen that I turned round, looked up and almost fainted. There, standing a hair's-breadth away from me, was James.

'And what does he do with his tongue when it's not creating tidal waves of saliva with yours?' she enquired, smiling so as not to appear jealous.

'*Well.*' Jo grinned, looking pointedly at her crotch.

'I was talking about conversation, Jo.'

'There hasn't been time for much of that,' she replied, smirking.

While Jess was given a further rundown on what exactly there *had* been time for, forced out a few fake squeals of enthusiasm in the process and convinced Jo, based on the crucial fact that he hadn't bolted at dawn, that very likely they had a future together, the heavenly lust-beast was inflicted with the human need to go to the loo. Jo was keen to use his absence to slap on a bit of mascara, hide an anti-thrush pellet applicator she'd tried unsuccessfully to kick under the bed, and flee downstairs for some tea – to give the impression she'd spent the last twenty minutes slaving over kettles rather than slavering over him.

'Wish me luck,' she said, springing to her feet. 'Orgasm number three . . . coming up.'

Jess gave a weak smile. It sounded like a game of bingo.

'Oh, by the way,' she added, turning back and handing Jess the envelope, 'this came – if you'll excuse the pun.' She threw back her head, roared with laughter and flounced out of the door.

Jess lay staring into space, reflecting on how unbearable Jo was when she was happy. She picked up the envelope and began to open it, then immediately chastised herself for being so evil and wicked. Jo was her friend. It was nice that she had found some phenomenally attractive male model, who happened also to be rich, sensitive, funny, kind, intelligent and fantastically good in bed. It was great. Truly . . .

'Oh, God,' she wailed. She had just pulled out a gold-embossed card decorated with the kind of thick cerise ribbon found glued to manufactured birthday cakes. Vanya and Toby

When your boyfriend puts you on trial separation under the pretext of needing 'Time', you suspect he might be trying to play the lad, wonder if he misses you, hope he isn't after someone else and certainly do not expect to find him staring at you over the breakfast table having just walked sexy and tousled out of your flatmate's bedroom.

I stood there in a state of stupefied shock while Jo, who in a quite unbelievable display of dim-wittedness hadn't made the connection, went round asking everyone how many sausages they wanted.

For an awful second I thought James was going to pretend he didn't know me, save his own bacon, as it were, and leave. Instead sexual jealousy got the better of him and he said, pointing aggressively at Medallion Man, 'Who's he?' forcing me to reply, 'James, this is Mark, Mark, this is James,' causing Jo to say, 'How come you know he's called James?' then let out a high-pitched yelp and drop all the sausages on the floor.

After that the brunch rather dissolved. Jo burst into tears, allegedly out of shock but I think it was more at the thought of never being able to shag James again. Mark ate eight rashers of bacon and four eggs, then left with tummy-ache, and James and I retreated to the bathroom from which we have just emerged three hours later vowing to resume our relationship on a day-by-day basis as if it is a drug problem and we are both in rehab.

Strong people, I know, would have told him to bugger off, but they do not know how difficult it is when he puts on his cute face and says sorry. Anyway, I have made it clear that I'm not going to put up with any more shit, otherwise I will be forced to run off and form a functional relationship with Mark – or possibly just Mark's medallion.

James is certainly trying hard at the moment, dashing to the corner shop when I said I really fancied some green Pringles and offering to put up into the loft the box that has been sitting in my room since I moved in. But he always makes such a song and dance about doing things like this, making out that he is performing were getting married. This was about as much as she could take. It seemed the whole world was doomed to form happy, functional relationships, even lesbians.

She got up and marched moodily through to the bathroom but Jo's lover was still in there, flossing his armpits or whatever Adonises did. She knocked impatiently and stood glowering at the floor, arms crossed in bitter contemplation.

'Sorry,' he said, emerging with a towel strung sexily over one shoulder.

Jess collapsed in horror. The Adonis was James.

some enormous, self-sacrificing favour, then uses it as ammunition months down the line, replying indignantly, whenever I moan that he never does anything for me, 'But I do lots for you – take that tube of Pringles I got you seven and a half weeks ago last Sunday.'

I think a large part of us getting back together – other than guilt and perhaps shock – has to do with the fact that, in a startling turnaround, Toby is getting married – Vanya, apparently, is not a lesbian after all. Obviously James and I are both invited to the wedding, which happens to be on the day we get back from our off-on-off-now-back-on-again holiday.

Right, must go. Cannot seem to shake off the idea that I must be in bed early on Sunday nights. Work's got really exciting recently because we're doing a commercial for a new shampoo called 'Tiffany' using the real Tiffany from EastEnders. I've been helping a lot with this, completely over-hauling the video library, relabelling and refiling every tape, which everyone thought was fantastic and I must say it did look rather impressive. Actually, without meaning to sound boastful, I think I'm doing rather a good job generally – it's always so much more enjoyable doing something you're talented at.

Lots of love,

Jess

xxx

Sam
Office Joke

In a state of trauma
Calming my nerves with a glass of Sophie's elder-
flower, geranium oil and sperm-of-Vietnamese-
pot-bellied-piglet juice
Listening to relaxing Pan-pipe music in an effort
to pretend I am swimming with dolphins on a
wildlife documentary

Dear Alex,

I have got Irritable Bowel Syndrome.

I have never had a serious illness before so I am finding it deeply distressing, although I must admit there is also something exciting about knowing you have a proper disease instead of just a hangover.

Of course I would not be ill at all if it wasn't for James. You are not going to believe this but I happened to bump into the bastard, not in a pub, tube station or even mutual friend's party but, to my sheer horror, my own house: coming out of my bathroom having just spent the night with Jo. I always knew he was more intrinsically evil than your average shit, but never in a million years would have thought him capable of such an emotion-wrecking atrocity.

They seemed to think that because neither of them knew who the other was this was some kind of point in their favour, that I was slightly weird for not immediately wanting to rush up and pat them both heartily on the back. Indeed, I would have liked to stab them heartily on the back but as the only instrument to hand was a bendy-headed toothbrush, I opted for the be-the-better-person-and-be-rewarded-in-heaven approach, as advocated by Mr Boogle, my handsome Sunday School teacher – who, come to think of it,

Office Joke

'You have fucked up!' Chris was sitting at his desk looking furious, occasionally picking things up and hurling them across the office floor. 'Do you understand?'

The room was deathly quiet. Even the phones had stopped ringing. Jess gulped. She had never seen him like this.

Apparently he had just had a complaint call from a large advertising agency who, after requesting a copy of their company showreel, had sat down to view it with a group of important clients and been 'humiliated and disgusted' by what they saw. Instead of the correct reel, someone had sent them that of an amateur filmmaker. It was unknown whether this had been a genuine mistake or a joke, but either way the agency were furious. What they had been expecting was a series of neatly edited samples of FunFilm's work. What they got was *Kama Sutra for Teletubbies*.

'No one is moving until I know who did this.'

Jess looked furtively about the office, wondering who the culprit might be. Even though she knew nothing about it, she couldn't help looking guilty. It was something she did involuntarily, usually when passing a policeman or going through customs.

Eventually a weaselly guy in the corner confessed, claiming he'd had no idea he'd sent the wrong tape. She felt a conflicting sense of sympathy, relief and also, she noticed disturbingly, glee. Could it be that she was enjoying watching someone else get into trouble?

'Jess, are you listening?'

Suddenly, inexplicably, everyone was looking at her. She smiled tentatively. It was one of those moments to tell the truth and own up, however terrifying and embarrassing. She lied.

must have encountered a momentary deviation from this approach somewhere along the line as he is now, unfortunately, in jail.

Anyway, I am being suitably offhand with Jo and resolutely refusing to talk to James, because even though they were both at fault he is the one I am angry with.

It is therefore of little surprise that I feel as though I've spent the last week astride one of those less enjoyment-inducing fairground rides at Alton Towers. In fact, my tummy has been making alarming Jurassic Park *noises for quite a while but I had bravely assumed this was just a result of drinking too much Diet Coke without burping – it is frightening how easy it is to overlook major symptoms when you are not a hypochondriac. Then I woke up with such agonising stomach cramps I thought perhaps I was having an ectopic pregnancy and the foetus had just been strangled by a Fallopian tube.*

I rang up work and told them and said I would be in as soon as I could. I could tell they didn't believe me. One of the infuriating things about having a real *excuse is that it never sounds convincing. Had I picked up the phone spluttering phantom phlegm, told them in a frog's voice that I was vomiting viscid green bile, squitting fluorescent diarrhoea and going into hospital later that afternoon for an emergency kidney transplant, they'd have been shipping Cellophaned chrysanthemums right away.*

As it was, I explained simply what was wrong and they listened without saying anything. Then the minute I stopped speaking, they left one of those hideous prolonged silences designed to make weak people like me back down, turn into a sheep and say, 'Well, I suppose I could struggle in if you really need me.'

Anyway, I managed to persevere and sit it out, and have now been off work for three days, languishing on the sofa eating grapes like paintings of fleshy nineteenth-century women on chaiseslongues.

I must say, there's something quite nice about being ill. It is one of the few occasions when you can lounge around doing buggerall and not feel guilty or lazy. And it gives you the opportunity

'Good. Two thirty sharp. Any problems I'm on my mobile.' Then he grabbed a gigantic file and stormed out.

Jess sat glued to her seat in terror. The longer she pretended she knew, the harder it became to admit that she didn't. Very soon, she panicked, it would *be* two thirty.

After rearranging the paper-clips in descending order of size, she embarked on an ingenious method of couching questions in the form of statements and eventually collected enough clues to work out what was going on. It came as a startling, yet joyous surprise to discover that Chris had entrusted her with the job of showing the agency the rough-cut of the Tiffany commercial. Though not sure what this meant, she had an intuitive feeling it would be exciting. She must be prepared, she told herself, and scurried off to the loo with her makeup bag.

'Jess!' someone shouted, hammering on the door. 'Steve's asking if you've wired the output frequency and checked the visual co-ordinates.'

'Just about to,' she called, trying to sound casual. Sometimes it seemed like she worked in television and at others it felt like a rerun of her physics exam.

Grabbing the proffered tape, she scuttled into the little side room and positioned herself in front of an enormous television set under which two terrifyingly complicated video players were stacked.

Tentatively, she pushed the tape into one of the machines. It seemed to be hitting against something and wouldn't go in. She pressed eject. Nothing. She pushed a bit harder. Nothing. She tried the other one. Nothing. She looked at her watch and nearly jumped out of her skin. It was almost two thirty.

Taking a deep breath, she tried again, really slowly. She'd read somewhere that during times of stress and frustration, force and panic were counter-productive. What was needed was a calm, gentle . . .

to do things you never normally get round to doing, like reading the newspaper. So far I've managed to force-read five articles from yesterday's Times as part of my recently formed plan to become knowledgeable about current affairs that do not just appear inside the cover of Hello!. To be honest, though, I don't know why I bother buying a newspaper. I hardly ever get round to reading it – it looms over the day like a Tolstoy epic, sits in my bag rubbing newsprint over everything, then makes me feel wasteful for chucking it away unread as if it is not something that can be bought again the following morning for a fifth of the price of a tube fare, but some precious fountain of invaluable knowledge that I will be intellectually and spiritually poorer for not having consumed.

I feel quite a bit better now, to tell you the truth, which is, I suppose, to be expected since no matter how dismal and wretched an illness can make me, I only need to think of making an appointment with a doctor to feel miraculously and almost instantaneously cured.

When I phoned the surgery I assumed I would be told they didn't have anything until next spring because being ill in London requires you to have a premonition about it three and a half weeks previously in order to book an appointment that actually coincides with the illness, so I was startled to find that they could fit me in today and decided to celebrate by going along.

In fact, it's so long since I've been to the doctor's that I was prepared for a rerun of university, expecting the equivalent of that awful woman (the one who asked you how often you had intercourse when you'd popped in to get antibiotics for earache) to sit me down and launch into similarly probing questions about my sex life.

Instead, a ruthlessly efficient Indian girl ushered me into a room and stared at me while I talked earnestly about my 'stools'. She had little round reading glasses and hair pulled back so severely her eyes had gone slitty.

After prodding around under the fleshy folds of my tummy with

'Oh, for crying out loud,' she yelled, throwing the tape at the floor and realising as she did so what was wrong. The machine had been switched off.

Suddenly everything was happening. Tapes were spewing out, lights were flashing, buttons were beeping and *Home and Away* was belting out at excruciatingly high volume. Reaching for the remote she turned down the racket, put in the tape, pressed play and waited.

For a long time nothing happened. She sat staring at the machine, too frightened to touch it, as if by willing it to work it would defy all technological logic and spring into action. Which was then, to her amazement, exactly what it did. There – hair sleek and shiny – was Tiffany! Even though she could be doing everything right with a piece of machinery, it always came as a pleasant surprise when it actually did what it was supposed to.

Triumphant, she flicked up the volume then started to panic again. Shouldn't there be some sound? She turned it up full but still it was eerily silent. Be calm, she told herself, and pressed the off button at which point *Home and Away* catapulted back into deafening action, causing her to drop the remote control and rear in fright like a startled horse.

'That's the agency on their way up,' a voice shouted from the doorway.

She'd now turned it back to the video function and was stabbing frantically and erratically at buttons. A menu for colour variance popped up then disappeared and was replaced by a flashing box in the corner of the screen and the words 'audio mode'.

'Fuck off audio mode,' she shouted at the gyrating icon, which, while clearly doing nothing of use whatsoever, refused to go. She was starting to sweat. The agency were in danger of watching three silent minutes of Tiffany with a box over her face.

She breathed in deeply. Often in situations like this it was me doing nervous giggling, she announced I had Irritable Bowel Syndrome, told me to cut out all dairy products, sugar, fruit, cooked vegetables, red meat, white meat, all meat, nuts, fish, yeast-based products, calcium, and – I forget what the other one was, then handed me a prescription and advised me to avoid any situations of stress.

Distraught that it wasn't just a liver cyst or strangled foetus, I left the surgery resolving to live a life of yoga classes and organic salad dinners. I would become a reformed person, I told myself, sporting long, floral, floaty skirts, sandals and Save the Dolphin T-shirts, who would be free from additives and stress. Then I walked into the chemist and the entire plan blew up in my face – the bastards were charging me £14.95 for six Irritable Bowel pellets!

I launched into a ferocious rant about the Americanisation of our culture and how soon poor people like me, unable to afford even the most basic medical treatment, would be found dying by roadsides, arms outstretched to passing ambulancemen who would stop briefly, rifle mercilessly through our wallets for any sign of insurance then head off empty-handed, leaving us, destitute, to splutter our final breaths.

I'd just got to the stage where I was almost dying – sweating and hyperventilating like a fat person trying to jog – when the chemist stopped me mid-sentence, reminded me I still had to pay for my prescription and suggested I take up these issues with the Health Secretary. Which is when I made a complete pig's arse of myself by saying haughtily, 'I think you'll find she'd take more notice of you,' at which point the corners of his mouth broke into a wry smile and he said, 'I think you'll find she is a man called Alan Milburn.'

I went bright red, fumbled angrily in my wallet, was 8p short and stormed out to the cashpoint, knocking over a display of aromatherapy stress-relieving oils in my fury.

No wonder my bowels are irritated. It's all very well for the doctor to tell me not to get stressed when she has no idea how fraught just something simple like an 'on' button, for example. Or a loose connection. In fact, she decided, that would be it: an important wire had probably just popped out and needed popping back in again.

Quick as a flash she dashed behind the unit where a seething mass of red and black leads spilled out of tiny holes in a quantity and manner not too dissimilar, she imagined, to what would happen if she ceased to shave her legs.

Scanning the line, she pinpointed the problem. Exactly as she'd thought: a disconnected wire. Elated, she reached over and plugged it back in. And then – horror. A loud, high-pitched tone screeched out of the machine.

'Fuck!' she yelled, grabbing the lead and trying desperately to yank it free. It wouldn't budge. It had somehow become locked in the socket. She flew round to the front again in the vain hope that the noise might be intentional – part of a test card sequence or similar – and shrieked in terror. The picture was totally distorted.

'Buggering *hell*!'

Panic-stricken, she raced back round again and, using all her weight, pulled as hard as she could. Smoothly, effortlessly, almost like a miracle, the lead glided out. But the noise hadn't stopped. In alarm she realised she'd pulled out the wrong one.

Furiously, she started battling with every connection until she located the right one and, in a single almighty tug, managed to loosen it, rip it free and send herself, with very nearly the entire turret of machinery, crashing to the floor.

'Everything OK, Jess?' Steve had just appeared, guiding a group of people with clipboards into the room.

'Fine, thanks,' she mumbled, appearing from behind the television like something out of *Fawlty Towers*. 'Just, um, checking the sound.'

Steve grinned. 'That'll be a tough job.'

'Ooh, well, you know, not really,' she replied, giggling modestly.

merely existing can be when you are me. Short of sitting in a white room all day nibbling raw broccoli, I can't see a solution.

Even nice, calming things are agitating me at the moment. This morning a lovely bouquet of flowers arrived with a note that said, simply, 'Sorry.' It should have been very exciting – after all, I do not get anonymous bouquets of flowers with mysterious and intriguing messages alluding to secret admirers and the like. I get nothing or three half-dead carnations from a petrol station.

But instead of just smiling, placing them artistically in a vase and admiring them, I got tense and obsessive about who might have sent them, oscillating violently between two emotional extremes. One minute I was dancing around entertaining the idea of a lovelorn suitor sorry that his love was unrequited. The next I was frozen to the spot in contemplation of stalkers and psychotic axe-murderers.

The logical answer, I know, is Sam. We had our first fight the other day because he found the poem I'd sent to James. But I cannot really fathom what reason he would have for not saying they were from him. Surely if you are going to fork out 40 quid for half of Kew Gardens you might as well get the credit for doing so.

Of course, the person I would really like them to be from is James. And certainly there are myriad reasons why he should have sent them: sleeping with Jo, snogging Zadia, being a wanker, to name just a few. But unfortunately there is one overriding reason why they will not be from James: James never sends flowers.

So the only other sensible option is work, but if anyone should be sending peace-offerings the size of a small goat it is me. And why on earth would they be saying sorry? Unless, of course, it is a premature sacking gesture to soften the blow. Oh, God – need more piglet juice.

Certainly, work is not going well at the moment. I don't know whether it's because of my irritated bowels, but I can't seem to do

He looked at her oddly. 'We haven't laid the audio yet,' he announced.

She looked at him blankly.

'There *is* no sound, Jess.'

Everybody started to laugh. As redundant as this piece of news now rendered the last five minutes of unparalleled horror, she was relieved. She hadn't messed up. Everything was fine. Completely fine.

'OK, folks,' Steve said, and invited them to take a seat. 'I've got to dash but I'll leave you in the more than capable hands of Jess here. Enjoy.'

Jess beamed beatifically as the video whirred into action and everybody began to make encouraging noises at a clear and undistorted Tiffany.

She could barely contain her joy. She was '*more than capable*'. She repeated the phrase again – 'more than capable', 'more than *capable*', '*more* than capable'. Taken to its logical conclusion this meant she was very capable, highly capable, perhaps even—

'Where the fuck is that imbecile Jess?'

She froze. Chris had just come clattering into the office next door and sounded furious. Terrified, she tried to work out what was wrong, craning her neck to the wall and smiling meekly at the agency, who were politely pretending they hadn't heard a thing.

'All wrong,' he was yelling. 'Every sodding label . . . all mixed up . . . can't even label a tape . . . *Teletubbies* . . . fucking up . . . fucking moron . . . fucking *hell*!'

For a blissful, peaceful, wonderful moment she didn't have the faintest clue what he was ranting about. And then it hit her. Her relabelling system. Her fantastic relabelling system. Her fantastic relabelling system, which was now clearly responsible for, among other atrocities, the sex-with-*Teletubbies* horror.

She recoiled in ·fear. Nothing, not even an imminently

anything right. The other day I was asked to deliver three lever-arch files to the lawyer. Despite being the kind of thing a two-year-old could do, it proved beyond my capabilities. First I had the bright idea of putting the wretched things in a Safeway bag, which, of course, split the minute I got to the bottom of the stairs, causing one file to plop into a puddle and another to ping open and all the bits of paper that I'd spent the last two hours laboriously putting in order to float off down the street. Then I had the brainwave of using my laundry bag, which I had taken to work because Jo had broken the washing-machine by wrenching open the door before the cycle had finished because she can't stand having to wait the ninety seconds for the auto-lock to click off. I transferred all my dirty clothes into Safeway bags, hoping that Steve (nice man in the office who I have developed a slight crush on, only because I need to fancy someone at work not because he is attractive) hadn't seen, then put the files into the laundry bag and trotted round to the lawyer's.

I then spent an interminably boring evening in a place frequented only, I had assumed, by people who didn't own a washing-machine and therefore, by extension, the entire cast of EastEnders: a launderette. In fact, it turned out to be the local hang-out for people who didn't own anything, as I discovered when a woman who looked alarmingly like a man attempted an Artful Dodger number with one of my pillow-cases.

After getting pound coins stuck in machines and burning my bras – not, alas, in support of the women's movement, but because the dryers were buggered – I eventually bumbled home with a selection of melted underwear and damp bed linen, only to find I'd lost a pair of pants. Decided, however, this was of negligible importance since they were vile things riddled with caterpillar holes.

The next thing I know it's two days later, I've just got into work and Chris – head producer, fat, looks like a meerkat – is throwing a telephone across the office and shouting loud swear words, while everybody else is trying not to piss themselves laughing behind blank computer screens.

exploding bomb on the seat next to her, could be worse. And then it happened. Her voice, clear as day, booming out into the room. Two words: 'Buggering *hell*!'

Dumbstruck, she turned to face the source. Tiffany's face was gone. The screen was blank. The agency were horrified.

It had suddenly and indisputably got worse. Much worse.

'. . . so what did he say then?' a consoling James asked three hours later, when Jess, red-eyed and sobbing, appeared unannounced at his office.

'Fucking,' she shrieked, as he winced and did nervous nodding to his surrounding colleagues. 'That's all he kept saying – fucking, fucking, fucking.'

'Well, he got his point across, I suppose.'

'James, this isn't funny, it's my career we're talking about.'

'You realise none of this would've happened,' he smirked, 'if you'd taken my advice about Tie—'

'This isn't fucking *funny*!' she yelled, as a couple of blokes doing sly sniggering seemed to suggest that it was.

'OK, sorry, carry on. What happened about the tape?'

'Well,' she spluttered, between sobs, 'luckily they had a master copy, but Chris says I've got to pay to get another one done.'

'And what did he say about the labels?'

'That I was on my last warning,' she sniffed, separating the only bit of dry tissue and blowing into it dramatically, 'as long as I wrote a personal letter of apology to all the people who'd been sent the wrong tapes.'

'Well, that doesn't sound too bad,' he said, relaxing back in his seat.

'James!' she exploded. 'There are forty-two of them.'

When it became clear that James was incapable of offering her what she wanted, she decided to go and search elsewhere, and found it, several hours later, in the form of a candle-lit alcove, a bottle of wine, a walnut risotto and Sam.

Sam

Rejoicing in the rare and wonderful phenomenon that nobody was doing a scrap of work, I started grinning too, looking furtively round the office, catching people's eyes, raising my eyebrows, shrugging, then grinning some more, loving every second of new work-free work, desperate to know what this hilarious thing could be.

And then horror. Chris got to his feet, hurled what appeared to be a cloth at the floor and stormed out, much to the amusement of the entire office, all of whom erupted into mad laughter while someone leapt up, picked up the cloth and pinned it to the noticeboard. Which is when I realised it wasn't a cloth at all. It was my pants.

It turns out they had still been in my laundry bag when I'd delivered the files and had somehow got stuck inside one during transit. The lawyer, rather than being offended, had thought it amusing and had sent them back with a note saying, 'Not quite the brief we were expecting. Too big,' which was in itself deeply embarrassing since they were, indeed, mammoth BhS affairs. I thought I was going to get away with it and carried on doing over-enthusiastic laughing until one of the blokes decided it'd be a hilarious idea to put the pants on his head. In the process of cavorting round the office looking as though he should be shouting 'get yer tits out' into the camera lens of an Ibiza Uncovered episode, someone noticed there was a label poking out. I assumed this would just be the BhS tag and prayed no one would discover they were mine, until all of a sudden my initials were being read out loud and clear, and I realised to my utter mortification that not only had I left a pair of pants that were (a) dirty (b) hideous and (c) from BhS, I had also succeeded in leaving the one surviving pair from girl guide camp complete with, for reasons known only to my mother, red-stitched embroidered name tag.

It didn't take long for the office to work it out and when they did, to piss themselves even more. In fact, everyone thought it was so hilarious I was tempted to claim I had done it on purpose, until I remembered Chris, who did not think it hilarious as he has the sense of humour of a kettle.

'. . . so I said, "No, Emily, *that*'s the vinaigrette," and what did the womble do but go and pour brake fluid all over her salad.'

They both laughed.

'So,' Jess ventured, when the hilarity died down and they were left grinning at each other over the table, 'is Emily the one, then?'

Sam picked up his glass and smirked. 'The one what?'

'You know.' She smiled, pretending to be coy. 'The one. The one for you. Your soulmate.'

Sam put his elbows on the table and leaned forward towards her. 'That depends if you believe in soulmates,' he said, raising an eyebrow sexily.

'And do you?' Jess replied, thoroughly enjoying the way things were heading.

'I didn't. No.'

'So what changed?'

'The wind, I think.' Sam drained his wine then reached for the bottle and refilled their glasses.

'I thought that just made you ugly,' she retorted, causing him to start flicking water from the jug in the direction of her chest. 'So, come on, then, what changed? What turned Sam the sceptic into Sam the believer?'

He grinned and put down the water jug, then cupped his face in his hands and looked her straight in the eye. 'I met someone, Jess. That's what changed.'

Jess felt as if every nerve in her body had combusted simultaneously. This was better than any kind of fantasy she could have dreamed up. And he'd used her name. There was something irreplaceably thrilling and intimate about hearing someone you liked using your name.

She sat there fixating on the stem of her glass, rigid with anticipation, terrified to breathe, terrified to blink, terrified to swallow, terrified to make even the slightest movement that might stop him from following this through, that might stop

223

Sam

Which reminds me. I must boil up Sophie's fennel leaves and hover over the pan with a towel on my head as a means, I am told, of effective stress-relief. I can think of more pleasurable ways of de-stressing but Sam is not around at the moment and, besides, lately, that too seems to cause me stress.

I thought we might have made a breakthrough with the whole bad-sex thing after last Thursday night's unnaturally fantastic bedroom performance. But – alas – it was just post-argument sex – always guaranteed to be fantastic – and now we're back as before: devoting the entire act to his enjoyment. (Bizarre baffling logic that James – a selfish bastard at all other times – becomes a sensuous, attentive Joy of Sex *lover when in bed, whereas Sam, a godly saint-like person, giver to the homeless and helper of the handicapped, turns into Ebenezer Scrooge.)*

It's partly my fault, I suppose, for not pointing out sooner that just because he's reached his *destination, so to speak, it doesn't mean the journey is at an end: the Intercity Aberdeen to London doesn't just terminate half-way through because most of its passengers get off at Newcastle. The trouble is, I was too shy to mention this when we first got together and now that we're more relaxed with each other and I could, it has become the accepted routine: Sam pounds his way to pleasure, collapses and snores, and I wonder whether I could get another day's wear out of my polo-neck.*

However, I am not going to let a small detail like passionless sex get in the way, especially as I'm doing such a good job of fancying him. Lust and desire are highly overrated anyway. Who wants to have their emotions boinging out of control like a yo-yo when you could have the comfort and security of a nice bed buddy? Not me. Hurrah!

Lots of love,

Jess

xxx

PS Misery. I have just got up to arrange the mystery flowers in the gigantic floor pail – the only vase available being an expensive him reaching over, grasping her hand and saying, '*You*, Jess, I met *you*.'

Then suddenly it was happening. She could feel it. She couldn't see him because she was still too scared to take her eyes from the glass, but she could feel him. Feel him moving. Feel his tension, his intention. Her heart was thumping over-time. She waited. Mustn't look up too soon, she told herself, mustn't look up too late. Must time it just . . .

'Hey there, womble.'

She looked up and let out a yelp. There, at the table, was Emily.

'Thought you two might like a free taxi service,' she said, jangling some keys.

'Thank you,' he said, looking nervously at Jess.

Jess stared in horror. To have an intimate moment inter-rupted by someone was annoying. For that someone to be an uninvited Emily was just too much for her to bear.

'I think we'd like that taxi now, Emily,' she said, and signalled to the waiter for the bill.

The minute they'd got into the flat the phone started ringing. Grumpily Jess picked it up.

'Where have you been?' It was James.

'Out,' Jess said, flatly.

'Oh, well, that's good,' he replied. 'I mean, it's not that I've been worrying about you or anything. Haven't been trying to get hold of you all night. Out where, then?' he said, when it became clear Jess wasn't going to rise to it.

'Dinner with Sam.'

'Oh. How romantic.'

'It *was*.' Jess seethed, as she watched Sam piggy-back a squealing Emily out of the room.

'What's that supposed to mean?'

'Well, it would be nice to do romantic things with my boyfriend once in a while.'

'I'm always doing romantic things,' James protested.

Sam

Conran one that leaks due to being designed not to hold water or indeed any liquid at all, but instead two designer twigs – and discovered the girl in the flat opposite is doing exactly the same. I have not got a secret lover or even crazed pervert. I have merely been the target of an Interflora promotion.

'Like?'

'Like . . . like . . . well, like the other day when I got you those Pringles.'

'James, if you had any notion of what it was to be romantic you'd be taking me away for the weekend, like any normal couple, not buying me sour-cream crisps.'

'OK,' he said, assertively. 'Fine. Let's go away.'

'When?'

'Well, it'll have to be after Toby's stag weekend.'

'When's Toby's stag weekend?'

James paused.

'When?'

'Well, it's . . .'

'When is it?'

'Promise you won't be cross?'

'*James!*' she exploded. 'When is Toby's stag weekend?'

Sam

Valentine's Day

'Interflora,' announced a selection of unnaturally orange flowers three weeks later. Jess was peeping through the crack of the chain-lock like a frightened pensioner.

'Gosh. Thank you,' she gushed, when she realised what was happening, fighting back a ridiculous urge to show off in front of the delivery-man. Flowers on Valentine's Day were like snow on Christmas Day – always hoped for, seldom got.

'No one answering next door. Don't mind, do you, love?'

Crestfallen, she took the giant satsuma and plodded through to the kitchen where SophienRichard were doing their best to remind everyone what the day was really about by spoon-feeding each other an M&S gooseberry pavlova.

'Woo-hoo,' Jo cooed, 'who's got an admirer, then?'

'The neighbour,' Jess said flatly, dumping them on the table.

'Boxer-shorts Man?' Jo offered hopefully, referring to the nameless wonder who'd earned his title by appearing on their doorstep in his underwear when Sophie had decided to Hoover the lounge at midnight.

'Boxer-shorts Man's girlfriend,' Jess replied.

Just then there was a loud clanging, and Sam appeared swinging two billycans. His hair was tousled, and he was dressed in an open shirt and baggy tie-dyed pantaloon things of the sort worn with leather necklaces and brightly coloured hair braids by people who'd just come back from their gap year and thought it cool to wander round autumnal British streets looking like Malaysian drug-dealers.

'Happy Valentine's Day,' he said, handing Jess, rather defeating the point of the day, a card. He'd been up since seven preparing some sort of surprise trip away which, Jess noted, from the fossilised drinking utensils and streaks of

Valentine's weekend
Having an uncannily fabulous time
Beginning to wonder whether I haven't got my
*   dates wrong and the real Valentine's Day with*
*   its attendant misery and feelings of rejection is*
*   still to come*

Dear Alex,

*   I have decided to take an entirely different and, some may say, slightly pessimistic approach to life. Instead of looking forward to things, getting excited, nervous and foolishly over-eager, I am henceforth going to assume the worst of every situation. Then ~~when~~ if it is good, it will be like a pleasant, yet unexpected bonus.*

*   I devised this innovative life-stance this morning when I realised I'd spent two weeks dreading what has turned out to be a really quite superb day of Valentine merriment.*

*   After witnessing the nauseous display of Sophie and Richard spoon-feeding each other a Marks & Spencer's Valentine Special Gooseberry Pavlova – invented, I can only assume, to make those without a loved one feel doubly left out – Sam and I decided to escape all further reminders of the day, packed some sleeping-bags, blankets and a tent without a fly-sheet and are now, six hours later, camped illegally in a field somewhere off the A264.*

*   I feel totally exhilarated. It is the kind of thing cool, exciting people do in films and although it is (a) bitterly cold (b) starting to rain and (c) becoming apparent that we have erected the tent on a miniature rock garden, it is great. I am currently crouched under swathes of bedding holding a torch that only works at certain angles while Sam, in an effort to pretend we are nomadic hunter-gatherers, has gone off with his penknife to forage for food.*

226

Sam

engine oil on his forehead, was not going to take place in Mayfair.

'Thanks,' she mumbled, opening up a mammoth flowery affair with gold-embossed 'To My Valentine' running diagonally along the top left-hand corner. It was difficult to know whether this was meant to be amusing in its vileness or the result of a mad dash to the corner shop. Either way, she realised, she had forgotten to get him anything.

'Your carriage awaits you, ma'am,' Sam said, leading her outside to where a battered tin Land Rover was parked, looking as though it should have little marmoset monkeys swinging from its broken wing-mirror and baby lions curled up on its roof-rack.

'Am I allowed to know where we're going yet?' she said, in a whiny are-we-nearly-there voice of the sort used by small children three minutes into long car journeys.

'Accident and Emergency.' He laughed as the rear-view mirror he'd been adjusting came off in his hands.

The journey, after an initial glitch when the car sounded as if a lung-cancer patient had inadvertently got stuck in the starter motor, went surprisingly well. Jess had been used to car trips with James, which were tense, silent affairs, a bit like funerals, punctuated by the odd bout of swearing when they were forced to travel forty miles in the wrong direction after she'd squealed at him to come off the motorway too soon.

'You check in, I'll get the luggage,' Sam announced, when they had ground to a halt in a little brambly country lane of the sort found sketched inside an oval floral border on the front of boxed gift-soaps.

Jess looked at him, perplexed. 'Where exactly?'

'Where do you think?' he said, leaping out of the vehicle as a gust of wind did unfavourable things to his pantaloons. 'There.'

She followed the direction of his finger, which seemed to

I slightly think I might fancy him again. It's just that he's being so nice and funny and attentive without being gagging and . . . Anyway, I mustn't think about it. I am here purely for platonic reasons and to cheer up Sam, who is purportedly upset, having just finished with the annoying Emily for being too keen (slightly terrifying concept). Apparently he did it yesterday because he couldn't stand the idea of being in a relationship on Valentine's Day. Although I do not sanction such a heartlessly mistimed act of cruelty – even towards someone like Emily – I can understand his reasons for doing it.

It is a much-understated fact that having a partner on Valentine's Day is complex: on the one hand you don't want to cheapen the relationship by sinking to the level of a Carlton-card event, but on the other you can't help feeling unloved and rejected if you don't mark the day.

But how do you celebrate? Do you make a special effort, e.g. lavish meal, quirky gift, etc., in which case if they have not done the same you just end up feeling a bit of a prat? Or do you go for the cheesy option, as promoted to maximum effect by florists, Thornton's and novelty knick-knack shops, thereby making a light-hearted and ironic statement about the true depth of your feelings, which could never be epitomised within the three-inch diameter of a chocolate praline heart?

Maybe the answer is to avoid all potential gift-gaffe horrors by a no-nonsense up-front prearranged consensus. That way everyone is clear from the outset as to what is expected of them. Admittedly, though, this would defeat the purpose of Valentine's Day, which is, after all, largely about the thrill of the unknown.

Mercifully I did not have to endure any of these quandaries because my boyfriend is so romantically unevolved that he chose this weekend, out of a selection of fifty-two, to go away. Thus, instead of spending the day taking an unhealthy interest in the postman, sneakily glancing at the doormat, holding out feeble hopes for second posts and Interflora vans while all the time pretending to be wholeheartedly indifferent to the occasion, I sat back and be pointing at a cow-pat. It turned out, moments later, to *be* the cow-pat: Sam had taken her camping.

Excited and laughing, they abandoned the car and squelched their way through someone else's field. Jess couldn't help reflecting on all the times she'd wanted James to do something like this. Something fun, spontaneous, mad. But as she watched Sam set about doing manly things with a tent pole against the frosted pink light of a wintry setting sun, she caught herself trying rather too desperately to feel slushy and romantic. Here she was in the middle of a cornfield, miles from nowhere, with a tent, a boyfriend, and the possibility of shagging all night under twinkly stars – a scenario that with some dry ice, backing vocals and possibly a grazing fawn or two would have made a marvellously tear-jerking Céline Dion video – yet something felt missing. It was like trying to bake a cake: all the ingredients were right but it hadn't come out like the picture.

'You thinking what I'm thinking?' Sam grinned, approaching her in a way that made it obvious the tent wasn't the only thing that had just been erected.

'Food?' she replied limply, to which he gave a wan smile and walked backwards into a guy-rope.

The trouble with camping, Jess thought, once they'd chewed their way through a rubber fish-and-chip supper, was that unless you were Patrick Moore or a tawny-owl enthusiast, there was little to do past seven o'clock other than go to bed. Which was her problem. It wasn't that she didn't want to have sex. It was just that she didn't want it with Sam.

'I think we need to do something,' he smirked, clambering on top of her in a green woolly hat and matching scarf, 'to keep each other warm.'

'I'm perfectly warm, thank you,' she said, curtly. But she knew she was losing. Sex with Sam was like encroaching flu: you could fend it off for a while with sleep and food but it got you in the end.

relaxed as there was no way on this planet that James, pissed on the ski slopes of Chamonix, was going to (a) remember (b) be arsed or (c) have any inclination whatsoever to send me something.

Which makes what happened this morning all the more superbly exciting. There, like a quivering arrow from Cupid's bow, was a Valentine card. Intriguingly, it had been hand-delivered, denying me the joy of a two-hour analysis of a postmark and instantly alerting suspicion to the possibility of a flatmate – pray to the heavens it is not Colin.

It was, slightly disappointingly I have to say, one of those ones you might get if elderly aunts sent Valentines, i.e. swirly flowers with gold-embossed 'To My Valentine' running diagonally along the top left-hand corner with nothing but the tragically over-sentimentalised rhyme inside.

The trouble with anonymous cards is that, however much you deny it to yourself, there is always one person you hope it might be from and they are usually the one person, quite frankly, who it is not from. Obviously that person is Sam. And obviously he would not have given me a disgusting petrol-station-forecourt-style Valentine.

Jo thought it was from Mark, at one stage doing such a good job in convincing me that when he innocently phoned up to arrange a drink with her, I couldn't stop myself asking him. The more he denied it the more I began to think it was him until I got to the stage of practically bullying him into confessing. I say 'practically', because I would've gone a whole lot further if he hadn't suddenly blurted out, in a fit of exasperation, that if I must know he had sent a Valentine – to Jo.

So I have resigned myself to the rather disappointing fact that it is probably from James (despite the bamboozling image of him organising for it to be hand-delivered) and rationing myself to one daydream an hour that it is from Sam.

I hope you had a successful Valentine's Day too – certainly from your letter it sounds like there isn't a shortage of admirers. In fact,

'You're not warm,' he grinned, licking his lips, 'you're hot.'

And that was it. It wasn't bad, she conceded, once she got into it. Like exams, the dentist and everything else she dreaded, the reality was never as horrible as the anticipation.

When she awoke the following morning she let out a high-pitched yelp of delight. Sam had laid out – rather incongruously given that there was a thin covering of snow – his beach towel, on which he had placed two *pains au chocolat*, some orange juice, a couple of bananas and a little bunch of ferns and snowdrops. In the distance a calor-gas stove was doing its best against February's frost to make a billycan of coffee.

'Oh, Sam,' she squealed, braving the sub-arctic conditions to join him. It was frightening how easily she could fluctuate from finding him unattractive and needing to finish the relationship immediately to having the kind of warm, fuzzy feelings associated with the end credits of a Meg Ryan film.

And this emotional ping-ponging continued all day. They went for a walk and she wanted to marry him. They went for a pint and she couldn't bear the way he slurped it. They read the papers and she imagined their children. They had dinner and she planned how to dump him.

By the time they got home she was absolutely shattered, which was, she conceded, little wonder: in the space of a weekend she'd split up and got back together again eighteen times.

'Don't strain yourself,' Sam called, as she entered the house swinging the tent-peg bag and made her way casually over to a ringing phone while he, in the manner of a donkey with saucepans round its neck, dragged behind her with everything else.

'You're the man,' she laughed, picking up the handset, 'or at least claim to be. Hello?'

There was a long silence, as if whoever it was had dialled the number then promptly keeled over and died.

you sound in excellent form generally, helped enormously I should imagine by bumping into that Swedish model again – so to speak. How amazing. I think you're definitely right about your foreigner's theory, by the way. They do seem to treat kissing as an end in itself and not, as frequently demonstrated by the likes of my bastard Beelzebub ex-boyfriend Craig, a means to getting their end away. (Would perhaps have to extend my experiences beyond Thierry, aged thirteen and a half on a school-exchange trip to Paris, before I could be fully entitled to make such a claim, however.)

Talking of snogging, where's Sam? I really wish he would come back. There's a funny rustling sound outside and although it is probably just the wind or a grazing baby fawn, I've watched too many horror movies not to assume it is a masked rapist who, just when I think he has gone, will slice a gigantic machete through the canv – I am not going to think about it. There is nothing to be frightened of. Nothing. I am in Surrey, not Psycho.

I am going to think of calming things instead, like my birthday. Or, more importantly, what I would like for my birthday. James keeps asking for ideas which is annoying on two counts: (1) because he should have the imagination and insight to know instinctively what I want, and (2) because six months ago I could think of a thousand things I wanted and now, when there's a chance I might be able to get some of them, I can't remember what they were.

And then there's the question of what I should do for it. This is always a hard one. One minute I will be feeling wildly confident and happy and decide that I am going to have a fantastic ginormous party, invite everyone I know and get hammered on tequila until six in the morning, then the next I am thinking, what's the point? No one will come, the house will be trashed and I would be better off doing nothing at all.

Occasionally, if I am feeling particularly mad, I entertain a third option – inviting a big group of friends round for dinner. But then I realise, ashamedly, that part of the reason I would be doing this, other than to reassure myself that I actually have friends,

Sam

'Hi.'

Now it was her turn to die. 'James!'

It was peculiar, she thought, as her heart started racing, how you could have a million things to say to someone and suddenly not be able to think of a single word.

'How are you?' he said, when the silence got too loud.

'Fine. How are you?'

'Fine.'

More dead people's silence.

'Did you get the flowers?' He asked this as if they had been some important documents he'd faxed through from New York.

'But . . . you . . . he said they were for next door,' she faltered.

'Who said?' he asked suspiciously. It was typical, she thought, that this was the only time she'd heard him sound jealous.

'The delivery-man.'

As they carried on in their stilted English, Jess couldn't help thinking it was rather pointless to give someone anonymous flowers then phone up the next day to check they'd arrived. Nevertheless she was happy. There was nothing better than knowing you were still desired by an ex even though she wasn't – obviously – in the slightest bit interested.

'Um . . . gosh . . . excuse me,' she stuttered, ten minutes later, when a smaller version of Jemima Khan without the headscarf came barefoot to the door of the neighbouring flat.

'Yes?' She was looking at Jess as if she was about to try to sell her some dishcloths.

'Are you . . . um . . . This is a bit embarrassing, but . . .'

Jemima's eyes had gone very large indeed. 'What's your point, dear?'

'You've got my flowers,' Jess blurted, going bright red.

'I'm sorry?'

would be to get presents. But it's all very well to be stuck in the primary school 'more people = more presents' mode of thinking if you are not also the one who must give up your entire day to cook *for these people.*

Jo thinks I should have a fancy-dress party, supposedly because it makes people feel more obliged to come, but I suspect because she wants an excuse to cavort around all night in her bikini.

I personally cannot stand·fancy-dress parties: you spend all week trying to think of something clever and creative to wear, ransack the depths of your wardrobe and rails of sick-animal shops, lament the fact that you could be looking a whole heap better in the dress you would have worn had it been a normal party, then find yourself, half an hour before you are due to be there, suffering a crisis of confidence that you will be the only one dressed as a schoolgirl/character out of Star Wars/*carrot, decide to forget the whole thing and put on instead something that shows you've made the effort but can be immediately discarded on arrival, like a tiny sparkly hair-clip. No, I am not going to have a fancy-dress party. In fact, I'm not going to do anything this year, I've decided. There's no point. It's just another day after all. Nothing –* ARGHHH!

The scary rustling was Sam all along. He'd lost his bearings and tripped over the guy-rope. However, his foraging, though lengthy, seems to have been successful. Instead of the feared foliage pickings, he has returned with two deliciously juicy-looking, tasty-smelling fish suppers.

I've decided I am *going to have a party – though just a normal one. Sam's reminded me that Sophie will be away that weekend so we should take advantage of it. He's right. She has become such a pain recently, especially over this stupid loo-roll thing. She's taken to leaving notes around the place saying, 'Toilet paper?' which everyone is making a point of doing nothing about with the result · that someone, perhaps Colin?, is using the Style section of the* Sunday Times. *This is something I will try not to think about as I munch into my newspaper-coated dinner.*

'The flowers I brought round yesterday,' she continued, 'were actually for me all along.'

'Oh, for goodness' sake,' Jemima snapped, disappearing into the house. 'Harold?'

Ergh, Jess thought. Sexy Boxer-shorts Man should not be called Harold. Not at all. Harold was completely wrong.

'Hey, there! What's up?' Harold was wearing running shorts and a bandanna.

'She seems to think I've stolen her flowers,' Jemima sneered.

Harold smirked. 'Is this true?'

Jess explained the mix-up. She could tell by the way he was grinning that he was on her side.

'I'll think you'll find they're hers,' he said. Jess gave a closed-lip smile of smugness then watched in horror as he put a protective arm around Jemima. 'I ordered them two days ago. Looks like your bloke's playing silly buggers.'

'Looks like your girlfriend's a bitch,' Jess was sorely tempted to say, and walked away mortified.

'Did you get them?' Jo chirped, sitting at the kitchen table, waxing her legs with the butter knife.

'They weren't mine.'

'Oh dear, and you went round there and—'

'Yes. Thank you, Jo.'

'So why did James lie, then?'

'Because he's a—' Suddenly she spotted something. 'Oh, shit.' She pointed at the wilting remains of the Kew Gardens delivery sitting with its 'sorry' tag in the corner. 'He didn't. He didn't lie at all.'

Hope you are well.
Lots of love,
Jess
xxx

*PS I'm not going to have a party. It's a stupid idea – like taking
an exam on popularity. No one will come till midnight, then a
whole horde of people I've never clapped eyes on before will march
in as if they own the place, demanding cans of Boddington's.*

Sam
Birthday Shower

Lying in bed wishing never to get up
Alarmed to discover that, despite last night's repul-
    sive birthday gorging and plans of not eating
    for a fortnight I am now, inexplicably, hungry
Too lazy and blobby to get food, though

Dear Alex,

    Why is it that whenever you plan a lie-in workmen start drilling outside your window at 7 a.m.? If it was a constant pneumatic drone I could at least incorporate it into my dream as a Metallica song, but the bastards insist on stopping just when you're at the point of throwing a chair on top of them, then starting again the second you have got back to sleep.

    I wouldn't mind if there was some visible improvement at the end of it, but all that happens is a large crater appears in a perfectly good bit of Tarmac, causing multiple traffic pile-ups and everybody to walk in the middle of the road. Then six weeks later it gets filled in and the process is repeated all over again a hundred yards further down the street.

    In fact, the only thing this lot seem to have achieved with any degree of efficiency is to cut off our water supply. This was some-thing they chose to do during *my shower.*

    I still can't believe it. I'd rushed back from work with the idea of relaxing before my big posh birthday meal and all was going swim-mingly. I'd just soaped up my hair while sipping calmly at a gin and tonic and smearing a tube of Immac over the shrubbery of my lower body, when the shower went into a piddle then stopped altogether.

    This is quite common. We have one of those shitty showers that go scalding when anyone uses the cold tap in the kitchen and are

'We don't have any, I'm afraid,' Jess shouted, over the din of a dance track with the kind of repetitious rhythm that made it difficult to know whether it was intentionally monotonous or the CD had got stuck. 'Heineken OK?'

At a quarter to midnight she was only just beginning to enjoy her birthday. Having spent the morning fixating on outfits, punch ingredients and whether the lighting was flattering enough, she'd gone into a state of high-energy neurosis whizzing round the house removing anything worth breaking, stealing or using as an ashtray, while stuffing all unsightly objects into the airing cupboard and writing large No Entry signs on everything short of the bathroom door and, at her specific request when she discovered how many men were due to turn up, Jo's bedroom.

Then, panicked someone might arrive on time, she'd raced to the supermarket, where she'd charged around grabbing own-brand booze and industrial sacks of crisps only to spend the rest of the evening staring at the clock, getting progressively pissed on her own, convincing herself that nobody was going to turn up, and wishing she had never agreed to have a party in the first place.

But now, as she looked about the room crammed to the hilt with fun, wacky people, she felt a swelling sense of pride. It was *her* party. They had all come to *her* party. She smiled at how, only hours earlier, she had slumped into a tortured spiral of self-doubt, believing she had no friends. It was funny what the brain could do in times of depression and stress. No friends indeed! She glugged her wine merrily and scanned the floor for someone to talk to. It was then she made the so finely tuned at all other times you only need to nudge the dial a milli-fraction in the wrong direction and you may as well be standing under a rapidly melting igloo.

I bashed it around for a bit, which usually does the trick, but nothing, not a dribble. It was only when I tried all the other taps and they did that vicious dry-retching thing that it dawned on me what had happened. I was covered from head to toe in foam and had half a G and T, some vile-smelling vase water and what was left in the toilet bowl with which to rinse it off.

Furious, I clambered out and dripped my way to the kitchen in the hope that some sensible person had had the foresight to fill all the saucepans. But Sophie is away at the moment. Consequently all the saucepans were full, just not with anything you would choose to throw over yourself, however desperate.

In a blind panic, I phoned Thames Water, which was a bit like going into Dolcis and being told they didn't have any shoes: they said they had nothing to do with my water supply and I would need to phone the council. The council, however, did not seem to have a phone. They appear to run their entire outfit from an answering-machine in the Midlands, which, given that they employ Colin, is little wonder.

So the whole thing culminated in me with cauliflower hair having to beg with the mini Hitler at the swimming-pool kiosk to let me in five minutes before closing time for a swim I had no intention of having until I skidded into a fat woman with a mop and the sign 'Showers Closed'.

From there a period of intense mortification ensued with me leaping into the pool and doing ferocious swimming, watched by an attractive yet clearly repulsed Baywatch bloke, as a trail of disgusting shampoo-scum plus bikini hair followed in my wake. By the time I made it to the restaurant everyone thought I'd been run over.

Sam had booked it, so I'd planned on a little offbeat Bengali number where everyone slummed around sitting on cushions banging their heads on tinkly wind chimes every time they got up somewhat unwelcome realisation: out of a room of fifty people, she recognised only three.

'Decided to dress for the occasion, I see.' Sexy Boxer-shorts Man had just perched himself beside her, and although not sporting his trademark outfit looked disarmingly sexy.

'You too,' she said, flashing a grin at his groin.

'It's a pity.' He smiled. 'You look good in a towel.'

Jess beamed, wondering whether she shouldn't have had a fancy-dress party after all. A toga party, perhaps, where she could have swanned around in a flimsy piece of cotton all night claiming to be a Roman goddess.

'Wow,' he said, looking round the room then back at Jess in an undeniably flirtatious manner, 'you know all these people?'

'Well, yes, most of them,' she said, giggling.

'Popular *and* attractive.'

She smiled modestly.

'So,' he continued, really slowly, as if at any moment he might move forward, part his lips and start to kiss her, 'what about that delectable beauty in the corner?'

Jess swung round in the direction of his gaze and immediately wished she hadn't. He was staring directly at Petra.

What was it about men, she wondered, as he started slavering, that they could be intelligent, discerning and even – some of them – sensitive, but put them in a room with a big-busted blonde and instantly they disappointed you?

She decided there was little point in hanging around – particularly as Petra, like a lean hound, had already picked up the scent – and fought her way to the kitchen where she helped herself to a superior bottle of someone else's wine. That, she was learning, was one of the best if not only perks of being the hostess.

'*There* you are, sexy!' a voice boomed from inside the freezer. It was Sam trying to cram in eight cans of Stella among the peas. 'Come with me,' he said, taking her hand to go to the loo. I was a bit taken aback, therefore, to walk in and find I had six spoons with which to eat my soup. Indeed, the whole thing was so ridiculously posh that you only had to pick your nose and an eager little Frenchman would appear with a silver brush and pan to sweep it up.

The food, whose presentation gave the impression it should really have been eaten with tweezers, was lovely. I had pigeon – fine as long as you didn't think of Trafalgar Square – followed by two strawberries and a grape, encased in a little sugar cage of the sort my mother would profess was too beautiful to eat, then make a big song and dance about taking a photograph of it.

The bill, however, wasn't quite so sweet, despite being proffered in an envelope as if it were a gift voucher, and caused me to run off to the loos in horror, where I was met with the entire perfume counter of Boots and a lady who handed me three tissues on which to wipe my bottom.

Why, when restaurants can get it so right in many other respects, do they insist on forcing some poor bastard to sit dishing out hand-towels to people like me who would rather not have to fork out a pound to look at themselves in the mirror? It's like shops that still think what the customers really want is to be pounced on with offers of assistance the second they have stepped through the door.

Luckily Sam insisted on paying my share – a heaven-sent miracle indeed, given that a debit of £52.80 to a restaurant in SW3 would not do much to convince my bank manager I was living the life of frugality and self-denial I had so emphatically promised him. He is being so nice to me at the moment – Sam, not the bank manager – and for my birthday gave me a beautiful big framed watercolour of the sea (because I'd said on one occasion four months ago how I'd love to have an ocean view from my window) plus a long polka-dot dress, which is, unfortunately, disgusting.

I hate getting presents I don't like because rather than saying thank you and moving on, I panic and launch into ten reasons and winking. 'I've got a friend who's dying to meet you.'

She followed him willingly into the hall, hope for the evening renewed. Maybe all was not lost. Maybe she would not be left mopping up pools of vomit, digging fag butts out of plug-holes and pouring salt all over the sofa, but rather making fascinating conversation with an attractive man who would coyly yet masterfully request her phone number, charm her into seductive tête-à-têtes in little cobblestone restaurants, be hilariously witty in chic wine bars and never be in the least bit interested in big-busted blondes.

She gawped. The friend *was* a big-busted blonde.

'Hi, I'm Melanie.'

Jess stared in a mixture of disappointment, envy and a startling revelation that not a single one of Sam's friends seemed to be male.

'Hi, I'm Jess.'

It turned out rather rapidly that Melanie's enthusiasm for meeting her centred not around friendliness, intrigue or a genuine desire to find out whose party she was at, but wholly and singularly around Melanie. She'd got it into her head that Sam fancied her and seemed to think that by talking incessantly about herself she could get it into everyone else's as well.

'He likes **me** coz **I**'m **me**, **myself**, do you know what **I** mean? **I** don't play games, or try to be anyone but **me** and in **my** mind, blokes like that, don't you think? Like the other day when he said **I** was sweet and **I** was just being, you know, just **me**, but sometimes, if **I**'m being honest with **myself**, **I** do have a habit of putting **myself** down, only when **I**'m feeling, you know, **self**-conscious or unsure of **myself**, doubting **me**, who **I** really am, do you see what **I**'m saying? But when **I**'m **me** everyone loves **me** and **I** think that's what Sam was trying to say, wouldn't you agree? **Personally I** think he's very keen on **me** and **I** think **I** should say something because after all, at the end of the day, it's all about **me** – **me**, **me**, **me**, **ME!**'

why it is the best thing I could possibly have been given. I went a step further with the dress, though, putting my foot in it when I said that I used to have one similar years ago but chucked it out because everyone said it made me look like a giant strawberry (it was red with white dots).

I realised the minute I said it this was a disaster (this one is also red with white dots) and for the first time could empathise with how Prince Philip must feel every time he opens his mouth. So I tried to counteract it by adding, 'Of course, that was when they were going out of fashion anyway,' which was a bit like playing one of those arcade racing-car games, crashing into one wall and, in an effort to correct yourself, swerving round and crashing into the other.

None of this was helped by the fact that James had sent me the most beautiful light blue silk dress I have ever seen, with a note that said simply, 'I miss us.' As much as this melts me to the core, I can't help feeling angry with him for confusing me. There was something a lot easier about him being the irredeemable bastard.

Sam, meanwhile, has gone entirely the other way and has become such an inordinate gagger that I could tell him to take a flying fuck at the moon and he'd probably set about making some wings. Recently I've been seriously considering splitting up with him but I think this might just be a pre-menstrual thing so I'm not going to do anything rash. After all, he's such a lovely guy, who is fun and likes me, that it seems silly to end it all because there is no spark. As my chemistry teacher used to say, just because potassium and hydrochloric acid create a big explosion it doesn't mean that there isn't a less important atomic transformation occurring in water.

Oh, God. Jo has just burst in like a Vitalite commercial, sporting fluorescent trainers and a bra top. She is showing off because she is going for a run. I can't help feeling jealous about this, even though the last thing I feel like doing is pounding the streets of Clapham doing asthma-breathing with a purple face.

Mind you, I've recently discovered there is a trick to jogging

She stopped. 'Anyway, enough about me.'

Thank the Lord above, Jess thought, with a feeble smile. It was good to know that even the most self-centred people knew their limits.

'What do *you* think I should do about Sam?'

Luckily Jess was spared the torture of being subjected to any more of **Me**lan**I**e's monologue by a wandering drug-addict, who grabbed her arm and said, 'Man, is this a happening party,' before disappearing up the stairs again with a six-pack of Boddington's. While overjoyed to attract such an accolade from a stranger, she couldn't help wondering whether she might not be missing out on something – a recent drug delivery in the toilet cistern maybe – and used the excuse of needing to refill the Hula Hoop bowl to escape and find out.

Eventually when she wove her way past stairloads of huddled couples baring their souls and, in the case of Jo and a muscular Nigerian from Slough, a lot else besides, there didn't seem to be much going on at all. A queue of bored people were standing outside the bathroom where a delivery in the toilet was certainly taking place – unfortunately, though, she deduced from the emanating retching sounds, not of the drugs variety – a girl was searching for a contact lens, someone was studying the skirting-board and two blokes were playing football with Sophie's shower puff. She was missing out, she assured herself, as she made her way towards the stairs, on absolutely nothing.

Then, just as she was about to begin her descent, she noticed something missing. The ironing-board, which they'd jammed across Sophie's door for fear of anyone entering, had disappeared. Either someone had experienced an urgent need to press their trousers or Sophie's room was occupied. She crossed her fingers for the former, pushed open the door then shrieked in horror to discover, catastrophically, the latter.

The room was bedlam. The entire radiator had come off

which makes it marginally less hideous. It lies not in physical endurance, aerobic ability or expensive trainers with air inside them, but merely in the art of fantasising. If you can focus your mind off what you are supposed to be doing i.e. getting up a hill, and on what you are not i.e. little fantasy scenarios about, for example, James, then the whole thing becomes a lot easier. The more you concentrate on the intricacies of the 'story', the more you forget that you are actually wheezing round Hyde Park with a stitch.

I know this is not normal and that I'm supposed to gain something wonderfully satisfying from feeling like death for twenty minutes, but I'm not sure what it is. Admittedly I do feel better once the ordeal is over but I'm convinced this has less to do with the exercise itself and more because I can have a nice long shower, eat lots of food, and feel virtuous and smug for the rest of the week.

Anyway, if anyone's being smug at the moment it's Jo. She is being a bit annoying generally, to tell you the truth. Some guy at work fancies her and although she claims not to be interested in him she is unable to utter a single sentence without mentioning his name. She keeps doing this irritating thing of telling me some compliment he's paid her then disguising the ensuing self-satisfied grin with a large, exaggerated yawn to give the impression she finds the whole thing unimaginably tedious.

Then the other day she told me she had this really juicy secret, something I could never guess in a million years, something that was so fascinating yet death-threateningly confidential I had to swear on the life of everyone I had ever met that I would never tell a soul. Colin, she suspected, was gay.

Why is it that whenever someone hypes up a secret like this it is either something you already know or something in which you had no interest in the first place? I don't know what I was expecting, mind you, but the sexual preferences of Colin was not it. Personally I don't think he's sexual enough to be gay. He's like one of those androgynous fourteen-year-old models, only fatter. Poor Colin. Oh, the wall and was lying on the floor like a sunken relic from the *Titanic*, while jets of murky water were spraying out in all directions from various severed pipes, giving the impression that it was not a bedroom at all but the set of a *Police Academy* movie, where someone had just ridden roughshod over a fire hydrant. The floor, once a fluffy lilac, now resembled a swamp in which two blokes, trousers rolled to the knees, were paddling barefoot. Sophie's favourite cuddly Little Mermaid doll was sitting up-ended in a puddle, a selection of her clothes were acting as islands of dry land upon which a dreadlocked girl was claiming to sunbathe, and the ironing-board was lying in the middle of the room flattened by a large bloke sprawled along the length of it wearing only boxer shorts and flailing his arms madly in the air in a dog-like paddling motion. It was, he assured her earnestly, a surfboard.

'Shit! Shit!' Jess yelled, sploshing through the marshland searching for anything absorbent enough to smother the sprays. The double duvet looked appealing until she calculated the resultant dry-cleaning bill and decided that, with the loan she would be taking out to rectify the rest of the damage, it probably wasn't worth it.

Frantically, she began opening and shutting drawers unaided by the swimmers, surfers and sunbathers, who seemed content to bask in their cherished Caribbean creation oblivious to the fact that anything was wrong. After a futile search in bedside cabinets and laundry baskets, she suddenly remembered SophienRichard's matching towel set, dashed to the wardrobe and started leaping wildly in the air in a bid to reach the overhead cupboard. Just as she was about to give up and go for the duvet option after all, the surfer, seemingly on the crest of a particularly good wave, hurled himself plus ironing-board smack into the side of the wardrobe, causing it to lurch forward, the cupboard doors to fly open and lots of white things to cascade into the air.

It was only when the bombardment ceased, and Jess realised

Sam

God, though, I must stop calling him that. Like famous people whose first name sounds peculiar if you use it on its own without their surname, I find it almost impossible to refer to him without the prefix 'poor'.

Anyway, Jo's purported reason for coming into my room at eight fifteen on a Saturday morning was to tell me she's unearthed the no-water mystery. It turns out we had been warned, but in the form of an uninteresting brown envelope which, because Sophie is the self-elected bills person and nobody else can be arsed, has sat for two weeks in the boring-mail pile along with some visa circulars, Jo's smear test reminder and 50p off new spring-fresh non-biological Ariel.

I must say, though, having our water cut off unexpectedly is a small price to pay for not having Sophie around. Obviously it's been anarchy – jammy knives and pubic hairs all over the place – but a damn sight more relaxing than having to live in the organic military camp we are used to.

She's going through a particularly anal patch at the moment, sticking all sorts of rosters on the fridge, the latest of which – to be ignored by the rest of us – concerns the telephone, the use of which she has insanely rationed to half an hour each per evening because otherwise someone, she said, looking directly at me, hogs it for the entire night. I find this senseless – like the government deciding to issue every household in Britain with a box of tampons: Colin, who does not have periods/friends/anything to say at all is allotted the same quota as me and Jo, who have large quantities of all three.

Hopefully, though, by the time she gets back she'll be too consumed with Toby and Vanya's wedding arrangements to remember about it. Certainly, it was all she could ever talk about before she left, obsessing to the point of absurdity about two champagne flutes she'd had to buy them because all the 'good things' on the list had been taken – these apparently being matching bath towels and a set of knives and forks from Habitat. I tried to reassure her that the glasses would be a great deal more desirable than my she was not going to die under several tons of oak panelling, that she was able to make out what the white things were. Scattered in all directions and soaking into the swamp like balls of cotton were rolls of toilet paper, which Sophie had clearly been hoarding. Jess stood in disbelief, stunned that anybody could be quite so petty and selfish, imagining Sophie, loo roll in hand, bowel movements synchronised with the dead of night, creeping stealthily towards the bathroom to lay her turd. Then, all of a sudden, the seedling of an ingenious idea began to sprout.

'OK, everyone,' she announced, grinning, turning to the assembled bunch of beach bums, picking up a roll and gleefully unravelling it. 'Let's make some waves!'

The following morning the decimation resembled something from a *Yellow Pages* commercial – and if it hadn't been for that particular party-aftermath manual offering up such delights as radiator-installation men, heavy-duty drying-machines and specialist carpet cleaners, Jess felt sure it would probably also have included mutilated bodies and large amounts of spilled blood. As it was, two weeks on Sophie was still none the wiser.

'How many socks d'you think I'll need?' Jess said, surveying a mound of clothes on her bed that had started off as a bikini and a pair of shorts and somehow grown into everything but her ski hat and waterproof fleece.

It was the night before her holiday with James – a time that should have been spent in dreamy anticipation of the fantasies that lay ahead of them, but because they were finding it increasingly hard just to string a civil sentence together, let alone a fantasy, was being spent in separate houses several miles apart.

'It's Greece, not Glasgow,' Sam chortled, filling out her baggage labels.

The problem with going away somewhere hot and living

present, which was going to be some nice crockery until I discovered I could only afford one Royal Doulton saucer, and therefore ended up being a brass candle snuffer for £14.95, but she persisted to fixate on the missed opportunity with the towels.

I am personally more concerned about stealing the miniature body lotions and using up all the hot water in the lovely big swanky hotel we will be staying in.

Hope you are well.

Lots of love,

Jess

xxx

somewhere cold, she decided, as she jettisoned a black polo-neck and pair of jeans, was that it took a great leap of the imagination to conjure up how you could possibly be able to wear anything less than eighteen jumpers and a headscarf.

'But apparently it gets nippy at night,' she said, reconsidering the rash abandonment of the jeans.

'That depends what you *do* at night,' he replied, with raised eyebrow, causing her to wonder, not for the first time that week, whether she mightn't be going on holiday with the wrong guy.

Suddenly a distressed Sophie appeared.

'*What* is this?' She was holding a small metal object in the palm of her hand.

'A ring-pull, I think.' Jess was more concerned that Sam's idea of zipping up a case seemed to involve fondling her right breast.

'And what's it doing in my clog?'

Sam began to hum the theme music to *The X Files*.

Jess squealed in delight as he pretended to zip up her finger.

'Why is there a ring-pull in my clog?' she shouted. Sophie never shouted.

'Because you left it there?' Jess suggested, laughing.

'Because your clog got thirsty?' Sam guffawed.

'Or because someone,' Sophie said, steely-eyed and angry, moving towards them like a snake about to lash out its tongue and swallow them whole, 'had a party.'

They stopped laughing and looked at each other.

The prospect of going away, even if it *was* with a moron, Jess conceded, as she hung her head and waited for Sam to invent a lie, now seemed an enticing one indeed.

Love Unstuck?

Boxed up in a hotel room the size of a large cornflake
Too excited to sleep but too hung-over to do
    anything else
Eating a packet of peanut M&Ms from the mini-
    bar having missed, as tends to be the case
    when I have paid a fortune for it, a delicious
    continental breakfast

Dear Alex,

I feel as if I have just woken from one of those dreams that stay with you all morning – nothing and everything seems real. Vanya, formerly a lesbian, is now married; James, formerly a wanker, is now nice; and I, formerly sober, collapsed in a coma at four in the morning swearing I would never touch alcohol again. To complete this blurry picture of confusion, I am now lying next to Jane, the girl who tempted Vanya down the path of homosexuality and who has clearly been sent, like Jesus to the blind, to work a similar miracle on me. It is hardly surprising that things seem a bit out of sorts.

I really wish she'd wake up so that I can put on the light and not fumble around in the dark, knocking over kettles and banging into trouser presses in an effort to be quiet. She keeps doing loud sighs, flinging herself melodramatically across the bed as if she was not under a brown acrylic quilt in a dingy twin room but rather in the penultimate scene of Romeo and Juliet. *It's bad enough that I am having to share a room with her, let alone that I cannot so much as wee without performing a gymnastic feat with the toilet bowl to silence it.*

It's so disappointing. When Vanya told me I would be doubling up with her ex, I imagined a bloke with teen-magazine good looks in faded Levi's and a baseball cap (Vanya once dated a model from

Love Unstuck?

Having a lovely time here in Syphilos
Weather beautiful, beach glorious, hotel charm . . .
Oh, God – what is the point?
Having a wretched time, feel suicidal, hate the
   horrid holiday

Dear Alex,

   What on earth possessed me to think that James and I, who,
let's face it, have not exactly had what one might term a func-
tional, let alone successful, relationship, could travel several hundred
miles to a tiny Greek island with a couple of stray goats and a
busload of overweight people in shell-suits, discover in a blinding
flash of revelation what it was that we loved about each other
in the first place and have a truly marvellous super-wonderful
holiday?

   It is day three and we have split up.

   I feel like those married couples who only stay together for the
sake of the children – in our case holiday – and that when the
children leave home – flight leaves Gatwick – they can do what
they should have done years earlier and separate.

   I now realise that all along I had subconsciously been assuming
that the reason we were not getting on was not because we didn't
want to, didn't know how to or simply couldn't, but merely because
we were living highly stressful lives in a frantic city. If we just
transported our relationship to a different location, I believed, all
our problems would be solved. Now, of course, I realise that James
is just a wanker, in London, Greece or – preferably – outer bloody
space.

   It was clear fairly early on – to be honest, before we'd even
boarded the plane – that things were not going to go well. James

Sam

Just Seventeen) *with whom I would prance about wearing a loosely attached hand-towel having shaving-foam fights. I did not think the ex would be (a) female (b) homosexual and (c) hang all her clothes in gigantic Cellophane condoms, place her tissue-wrapped underwear in the never-before-used chest of drawers, align her makeup like surgical implements on the bathroom shelf and generally make me feel that just because my shampoo bottle has leaked over everything in my washbag and my suitcase is erupting like Vesuvius all over my bed, I am the one with the personality disorder.*

When I first arrived she thought I had come to empty the bins. When I told her, sweaty and panting, that I was one of the guests, she blanched at my jeans and put-in-the-wrong-wash T-shirt and reminded me we were due at the church in seventeen minutes. In a surge of panic, I realised I'd taken 1300 hours on the over-ornate invitation to mean 3 p.m. – the twenty-four-hour clock being something, along with remembering that nineteenth century actually means the eighteen hundreds, that I am spectacularly slow to get the hang of.

So by the time Reception called up with our taxi, Jane was looking stunning in a lilac chiffon number, attaching a little sprig of berries to her delicate flopsy hat and gliding her feet gently with the aid of a shoehorn (suspect she is also someone who uses quilted coat-hangers) into a brand-new pair of designer sandals, while I, lurching semi-dressed off the end of the bed, hair dripping wet, toothbrush jutting out of mouth, was trying alternately to sew the lining of my dress to a strapless bra twisted somewhere around my midriff and apply cream upholstery-dye to a pair of navy shoes.

The shoe-dyeing in particular was a disaster. No matter how often I do this kind of thing I seem incapable of learning that however terrifyingly expensive the real thing might seem at the time (£69.99 in Jones), it is never a good idea to attempt an ersatz model, which will take hours, look shit and ultimately work out just as expensive as the original. It derives from the same kind of perverted logic that allows you to think you are saving *money by buying something because it is in the sales and not because you would have* thought I had the tickets and I thought he had. After a session of blame and counter-blame, with me beginning, as I always do in such situations, to think maybe I did have them and had left them on top of the hand-dryer in the ladies' toilets or, worse, at home, we remembered that Shelly, the tour rep from BlueSky had taken them from us as we'd entered the terminal – presumably in the belief that anyone stupid enough to travel BlueSky would not be intellectually equipped to cope with the rigours of check-in (which turned out to be true, as James and I discovered when we had spent half an hour waiting for a flight to Afghanistan).

Then, no sooner had we made it to the departure lounge, the second argument of the holiday kicked off. James was pissed off that I'd brought my wallet with me ostensibly because I would get my 'Greek money confused with my British' but really because, for no logical reason, he hates my wallet. He claims I don't use it as a place for keeping money but instead as a safety-deposit box for my entire life.

This is just not true, especially as I've just purged it of an invalid Boots Advantage card, membership of the local tennis club, which expired 1.7.85, a French phone-card with three units left over from Interrailing days, an organ-donor card, filled out when I was going through a generous phase, and several passport photos taken when I was fourteen and it was cool to cram as many people as possible into tiny railway-station photo booths, pull stupid faces into the camera and do devil-horns finger signs behind everyone else's head.

He says it's not practical to carry a library around every time I leave the house, but what, pray, is practical about having large quantities of change jangling around in trouser pockets, which then spills out all over sofas and has to be transferred from pocket to dressing-table to pocket twice, if not three times, a day?

Hold on, must just manoeuvre my right arm a fraction of an inch to the left so it doesn't block the sun on my stomach . . .

I must say, whoever said lying in the sun was relaxing was obviously not in search of a sun-tan. Getting a tan is not, as *bought it anyway. As a result, I ended up looking like a prostitute who, in a moment of boredom, had decided to Tippex her feet.*

Just as I'd got to the door congratulating myself on remembering not to leave my absurdly gigantic room key locked in the room, Reception called up again to say the taxi had gone without me but that a rather charming gentleman was downstairs waiting to escort me. Not convinced that I knew a charming gentleman, the thought was appealing nevertheless and I skipped downstairs to meet him.

When I got to the foyer, however, no one was there except a pissed sixty-year-old staring at the imitation coal fire. He might have been charming and I might have resembled a hooker but this was not what I'd understood by the term 'escort'. Then just as I was turning to flee, a figure bounded out from behind an imitation pot plant and nearly sent me flying into the revolving doors. It was Sam, grinning and holding a beautifully gift-wrapped present.

For an awful moment I thought he'd decided to invite himself to the wedding as my guest and was just about to tell him that I had already been allotted a lesbian for that purpose, when he announced the present was for me: a shawl – because he'd seen what I was planning to wear (James's light blue dress) and said it was as good as going naked, which had been, I must confess, entirely the point. He then drove me to the church and gave me such an adoring goodbye look that for a second I wondered whether the spark of passion was the all-important ingredient I had made it out to be when you could have someone who loved you as uncon-ditionally as Sam loved me.

And then: ding dong! My body gave one of those violent lurches that tells you the person you have just spotted two feet away is not a great aunt or your old geography teacher: James – looking so ravishingly attractive it was all I could do not to rush up, pin him against the pulpit and do unholy things to him on the altar. He was the best man in every sense, and when he saw me and gave a little wink I instantly forgot every negative thought I have ever had about him. It struck me as rather dangerous to meet your ex-boyfriend like this at a wedding, though – a bit like holiday brochures and adverts for Nivea moisturiser would lead us to believe, simply a case of dancing around smiling at the sun, but a torturous full-time job, made worse because it is unseasonably hot at the moment, which is in itself both mentally and physically exhausting.

To be honest, I'm worn out by the whole thing. I keep finding myself lying in an anxious state of neurosis wondering, Is it safe to bring my shoulders down from factor thirty to factor eight yet? Have I covered up the burnt patches from yesterday's slapdash lotion-applying? Is my head tilted at the most productive angle? Should I be doing my back now? Have I managed to match up the tan lines of my bikini correctly? Can I feel a new burnt patch? Did I remember to put anything on my earlobes? How impressive do my white bits look? Am I going brown?

Added to this is the extra trauma that James, unconcerned as to whether he gets a tan or not, is turning mahogany without even trying, thus sparking a ridiculous competition, which has me, at every opportunity throughout the day, obsessing over who is browner.

But what is so deeply depressing about the process, however, is that while it may finally, after many arduous hours' work, offer up a beautiful deep tropical sun-tan – or in my case, cancerous-looking orange tint – no matter how much nurturing, moisturising and bath-avoiding you do once you're home, it is an inevitable, undesirable and distressing fact of nature that, three weeks down the line, you will look pale, pasty, anaemic and, quite frankly, as if you have never been away at all.

Naturally, this did not prevent me taking a mini heart seizure when three and a half hours after take-off BlueSky defied all the logic of its name and landed us on an island surrounded almost entirely by thick grey cloud. There is nothing more disappointing than travelling hundreds of miles to be somewhere that could just as easily, give or take a few olive groves, be your own back garden.

Considerably more annoying, however, was that in the process taking a woman recovering from an abortion straight to a crèche.

Anyway, the ceremony was lovely, although it wasn't until it was over that I realised I had not spent any of it thinking about Vanya and Toby. Instead I had been consumed with my own marital likelihood, oscillating wildly between attempts to see myself bedecked in white lace grinning at a handsome husband – or any husband, for that matter – and a sick, panicking sensation that I will never be capable of feeling sure about anyone, given that it is hard enough sometimes just to decide what to put on in the morning. The whole thing was like watching a slushy film that feels at once entirely within reach yet so divorced from the reality of your own life that it might as well be taking place on deepest Mars.

Obviously, though, I did not point this out when congratulating the newly-weds. To the contrary. By the time I'd stumbled my way to the reception – the heel of one of my shoes had snapped off in the middle of the Lord's Prayer – I had said 'beautiful' and 'very special' so many times that they had lost any sense of meaning.

I take pride, however, in not having sunk to the level of the feathery-hat brigade, who passed off several catty remarks about the colour scheme of the spray carnations with the we-must-remember-it's-the-bride's-day line. I find it unbelievable that people can say such things, given that with a guest list open only to those she has been instructed to invite, the expectation she will do the twist with a selection of leery-eyed sixty-year-olds who claim to have looked after her in the paddling pool, and a post-dinner speech detailing her new husband's antics with Cherie, the blonde stripper from the stag weekend, it would seem that the bride is the last person the day is for.

One look at the seating plan, though, assured me that the day was clearly not for me either. I had been sandwiched between Toby's uncle – a computer-software programmer from Liverpool who called everyone 'buddy', under the misguided impression that this would make him seem interesting, and Vanya's niece Hope, a tiny little thing who, after several condescending attempts on my part to cajole her into conversation, looked me up and down so of delivering us, they had failed to deliver our bags. Thus, without the foresight to pack a bikini in my hand-luggage, I was forced to spend the first two days of the holiday sweltering by the poolside in a pair of rolled-up jeans and James's Manchester United top, which, I soon discovered, with the addition of knee-length Hawaiian shorts and black Adidas trainers, is the national dress of the island.

Despite frequent attempts on my part to see the funny side of our situation – our hotel is a concrete tower block, overlooked by a slightly taller concrete tower block thereby obscuring all sunlight – James refuses to crack a smile. He keeps describing everything as vulgar and sat sneering aloofly throughout Tanya's welcoming speech, which admittedly seemed to suggest that you could spend a week on the island without ever leaving the hotel.

I don't know what it is about package-tour operators that makes them assume what people really want out of a holiday abroad is not culture, new experiences and a different country to explore, but a steadfast assurance that they have never left England. We have yet to find a single restaurant that does not sell chips, speak English and play something other than Robbie Williams.

Indeed, the only thing that makes you stand back and realise that, yes, you are in a foreign country after all is that everything has a price tag somewhere in the high hundreds. But even here you are rarely able to forget England, forced to spend your holiday doing complex division sums to find the pound equivalent of a cheeseburger and fries at 1962 drachmas. Or, as happened yesterday, fainting over a T-shirt you've just bought for what at first calculation seems to be £485. (Have no idea what makes me want to buy T-shirts on holiday anyway, when everyone knows that if there is ever a more unflattering garment it is a T-shirt).

In my experience, however, you don't fully master the converting thing until you have left the country and arrived back home, at which point a cheeseburger and fries for £9.95 immediately seems an impossibly cheap and tiny sum.

The other day, in a foolish quest for something Greek, I dragged *contemptuously that I felt like scuttling under the tablecloth.*

As a result, the speeches came as an unusually welcome relief, especially when James took the stand and delivered a funny account of Toby's last days as a bachelor, making it sound as though he was about to enter ten years' community service as a park-litter attendant rather than a loving marriage. I started to feel all warm and proud of him, but more especially of myself, in awe of the person I used to be when I went out with him.

(Why is it that things you have done in the past always seem much more impressive than things you are doing in the present? I am forever stumbling across rather ingenious drawings of garlic bulbs that I did aged twelve, or university essays, the subject matter of which is so sophisticated and erudite I feel sure it must have been written by someone else – which, of course, did tend to be the case.)

By the time we'd all been ushered on to the dance floor I had become so besotted with James that, at any given moment, like a finely tuned aircraft radar – one aiming to crash into rather than avoid its target – I knew exactly where he was, what he was doing and who he was doing it with. This was more of an achievement than it sounds given that the place looked as though an unfortunate clash of the church-hall booking system had occurred, with the senior citizens' bowls team, the women's guild, the church elders, the local playgroup and the entire Scouting movement all turning up on the same night.

Luckily, though, James's radar was transmitting very clear signals indeed, in the form of an unmistakably large bulge in his trousers whenever we danced together. And even though I'd had quite a lot to drink, suddenly everything seemed clear, as often only alcohol can make it.

It wasn't so much what I felt for James that was the pressing issue, so to speak, but what being with him made me realise I didn't feel for Sam. James does not just seem attractive in brief moments when the light is switched off. James does not do desperate eager gagging whenever I appear uninterested. James does not fill me with revulsion when he stands in boxer shorts and

James to a remote little cove described in the brochure as an 'idyllic hideaway'. When we got there, however, though clearly idyllic in a scenic sense, there was little in the way of the hideaway element going on. Everyone as far as the eye could see was stark bollock naked.

While I had no desire to have twiggy little penises dangled in front of me, I had a sneaking suspicion that James fancied a look at their ample-bosomed counterparts, so I hurriedly ushered him back to our regular beach, where he stubbed his toe and trod on a washed-up condom. He spent the remainder of the day refusing to go in the sun, claiming to be suffering from severe prickly heat and moaning to the point of tedium about a couple of minuscule red blotches on his upper arm.

By night-time this had turned into skin cancer, with the added possibility of malaria when he heard, at two thirty a.m, a mosquito he claimed 'had it in for him.' Rather than just ignoring it and putting a pillow over his head, he insisted on getting up, switching on the light and charging around the room with a newspaper. Come dawn, I felt sure it would not be a fatal disease that would kill James, but me.

And now I've just turned over to do my back and spotted him further up the beach sitting arrogantly under a parasol studiously reading A Passage to India. *He is such a berk. Why can't he be normal and splodge around in the sun doing bugger all like everyone else? I wish I was going home. This holiday is a disaster.*

Where is Sam when I need him? Lovely Sam. I just know the whole thing would be unbelievably better if he were here – though obviously instead of, rather than at the same time as, James. He would not be taking himself off to the other end of the beach to prove to the Sun-*reading population of Manchester that he has a degree. He would not glower menacingly at the concrete tower block and refuse to sit on any of their toilet seats. He would not have regular bouts of hypochondria and rush for shelter at the merest glimmer of sunlight. Instead, he would be fun, funny, three-quarter-length black socks making sexual advances over the toothbrush holder. In short, I fancy James with every single cell in my body, including the ones I have just killed off in last night's debauched drinking frenzy.*

I always had doubts about Sam and just assumed that they would disappear like pubescent acne. But that's the problem with doubts, isn't it? They don't disappear. Like energy they can be converted from one form to another – ignored, substituted, convinced out of, temporarily suspended – but ultimately never destroyed.

Obviously before I can embark on my delicious new doubt-free dating début with James, I will have to finish with Sam, which I attempted to do over the phone, plastered, at three in the morning until I discovered I'd just spent fifteen minutes dumping Colin. Apparently Sam was still at a party being chatted up by some girl who sounded suspiciously like the Emily person from that party way back – the party, funnily enough, at which Sam and I first got together. (Spooky situation that the minute I decide I no longer want him, someone else decides they do. Like second-hand clothes, I suppose.)

Ever since I've been with Sam it's like I've been eating those dry crackerbread biscuit things, convincing myself I enjoy them, occasionally finding them tasty if I'm starving, always feeling empty and unsatisfied afterwards. Then, all of a sudden, a slice of double chocolate gateau has been put in front of me and I want it even when I'm full.

Ooh, I love my slice of double chocolate gateau, even though I left him six hours ago splayed out on the bar floor with his hands down his trousers. (Is it just the ones I meet or do all men fall asleep with their hands on their genitals?) He has promised me he is going to take me somewhere nice to make up for all the horrible things he has done. I hope this means an idyllic little Greek island in the Mediterranean, not a day trip for two to Bognor.

It may have taken the perspectives of distance, time and a wonderful wedding without Sam, but I realise now what I should have realised long ago, that James is the bloke for me. I can just nice, sane and an altogether preferable holiday companion – and, as I am becoming more and more certain by the second, boyfriend.

Obviously I mustn't get too carried away with this idea – however appealing it might seem – as I am still officially within the ten-hour rebound territory, but I must say, I do have a bewildering and dazzling feeling that, after suffering at the hands of such an atrociously dire and confidence-wrecking relationship, I am going to rise phoenix-like from the debris and soar to the magnificent, breathtaking heights of perfect coupledom with Sam.

In anticipation of this, therefore, I have decided I will not be going with James to demonstrate our failing as a functioning couple at Toby and Vanya's confirmation of theirs, i.e. their wedding, but instead to a party with Sam with the express and thinly disguised purpose of snogging the living daylights out of him. I have just spent the last of my drachmas phoning him to insinuate this. In the meantime, however, I am going to brave the floating panty-liners and go for a little swim.

I hope this letter reaches you. When I tried to explain to the lady in the post office that I wanted stamps for China, gesticulating madly at a china tea-cup behind her, she looked confused then scuttled away, returning seconds later with a steaming cup of tea.

I suspect it will be the only thing I send. Despite having every intention of writing the fifteen postcards I have spent all morning choosing, I know they will just loom over the rest of the holiday like maths homework over a weekend and I will end up in a foul mood on the return flight home copying out an identical message on six of them then posting them at Gatwick Airport.

Hope you are well. I'll write again after the party. Yippee – can't wait.

It may have taken the perspectives of distance, time and a disastrous holiday with James, but I realise now what I should have realised long ago, that Sam is the bloke for me. I can just tell we are going to work. It's such a relief when you know that finally, after so much heartache, you have made the right decision.

    Lots of love,

    Jess

    xxx

The right decision: go back to *James*, page 159 . . .

tell we are going to work. It's such a relief when you know that finally, after so much heartache, you have made the right decision.

Lots of love,
Jess
xxx

The right decision: go back to *Sam*, page 159 . . .

EPILOGUE

The plane had landed and with it the realisation that she wasn't so much waiting for its passengers as losing the blood supply to her upper body. A railing, clearly made by pygmies, had sandwiched her between most of London's Chinatown, chattering to each other with about as much coherency as a tape on high-speed rewind, and a selection of morose men in suits who, she concluded from the fact that they were all holding name placards, couldn't speak at all.

Suddenly Jess felt nervous. What if she and Alex didn't get on any more? She'd read somewhere that real friendship transcended distance and time. Did this still hold true if one person had travelled extensively in a fascinating country, experienced diverse cultural customs and practices and integrated themselves into an entirely new social, political and economic climate and the other person had done, well, nothing at all, really?

Before she had time to dwell on the implications of Alex rounding the corner on a bicycle with sleek shiny hair and a frightening desire to hold sophisticated conversations in fluent Mandarin, a stream of people was flooding towards her, looking more as though they'd travelled on the back of a disabled mule rather than on anything that offered miniature toothbrush sets and tweezer-delivered hot towels.

Within seconds the awaiting crowd dispersed, giving way to sentimental scenes of reunion: laughter, tears and a rather too enthusiastic display – given that the couple in question were at least seventy – of snogging. It struck Jess that an airport, with its institutional floor-tiling, artificial strip-lighting, anonymous food halls and yellow neon toilet signs was a rather incongruous setting for the expression of so much emotion. Like holding a wedding ceremony in a McDonald's drive-thru.

She continued to scan the approaching mass of strangers feeling the kind of mounting panic normally reserved for when she couldn't spot her bag on the luggage carousel while her fellow passengers were merrily trotting out of the terminal with theirs. And then it happened. Alex's head loomed into view eclipsing everyone else's like a famous person's.

Jess watched, doing excited manic grinning, as the familiar figure, thinned down and browned up, came bobbing ever closer. She'd forgotten how attractive Alex was, despite the apparent shampoo deficit and peculiar – presumably bought in the belief it would be trendy back home – mandarin-collared silk shirt.

'Oh, my God,' they shrieked in unison, the second they were within touching distance, jumping up and down on the spot, squealing and hugging each other as though engaged in a complex tribal greeting ritual. Two little boys sitting on a nearby trolley joined in, clapping hands and cheering. Alex's return had evidently had a happy effect on the airport generally, Jess thought. Either that, or they were hoping to be spotted for the next Dairylea commercial.

'Obviously didn't quite master the chopstick thing, then,' she joked.

'Or the language thing,' Alex said, laughing and gesturing to a collapsing phrasebook.

'Or even the haircut thing,' Jess added. Alex's hair, far from resembling a Pantene Pro-V advert, looked as though it had been given over to a family of nesting pigeons.

They stopped hugging and stood grinning at one another inanely.

'You look fab, Jess.' Fab would not have been the most obvious choice of word for someone who'd arrived at the airport at six in the morning, unwashed and sweating, still wearing remnants of the previous night's mascara, Jess thought. 'And I can't believe you're here. I thought I was going to be punished.'

Jess stared blankly. 'Whatever for?'

'For making the wrong decision on your bloke front.'

She looked up and suddenly felt an unexpected sense of clarity. 'Two wrongs make a right.' She smiled. And in a way that suggested this might just prove to be true, he smiled back.